c:4/12 L:6/13 3X

D0908104

Caged
INNOCENCE

Withdrawn from
Toronto Public Library

Withdrawn from
Toronto Public Library

Caged INNOCENCE

A. P. RI'CHARD

SBI

STREBOR BOOKS

NEW YORK LONDON TORONTO SYDNEY

SBI

Strebor Books
P.O. Box 6505
Largo, MD 20792
http://www.streborbooks.com

This book is a work of fiction. Names, characters, places and
incidents are products of the author's imagination or are used
fictitiously. Any resemblance to actual events or locales or persons,
living or dead, is entirely coincidental.

© 2008 by A. P. Ri'Chard

All rights reserved. No part of this book may be reproduced in
any form or by any means whatsoever. For information address
Strebor Books, P.O. Box 6505, Largo, MD 20792.

ISBN 978-1-59309-214-6
ISBN 978-1-4165-8587-9 (ebook)
LCCN 2008935884

Cover design: www.mariondesigns.com
Cover photograph: © Keith Saunders/Marion Designs

10 9 8 7 6 5 4 3 2 1

Manufactured in the United States of America

For information regarding special discounts for bulk purchases,
please contact Simon & Schuster Special Sales at 1-866-506-1949
or business@simonandschuster.com

The Simon & Schuster Speakers Bureau can bring authors to
your live event. For more information or to book an event, contact
the Simon & Schuster Speakers Bureau at 1-866-248-3049 or visit
our website at www.simonspeakers.com.

Acknowledgments

To Zane, Charmaine and the rest of the Strebor family, thank you for opening your hearts to me. I will always be grateful to all of you wonderful people for taking a chance in bringing me into your world. Pamela Crockett for taking me on as a client and a friend. You've waited patiently for me to develop; I've yet to reach my full potential, but you know that I will continue to work hard. Thank you for believing (Go, Wolverines).

A special thank you to one of the strongest individuals that I have ever had the pleasure of meeting, Mr. Larry Floyd, for providing me with the inspiration needed to put this story on paper and film. Archie Floyd, for providing prayer. You are truly my brother from another mother.

I would like to thank John Andino, Durie Purvis, Joel Phillips, Greg Bumpass, Maxwell Taylor and Regina John along with the rest of the United Spirits family for your hard work in helping to prepare our future endeavors. To Julie Davis and Janet Miranda for all your help and encouragement. Ian Surrey, Lubangi and Beatrice Muniania of Tabilulu Productions, you two are the best. I appreciate your support and friendship.

Fred Caruso, Gary Donatelli, Kim Tumey, Joycelyn Engles, James Ruggiero and Terrence Gordon for coming aboard to help with the filming of *Caged Innocence*.

May "Gypsy" Ri'Chard, for being the greatest mom in the world. Michael, Darwin, Larry and LaTanya, couldn't ask for more supportive siblings. To my two younger brothers, David and Bernard, who watch over me from above, I love you. James "Young Blood" Ri'Chard for teaching his third child the meaning of determination.

Anita, thanks for taking the time to help Zane edit this book. To Pamela, Carita, Karla, Charlotte and AJ for putting up with Daddy not having a lot of time to spend with you during this process. Mark Childress, Hazen, Kyle and Curtis Mahon, Leisha Slater-Hagerman, Darryl and Letrice Slater, Tony Womack, Aaron, Kenny, Bobby and Vanessa McCray, what a family. To my Suriname family, Charlotte Jackson, Tyrone, Guy, Maxie, Ray, Richie and Raul Ouseley, to Lana, Stephan and Ryan Dicou, Urani John, Sasha and Raul Persuad, thank you for accepting me into your family.

To my manager and friend Phil Arnold, keep up the good work—we have a lot to look forward to. Michael and Isabelle Glover-Phifer, you and Mekhi are all special people. George Burks and Freddy Contreras for always looking out for your boy. To Ramadan Nanji, Cliff Benton (Audacity Literary Agency), you were the first to believe.

And to the most special of all—to the person who

went through the struggles of me changing my career path, the one who inspired me to pursue my dream no matter how hard things got—the absolute love of my life. Lia, I love you more than I can express in an acknowledgment. Thank you for encouraging me to stick in there—for having my back no matter how hard times got. I promise that I will continue to work as hard as I can to make you proud to be my wife.

Deep
SOUTH

The brown cotton robe that sheltered her slightly overweight frame was shoddy at best. Her dirty brown slippers looked like they had been passed down through many generations.

Before the moon completely gave way to the sun, Margaret Henderson found herself standing on her back porch, scanning their one and a half acres of property.

The refreshing early morning country air invigorated her lungs, mind and spirit. Each time she drew in, and then slowly exhaled the tranquility of a brand-new day, she'd whisper, "Thank you, Jesus."

This day was special—for this was to be her son's day; his turn to be acclimated into family traditions. Her preparation would initiate the beginning of his rite of passage.

A knowing sigh chased her from her relaxing state.

There was a lot to do, and she had less than an hour to get things done. She had to finish breakfast, iron clothes, and bathe the little boy who was taking his first step into manhood; at least, according to the Henderson doctrine. But first, fresh eggs needed to be gathered, so she descended the wooden stairs and headed toward the chicken coop, some twenty yards away.

Breakfast was on the stove, the ironing board was placed in the kitchen, and she had already awakened the young man for whom the day was dedicated.

Margaret rarely had to physically wake anyone in the house, as the crackling bacon, boiling grits and freshly cooked biscuits, more often than not, worked as their alarm clock. The aroma sent signals to her family members' stomachs, which instantaneously ignited their urge to eat. On most mornings, the kitchen would fill as fast as a truck stop diner. However, due to her earlier than usual start, this particular morning was the exception. Not even her highly regarded blueberry pancakes would break her family's slumber.

Several minutes into her chores, Margaret noticed a shadowy, elongated figure making its way along the side of her home. A bit uneasy, she stood in silence. The mother of five watched the silhouette slowly reduce in size. Margaret wasn't expecting anyone so early in the morning. It wasn't until she realized that it was her nephew who had entered the backyard that she was able to relax enough to continue with her chores.

Terrell didn't appear to see his aunt tending the fowl. His attention was clearly on the open screen door. The teen inhaled; the allure baited him. He rushed up the porch and into the house.

He was enticed by the familiar aroma emanating from several pots and a skillet, sitting on top of the stove's burning eyes. He walked over to the range and began rummaging through the cookware.

The screen door opened, causing Terrell to promptly pull his nose from the pot. He snapped to attention, picked up a spoon, and began stirring the grits.

"Boy, what you doin' wit yo' nose in my pot?" Margaret announced as she placed several eggs atop the kitchen counter.

"I didn't see you outside, Aunt Margaret," Terrell said as he calmly peered over his shoulder.

"How you doin', boy?"

"I'm doin' good. How 'bout you?"

She glanced at her favorite nephew before turning the corners of her lips upward; her Southern drawl as delightful as her cheerful expression. "'Bout the same as the last time I saw you. What was it…five, six hours ago?" Margaret continued as she removed the spoon from her nephew's hand. "If you really wanna help me, go make sure yo' little cousin is up. I woke him a while back."

Larry's mother had awakened him before the sun had a chance to dry the dew that covered the ground between nightfall and morning. With a childlike innocence, he gently rubbed the sides of both index fingers to the corners of his dark brown eyes in an attempt to remove the cockcrow crust. The baby boy then slid out of bed, stood in the middle of his room, and reached to the heavens. The five-year-old's contorted body and wide yawn were his way of introducing his tiny frame to a brand-new day.

Losing his footing, he began to wobble. "Woo…"

The child was startled when his cousin's gentle hand steadied him. Larry jumped in fear. "WHO…!" He quickly turned. "Oh…you scared me. Good mornin', Terrell."

"Mornin', little man…yo' momma told me to come in. You okay? Can you stand without fallin'?"

"I'm okay."

Terrell began to tickle his pudgy cousin to ensure that he was wide-awake. Little Larry broke free, and then dove back into bed. He grabbed the youngest male in the family before he could cover himself. Terrell hugged Larry and planted several kisses all over his face.

"Well, let's get you ready. Today's yo' big day!"

The first-year junior college student's special kinship with his little cousin was established at birth. Terrell had no siblings, and his relationship with Larry's two older brothers was strained at best. Both seemed destined for troubled lives. The two were discreet with their shenanigans around adults, but Terrell was very much aware of their deceptions, and he wanted to ensure that Larry chose a different path.

The little boy giggled and squirmed as his big cousin held him snug in his arms. "I'm goin' fishin'…I love you, cousin Terrell. You're the best."

Terrell smiled. His embrace was firmer. "If I had a little brother, I'd want him to be exactly like you. Come on, I gotta get you to yo' momma; she wants to wash you up."

"Can you do it? Can you wash me?" The boy's smile was infectious.

Terrell lifted his cousin over his head. "Sure, little man…" He kissed Larry's cheek once again.

"I'm goin' fishin'…I'm goin' fishin'…" he sang in delight at the thought.

The five-year-old was finally going to get his opportunity to stand at the edge of Morris Creek with his very own pole, and cast his line into the cool, shimmering waters.

For over forty years, the Henderson men would assemble every other Saturday at the bank, before the birds could catch a glimpse of the beauty that the horizon inherited each morning. Pulling bass from the narrow inlet, which gave way to the Mississippi, was their way of bonding.

Terrell lowered his little cousin into the tub. He used the rag that was draped over his shoulder to wash the eager little boy.

"Larry...yo' mom and dad didn't think you was ready to go fishin' yet, but I convinced them otherwise. I told them that I won't let nothin' happen to you—ever! I'll always be there for you...always!"

He continued with a smile as he scrubbed his cousin's back. "Everyone thinks that I didn't go away to school because of my momma bein' sick...but it was really because I would miss you too much."

"Terrell, you really stayed for me? And you always gon' be there fo' me? What about when you get a girl-friend, you still gon' find time for me?" His wide eyes and tilted head exposed the child's curiosity.

"What do you know 'bout havin' girlfriends?" Terrell gazed lovingly at his cousin's cute expression before saying; "Yeah, I'll always be there for you. I mean that, little man. I've been lookin' out for you since the day you was born. That's never gon' change. Never, I swear!"

"You not suppose ta swear."

"I'm sorry, but I promise."

"Promise what?" Larry questioned, before splashing water.

Terrell used his sleeve to dry the bathwater from his face. "I promise that I'll always be there for you. You believe me?"

"I believe you."

Every time Terrell dried himself, Larry would splash more water. Terrell laughed and then turned the tables on his mischievous little prankster.

Although young Larry didn't know what to expect, new experiences weren't unique to him. After all, he was only five. Every time he rose to a brand-new day he was assured of experiencing something different.

Fishing for the first time was not what excited him.

Standing in cold water, and not being able to say a word, in fear of scaring the day's catch, really didn't sound like that much fun. Nevertheless, the whole idea of spending the better part of the morning hanging out with his dad and cousin is what brought about his enthusiasm.

The rambunctious little boy was dressed in similar attire as his father—orange boot-type galoshes, blue jeans, and a combination red and blue flannel shirt. Larry would take the imitation of his hero a little further. He, like the man that led the way, carried his fishing pole over his right shoulder.

With a tackle in one hand, and his rod in the other, mindful of the steps he had taken over so many years, Terrell brought up the rear as the three trudged the narrow path that led toward the creek.

"Uncle Perry...the family tradition is destined for extinction. Ain't nobody interested in fishin' with us nomo since Grandpa died."

"My two older boys think that fishin' is lame. Don't worry 'bout them; we don't need 'em," Perry replied as he led the two boys through the clearing and into what seemed like paradise.

The line for which the sky and river met was adorned with a beautiful rust color that reflected brilliantly off the waterway. The cool air hung heavy as several mayflies skipped along the surface in an effort to avoid falling prey to winged predators. The pure exquisiteness and splendor of this picturesque setting could not fully be appreciated, if it were replicated on canvas.

Perry immediately walked to the edge of the creek. His eyes were wrapped up in the stately splendor of the sunrise; and his mind was inundated with fond memories of previous Henderson outings.

Perry, his father, and two brothers, Sammy and Arthur, were very competitive in those days. They exhausted most of those mornings arguing over who would stand where. If they hadn't used up so much time battling over positioning, the men might have been able to catch more fish. However, the mêlées were part of their fun.

Perry's memories brought about a smile.

What he saw as a place of peace and solitude, a place of escape from the racial discord that ravished his community, others took as a racial divide. The side of the stream in which he stood was known as the Bottoms. Although white folk ran businesses in that area of Morris County, others felt that it was taboo to wander across the creek.

Every now and then, the Klan would use the cover of darkness to make their presence felt. On those occasions, the residences of the Bottoms were reminded by the white supremacists that nothing had changed.

Most Blacks that worked outside of the Bottoms did so on dairy and cattle farms, which aligned unpaved Junction Three's route toward downtown Jacob. Perry was one of the exceptions from his area that made the commute up Junction Three, across the bridge, which extended over Morris Creek, and into the center of the metropolis. The six-foot, thirty-six-year-old father of five held a position in the heart of the city that gave the citizens of the Bottoms hope, and a feeling of pride.

Terrell and Larry made themselves comfortable on the ground before Terrell opened his tackle box and began rummaging through it.

"I remember when your father first brought me out here. I was a little older than you. You're gonna need to learn how to do this, so pay close attention. Now, if you want, you can use one of these." Terrell pointed to his array of dry flies.

Larry marveled for several seconds before he reached for a beautifully crafted dark-winged lure. "What's this?"

"Be careful; you'll stick yourself if you don't handle it right. That's called a black gnat. That one seems to work best for catching trout. The best thing for bass, which we're gonna be tryin' to catch...is this."

Terrell pulled a wiggling worm from a jar, and dangled it in front of him. "A dark-colored senko finesse worm. If we were really tryin' to catch a bunch of fish, we would have to get on the boat and go into the middle of the creek. Thing is, when we come here, it's really to talk and hang out. We have more fun tryin' to catch as many as we can without gettin' out there. Every now and then, standin' on the edge of the creek, we might get a half-dozen or so."

Enamored with the serenity produced by the chirping birds as they glided in the foreground of the rising sun, Perry heaved a tranquil sigh before his brown eyes briefly veered in the direction of his son and nephew.

His Southern inflection was as calm as the creek. "Terrell, I still think that you should've gone to Michigan. Track and field at Michigan State University could afford you some very good opportunities."

Terrell hooked the worm to Larry's line. "I know, but I can still go next year. I'll still get the track scholarship. I'm gon' hang 'round and help my momma. I don't wanna go away to school and be thinkin' 'bout her bein' sick and all," he said as he and his little cousin got to their feet.

Terrell immediately brushed the dirt off of his brown corduroys, then removed a rag from his trousers and began to wipe his hands neurotically; he had a compulsive nature. Terrell noticed a speck of dirt that had fallen off of the worm and onto his blue cotton shirt. He wiped at it before he stuffed the rag into his back pocket.

"Yo' mother is okay…she had walkin' pneumonia… me and yo' daddy are more than capable of lookin' after my sister," Perry replied.

"Daddy, why did we get up so early?" the inquisitive

offspring interrupted as he approached his father with pole in hand.

Perry handed his rod and reel to Terrell before he glanced down at his baby boy. "You remind me so much of Terrell, always with the questions. The fish go to school early in the mornin'. We want to try and catch them when they're on their way to class," Perry said with a smile.

Returning his father's smile, Larry offered, "I wanna be like you, Daddy. I wanna be a policeman."

Terrell watched on as his uncle began to instruct little Larry on how to cast his line. "He ain't the only one. Uncle Perry, I wanna be like you, too."

Honor, gratification and pride overwhelmed the senior member of the fishing expedition. He could tell that both boys were very proud of what he had accomplished.

Being a pioneer always brings about struggle; it's nothing to take likely. However, to be the first person of color to tread in uncharted waters, at a time when discrimination was blatant, and considered the norm, that took more than guts; it took a divine hand. For two years, Perry Henderson, Jr. held the distinction of being the only Black law enforcement officer employed by the Jacob Police Department. In fact, Perry was the first Black officer in the history of Morris County.

The policeman carried on his slender shoulders the hopes and dreams of nearly fifteen thousand residents, which made up the county's population of Blacks. Perry not only had to deal with the jealousy and ridicule of his own community, he had to deal with the arrogance of a people who felt that his position meant absolutely nothing. To arrest a white person would bring on more problems—not necessarily from the individual in handcuffs—but from the very people that he worked with, and reported to.

Perry reached over his son's shoulders and placed his hands on the boy's pole. "Larry, you have to bring yo' pole back like this and then fling it forward."

"Wow…look at it go…" Larry's joy was obvious as he watched the worm fly through the air and come to rest on the creek's surface.

The trees that aligned both sides of Junction Three obstructed the view to the worn shack-like trailers in a rural area less than a mile from the Bottoms. This was a region in which the white lower class of Jacob took refuge.

The activity of several children that played in front of these neglected dwellings was interrupted. They stopped in order to catch a glimpse of a vehicle as it tore recklessly through their neighborhood.

A gray 1967 Lincoln Continental kicked up the dust in its wake as it traveled the two-lane dirt road at an ungodly speed.

Miran Thompson barely maintained control of his car; it periodically fishtailed on the unpaved thoroughfare. He was obviously determined to reach his destination, so he continued to press on the gas.

🌼

Lee Thompson was attempting to make repairs underneath one of several wrecks that sat in front of his residence when his stepbrother's luxury vehicle barreled onto his property.

Lee jumped, nearly hitting his head against the oil pan after hearing the car door slam. "Damn...that son-of-a-bitch is mad," he whispered to himself.

Miran yelled as he angrily yanked his little brother by the legs, and pulled him from under the car. "Damn it, Lee...you one stupid son-of-a-bitch. I told you how I wanted this thing handled."

Lee squirmed as he was being dragged. "What the hell you doin', Miran...let me go."

"You was suppose'ta take care of that nigga...nah my boss thinks that I can't do my damn job," Miran ranted as he threw his little brother's legs to the ground.

Lee quickly got to his feet. He took a rag from the pocket of his overalls and attempted to wipe the grease from his face. "I told the boys that we gon' take care of that on Monday. You gon' be there...right?"

"You damn right I'm gon' be there. You just make

sure that this don't happen again...do the jobs when you're told."

Lee angrily threw his rag in Miran's face before he attempted to walk away. "I'm tired of you always tellin' me what to do. While you workin' with him and livin' in some fancy house on the hill, I'm stuck here doin' yo' dirty work."

"You ungrateful redneck...I been carryin' you ever since Daddy died. I gave you his house, and I give you an allowance." Miran grabbed Lee by the shoulder and spun him around. "You look at me when I'm talkin' to you, boy! I even brought you into the Knights when Daddy said that you were too damn stupid to understand our mission. Is it true that you told Jasper and Red to handle this?"

"Yeah...so?"

"You know that I don't trust Jasper. He too soft! You better keep your eye on him," Miran insisted.

Monday NIGHT

Local and national meteorologists' forecast of a hurricane could barely be heard over a transistor radio due to the roar of thunder that played like a bass drum.

Lightning introduced a buildup of dirty gray clouds that were forced in from the gulf. The predicted fifty-five-mile-an-hour winds were scheduled to touch down within hours. A steady breeze began to flirt with leaves that danced a circular tango above foliage that carpeted the ground; a sure sign that a severe storm was brewing.

The deejay's deep Southern enunciation was barely audible against the static that was produced by the bad radio reception.

"Take every precaution necessary. This storm has intensified and will undoubtedly cause massive damage. This here, it be a hurricane fo sho... Now, for the local news, we have a hurricane of a different sort brewin' in these parts. From the moment that The Montgomery Bus Boycott, the sit-ins...The Freedom Rides, Birmingham, The March on Washington, Selma, Medgar Evers and Martin Luther King have attempted to initiate a change in our way of life. This reporter has come to the conclusion that most white-folk feel the same. We're all against, and will never accept segregation. I'm with Wallace. Everyone should know their place."

The individuals gathered in an isolated wooded area some thirty miles from the nearest hint of civilization strongly objected to any suggested modifications in their way of life. Their attitudes were engraved from childhood. They were taught to hold true to their idealistic beliefs of superiority.

The demonstrative group began to move with a sense of urgency upon hearing the broadcast. Nothing, not even the expected heavy winds and rain—in any way— would interfere with the abhorrence about to be unleashed. Those that had assembled were hell bent on dealing with the detestation they felt toward their guest of honor.

His eyelids encased his worst nightmare, but knowing that he would have to open them in order to authenticate his demented thoughts (his belief that he was about to become an unwilling participant at the end of a Klansman's noose), frightened him more.

The throbbing and stinging sensation that electrified his tattered body persuaded him that he had to feign unconsciousness, so he continued to lay dormant in the bed of the pickup truck after awakening to the sound of laughter around him.

He'd already been kicked, stumped and bashed in the head several times with a baseball bat; so the young boy wouldn't dare make the slightest movement in fear that he would receive more of the brutality previously inflicted.

The child was able to distinguish with certainty that only one of his assailants was in the truck with him. He quickly realized that another stood outside the bed when the horrid aroma of manure, liquor, fish and tobacco tortured his nostrils after that individual leaned in and blew cigarette smoke into his face.

As hard as he tried, the youngster couldn't make out what was being said—blows to the head had damaged his eardrums. It was like someone held their hands over his ears while they whispered.

"We gotta get this little porch monkey over to Miran—

and change into our uniform like the rest of them before we get this lynchin' under way."

He didn't have to be able to understand what was being said because the aroma of death was in the air. It was really eerie to him. At such a young age he'd already experienced being on the brink—so he was very much aware of death's odor; its aura.

Suddenly, the Black youth felt the weight of the truck shift as Lee Thompson hopped onto the bed.

Jasper began to have second thoughts when he looked down at the little boy that frequented his store. Before him was a kid that he had grown to like—a child that would occasionally help him out around his place of business.

Jasper did business with the kid's family. He looked at them as being good people, God-fearing people. A grocer during the day, and a wannabe racist by night, Jasper wasn't sure whether he would be able to live with what was about to take place. He wouldn't be able to live with the boy's death on his conscience.

"Looky here, Lee, I can't do this."

The frail racist directed his attention back to his captive before removing his baseball cap. He used his free hand to wipe the perspiration from atop his half-bald head.

Lee snarled as he then glared at his partner. "Miran told me that you was too soft." He insisted, "Get that boy's feet."

Jasper refused to move. He lowered his head in shame.

Lee shouted, "JASPER…YOU BETTER GET THAT BOY'S FEET!"

The boy kept his body limp as the two Night Hawks lifted, and then tossed him from the bed of the '59 Ford. His body bounced as it made contact with the ground. The air that escaped from his lungs forced him to heave a sigh.

With a cigarette dangling from the corner of his lips, Lee smiled. "Damn! If that boy wasn't out…he is now."

Jasper stood petrified.

For the first time since he'd become a member of the Knights—a group dedicated to the preservation of their race—he had a feeling of regret.

Both members of the Klavern security team stood on the back of the pickup and glared at the activity taking place around them for several seconds before they leapt to the ground.

The two rednecks immediately hooked their arms under his armpits and lifted Terrell Johnson's lanky, lifeless body from the earth's surface. Blood was visible on his exposed torso. The crimson fluid also trickled from his ears and the corner of his mouth.

The lean, cratered-face leader of the security team took a long toke of his cigarette before he attempted to extinguish it on Terrell's mutilated chest. Lee filled the night with demonic laughter as he listened to the sizzle of burning flesh.

It took every ounce of fortitude that the eighteen-year-old could muster for him not to flinch as the heat generated from the Pall Mall scorched his skin. Terrell courageously continued to dangle his battered cranium as lifeless as a worn rag doll.

Lee was extremely disappointed that his attempt at torture didn't seem to wake the Black youth from his stupor.

"This *son-of-a-bitch* must be dead," Lee mumbled as he flicked his cigarette. He attempted to wake Terrell by slapping his face several times. The heartless racist wanted Terrell to feel the anticipation of death; he wanted him to be aware of his fate.

Snot and saliva dribbled from his nose and mouth. Terrell faintly whispered as he continued to dangle his head. "Mr. Jasper, I told Larry that I would always be there for'em…I promised him."

"What did he say?" Lee asked.

Jasper's hunched shoulders and lost expression prompted Lee to put his ear closer to the boy's mouth.

"What did you say, nigga?"

Terrell didn't respond. He attempted to once again feign unconsciousness. Lee immediately slapped him several more times while yelling in anger, "Wake up, boy! Wake yo' black ass up! I want you to see this."

Unable to bring the Black youth around, the two rednecks began to drag the youngster through the dark of night. Terrell could feel the bony men weaken with every step as they yanked and tugged at his battered frame.

Barely able to open his eyes due to the swelling, Terrell's trepidation was exaggerated as he raised his head enough to see a portion of the densely wooded area suddenly light up.

The intensity of the flames, which consumed several make-shift wooden crosses, seemed to ignite the ire of Lee. The men stopped and released Terrell. His body once again hit the ground with force.

Filled with a rage that he didn't fully understand, Lee cowardly began to kick Terrell. "Goddamn *nigga*...!" he grunted.

Terrell was about to give in—he couldn't take it.

He was ready to cry out but Lee suddenly stopped his attack.

Lee nonchalantly reached into his shirt pocket and pulled from it a pack of cigarettes and a lighter. He lit a cancer stick as both men marveled at the inferno's battle with the slight drizzle. For that moment, their symbol of superiority seemed a cut above Mother Nature. The frightened youngster's mind immediately registered the bizarre images.

His parents spent many tireless hours trying to explain what was before him. He finally realized what was being preached. The world was not yet ready to accept him as a person, let alone an equal. At that moment, his optimistic outlook of the world, which had caused many debates within his household, changed. It didn't matter that the courts had abolished segregation, and it certainly didn't matter that he was allowed to attend the city's community college. It mattered only that he had crossed the line—and crossing that line meant that he had to pay the ultimate price.

The combustion provided enough light for the youth to see dozens of individuals cloaked in Klan attire. Terrell shifted his eyes to his right. The man that stood next to him wore blue jeans and a red flannel shirt. The youth saw this man every day. This individual had always been nice to him. Terrell quickly realized that he couldn't allow his mind to get caught up in trying to understand why a man that his family did business with on a daily basis was readying himself to commit murder. He had to find a way to escape. The reality before him sparked his survival instincts.

One hundred yards or so from where he lay were several other wraithlike shadows. He quickly shifted his attention to his left; the man who'd tried to burn him with cigarettes donned similar attire as the other.

Terrell could see several dogs tied to a tree some sixty yards away.

Suddenly, he caught the two men responsible for carting him to the bonfire completely off guard when he got to his feet and broke into a full sprint.

"What the...catch his ass, Jasper! The truck...I left the keys in the truck—that *NIGGA*, he...he...he's gettin' away," Lee shouted as both watched Terrell run in the direction in which they'd come.

Jasper was relieved. His hope was that Terrell could actually avoid capture. The grocer knew that his life would be over if Terrell escaped, but he didn't care. If he could have, without drawing suspicion, the storeowner would have assisted the frightened youth in his flight.

The terrified youngster made his way to the pickup. He jumped into the driver's side and frantically tried to start the old Ford. Three, four, five turns of the key—he had to be careful not to flood the engine. On his panic-stricken sixth attempt, the truck finally roared to life. Terrell quickly shifted the pickup into reverse—he shifted into drive and stepped on the gas.

Lee fired his revolvers at the vehicle as its spinning tires kicked up mud.

The redneck couldn't believe what had happened. He knew that his stepbrother wouldn't hesitate to make him the evening's activity if the kid he was firing upon were to disappear into the night.

The sound of hot lead piercing metal caused Terrell to panic. He briefly removed his hands from the steering wheel—the errant pickup immediately grazed several parked vehicles, but he never let up off the gas. He promptly grabbed the wheel, but the truck continued to swerve recklessly as he attempted to gain control. Terrell ducked as the smoldering projectiles began to strike the vehicle.

Suddenly, the driver's side window exploded. Several pieces of glass embedded themselves into Terrell's high cheekbones.

The commotion didn't spark an immediate reaction from the other members. Preoccupied with drinking, smoking, and all out rebel rousing, they felt that the gunfire was a part of their festivities. It wasn't until someone was heard yelling, "*HE'S GETTING AWAY!*" that they grabbed their weapons and rushed toward the uproar.

Exalted Cyclops, Miran Thompson yelled as he made his way toward the mayhem. "Don't kill 'em...don't kill 'em...I wanna hang his black ass...Goddamnit, Lee, you can't do nothin' right!"

A bullet ripped through the front tire, sending the vehicle on a reckless out-of-control journey down the very narrow trail, which was completely surrounded by a sea of thick redwood. Terrell fought as courageously with the wheel as a sailor would trying to maintain control of his vessel through turbulent twenty-foot-high waves.

"Oh no..." Terrell yelled, as he inadvertently smashed the truck into a tree and his head against the steering wheel. "Huh! Oh—shss!"

Confused and dazed, the young man desperately tried to exit the smoking wreckage but the driver's side door was wedged against a tree.

"My God! Help me! I gotta get out of here," he shrieked as he frantically smashed his shoulder against the door in hope of forcing it open.

Although his focus wasn't clear, he was well aware that the platoon of ghostly silhouettes that approached would gain some sort of morbid pleasure watching him die. He wanted to prevent that—he had to. So, Terrell quickly slid to the passenger side, and out the door.

Fear fueled every stride as he attempted to maneuver his way through the dense forest. If Terrell stood any chance of survival, he had to convince his mind that the excruciating pain was a non-factor.

He lost the light of a once full moon as it took refuge behind the overcast night sky, so visibility definitely added to the list of obstacles that he had to overcome. His eyes veered unknowingly into unfathomable darkness, which caused his stomach to tie up in knots. He hadn't experienced anxiety on the level that had overtaken him since his mother had fallen victim to pneumonia.

Strained cries of hounds approaching reminded him to run, and run fast.

"You think they'll still let us hang that black son-of-a-bitch?" one of the rednecks asked, as he was being led through the woods by an aggressive hound.

"Of course they will…he was tryin' to kiss a white girl. We gotta teach them niggas a lesson!" Jasper replied in an effort to keep up appearances.

The redneck that held the dog pointed. "Billy said that the little *nigga* ran off in this direction."

With a shotgun in his right hand, Lee knelt beside

the very spot where Terrell had fallen. He picked up some leaves and twigs that were covered with blood. "Hey, ya'll…he was here."

Lee tossed the foliage to the ground before he got to his feet. He stared intently through the drizzle. Using his left hand, he pulled the collar to his shirt up; he then yanked on the bill of his baseball cap, pulling it snug to his head in an effort to protect himself from the rain.

Barely able to maintain his grip on two hostile hounds, one of the hunters cried out, "You want us to let the dogs go…?"

"Yeah," Lee replied as he lifted his shotgun.

He knew that his brother was going to blame him for the Black teen's escape; and Lee also realized that if they didn't catch Terrell, Perry Henderson would come after him and his brother with a vengeance. If Terrell got away, a house of cards would come tumbling down.

Four hounds were released; they immediately ran in Terrell's direction.

Lee and five other men—three carrying shotguns— attempted to keep pace. Their robes flowed freely in the wind, which gave the impression that Terrell was being hunted down by angry spirits. When the clouds opened, the heavy rains further disrupted Terrell's visibility. He was soaked, confused, tired and very scared. He felt like all that was taking place was his fault. How could he believe that being best friends with a white woman would render absolutely no consequence? After all, it was 1967; he lived in the Deep South—Blacks and Whites lived separate lives. He had been taught to keep his distance, but Sara kissed him. Although he wanted her to, he would never have initiated it.

He made it to the clearance and spotted a cargo train.

Terrell abandoned every technique that he'd ever been taught as the city's top sprinter by using his left arm to clutch his aching stomach. Terrell stumbled several times. Without the use of his arms as leverage, it became increasingly difficult for him to maintain his balance. The constant gulps of air began to take its toll; Terrell's lungs felt like they were about to burst. His arms felt like bricks and his legs tightened, which caused his pace to shorten even more.

He glanced over his shoulder but was unable to see the hounds whose unrelenting cries were becoming louder.

TOOT…TOOT…the train's horn blasted.

"Damn… It's movin' kinda fast," he managed to say in between desperate attempts to relieve his lungs.

Now was the time. He had to deal with the pain if he were to have any chance at escape. Terrell's determination was evident. He took a deep breath, tightened his fist, pumped his arms and lifted his legs. His stride was back. He puffed and blew as he pumped and lifted. His legs began to cramp, but he ignored it. He'd never lost a race in high school, and if he lost this one, it would be his last.

As he ran alongside the cargo transporter, he once

again peered over his shoulder. Terrell could see four hounds dash from the wooded area like they had a bet which would catch him first.

His hand slipped as he tried to jump into an open car. The dogs were gaining fast and he was extremely tired. As his pace began to shorten, the hand of a hobo appeared from the darkened railroad car. Terrell was barely able to grab it.

The white man pulled. "Hold on, son...I got you," he said as he attempted to lift Terrell into the empty shipment container. The severe downpour and heavy winds, combined with the freight traveling at a twenty-mile-an-hour pace, made it extremely difficult for the hobo to hold on. Terrell's body swayed wildly; the Samaritan struggled to pull the youngster's one hundred and sixty-eight-pound frame to safety.

"Help me...please," Terrell begged.

Thirteen
YEARS LATER

Several officers from the Jacob police department patiently walked the perimeter around Harry's Liquor Store. A search was underway for evidence, and or witnesses, that could lead them to the person responsible for a reported homicide.

Curious spectators began to gather; they were all a bit on edge.

Morris County residents had a right to be concerned because a number of white males had been mysteriously murdered over several months and law enforcement wasn't even close to identifying a suspect. A sense of panic could be felt from those that had congregated at the site of the most recent slaying.

The victim's face was unrecognizable due to the blood and swelling caused by a single gunshot wound to the temple; his body lay sprawled on the cool pavement of the parking lot. Pieces of a broken whisky bottle escaped from a brown paper bag, which lay next to the corpse. One officer carefully stepped over a trail of liquor.

A second officer sat with his legs dangling from his open patrol car. Twenty-three-year-old rookie patrolman Nolan had a two-way radio to his lips, his Southern infliction deep. "I was the first to respond. It seems like a robbery gone bad. The victim looks to be 'bout five-nine or ten; white male…he's wearin' a black suit, minus a tie, black loafers; neatly trimmed gray hair. The fatal wound was a single gunshot, up close and personal on the left side of his head."

The patrolman went on to say, "His face is covered with so much blood, and is seriously swollen, so I'm unable to give an accurate description at this time. I didn't touch any of his personal effects because I didn't want to disturb the crime scene… over!"

There was static, which accompanied the pause. The dispatcher interrupted the silence. "Four-sixteen… four-sixteen, secure the scene and don't let anyone touch anything…Jake is on his way…over!"

"Ten-four…" the officer replied.

"Four-sixteen…have you got any other details? Over!"

"I was told by the clerk that the victim's name is Miran Thompson…over." The officer listened to the static created by his two-way radio as he awaited a reply.

Confederate flags covered the dirty brown paint peeled walls behind the well-stocked, L-shaped bar. Johnny

Cash's down-home country lyrics blared from a jukebox that sat in the corner of Nobles, a high-energy, dimly lit, smoke-filled, watering hole.

Several inebriated regulars jeered and cheered as they watched a female patron hold on for dear life in the midst of being tossed around by a mechanical bull. A dispute over the female's ability to ride the mechanized creature caused three customers to push and taunt one another.

A drunken ruckus erupted.

Everyone in the establishment, apart from the diligent bartender, seemed captivated by the intoxicated gladiators. Working around fisticuffs was a part of the barkeep's nightly ritual; in fact, several times a night, the rowdy patrons of Nobles would butt heads for one reason or another. The saloon owner was used to the altercations. What he wasn't used to was seeing one of the biggest instigators in the entire town not attempt to get in the middle of a dispute. This was the case when dogmatic extremist Earl "Red" Peters burst into his establishment. The bartender continued to pour drinks but wondered why the known rowdy racist ignored the barbaric display of manhood. He kept his eyes on the frail man as he marched directly to, and then pulled the plug of, the automatic slot machine that played records. Everyone froze in their tracks when the needle created an annoying scratching sound as it slid across the recording.

Red's unsettled Southern drawl exploded, "HEY YA'LL! SOMEBODY KILLED MIRAN!"

Several of the patrons aimlessly hurled their drinks in response to Red's announcement.

Everyone respected Miran Thompson, and they quickly surrounded Red before bombarding him with questions.

"Where...?" one of the men involved with the pandemonium that had taken place asked, holding a bottle of beer to his swollen eye.

A man in his forties, who had had his lip busted, shouted, "Who did it?"

Out of nowhere, Miran's infuriated little brother pushed his way through the crowd that had congregated around Red. Lee Thompson grabbed the flimsy messenger by the arm with firm determination. "What happened?"

"He was shot outside Harry's Liquor Store." Frantic, the wiry hillbilly motioned for everyone to follow. The liquored up mob scurried to the door.

Bright flashes of red and blue lit up the area.

A plume of white exhaust swirled from the tailpipe and around the array of antennas; it was obvious that the black unmarked vehicle was official as it pulled up to the crime scene. A uniformed officer lifted the tape used to cordon the area and allowed the automobile access to the parking lot of Harry's Liquor Store.

Patrolman Nolan immediately recognized the veteran cop's squad car. "Here comes Jake…he's really gonna be pissed," Officer Nolan said, tapping his partner on the shoulder.

Detective Jake Aaron pulled directly in front of the entrance to the store and cut his engine.

Both rookie policemen stood at the side of the building where the body lay. They stopped their search for evidence and glared at the veteran detective's car.

"Why would he be mad?" Nolan's partner asked.

He responded, "I was told that the murder victim was Aaron's best friend."

Jake Aaron's grasp of investigative tactics was legendary in law enforcement circles. The twenty-year veteran was wearing a long black trench coat as he stepped from his vehicle. A cigarette hung from the tip of his lips.

The rookie cops on the scene stood in awe as the wind seemed to pick up just enough to force Aaron's coat to flutter like Superman's cape, which in their view, only added to the homicide detective's mystique. Jake's strong chin and mountain man rogue appearance was the look of a man who was not easy to talk to.

As he closed his car door, Jake immediately spotted six pickup trucks approaching—their headlights nearly blinded him. The detective flicked his cigarette, and then squinted. He used his right hand in an attempt to shield his eyes from the gleam of headlights while trying to identify the angry citizens he heard shouting vulgarities from the bed of the vehicles that recklessly sped toward his crime scene.

The trucks abruptly stopped right behind the yellow crime scene tape. Lee quickly hopped out of his red '74 Hi-Lux pickup truck and attempted to lead a group of irate citizens toward the detective.

He wanted answers. Someone was going to pay for Miran's death.

Jake made his way toward the fuming posse.

Lee's monotone was filled with a tremendous amount of stress. "Jake...

What the hell happened to Miran?"

"I just got here myself. But, from what I was told, yo' brother was gunned down in what looks to be an attempted robbery."

Doubt saturated Lee's response. "Robbery...no one in their right mind would try to rob him."

He tried to force his way past the detective. Jake immediately grabbed him by the arm. "You can't go over there...we'll handle it."

While the detective attempted to calm the victim's brother, several of Lee's friends noticed a Black man kneeling beside the corpse.

Red pushed his way through the tense mob and headed toward Lee and Jake. He tapped Lee on the shoulder—then pointed in the direction of the Black man who was wearing blue jeans and a light-blue cotton shirt, "Hey, Lee...look over there."

His anger once again flared. Lee's antagonist was stooped over his brother's body, and he was not at all comfortable with the Black officer being involved with the investigation into his death. "What the hell is that nigga doin'?" Attempting to pull away from Jake's grip, he blasted, "Let me go! He's the one that did it! I'd bet anythin'… Get him away from my brotha… He said that he was gonna get Miran. Let me go! I'm gon' kill his black ass…"

Jake motioned for the uniformed officers. "Nolan… you guys…get these people out of here."

The Black man completely ignored the commotion that was taking place at the front of the store. He used a pencil to open a wallet that sat in a pool of blood next to the body. Several seconds later, he used his pencil to open the victim's blazer; after which, he carefully observed the body. He wasn't going to lose any sleep over this homicide. Miran Thompson was the leader of a group Perry believed was responsible for the murder of his nephew thirteen years prior.

The police lieutenant was delighted that the bigot had a bullet in his skull. As he gazed at the bloody gash, the cop wished that the entry wound was bigger. In fact, he wished that the burly corpse that lay before him was missing his entire head.

Images of his favorite nephew's million-dollar smile played about Perry's thoughts as he continued his investigative search for evidence. Memories of their last fishing trip the weekend before Terrell's murder seemed to light a fuse.

Perry reached and then clutched the handle of his weapon.

The officer's intent was clear. If he hadn't been interrupted, the fifteen-year veteran would have emptied the chamber of his .38-caliber revolver into the extremist's lifeless body.

Jake mouthed as he approached Perry from the rear, "Hey, Perry...what the hell are you doin' here? You need to get away from that body before you compromise my crime scene."

"I was in the neighborhood...I responded to the call," Perry replied. He removed his hand from his weapon and stood up. He tried to sound sympathetic. "I'm sorry...I know how close you two were." Perry stepped away from the body in order to give the lead detective a clear view of the victim.

Jake's eyes watered. He discreetly wiped at them.

The veteran cop had been to many crime scenes but none was as personal, so he could barely stomach the gash in his friend's head, nor the blood, which formed a puddle around Miran's nearly unrecognizable face. Jake lowered his head before using the tips of his index and ring fingers to once again wipe the mist from his eyes.

"Damn...I can't believe this."

For a brief second, it seemed that the lifeless corpse of his childhood friend was too much for him to bear.

They'd known each other for over forty years. Although an unsolved lynching had threatened their friendship— a murder that Jake suspected Miran had taken part in— they had endured. The two had gotten back on good terms when Miran asked Jake to be the best man in his wedding two years after the murder.

The two shared a special kinship. No matter what, they always found a way to be there for one another. Miran had been the first to provide support for Jake after the detective buried himself in the bottle during his wife's lengthy battles with ovarian cancer. Unfortunately, she eventually passed from the disease.

Jake knelt beside the body before asking, "You got anythin'?"

"I spoke with the store clerk...Miran ordered several cases of liquor and beer. He asked that they be delivered to his house by Wednesday. The clerk said that he paid for that order by credit card." Perry pointed toward the broken bottle before he continued. "He paid cash fo' that bottle. The clerk said he heard a shot about three minutes after Miran left the store. He ran out, that's when he saw someone runnin'."

The detective slowly shook his head in disgust before asking, "Was he able to give you a description?"

Several DAYS LATER

The silence was a welcome departure from the ruckus that took place during the day when the students of Fitzgerald High would gather for American History. Two nights a week, several individuals who had missed out on their daytime education assembled to prepare for a chance at obtaining their high school diplomas.

Tick tock, tick.

Each second was clearly heard as the second hand of the clock that was mounted on the wall of Room 212 made its sixty-second revolutions.

Mr. Jerry Careri, the assigned educator, sat at his desk grading papers. The night instructor was the best in the city at preparing high school dropouts for General Educational Development testing. Before him sat fourteen students, each was completely immersed in a pretest.

Careri attempted to concentrate on the papers before him, but his eyes kept swaying back to the clock. The test that was being administered was on time restraints and the instructor didn't believe in allowing the students one second more than the forty-five minutes permitted.

It took the college professor nearly the entire allotted testing period before he was finally able to complete his task. He gathered the papers, checked the clock, and then directed his attention toward his students.

"Okay...everyone...put your pencils down and pass

your test up to the front," the volunteer ordered as he
got to his feet.

While collecting the test papers, he said with joy, "I'd
like to say that I'm really proud of all of you; especially
Scott." The teacher sat on the end of his desk with
papers in hand.

Scott Billings was a twenty-seven-year-old Caucasian
who had been heavily involved in drugs and alcohol
when he was in high school. Of course, his addiction
became a hindrance; he dropped out at sixteen and
spent much of his youth in and out of juvenile.

"Scott…ever since Larry has taken the time to work
with you, your chances of obtaining your GED have
improved substantially."

Careri directed his attention toward seventeen-year-
old Larry Henderson, who was seated to his left. "Mr.
Henderson…I really appreciate you giving of your time
to help a fellow student."

The teen acknowledged his instructor's sentiments
with a nod.

Larry was proud that he was able to help. He'd always
loved school, but circumstances had made it impossible
for him to graduate with his class. Valedictorian was not
out of the realm of possibility, if he had been able to
finish school with his peers. Larry was ranked third,
only percentage points behind. He would have had
plenty enough time to surpass his competition, if he
wasn't forced to leave his hometown.

The instructor addressed the entire classroom. "I feel that every one of you will have absolutely no problem passing the test...you guys can leave early...go home, get some rest...I'll call you after I finish setting up your testing with the board."

The murmuring students got to their feet and began to gather their things.

Careri stood.

He looked younger than his fifty-three years. His salt-and-pepper hair, black slacks and white turtleneck sweater, made him look like a *GQ* magazine model. The popular educator opened his briefcase and began to stuff papers inside.

As Larry passed, the professor of art history summoned, "Larry...I'd like to speak with you...can you hang around for a few?"

Larry nodded.

He immediately took a seat and watched as everyone headed for the exit. Careri was delighted with the conversation of several of his students as they talked amongst themselves while passing him.

He heard a young woman say, "I think that we're all going to pass. Jerry is a wonderful teacher."

"Yeah...I thought I was stupid before I met him," said another.

An elderly student said, "He makes things so simple. If he were my teacher thirty years ago, I wouldn't have dropped out."

The corners of Careri's mouth turned up as he watched his eager students exit his classroom. The professor had a moment of self-gratification—it was a feeling for which all dedicated educators strive for. To unleash a student's desire to seek and obtain knowledge is a glorious feeling, but to do so with someone that had once given up on education is the crowning jewel. Careri felt like everything that he ever wanted to accomplish as a teacher had been engraved in the hearts and minds of the individuals that had walked past him.

After the classroom emptied, Jerry turned his attention toward Larry. However, before he could speak, Scott peeked his head back in the open door.

"Excuse me, you guys... Larry...you want me to wait? I'll drop you off at work, if you still want me to."

"I'll take him..." Careri interceded.

The professor's black Cadillac motored northwest up Route 515. He rolled his window down before he lit a cigarette.

Larry's eyes wandered around the vehicle. He was impressed with the car—a brand-new Cadillac with all the extras. The butter-soft black interior was so comfortable that he couldn't stop the slight wiggle of his bottom as the leather literally engulfed his entire body. The more he moved, the better the feel. While he nodded his approval, his hands glided lightly across the door panel.

"Like I said, your potential is unlimited. I'm very impressed with how intelligent you are. I'm more than willing to help you get into college," Professor Careri said.

Larry caught part of Careri's conversation, but for the most part, what his instructor was saying went in one ear and out the other. He was totally enamored with the vehicle he was riding in.

The professor exhaled; a stream of cigarette smoke was yanked from the car by the midday's air. Careri's eyes briefly swung from the road and toward his passenger. "So, would you be interested? I'll help you with finding scholarships...and I'll also help you prepare for your entrance exams. If we aren't able to find enough scholarships, I'll make up the difference."

"Sure...I wanna go to college...and I would appreciate any help you can give me. I'd like to be able to go without having to involve my parents. I really wanna surprise them," Larry responded with a smile. "But... why are you willin' to do all of this for me?"

"I find that learning comes easy for you. Plus, I see how you go out of your way to help others in the class. I feel that you'll make a hell of a professor one day."

Larry redirected his attention to the dashboard. He placed his hand on top, and gently ran it over the leather before continuing, "If being a professor means that I could buy a car like this...where do I sign up?"

Several minutes later, the black sedan pulled to the curb in front of the Vegas Hilton.

Larry reached into the backseat and grabbed his gym bag. He opened the door before he extended his hand to his professor. "Thank you for everythin', Jerry..."

Jerry Careri firmly shook his favorite student's hand while saying, "You take care...I'll see you later this week. We'll go over everything then."

Larry changed from the blue jeans and yellow cotton shirt that he wore to class into the white wool pants and shirt that made up his work attire. He grabbed his apron and made his way over to the large sink positioned in the back of the kitchen. The silver bake and cookware, cutlery, gadgets, utensils, thermometers, timers and other necessities that hung from racks and or were scattered about was a welcome sight.

His life seemed to be headed in the right direction. He had a good job. He was about to get his GED, and he was away from the madness that surrounded his hometown. However, for some reason, Larry felt it wouldn't be advantageous to get excited about the direction his life was headed. He wasn't a pessimist by any means; he just strongly believed that every time he had relaxed in the past, something went wrong.

Larry decided that he wasn't going to allow the troubles of his past to follow him the eight hundred or so miles that he had traveled in order to live with his aunt. His mind had found a peaceful place, a place that he felt he would eventually one day be a place which would afford him endless possibilities; his place called "there."

"This is cool," Larry said. "Yeah…" He nodded his head up and down while tying his apron around his waist. He whispered again, "Yeah…this is it…finally."

As he was piling dishes into the double sink, someone tapped him on his shoulder.

"Larry…what the hell are you doing here this early? You weren't supposed to be here until ten o'clock tonight," said the executive chef.

"I got out of class early…thought I'd come in and help out." He turned on the faucet, picked up a bottle of Joy liquid soap, added some to the water, and began scrubbing a pot.

The chef smiled and then said, "You've only been here for a couple weeks but I wouldn't trade you for anybody. You've reported to work at least an hour before your scheduled time every day since you've worked here…and, you're usually one of the last to leave from your shift. I like that. Keep up the good work." The chef patted Larry on the shoulder before whispering, "Look, don't tell anybody that I told you that…they might think that I've gotten soft."

A Latino coworker was mopping the floor, but his attention was clearly split between his chore and the conversation taking place with the chef and Larry.

After the boss left, the coworker mopped his way toward the whistling dishwasher.

"Hey, Larry, do me a favor, would you?"

"What'cha need…?" he asked, tending to his dishes.

The young Dominican leaned closer. "I know that you're off tomorrow…but can you work for me? My wife's labor is gonna be induced in the morning."

"No problem…" Larry replied before he would wipe his hands off on his apron and extend it to his coworker. "Con-gratulations!"

Forty-five minutes had gone by and the tension was thick. The executive chef's anger was evident. The culinary genius attempted to direct traffic in what had, in a matter of an hour, become a very chaotic working environment. The staff of the Las Vegas Hilton frantically hustled about. They were behind in their efforts to meet the dinner rush.

"I really don't think that you people understand how important it is that you live up to my name. Now, get it right…every one of you can be replaced, but my reputation can't survive the mess that you're trying to pass off as Italian cuisine." The chef yelled, "The base of the fennel bulbs haven't been cut, the core isn't whiter than the surrounding green." He tossed the dish of baked fennel with parmesan into the trash. "I have a standard, people…those that can't live up to that standard should get the hell out of my kitchen."

Most everyone's attention was suddenly drawn toward the kitchen's entrance when two men in wrinkled suits entered. The two official-looking gentlemen were not authorized to step foot into the chef's domain; it was totally against policy. The employees braced themselves for the hurricane that would be their boss. The diligent staff was sure that shit would hit the fan once the chef noticed the unauthorized individuals who were scanning his kitchen during the peak dinner rush. The intruders immediately took note of the ranting manic responsible for preparing the exotic cuisine that the establishment was best known for.

"The very next time someone attempts to serve a substandard dish, I'll serve them up for unemployment." The chef realized that his entire staff's attention had been diverted away from him. He allowed his eyes to follow that of his employees.

The men were nearly upon the chef when he turned and noticed them removing wallets from the breast pockets of their off-the-rack attire.

"Excuse me…is there a Larry Henderson working here?" one of the men inquired.

Before the chef could go into a rage, the two men flashed their badges.

"What the hell is going on…why are the police in my kitchen?"

One of the officers countered, "It's police business…"

The chef pointed to the sink in the far corner. "He's over there…but he's very busy right now."

"This won't take long," the officer stated before the men made their way through the commotion.

The chef was close behind the two law enforcement officers as they approached the teenaged dishwasher.

"Are you Larry Henderson?" one detective asked.

Larry looked about in confusion. His eyes landed on his supervisor.

"Are you Larry Henderson?" the officer questioned again. He flashed his badge; Larry's dark brown eyes widened.

With dish in hand, Larry replied, "Yes, sir…what's this about?"

The second officer removed the plate from his hand while his partner spun him. "You're under arrest."

Larry was stunned. "What… For what…?"

"Murder!" replied the officer who was cuffing him.

I Blame
MYSELF

L ieutenant Perry Henderson, Jr. felt that everyone in the police station had their eyes fixed on his dark six-foot physique when he reported for the morning shift. It wasn't something out of the ordinary; being the first person of color to wear the charcoal gray and blue uniform had him accustomed to the piercing gazes.

However, this felt different.

It wasn't the same hate-filled indignation that he had become accustomed to, this felt more like pity. It was compassion rare for an environment known for racial intolerance; narrow-mindedness spearheaded by some of the very people that couldn't seem to take their sympathetic eyes off of him.

For years, Perry had struggled to deal with the mockery and injustice that had plagued his life from childhood; appearing resolute through the ridicule was now second nature. For over fifteen years, Perry endured the hostility that surrounded his pledge to *Protect and Serve*.

The officer's dedication to being steadfast, no matter what the circumstances, could be attributed to his determination in seeking retribution. He felt that someone had to take responsibility for the murder of his high school best friend in the summer of 1950, and of his nephew in 1967. Although thirty years had passed since the death of his friend, Perry never gave up the idea that he would eventually find the proof necessary to seek an indictment.

He always felt that one person organized both hate crimes—and his best chances of exposing the culprit meant that he would have to stay on the force, no matter what. He wouldn't even consider retirement as being an option until someone was made to pay for his or her misdeeds. Although both murders were long forgotten by law enforcement—they still haunted Perry.

The desk sergeant broke the awkward silence that had engulfed the squad room upon Perry's arrival when he said, "Lieutenant... Chief Bailey wants to see you."

"Tell him that I'll see him after I check my messages," Perry mumbled after breaking the hypnotic glare of his coworkers.

He headed toward his own office.

"LIEUTENANT...he said as soon as you got in..."

Perry stopped, and then directed his attention toward the messenger. The desk sergeant's obstinate expression, as he nodded toward their supervisor's office, sparked the lieutenant's curiosity.

Perry headed toward Bailey's workspace.

Everyone in his path apprehensively directed his or

her attention elsewhere when he approached. They were all very much aware that Perry's life was about to change.

"Hey, chief...you wanted to see me?" Perry asked upon entering the cluttered domain of his short, heavy-set supervisor.

Robert Bailey, who'd left New Orleans three years prior in search of a simpler way of life, sat at his mahogany desk with his trademark bifocals resting on the end of his nose. "Yeah, Perry...move those files off that chair and take a seat."

Bailey began to search through the files that were scattered on top of his desk. "The ballistics report is back. Your backup revolver was positively identified as the murder weapon."

"I can't believe it," Perry somberly replied.

He removed the files from the chair. Unable to find a clean spot atop his boss's disorderly desk, Perry placed the records on the floor, and then made himself comfortable.

Bailey stood and he handed Perry the ballistic report. "We had your son brought back this morning."

"He blamed Miran for what happened to his cousin," Perry said as he opened the report and began going over it.

The chief questioned, "How old was he...five...six?"

"It was the stories that he was told about his cousin... he wasn't old enough to remember...I blame myself."

"Why do you blame yourself?"

"Because I couldn't let it go. I had to find out what happened to Terrell. I thought that my family should know the truth…so I told them about the information that I had gathered durin' my investigation. That truth may cost my son his own life."

"I was told that you found out what happened to your nephew from someone named Jasper Collins." Bailey removed his glasses, and laid them atop his desk.

"Yeah, he told me. When Jasper took me to where they had dumped that bullet-riddled truck, I could only image what that boy went through that night."

Perry handed the report back to his supervisor; he took several seconds in an attempt to gather his thoughts before he would continue. "Jasper's conscience had gotten the best of him…he told me everythin'. We dragged the river a few weeks after Terrell was murdered…that's when we found his body. I guess the others involved found out that Jasper had spoken with me…we found Jasper's body that same day."

In a desperate attempt to keep Perry focused, Bailey stood. "Let's go see your son."

Larry Henderson was the spitting image of his father, tall, thin, mocha skin. He also, like his father, sported a tapered Afro.

The boy seemed bewildered as he sat alone at the long gray table in the drab interrogation room; his eyes nervously darted around. Larry hadn't been in his hometown in over three weeks—ever since his mother put him on a bus for Vegas to live with her sister. He hadn't a clue as to what was going on because the state police officers responsible for transporting him back to Jacob would not provide him or his aunt with any information, other than that a charge of murder had been levied against him.

MURDER...I can't believe that they think I murdered someone, he thought to himself.

Detective Jake Aaron and his forty-year-old graying partner, Detective Simon Harris, stood outside the interrogation room and watched Larry's nervous behavior through the two-way mirror.

"I don't believe that that boy had anythin' to do with what happened to Miran. Okay...ballistics indicates that Henderson's backup revolver was the murder weapon, but that doesn't put the weapon in that kid's hand," Jake mumbled.

Harris countered, "The kid told me that he was at work in the Vegas Hilton the night that Miran was gunned down. I find it hard to believe that he traveled that far to rob and murder Miran...then turned and headed back to Vegas in time for work."

Harris directed his attention toward Jake before he continued, "That scene looked staged. The position of his wallet, the dropped money, and the fact that his wristwatch and wedding ring weren't touched. If it were truly a robbery gone bad...then it was done by someone that had never committed that kind of crime."

The two detectives were so caught up in their exchange of ideas and concerns surrounding the crime scene that they were completely unaware that Chief Bailey and Lieutenant Perry Henderson were approaching.

"How's he holdin' up?" the chief asked.

"Looks confused...kind of antsy," Harris replied.

Perry peered through the two-way mirror.

His son appeared to be very nervous, out right fidgety. After several seconds of silence, the police lieutenant finally spoke. "Chief...I'd like to speak to my boy alone...if that's okay with you guys."

"Sure, Perry..." Bailey agreed. The chief turned his attention toward Harris and Jake. "You two...come with me."

Perry didn't attempt to enter the interrogation room until the others stepped away.

Larry's once solemn expression immediately changed to optimism upon seeing his father standing at the door. The nervous youth got to his feet and, without delay, began to babble. "Hey, Pop...what's goin' on...why are they sayin' that I killed someone?"

The lieutenant took a seat across from his son. Young Larry was very familiar with the stone cold expression that was etched on his father's face. His youthful eyes began to water.

Larry retook his seat.

"I didn't do it…I didn't kill nobody. Don't let them do this to me, Daddy."

His father whispered, "They have proof that you were the one that pulled the trigger."

"No way…how could they? You know I hate guns… who was it that I was suppose'ta have killed?"

"Miran Thompson, the man that murdered Terrell. They've placed you at Harry's Liquor Store at the time of his murder."

"Like I told them detectives…all they gotta do is check with my job. I was in Vegas, Daddy. Tell 'em…get me out of here."

"It's not that simple, son. They have witnesses…Larry… they got a lot of proof that you committed this crime."

Larry fired back immediately, "They can't have proof against me. I wasn't in town when this happened. I got proof!"

"Look, son…if you go to trial for this…they're gonna give you the death penalty. With the proof they have… in this town…you don't stand a chance. I don't care what kind of proof you have. I'm a cop…I know how the system works."

His father stood, and then leaned on the table before he said, "Look here, boy…someone gave your description…on top of everythin' else that they have. You're goin' down for this."

"You won't let them put this on me…will you?"

"Ain't much I can do right now, boy. I wish it was."

He walked to the mirror. "All I know is...if you don't admit to the killin'...they're gonna give you the death penalty." He turned suddenly and added, "...it was a white man that was killed, boy! A Klansman at that...they gotta blame somebody."

"Why me? You hated that guy...I didn't even know him."

"Son...listen to me...you're only seventeen...if you plead guilty...you'll be out in about four years. I'll do everythin' I can to help you...but if we go to trial...there ain't nothin' I'm gonna be able to do to help you. Your proof is not gonna be enough. All they gonna say is that you come here, committed the crime...and went back to Vegas."

Larry leaned forward in his chair; he folded his arms atop the table before he buried his head between them. "You sayin' that I should plead guilty to somethin' I didn't do?"

"I'm sayin'...if you don't...you gon' die," Perry said as he took a seat on the corner of the table.

"Daddy...I can't plead guilty...I'm not guilty!"

"You think that a bunch of white folk gonna believe you? You came back to town and tried to rob that man...*boy*!!! That's what it looks like to them."

"Do you believe me?"

"Sure, I do...but that ain't gon' get you free."

"Should we talk to a lawyer?"

"We don't need no lawyer, boy...ain't no lawyer gon'

help you if the system wants you to go down for this crime."

Larry raised his head.

His faced filled with tears. "Why me? I still don't get it."

"I don't know, son."

"What should I do, Daddy? I'm scared now. At first I wasn't scared 'cause I have an alibi; but now, you tellin' me that they gon' give me the death penalty...and that my alibi don't mean nothin'. What am I gon' do?" Larry's helpless expression pleaded for parental guidance.

"You gon' do what I tell you." The law enforcement officer leaned closer to his son before he continued, "Listen...I'm gon' talk with the DA. I want you to plead guilty. I'll make sure that the DA takes your age into account."

"*What?*"

"Listen...don't panic. You plead guilty...because you're a minor...they should put you away for a couple years... that's all. I'm tellin' you...we don't stand a chance goin' to trial."

"*Daddy!!!*"

"Just do what I say, for once in your life."

Larry wiped tears from his watered eyes. "It's not right... I shouldn't have to do this...I didn't do nothin'."

"Do you wanna die?"

"*NO!*"

"Well—do what I say." He leaned closer to his son

before whispering. The police officer spent the next several minutes attempting to convince his son of the validity of his plan.

Chief Bailey divided his attention between his paperwork and Detective Aaron, who had pushed some of the clutter aside so that he could make himself comfortable on the edge of his supervisor's desk.

"Jake...I need you on this. The media is gonna have a field day with this, if it's not handled correctly," Bailey said. He handed Jake a file.

Jake opened the manila folder. "So...what's goin' on?"

"It seems that Henderson's son has been a problem for quite some time. I've been told that he's a pistol. The lieutenant hasn't been able to control him...that's why he was sent to Vegas to live with relatives," Bailey announced before he turned his concentration on the paperwork before him.

"So you're tryin' to tell me that this boy killed Miran. That's kinda hard for me to believe. Bobby...somethin' 'bout this don't feel right."

"What's on your mind?"

"I don't know..." Jake stood. He had one important question that he felt he needed answered. "How the hell did his son get his hands on that weapon? We all know how anal Henderson is 'bout weaponry. He would never allow kids around guns. You'd have me believe that it's a coincidence that, on the very day that Perry was careless with one of his weapons, his son used it to murder his father's enemy. I don't believe in those kinds of coincidences. "

Bailey's curious expression was followed by a question of his own. "Where you goin' with this?"

Four DAYS LATER

He had been bombarded with phone calls from the press the entire week; the question swirling around, *'had Larry been pressured into his confession?'* He'd also fielded calls from Miran's family and friends demanding that Perry be relieved of duty. The chief made it clear that Perry was not responsible for the actions of his son, and would not be asked to step down.

Chief Bailey peered out of his office window while engaged in a telephone conversation with members of a white supremacist group. They had him on speakerphone. Several high-ranking officials demanded that a full investigation be conducted.

"I'm really sorry that you feel that way, but Lieutenant Henderson is a dedicated law enforcement officer. If it wasn't for him, we would not have found his son so quickly."

He listened to the rhetoric of the assembled hate

group for several seconds before whispering into the receiver, "Well…I am convinced that the right man is behind bars…so I wouldn't suggest that you do anything like going after my lieutenant."

Detective Aaron entered the office of his commander. Jake had no idea that his boss was on the verge of losing his cool, until he heard him scream, "If I hear another threat against my officer…I'll come and put the cuffs on all of you my damn self!

Bailey held up a finger, prompting the detective to wait until he concluded his call. "Well…I really have to go. I would seriously suggest that you people let it go…" the chief insisted. "Look… it's over. I gotta go…" he said as he rested the receiver on its cradle.

"Jake…I want you to drop your investigation. Henderson's son has copped to the murder and is being sentenced today."

"If it's alright with you…I'd rather stay on this," Aaron said as he took a seat.

Totally stunned, Bailey opposed, "No…I'm not gonna say it again. This case is closed. Perry's son confessed…I'm not going to allow this department to waste man-hours on a dead end." The chief walked over to his file cabinet before saying, "What do you care anyway? From what I was told, you never liked Henderson. What do you care if his son admitted to this?"

"I want the person responsible for killin' Miran…and I don't believe that the boy did it!"

Both of the officers were surprised when Jonathan Edwards, a reporter from the *Daily News*, sashayed into Bailey's office. He made it obvious that he had over-heard their conversation. "So, you don't believe that that kid murdered Miran either, huh?"

Jake hated the press—and he wasn't a big fan of the reporter.

Jonathan was known for digging as deep as he had to in order to get to the root of a story.

Jake wasn't the least bit interested in hearing anything that the award-winning reporter had to say. Without so much as a word, the detective exited his supervisor's office.

Fresh brewed coffee was more distinguishable than the perfume that emanated from the woman in the black robe. She sat behind her large red oak desk and allowed her mind to track the history of her family's ties to jurisprudence—she was hoping that it would bring clarity to her dilemma. Judge Marsha Elliott was going over an allocution related to the death of Miran Thompson. She found this to be one of her more troubling cases because someone she had grown to respect had a child that admitted to homicide.

Sending a teenaged boy to prison for the better part of his life didn't sit well with her. After all, she was a mother herself—she understood the pain that her decision was going to cause; but the perturbed judge knew that she had no choice. She was obligated to set forth sentencing according to the statute as it applied toward the crime committed.

First-degree murder was not a charge that could be dismissed with a mere slap on the wrist, no matter how much the judge loathed the victim.

The adjudicator looked up from the allocution and responded to a knock at her door. "Come in…" she said.

Larry was dressed in a county orange jumpsuit; his hands were cuffed to the front. Perry wore his police dress blues: two members of the District Attorney's Office, and two bailiffs accompanied the father and son.

Larry's nervous energy filled the room.

His legs twitched uncontrollably. The confessed murderer's wandering eyes strayed. If he wasn't caught up in his situation, Larry would have had an appreciation for the décor that populated the judge's wood-stained space. He had a keen eye for interior design and architecture. Larry's dreams of one day attending the School of Architecture at the University of Arizona was now in the hands of a complete stranger.

There were several seconds of silence.

The moderator presiding over Larry's confession looked up from the written allocution because she was prepared to address her invited guest.

"Larry Henderson…I know your father well…he's a

good man. He's done so many good things since he's put on that uniform. I admire his struggles and his determination. He is truly a trailblazer…and a credit to this city. His outstanding service to this community is why I decided to give sentencing here in my chambers. But before I pass sentence…is there anything that you would like to say?"

Larry's eyes passively veered toward his father for several seconds, and then back to the judge before he nervously whispered, "No ma'am."

The judge continued, "Because of your father's tireless dedication to this city, I'm forced to sit here and contemplate your future. My problem, young man, is that you are the son of a man that's worked real hard to maintain law and order within this community. Of all the children in this city, you should be held to a higher standard because of who your father is."

The judge made a hand gesture toward Lieutenant Henderson before she would go on to say, "Being raised in a policeman's home, you should understand the pain that this crime has caused not only to the victim's family but to your family as well. While I do appreciate your willingness to stand up and admit to what you have done, I find that you have committed a deplorable crime. This being said, I hereby sentence you to be held at the state's maximum penal facility for a term of twenty-five years."

Larry's knees almost buckled. His eyes began to water—he once again directed his attention toward his father and couldn't believe what he had heard. He wondered how he had allowed himself to be in his current situation. His mind was overwhelmed with thoughts; most of them geared toward his father's strategy.

Lieutenant Henderson ignored his son's pleading expression.

The judge continued, "Since your eighteenth birthday is in two days, your sentence is to be carried out immediately. You are to be placed in the custody of the state's maximum security penal facility without delay."

She made eye contact with Larry before saying, "Young man, I have no idea how the son of a police lieutenant could bring himself to commit such a horrible crime, but you'll have a lot of time to think about what you've done."

"*DADDY*! You gotta help me!!! You said I wouldn't have to go to jail long. You know I didn't kill nobody!!!" Larry insisted.

He desperately attempted to pull from the bailiff's grip as they began to escort him from the judge's chambers. His father showed no emotion. Nor did he make any attempt to look at his son.

Next MORNING

At six in the morning the sun hadn't eliminated the early morning dew, but the orange inferno was bright enough to create a rich golden shimmer, which reflected sharply off the two broken tractors, a combine, rotary cutters, and a shredder, that were scattered about the open field. The abandoned farm equipment was buried by grass so high that, if not for the sun reflecting off of it, no one navigating the isolated dirt road would have paid any attention to it.

A dust-covered Department of Corrections bus traveled at a moderate speed through the open country—it rumbled over the rough terrain and passed what was once considered prime farmland.

Two armed guards sat opposite one another outside the caged portion of the bus's interior. Dressed in penitentiary orange, twelve shackled convicted criminals occupied the seats within the cage.

Whispers from Wesley Hobbs, a bald thirty-year-old Black, two-time loser; and his partner in crime, thirty-two-year-old Leroy Burns, ignited rage from the guards.

One guard sternly interrupted the inmates. "You two had better shut the hell up!"

With cuffed hands resting in his lap, baby-faced Larry Henderson occupied the window seat directly behind Hobbs and Burns. The bewildered youth stared intently out of the window.

He was lost—his mind racing, his thoughts going nowhere.

Although Larry and his father's relationship was strained, he never, for one second, could bring himself to believe that the man he had once pegged as his hero; the man who taught him how to fish at the age of five on the bank of Morris Creek, would do anything less than protect him in a crisis. The youngster needed to believe his father's reasoning. He needed to believe that his father's insistence that he plead guilty to murder was a strategy.

His father needed time to find the proof that would exonerate him.

Perry also explained to his son how difficult it would be to get someone off death row—even if uncovered evidence established that person's innocence. Therefore, copping to the murder of a noted bigot made more sense than standing trial and facing a jury pool that would obviously be tainted against him.

The death penalty would have been inevitable.

Larry wanted so badly to believe his father's assertion; but the entire situation didn't sit right with the young, soon-to-be inmate. Larry felt that the only person that could bring clarity to his state of affairs was his mother.

Why hasn't she tried to see me? he asked himself as he continued to glare into the luminous rising sun.

You said that you would never leave me…why can't you be here to help me, Terrell…my life has never been the same since you died…

Larry closed his eyes before resting his head on the cool window. Thoughts of Terrell began to relax him.

No one believes that I remember you…but I do…

Larry's mind drifted to that last morning when Terrell lifted him in the air and over his head. He remembered his cousin's warm hugs and soft tender kisses across his face. Those memories provided him with a brief escape.

Reminisce

God was her primary source of comfort. Being raised in the church, the soloist of the choir was embedded in faith, so the deeply religious woman knew that she needed to clear her mind in order that she *hear* from Him. No matter how bad things got in life, and no matter how hard the devil worked on her mind and body, she knew that the *Almighty Father* would never, ever, forsake *Thine whom Believeth*.

Over the years, whenever she felt that her faith was being tested, Margaret Henderson performed the same ritual; sprinkled Holy Water into a warm bath with the hope that the anointing would somehow bring relief and clarity.

Margaret knelt beside the tub and gently clasped her hands together. She whispered, *"Lawd* …I know that You don't give us more than we can handle…so please, forgive me when I say…I no longer have the strength. I'm sure that the burden that I have been given is too much."

She tilted her head upward and, with closed moistened eyes, she continued with her entreaty. The troubled mother asked that the Father continue to watch over her—that He bless her child, by pulling him close to His bosom. She needed to believe that God Himself would personally guide her son through his turbulent times.

"I need, and I ask that You…Almighty Father, be the source of his strength. Bless him, my Father…and help him through this unimaginable crisis. I ask that You stand by him wherever he may be. He has given so much of himself to others; my baby is a very good boy.

"Father…he's done nothin' but good things in Your name. Please touch my family, and let Your blessings touch each and every member of Miran's family." Margaret ended her prayer. "In Jesus' name…Amen."

She got to her feet, wiped her watery eyes, and then used the toes of her right foot to check the temperature before stepping into the tub.

"Ouch…Sssh…oh my God…" she agonized in the midst of dabbing a washcloth around her contusions.

Margaret truly believed that in order for the healing process to begin, enduring the burning sensation, which was triggered by the blessed water as it trickled from the fabric and into her open wounds, was necessary.

As she had done so many times in the past, the volunteer crossing guard took a deep breath before leaning back. The battered woman squirmed as she submerged her aching body under the warm water.

A single tear found its way down her swollen caramel cheek.

After several minutes, overwhelmed by pain, and riddled with the frustration infused by her youngest son's predicament, Margaret Henderson stood, and then dried her dripping wet body before stepping from the bathtub.

The wife of the first Black law enforcement officer in their community wrapped a robe around her nakedness, turned on the faucet, grabbed her toothbrush, and immediately began brushing her teeth.

She stared in the mirror; her thoughts still on her son.

How could this be happening? How could she not know where her offspring was? Perry was keeping something more than his location from her. She still wasn't sure how Larry was tied to Miran's murder. Her husband had held onto that information like a government secret.

She needed to wipe the sudden burst of emotional leakage from her eyes before leaving the bathroom. Margaret didn't want her younger children to see her vulnerability or be frightened by her poignant state. The kids had always looked at her as being strong, as being unflappable. No matter how bad things had gotten in her marriage, Margaret made it a point to show strength.

The distraught mother made her way down the darkened hallway.

She, as always, checked in on her children. Her five- and seven-year-old daughters lay peaceably in twin beds, fast asleep.

The teary-eyed mother continued toward the second of four bedrooms in the tenement that she'd called home for six years. In that room slept the only other child still under her roof.

She quietly opened the door and peered lovingly at her thirteen-year-old daughter.

Lawd...these children have had to endure so much at such young ages, she thought. Margaret was disappointed in herself; she felt like she hadn't done everything in her power to protect her son over the years. *Where's my baby...what must he be thinkin'?* She closed the door and then leaned against the wall.

With a sigh, she shut her eyes and allowed her mind to be inundated with thoughts of the birth of each of her nine children. Margaret had always been able to use those images to console herself, no matter the situation. Her youngest son's birth was the one that brought a smile to her face. Of all the labors she had to endure, Larry's was the easiest. Because of that, she had always felt that he would give her no reason to worry.

She took a deep breath, sighed, and then headed toward the far end of the hallway. Her room was always immaculately kept. She was a firm believer in the old adage *everything has its place*. Perry didn't mind that his wife had basically turned their bedroom into her personal sanctuary. The décor was more on the feminine side—the lace, fluffy pillows and vanity would give one the impression that she lived alone.

Upon entering, her eyes immediately locked onto one of several photographs that sat on top of her dresser. At that moment, she reached for but quickly backed off the picture that depicted her husband. It was a stately photograph of Perry dressed in his patrolman's uniform. At the time that the image was captured on film, the couple was living in marital bliss. So much had changed since then. He was no longer the loving, caring man that she had fallen in love with in high school. He was manipulative and vindictive. He was a mean-spirited drunk.

She was angry when she turned her attention toward the mirror. Margaret peered for several seconds before she removed her gray cotton robe. The once stunningly attractive high school prom queen looked far beyond her forty-seven years—she herself couldn't believe how she had aged.

She gazed in confusion at her reflection, examining every wrinkle and inch of cellulite. But her anger grew at the sight of the discoloration that covered her body— the black eyes and busted lip disturbed her immensely. The more she viewed the results of her battering, the angrier she became. Without warning, she threw her robe at her husband's picture. The housecoat knocked the photograph, along with several other items, to the floor.

Fearful that the noise caused by her anger would awaken the children, the frustrated wife picked up, and immediately put her robe back on before attempting to retrieve the photo along with several perfume bottles that lay scattered about.

"Who is it?" Margaret nervously questioned in response to a tap at her door.

"Are you okay, Momma?"

"Val…is that you, baby?"

Her nineteen-year-old daughter, whom had been the most recent of her children to fly the coop, replied, "Yeah, Momma… can I come in?"

"Yeah, baby girl…are you okay? Come in," Margaret eagerly responded.

When Val entered, she noticed her mother kneeling beside a cluster of items that would, on a normal day, be resting atop the dresser. With her back to her daughter, Margaret placed the photograph in its rightful place.

"What happened?" Val questioned, making her way over to the mess. She noticed that her mother made it a point to turn away every time she got close to viewing her face.

After Val and her mother completed their recovery efforts, Margaret slyly hugged her fifth child before saying, "Girl…I don't know what to do." She kissed Val's cheek before asking, "…how long you been here?"

"I got in a few minutes ago." Entangled in her mother's embrace, Val sarcastically continued, "Where's your husband?"

Val noticed a welt on her mother's neck. She quickly pulled back and noticed the bruises. Margaret's daughter promptly broke free from the hold of her mother's arms. "What happened to you! You let him beat on you again?"

Margaret pulled her daughter back into her embrace and immediately changed the subject. "They won't let me see your brother."

"Momma, why did he beat you?" Val questioned. She gently rubbed her mother's back in an attempt to console her.

"I'm okay… You don't have to worry 'bout me…we have your brother to worry 'bout," she said as she escorted her daughter to the bed.

They both made themselves comfortable.

"Momma, look at you…" Val gently stroked her mother's face. "You gotta leave him before he kills you."

Margaret took her daughter by the hands. "Baby, I love your father. He's the only man I've ever loved. We had nine beautiful children together and we were happy for a very long time. You, your three brothers, and five sisters are blessings that your father and I share. It wasn't easy for him; he worked hard tryin' to save enough money to move us out of the Bottoms.

"We were one of the first to leave that area when we packed up and moved into the heart of Jacob. That was because of him. He endured a lot, bein' the first Black officer in these parts. I'm not tryin'ta make an excuse for the way he is now. Believe me, I'm prayin' that the man I fell in love with will find his way back to me."

"Momma, that ain't gonna happen. Somethin's wrong with him. He ain't right."

"He wasn't always like this."

"That's beside the point. Why did he beat you?"

Margaret gazed into her daughter's limpid light-brown eyes before saying, "They're apparently following your father's instructions. He got mad at me when I went to the station and demanded to see Larry. They told me that I couldn't because he had been transferred. When I spoke to your father about it…he blew up. He's under a lot of pressure."

"Why do you always make excuses for him? The reason I moved is because of what happened last year. Out of everythin' Daddy has done. What happened to Larry that night is somethin' that I'll never forget. You made an excuse for him then. I couldn't stand you after that, and I couldn't wait to move out of here. Your husband has chased out damn near every one of your children."

A Year PRIOR

Consumed with anger, Larry protectively held his frightened eighteen-year-old sister. He and Valeria sat in her bedroom listening to their mother being beaten by a man who had sworn to protect and serve.

Val tried to concentrate on the moonlight that crept

into her room through slits in her blinds. She wanted so badly to escape her reality. The woman that raised her with love, the woman that taught her to believe in herself even when she was being teased by classmates because she was slightly overweight, that beautiful person had to endure yet another beating.

Her father was inebriated once again and his intoxication was always accompanied with violence. The children could hear his slurs, which played in their heads like a horror film.

"WOMAN...I TOLD YOU A THOUSAND TIMES! JUST 'CAUSE I DRINK...DON'T MEAN I'M A DRUNK!"

"Baby...I'll fix you another plate. Calm down. The kids...you're scarin' them!" Margaret Henderson pleaded.

Val cringed when her mother's calm reply suddenly turned to a fearful scream. "NO! DON'T HIT ME!"

The sound of glass shattering was followed by a tremendous thud, which echoed throughout the bedroom. Somebody had fallen to the floor; and of course, both children knew that their mother was that someone.

"NO, PERRY! PLEASE, BABY!" Margaret continued to beg.

Sergeant Henderson's response was menacing. "DON'T YOU BABY ME. I DON'T WANT NO DAMN FOOD!"

Dishes could be heard crashing to the floor.

The frightened teens jumped in total fear; something

had collided against Val's bedroom wall with such force that it dislodged a framed picture of The Jackson Five; the glass-encased autographed souvenir shattered as it fell to the floor.

She held her brother tighter, her pudgy face covered with tears.

"Calm down, Val, everythin' is gonna be okay," Larry whispered in the most reassuring tone he could muster. He gently kissed his sister's forehead, then said, "One day, I'ma kill that bastard. You watch; I'll get his ass."

Perry Henderson never really had a problem with any of his other children. They all knew to stay out of his way, especially if he'd been drinking. But Larry simply couldn't. When it came to his mother, Larry would never back down from the man he once pegged as his hero—a man looked upon as a pioneer. In the mind of the one hundred fifty-seven-pound sixteen-year-old, the man that stood for strength, courage, and pride for Blacks in his community, was no more than an abusive, wife-beating alcoholic.

Both children continued to cringe as the sound of heavy objects crashing to the floor persisted to echo about the room.

"Nooo…! Ouch! Please stop!" Margaret implored her husband to discontinue his assault.

Suddenly, she screamed at the top of her lungs, "HELPPP ME! PLEASE…SOMEONE…HELPPP ME!"

Larry quickly released his sister and got off the bed. Val held on to her little brother with everything she had.

The petrified girl screeched, "No, Larry! He said that he would kill you if you interfered again!"

Larry desperately tried to free himself from his sister's grip, but Val maintained her hold on him like a vicious dog anchored on a burglar.

Every time a scream came from the kitchen, Larry's hatred for his father was magnified. He began to drag Val off the bed like a rag doll.

"Let me go, girl! I'm gonna kill him! I hate him! Let me go, Val!"

The youngest male in the family slowly made his way toward the bedroom door.

His sister couldn't stop him; he was going to face off with their father once again.

Finally able to free himself, he rushed to the door, opened it, and ran out before his sister could gather herself.

Larry angrily made his way to the kitchen, where he spotted his mother.

She lay on her side, in a fetal position. Her face showed signs of a significant beating. Her eyes were swollen. There was a combination of tears mixed with blood that eased from cuts on her face. Along with the blood that trickled from her nose, she seemed in desperate need of medical treatment.

Broken dishes were scattered about the entire kitchen.

The feast that Margaret had painstakingly prepared, which consisted of Southern fried chicken, collard greens, cornbread, macaroni and cheese, yams, and peach cobbler, covered the floor. A shattered wooden chair, apparently the source of the tremendous thud against his sister's wall, lay at his mother's feet.

When Larry was finally able to break his terrified glare from his helpless mother, he turned his attention in the direction of his drunken father. Perry, still in his patrolman's uniform, sat at the kitchen table with a fifth of Ole Grand Dad to his lips. Next to a shot glass, in plain view, was Sergeant Henderson's service revolver.

Larry ran over to his mother and knelt beside her.

He wanted to reach for her; however, he was too paralyzed with anger to touch his battered parent. The enraged teen began to tremble. After getting to his feet, he turned slowly toward his father like he was possessed.

Perry ignored Larry's threatening glare. The lieutenant's empty gaze was locked on his whiskey bottle. He had a drunken scowl on his face.

"You bastard…" Larry growled, as he stood frozen with anger.

Lieutenant Henderson, with hung head, shifted his eyes upward, his bloodshot piercing gaze directed toward his son. With slurred conviction, he announced, "I've been expecting you."

Never taking his eyes off his father, Larry slowly made his way toward the kitchen counter.

Everything seemed to be happening in slow motion. Margaret watched her son grab a knife off the counter and head toward his father. She couldn't seem to get herself to move; her mind couldn't process what was going on fast enough.

It wasn't until she saw the murderous gleam in Larry's eyes that she finally managed to get to her feet. She stood frozen for a second. The muffled words spoken by her unhinged teen really frightened her. The concerned mother extended her hand toward her angry little boy. With motherly sincerity, she insisted, "Give me the knife, baby…momma's okay."

Larry ignored his mother's order.

"I told you never to put your hands on her again!" he growled.

Out of nowhere, Val came running into the kitchen at full stride. She immediately spotted her younger brother with a butcher's knife firmly gripped in his right hand. The look in his eyes paralyzed Val. She stopped and glared at him with her mouth suspended open. At that moment, she felt that her entire family was about to fall completely apart. Val understood that her father was not the same man that she remembered, and once cherished, as a little girl. He had changed drastically over the years.

The eighteen-year-old felt that her father had intentionally tried to distance himself from the rest of the family. She just didn't understand why.

Perry suddenly stood, grabbed his whiskey bottle with his left hand and his pistol with his right. He took a long, sloppy swig. Whiskey overflowed from his mouth. He slammed the whiskey bottle atop the table before wiping his mouth with the back of his pistol-toting right hand.

Without warning, he fired three shots past Larry's face.

Margaret and Val screamed.

Stunned, Larry stopped—fear overtook him and before he realized it, the butcher's knife had fallen from his hand. Margaret quickly grabbed her son and attempted to shield his body with her own.

Perry barked with clear-cut determination, "Get the hell out of my way, woman! I'm gonna kill that bastard before he kills me!"

"Get out of here, boy! Go! He's really gonna kill you this time!" Margaret pleaded as she swiftly pushed her son toward the back entrance. The mother continued as she forced her son out of the door. "Get out, now!"

"No, Mama…he's just gonna have to kill me!" Larry insisted while his mother continued to force him onto the back porch.

The panic-stricken mother countered, "If he does that…he'll have to kill the rest of us…do you want that?"

In a drunken rage, Perry flipped the kitchen table. He threw it with such force that the whiskey bottle and shot glass flew across the room. The bottle shattered upon making contact with the wall. With pistol in hand, the inebriated cop slowly made his way toward his wife and son.

Larry hastily kissed his mother before he ran off the back porch, through his mother's garden, and past the chicken coop.

Perry tried to take aim as he stumbled out the back door.

Margaret, once again, stood between the two of them—her intent was to buy Larry enough time to get away. But her husband pushed her aside, causing her to viciously strike her head on the edge of the screen door as she fell helplessly to the wooden porch.

Larry hauled ass toward his bike, which was positioned at the far end of the fenceless yard. He grabbed his bicycle and jumped on it, beginning to pedal with urgency.

His father took aim.

Perry screamed; saliva sprayed from his mouth on every word. "I'M GONNA PUT A BULLET IN HIS NARROW BLACK ASS!"

The smashed police officer redirected his pistol toward the heavens and fired off his four remaining rounds while he watched his frightened teenage son disappear into the night.

PRESENT

Margaret stood—she walked slowly over to her dresser to retrieve lotion.

The mother of nine always believed that there were several events that her children would never get over and she blamed herself. If only she could have been a better wife. If only she could understand why her husband changed from the sweet, loving, Southern gentleman that she fell in love with into the crazed maniac that seemed to get off on terrorizing her and their children. She didn't understand why everything seemed to anger him—why he seemed so willing to take his own son's life.

Margaret realized that what Val had witnessed the night that Perry chased Larry from the house with gunfire ranked high on the list of unforgivable actions.

"I realize that I didn't handle that whole situation the right way, and I'm very sorry because I know that you've looked at me in a negative light ever since. I tried to talk with both you and Larry about what happened. I realize, in my heart, that neither of you will ever forget that moment."

She continued as she applied lotion to her legs, "I've always done what I felt I needed to do to protect all of you."

Val seemed unwilling to accept her mother's reasoning.

"If you felt that you had to protect us, why didn't you leave him?"

"Because your father would have found us; he's a very vindictive man. Look, Val, no one feels as bad as I do about everythin' that you children had to pay witness to over the years. I can't apologize to you children enough. But right now, I have to figure out what's goin' on with Larry."

Margaret sat back down on the end of her bed. She looked closely at her daughter and her eyes began to water. "I need you to get your sisters ready for church. Will you do that for me?"

"Sure, Momma," Val whispered shamefully.

The well-manicured lawn surrounding the two large flourishing oak trees in front of the church made the house of worship look as if it were in better condition than it really was. Greater Faith Baptist Church was a hallmark in the Bottoms; its forty-year-old structure was oblique and in desperate need of repair. A good paint job would have gone a long way to restoring the spiritual cathedral to its original state.

As usual, the church was packed.

Several conservatively dressed members of the congregation stood with their hands raised to the heavens; they were filled with the Holy Ghost.

Pastor John James stood at the pulpit. He was wearing a purple robe with gold trim. The senior member of the church was a much-respected man whose mere presence radiated spirituality.

The religious leader's Sunday sermons were legendary. It was said that the word resonated through his spirit. Reverend James' distinctive praise was known to light a fire in his congregation. The divine murmur, when accompanied by a few chords from the organist, sent chills up and down the spines of those in attendance.

"The contribution of a people is finally being recognized by the rest of this beleaguered country. Hallelujah..."

The organist played several chords.

"I say...every one of you hold some responsibility for recognizing our struggles each time that God blesses you with the ability to open your eyes each morning... can I get a Hallelujah?"

The congregation screamed, "Praise the LORD!"

"Teach your children. Ensure that they know of our responsibilities toward not only our communities, but to everyone for which they come into contact." The pastor stepped from behind the pulpit before he continued, "Before we get into today's sermon...how 'bout us hearing from our choir..."

The jubilant congregation exploded once again, "Praise the LORD!"

Behind the pastor sat a group of individuals dedicated to praise and worship through song; and their combined voices were truly virtuous. Draped in black robes with purple and gold trim, Greater Faith's choir prepared to heighten the spiritual awareness of the entire audience.

Everyone in the choir rose to his or her feet as Margaret stepped forward—she was handed a microphone. The battered wife and mother knew that everyone in the congregation was aware of her troubled marriage, so she didn't want to use embarrassment as an excuse for not attending Sunday services. She had become accustomed to camouflaging her wounds behind Maybelline products.

Praising the Almighty was a part of who she was— praise and worship uplifted her in her times of despair. She felt that through song she could achieve oneness with the Father, so nothing that her husband could do would stop her from seeking the peace that came through rejoicing.

God's faithful steward immediately locked her eyes on Val and her well-behaved three younger children, who were all seated in the front pew. The choir's soloist raised the microphone. An angelic rendition of "His Eye is on the Sparrow" reverberated from her diaphragm and escaped from her vocal chords.

It was said that every single time she sang, everyone within earshot was besieged with goosebumps. All that knew her considered her one of the Lord's more blessed, devoted, courageous and dedicated soldiers.

After Sunday services, Pastor James made it a point to stand at the entrance to the wood and brick structure so that he could personally shake hands and bless each and every parishioner as they exited.

As Margaret stepped from the church with her children, the pastor immediately broke protocol and excused himself from a conversation with a member of the congregation.

Reverend James pulled his soloist to the side.

For months, the leader of Greater Faith had contemplated reaching out to Sister Henderson. Several members of the church even suggested to him that he was the only one that would be able to convince her to seek help. But, the pastor felt that any intervention on his part might cause Margaret more problems with her husband.

"Sister Henderson…let your husband know that we miss him…we would really like to be blessed with his presence."

He took both of her hands into his, and the pastor cleared his throat before saying, "I, and the rest of Greater Faith, wish to extend to you and your family our full support in your efforts to clear young Larry of these terrible accusations. Everyone in this community knows that that boy isn't capable of committing such a crime.

"He has always been one of my favored young people… always willing to give his time to help around the church. If there is anything that I can do to help, I pray that you won't hesitate to let me know."

Margaret's eyes watered; she felt the sincerity. "Pastor…I and my family really appreciate your sentiments."

Before she could continue, her attention, like everyone else's standing in front of the church, was drawn toward a white man who had gotten out of a car that was parked in front of the place of worship.

The man was dressed in a blue, off-the-rack suit.

It was very unusual for a white man to be seen at Greater Faith—not that invitations hadn't been extended.

Curiosity made up everyone's statements as the white man strolled the walkway leading to the church. His blues eyes were locked on the chapel's doors.

As he stood at the steps leading to the cathedral, the stranger directed his inquiry to the pastor. "Excuse me; I'm looking for Mrs. Margaret Henderson. I was told that my best chance of catching up with her would be for me to come here."

The pastor turned his attention toward Margaret. That's when the man realized that the medium-height, heavyset woman in the black dress with hat to match, whose face was caked with makeup, was the person that he was in search of.

"I'm Mrs. Henderson. Who might you be?" Margaret

asked as she descended the stairs with hand extended.

The man took her hand into his.

"I'm honored to have your acquaintance, ma'am. I'm Jonathan Edwards from the *Daily News*. I've had the darndest time trying to catch up with you. I apologize for coming to your house of worship, but I was told that if I really wanted to catch up with you, I would be able to do so on Sunday…right here at Greater Faith."

Margaret smiled. "Why have you taken the time to search for me?"

"I want to speak to you about your son," said the reporter with a smile.

She hoped that this man wasn't trying to write another story about a Black man being accused of a crime that he didn't commit. She didn't want to speak about Black men being sent to prison—that sort of thing happened on a daily basis. The statistics spoke for themselves; out of the 319,598 prisons across the country, 75% of the penal population was Black.

The more she looked into his eyes, the more relaxed she became. There was something warm and gentle about his handshake. His eyes were filled with sincerity. The way he looked at her, she felt that he wanted to help.

Margaret didn't know what was going on with her son—she certainly wasn't about to get any answers from her husband. So, she was going to eventually have to trust someone. Her hope was that the handsome news reporter was a topnotch journalist who was looking to uncover the real truth.

"What would you like to know about him?"

"I'm interested in knowing why you allowed your son to plead guilty to a murder that he obviously didn't commit?"

Shock made up Margaret's statement. "WHAT! What'cha talkin' 'bout?"

"Your son's confession. He was sentenced to twenty-five years behind bars," the reporter offered while using his right hand to shield his eyes from the blazing sun.

Margaret had suddenly become weak-kneed. "I wasn't told that. What in God's name is goin' on?"

Jonathan steadied the distraught woman. "You really didn't know?"

Margaret leaned against the railing. "I was told that he was in county. They wouldn't allow me to see him." She looked like she was about to faint. "My *Lawd*… my baby."

"Are you going to be okay? Maybe you should take a seat on the steps." The reporter took her by the elbow and attempted to assist her.

What Margaret had become privy to wasn't something that she was at all prepared to deal with. Her husband had deceived her by not revealing the full gravity of her son's situation. Guilt hit her like a ton of bricks. She felt that she herself had committed the ultimate betrayal by not doing everything in her power to protect her baby.

First DAY

H e'd been in a trance for much of his journey—a daydream that lasted until the cling and clang of steel gates rang in his ear. Upon realizing what was before him, the confused teen's posture changed as he sat straight up in his seat.

The first thing he noticed was the concertina wire, which seemed to stretch for miles atop the red brick and steel gray fence that surrounded one of the largest facilities in the South.

The fact that he was going to prison hit him like a ton of bricks; his panic-stricken eyes darted about the ominous fortress. Suddenly, as if drawn by a neodymium magnet, his weary eyes were locked upward. The beleaguered youngster was overwhelmed when he saw several towers, each armed with guards holding rifles.

The boy became even more fidgety when the bus pulled onto the grounds.

To his right, one hundred yards away, he saw what seemed like thousands of inmates enclosed by two very large electrified fences. The drawling hardcore convicted criminals all seemed intent on having their pick of the litter.

The inmates jeered and cheered as the bus came to a halt in front of the administration building. Heckles caused Larry's fears to intensify. He'd watched the exact scene that played before him on television but never had imagined in a million years that he would end up in such a place.

The doors to the bus opened. In stepped one of the most heartless-looking individuals that his young eyes had ever encountered. Dressed in a gray Department of Corrections issued uniform, with a drill sergeant's hat that tilted forward atop his military-style haircut just enough to draw attention to his menacing gray-blue eyes, was Sergeant Hank Morris, a physical specimen whose face had more craters than the moon.

"GET THE HELL OFF MY BUS, YOU SEWER RATS!" he shouted. The sergeant exited before he would continue, "RIGHT NOW...YOU PIECES OF SHIT...YOU THINK I GOT ALL DAMN DAY TO FUCK WITH YOU? GET OFF...GET YO' ASSES RIGHT HERE."

He pointed to a spot on the pavement, one that gave the entire prison population a perfect view of the new inmates.

Resounding cries of *"NEW FISH!"* reverberated across the facility as an echo would in the Grand Canyon. The shouts overshadowed the chain gang jingle that accompanied the new inmates' ankle shackles as the convicted criminals hurriedly exited the bus.

As dictated by Sergeant Morris, the prisoners took their position on the grounds directly in front of several other guards who stood at parade rest.

A convict from the yard noticed Wesley Hobbs and Leroy Burns taking their place in line. He pointed toward both of the misfits, then shouted, "I'll be damned!… hey, guys…guess who's back? It's Black Cassidy and the Caramel Kid!"

Wesley whispered to Leroy, "This same old shit all over again. You know them fools gonna wanna get with us. We busted they ass last time…they gonna want payback."

"You two…SHUT UP!" Sergeant Morris ordered.

The sergeant stepped to the criminals, but before he could say another word, an unexpected eerie silence seemed to hang over the entire eighteen hundred acres that surrounded the seventy-nine-year-old prison. It was like all four thousand, four hundred and eighty inmates had been hit with a giant mute button.

Larry was confused.

Just seconds prior the entire yard was crazed, but in a matter of a moment, complete silence. *What the hell is goin' on? Why are they leavin'?* Larry thought to himself. He watched on nervously as the prisoners dispersed from what was known as "The New Fish Watch Spot."

Wesley and Leroy immediately recognized why the

inmates hightailed it from the Watch Spot. Lieutenant Frank Small had stepped from the administration building.

Small was a muscular, six-five corrections' supervisor who was feared by all. The ex-marine was the most intimidating figure behind the walls. His presence demanded respect—anyone that ever spent a day in his company would certainly attest to it.

Burns nearly pissed himself when he saw the one time military captain. "Oh shit!!!…Wesley, I thought that Small was gone."

"Somebody told me he didn't work here nomo…" Wesley whispered.

Sergeant Morris interrupted. "INMATE!!! Didn't I tell you to *shut the hell up*…?"

Lieutenant Small casually made his way over to the detainees. He gazed knowingly for several seconds before he began to pace the line, a routine he had followed for over twelve years.

His Southern drawl was strong and commanding. "You mean to tell me that the judicial system has saw fit to send us mo' garbage?"

The supervising guard stopped suddenly—he was thrown completely for a loop when he noticed two familiar individuals standing before him. "Looky here… if it ain't Leroy Burns…" He shifted his eyes toward Wesley Hobbs. "…and his partner in crime."

A wicked smile materialized on the CO's face. He deviously began to rub his hands together, like he had hit the jackpot. "Hobbs, I bet you regret comin' back to my house…you gotta lot of mouth, boy…I got a new surprise fo' yo' ass! I told you before you left here that I was gonna get another shot at you. What was it that you said the day that you walked from these gates, just over a year ago?"

While keeping his eyes locked straight ahead, Wesley Hobbs replied, "Nothin', boss…!"

The brass disciplinarian nodded several times before he resumed pacing the line.

"For those of you that don't know me, I'm Lieutenant Small. I'm the MUTHA that you all had better fear. I'm the one that tells you when to piss, when to crap, when to eat, and when to sleep. If I don't like you, you'll know it. If you disobey the rules in my house, I'll know it… and you'll regret it."

He stopped in front of Larry. They locked eyes. "What's yo' name, boy?"

"Larry…sir, Larry Henderson," he replied nervously.

"Boy…you look like you still got titty milk behind your ears. How old are you?"

"I just turned eighteen…sir."

"You da boy in here for murderin' a white man…ain't ya?"

"Yes, sir!!!"

"You proud of that?"

Larry wasn't sure whether he should wear the crime as a badge of honor; he wasn't sure if an acknowledgment in front of an entire prison would help or hinder him. If he sounded proud, would the prisoners be more or less likely to comfort him? Would the white guards seek out revenge? Would it be an admission of his guilt and hurt any chance at parole?

Larry solemnly lowered his eyes before he whispered, "No, sir. I'm not proud…"

"Do what you're told, and hopefully…you'll be able to survive," said Small before he continued with his New Fish speech.

"All of you will be escorted to the R&D Center where you will be processed and assigned your sleepin' areas. Unless you break the rules and are sent to the big house, you will not be housed in cells while you're at this facility. Believe you me…you don't wanna be sent to the Hole… or to the Big House," Small said as he gestured toward the giant structure that cast a menacing shadow behind the electrified fencing.

He pointed to Sergeant Morris before continuing, "All prisoners under CO Morris's watch are housed in open bays. CO Morris…along with all the officers that stand behind you…they're my eyes and ears. You will obey them, just like you're bein' ordered by me. If you don't…you will be sent to the Hole. While in the R&D you will also have to go through orientation, at which time…you will be instructed on how to live in my house."

Television was absolutely no help.

Prison life was always depicted differently in a motion picture or in a television drama. Larry didn't see any dirty gray walls—or any psychologist protesting that the dreary walls were depressing and could hamper the rehabilitation of the inmate. What he did see was flooring that had a polish that would put the White House to shame. He was nearly blinded by the bright lights that reflected brilliantly off of walls that were glistening because of the white gloss that covered them. Larry was truly blown away with the thought that he was in a prison.

This is a prison? He continued his thought, *what happened to receiving your sheets and toiletries, then immediately being led into an eight-by-ten cell where the steel bars slam behind you?*

On television, being processed into the system never took all day. Larry never saw inmates going from one medical checkpoint to another. He never saw the cavity searches, or the checking for STDs to ensure that the population wasn't exposed to anything from outside the walls.

This has to encourage sexual contact between inmates... them horny bastards can't wait. Larry's thoughts were all over the place as he watched Wesley Hobbs bend over and spread his cheeks.

Leroy Burns was next; then Larry would get his opportunity to stand naked next to the man in the white doctor's smock and watch him put on a surgical glove in preparation of ramming a finger up his rectum.

"Next," Dr. Freeman announced as he snatched the surgical glove from his hand and tossed it into a trashcan.

Freeman was in his seventh year at the prison. He took over responsibility for cavity searches because he was fed up with treating inmates with tears in the final section of their large intestine—injuries caused by over-aggressive searches.

Leroy's unclothed charcoal black sculpture was opposite only in shade to his best friend Wesley's caramel complexion. Both spent a great deal of time in the weight room—their physiques made that obvious. Their haircuts and clean-shaven faces made the two look more respectable than the raggedy beards and the Afros they sported when they stepped from the bus upon arrival.

It was obvious to Larry that Leroy had participated in cavity searches in the past.

The inmate causally walked up to Freeman, spun around, bent, grabbed—and then separated his buns. "Go ahead…you might as well stick it to me, too, Doc… the system has."

Freeman used his left hand to hold the glove as he wiggled the fingers of his right into place. When he released the glove it immediately made a snapping sound. The doctor dipped his finger into some gel and then proceeded with the procedure.

"Huh…Doc." The inmate flinched ever so slightly. "You could've at least given me a Pepsi and a pack of Kools."

"Keep ya ass still, Burns," said the doctor, "I think you like this because you keep coming back for more. You told me that you weren't comin' back. What happened?"

"Well, Doc...I missed this...no one has a finger like you."

Was Leroy Burns some kind of freak? Was the criminal standing before Larry really enjoying the doctor's examination? Larry didn't realize that he had spoken aloud, at least, not until Leroy's examination was complete.

Leroy whispered into Larry's ear as he passed, "You're gonna get a chance to see what a freak I really am."

"Next," Freeman broadcasted in an attempt to get Larry's attention, but his focus remained on the man built like a miniature Hulk, the guy he had offended.

It took Larry all of five hours to make an enemy—not just any adversary, but one that was very familiar with life behind bars. On top of that, this antagonist came to the party with help. Larry was very much aware that he would have to deal with Wesley and Leroy for the entire time they were locked up together.

Lieutenant Henderson's impression of the dark mushroom cloud, which besieged the early morning sky, was that of a nuclear explosion taking place in a residential neighborhood. The law enforcement officer stepped on the gas, then flipped on his siren and sped toward the epicenter of the ashy spectacle, several blocks from his location.

As he bent the corner, his screeching tires and flashing lights caught the attention of the spectators who had congregated. The panic-stricken inhabitants of the block, still in their nightclothes, stood in front of a tenement that had been completely engulfed.

Flames shot out from the third floor windows of the tri-level tenement. The blaze had already engulfed the roof. Thick smoke billowed out of the second-floor windows; more smoke spiraled from the front door.

A panic-stricken, ten-year-old child observed the patrol car.

The kid forced his way through the gathering of onlookers and rushed into the middle of the street; he stood directly in front of the squad car. The child shouted while waving his hands frantically.

"OFFICER! OFFICER! HELP! My brother and mother are still in there!!!" He pointed to the house as Henderson broke quickly.

"What did you say?" the officer asked upon exiting his vehicle.

The boy shuddered as he continued to point at the burning inferno. "My... My momma and my brotha are up there." He babbled; his feet moved like he was standing on hot coals. "They won't let me go get 'em. I have to go get' em. Nobody'll help me!!!"

Henderson placed his hands on the boy's shoulders.

"Calm down, son…did anyone call the fire department?"

"Yeah! But, they always take their time comin' to this neighborhood."

The officer asked while staring at the raging flames, "Are you sure that your mother and brother are in there?"

"Yes!!! Yes!!! They're on the third floor…my mother told me to crawl." The panic-stricken child jumped and pulled at Perry's arm. "They told me that they would be right behind me. When I got out…I heard my brother yellin'…he said that his foot was stuck! I think my mother was tryin' to help him! They're both trapped. You gotta help 'em!"

Lieutenant Henderson once again turned his attention toward the burning inferno. The public servant removed his gun belt and placed it on the front seat of his patrol car. He locked the car before rushing through the crowd and toward the building.

Perry stepped into the residence.

The crackles of the flames, as it devoured its prey, was deafening. The officer was immediately robbed of oxygen—the smoke firmly gripped his throat. The intensity of the heat and smoke caused his eyelids to close to prevent further irritation.

The officer spat on his hands and applied the saliva to his eyelids in hope that the slight moisture would allow him enough relief to locate the staircase.

He opened, and then managed to adjust his eyes to his surroundings long enough to notice smoke billow down a stairway to his right. Perry dashed toward it—he headed up, his mind completely void of the danger.

As he approached the second floor, Perry noticed that the flames and smoke were more severe. The staircase had weakened and was about to collapse. Henderson skipped several steps at a time and continued in the direction of the third floor.

After reaching the top of the staircase of the third floor, he found himself face to face with a wall of fire blocking access to the hallway. Lieutenant Henderson stopped, and stared into the firestorm—it was thick, and very intimidating.

Suddenly, his nerves began to play with his head.

Officer Henderson realized that he wasn't thinking when he made his decision to rush into the fire. He didn't do it because he was trying to be brave. It wasn't his job—he wasn't a fireman.

Why the hell did I do this? he thought to himself.

His eyes swayed to his rear in search of a way out—but the officer realized that he couldn't turn back, even if he wanted to. Without warning, the pleas of a little boy who was frightened for the safety of his mother and brother, the same child that had confronted him seconds prior, played in his head. His conscience wouldn't allow him to let another boy down.

After shaking off his weariness, he attempted to scan his smoke-filled surroundings. Gradually, his vision adjusted; there was a very small opening in the wall of flames. As he prepared himself to barrel through the intense inferno, he could hear the staircase behind him give way.

The smoke steadfastly ripped oxygen from the officer, causing him to cough uncontrollably. He attempted to use his hands to shield his eyes as he continued to press forward through the dense smoke, and yellow-orange, monstrous blaze.

"IS ANYONE IN HERE?" he yelled between coughs.

In the distance, he could hear a female's faint scream. "HELP!" She coughed. "HELP US...PLEASE!!!"

"I CAN'T SEE WHERE I'M GOIN'! KEEP YELLIN'!!! I'LL FOLLOW YOUR VOICE! YELL LOUDER!!!"

"MY SON'S LEG IS TRAPPED! HE'S LOST CONSCIOUSNESS!!! HELP US! WE'RE SURROUNDED BY FIRE! I CAN'T SEE..."

A big boom rang out. Parts of the floor around Lieutenant Perry Henderson had given way. Seconds later, a huge flaming beam crashed down in the very spot from which he had moved. But he was not swayed. He squashed any thoughts of turning back the moment that he realized the woman and her child were still alive.

Upon hearing her voice, the officer was more determined than ever.

Perry felt obligated to fight through the flames—he was going to finish what he had started. The officer wasn't sure how he would accomplish that feat—but he knew that he would not leave without them. With his right arm shielding his face, he kept moving toward the voice.

The woman's panic-stricken cries roared above the crackle of the blaze.

"WE'RE IN HERE!!! WE'RE IN HERE!!!" she screamed.

Perry could see the residue produced from the out-of-control flames being wrenched toward the early morning sky through a gaping hole in the roof. While peering through the smoke and fire, he was finally able to see a woman frantically trying to give mouth to mouth to a child. After several seconds of CPR, the woman subsequently tried to lift the beam that entrapped her helpless son. Perry could see the woman weaken with every attempt at lifting the smoldering shaft.

As the policeman made his way toward the helpless youngster and his mother, he yelled, "Look, lady!!! I'm gonna lift this beam. I want you to pull your son out when I say go!!! Got it...?"

The woman coughed several times before she was able to reply, "Yes!!!"

Lieutenant Henderson positioned himself in a way to get the best leverage in trying to lift the wooden support plank.

"Okay...ready???" He grunted as he lifted. "Go!!!"

After two tugs, the lady was finally able to free her thirteen-year-old son. Upon doing so, she once again immediately tried her hand at CPR.

The heat intensified; the smoke overwhelmed.

"Your front staircase is gone…we have to find another way out!!!" Henderson said in between coughs. The officer stood over the woman and her child. His wondering, irritated eyes scanned their surroundings in search of a way out.

The woman, once again began to panic. "We have to hurry…I can't get him to breathe. Let's try the WINDOW!!!"

"No…we're too high up. Plus, I don't think the fire department has made it here yet. Do you have a back staircase?"

Although the woman was choking—being strangled by the thick black smoke that had taken over the entire dwelling, she managed to reply, "Yes!!!"

Lieutenant Henderson knelt down and began doing CPR on the child himself. After several seconds of applying the breathing technique, he picked up the unconscious teen, and threw him over his shoulder.

Detective Jake Aaron was headed down the steps of headquarters when he noticed Lieutenant Henderson getting out of his squad car. Soot covered Perry's face and uniform. The officer was a complete mess—he looked exhausted.

The detective had never liked the Black officer. He felt Perry was self-centered and arrogant. Perry believed that Jake's Southern gentleman persona was as much of a sham as the rug that sat atop his bald head. Perry and Jake's dislike of each other began when they were in high school and had continued throughout the fifteen years that they had worked together.

The police lieutenant felt that Jake's ties with the Klan went deeper than simply being Miran's best friend. Although he couldn't prove it, Perry sensed that Jake was somehow involved in the murder of his childhood best friend three decades prior.

Both men accepted that they had to be cordial and professional toward one another; and for the most part, they were successful in doing so the majority of times.

Jake stood frozen on the bottom step. The curious detective asked, "What the hell happened to you?" as he watched Perry approach with his gun belt draped over his shoulder.

"There was a four-alarm fire on Garrison Avenue," the lieutenant said, attempting to wipe soot from his face with the back of his right arm.

The detective's response was playful. "You know that the city's not gonna pay you for playin' fireman...are you okay?"

"Yeah...I'm just a little tired...I spent much of the mornin' at Mercy Hospital. The doctors wouldn't let me out until they examined me," Perry Henderson whispered as he began to make his way up the steps.

Jake called out, "Perry...!"

The lieutenant stopped; he then directed his attention toward the detective before he uttered, "What...?"

"Why did you allow your son to cop to Miran's murder? That boy didn't kill him!"

"Jake...you know as well as I do...if my son had gone on trial, he would have been convicted of first-degree murder and given the death penalty. Him pleadin' out gives me a chance to find the evidence needed for exoneration. You know that I could collect all the evidence in the world to prove his innocence...but if they had convicted him, my chances of gettin' him off death row would be next to impossible; no matter what evidence I uncovered. As it is, he can always say that his plea agreement was coerced."

The excitement that filled the squad room disturbed Chief Bailey.

He flung his door open and stepped from his office. "What the hell is goin' on out here?" The irritated man caught a whiff of something as he entered the squad room. Bailey shifted his green eyes upward over glasses that rested on his nose like a studious librarian.

"What's that smell? Is there a fire?" he inquired, as his wondering eyes scanned the squad room for any signs of smoke.

Perry sat at the edge of a desk surrounded by several officers. They moved aside in order to give the chief of police a clear view of the man that was responsible for the rescue of a mother and her child. The chief realized that the grunge that covered the man who served as his director of public affairs' uniform was the source of the smoky stench.

Officer Nolan stepped forward and quickly explained, "Hey, Chief…Henderson here…he went into a burnin' house and pulled out a woman and her child." Excited, he babbled, "You won't believe how he got 'em out…he sent 'em down the dumb-waiter. Then he had to give the child CPR in order to save his life."

Henderson hung his head in humility.

When he looked up, he saw his wife. She stood at the entrance to Chief Bailey's office. Surprised, Henderson immediately got to his feet. "Hey, baby…what are you doin' here?"

Margaret didn't respond.

Bailey broke the awkward moment, "Well…I'm glad he did his damn job…now ya'll do yours!" He stared everyone down, and then locked eyes on the lieutenant. "Perry…I need to see you, now!" Bailey ordered before he reentered his office.

Perry wasn't used to his supervisor's tone—the chief had never been so harsh toward him in front of a squad room full of his subordinates, let alone in front of his wife. Then there was his wife; he couldn't figure out why she was at the station. He followed his boss, more so out of curiosity rather than being ordered.

Bailey took a seat on the corner of his desk and waited for Perry to enter. Margaret had already made herself comfortable in a chair, which faced the police chief. Her back was to the door so she was unaware that her husband of twenty-eight years had entered until she heard Bailey ask Perry to close the door behind him.

The officer did as his supervisor requested, and then leaned his back against the closed door before folding his arms. "What's this all about...?"

"Perry, why didn't you tell your wife about your son's allocution...and the fact that he was transferred to state prison this morning?" Bailey asked. The chief removed his glasses before he folded his arms.

Margaret could feel her husband's eyes locked on her; like a knife was cutting away at her spine. She wanted to turn—she wanted to look him in his eyes, but she wouldn't dare. The backlash, the consequences that she would have to deal with for being there would be evident in his dark eyes. But this wasn't about his intimidation. This was about her son—and her determination to find out what was going on with her baby.

Margaret hadn't been allowed to see Larry since his return from Vegas on murder charges. Moreover, she had no idea that her son had confessed to the crime until a reporter approached her earlier that morning. She knew that in order to find her child, she needed to be strong.

"Chief...that's somethin' that I think I should discuss with my wife."

Fifty Years
OF NEWS

F or a Sunday afternoon there was an abnormal amount of activity on the pressroom floor at the *Daily News*. The paper was not only celebrating fifty years of existence, but it was also covering statewide elections, so the entire staff was on hand.

One of the most prominent investigative reporters the paper had ever employed was Jonathan Edwards, recipient of the ICIJ Award for Outstanding International Reporting.

J.E., as he was affectionately known around the office, was considered the Columbo of his profession because he left no stone unturned in his pursuit of the facts; no matter where that hunt led him.

The man, who bore a striking resemblance to actor Alec Baldwin, attempted to maneuver past celebrating coworkers as he carried a piece of cake in one hand and a mug filled with coffee in the other.

"J.E., wonderful piece on the Harrison kidnapping…I really think it's Pulitzer material," another reporter conveyed. He stuffed a piece of cake into his mouth and nodded in approval at the handsome journalist as he passed.

Jonathan returned his coworker's acknowledgment with an appreciative nod of his own. He then sipped on his steaming hot coffee, continuing on his way to his work area.

Before he was able to place his java on top of his desk, Eric Maxwell, editor-in-chief, stepped out from his office with a cup in his hand. "J.E., I need to speak with you."

When Maxwell motioned for his most experienced reporter to enter his workspace, he accidentally spilled coffee on his white shirt.

Jonathan devoured what was left of his chocolate cake—after which, the reporter wiped crumbs from the corners of his lips, then took a sip of his morning pick-me-up before he headed toward his boss's office.

With mug in hand, Jonathan made himself comfortable on his couch before asking, "What's going on, Eric?"

The Daily News spared no expense when it came to the chief editor's office. The smoke glass desk and black leather furniture, accented in silver chrome, was exactly the décor that Eric Maxwell dreamt he would one day have. From the very first day that he stepped foot in the building, he felt that his destiny was to become editor-in-chief. When he accomplished his goal, Eric had the newspaper recreate his office the way it had always appeared in his dreams.

Eric walked over to, and then pulled a piece of Kleenex from, a container which sat on top of his desk. "The Henderson story...I haven't seen your follow-up.

I heard that the kid was transferred to the State facility this morning." As he placed his cup down, he asked, "Do you plan on concluding your original piece?"

Jonathan sat back and crossed his legs. "Look, Eric, this story is far from over."

"What are you talking about? If the kid confessed to the crime, and he was sentenced to twenty-five years, what more could there possibly be?" Eric dabbed the Kleenex to his stained shirt.

"There's a lot more to this story than what is on the surface. I'm gonna dig a little more before I conclude it. I'll speak with the DA once more tomorrow...after which, I'll write a piece announcing his sentence. But, I'm gonna leave this story open until I finish my investigation." Jonathan took a sip of his coffee.

Intrigued, Eric walked around his desk and over to the couch. He made himself comfortable next to Jonathan. "Tell me more."

The journalist uncrossed his legs and sat forward.

He gripped his coffee mug with both hands. "This whole thing is very peculiar. First, the cops quickly pegged their prime suspect as a youth who fled to Vegas. Second, the suspect's father is a police lieutenant who didn't look to get his son counsel. On top of that, the cop never told his wife that their son made a plea agreement with the DA's office. Then the mother...she looked a little beaten up."

"What do you mean?"

"When I saw her earlier today at the church she attends, her face was packed with makeup. She was trying to cover injuries. I know that what I said doesn't sound like much...but my gut tells me that something's not right." Jonathan nodded several times. Within seconds, he found himself deep in thought.

Eric's Southern drawl pulled the award-winning journalist back from his trancelike state. "What do you need?"

Jonathan stood. He began to pace.

"First, I need to get to Vegas...the kid's mother told me that he was working at the Hilton in Sin City the night that that Klansman was murdered."

He took another sip of his coffee before he continued, "I don't understand why the father didn't try to follow that lead. If that kid was working that night, why didn't a veteran cop like Lieutenant Henderson try to follow up on that? That in itself would have been enough to prove his son innocent."

Jonathan and Eric both turned their attention toward the door after the receptionist tapped lightly.

"Excuse me. J.E., you had a phone call...it sounded urgent. Her name was Valeria Henderson. She left her number," the office assistant said.

Jonathan responded with appreciation, "Thank you, Patricia."

Eric's hand gesture prompted the receptionist to wait. "Pat, tell Gene that I want him to get to Willington's campaign headquarters—they're working today. He might be able to catch Gavin Willington there."

Valeria escorted her invited guest toward the living room of her neat, modestly decorated trailer house. The nineteen-year-old nurse's aide rented the place from her paternal grandmother.

"Thank you for comin' so quickly, Mr. Edwards. I hope you don't mind that I copied your number from the card that you gave to my mother. When I saw you at the church earlier this morning I felt it was a sign."

The two made themselves comfortable on the sofa before she continued,

"I'm sorry, where are my manners? Can I offer you something, juice, water, coffee...tea?"

Jonathan removed a pad and pencil from the breast pocket of his blazer.

"No, thank you, Ms. Henderson. And please, call me Jonathan." He flipped open his pad. "I have a few questions that I would like to ask. First...what do you expect from me?"

"I want you to help me prove that my brother is innocent." Her eyes showered him with sincerity.

The reporter touched the tip of his pencil to his tongue. "If we're gonna do this, you're gonna have to be completely honest with me. Some of my questions are going to be very personal. I'm going to have to know everything about your family. I need you to be completely truthful. If I feel that you're not being truthful in any way…you're on your own."

"I understand. Look, Jonathan, my brother is innocent. I could not care less how many skeletons are let out of the closet."

"Well, let's get started. First, is your brother capable of committing murder?"

"Not at all. Larry is one of the…" Val stopped suddenly. She lowered her eyes. Her hesitation sparked an immediate response from the reporter.

"I take it that your honest response is that he is capable…"

She shamefully covered her face with both hands. "It's just that…"

"Just what?"

"Well…Larry and my father." She paused once again.

"Ms. Henderson…we don't have time to be coy."

He put his pencil behind his ear, and then reached for Val's hand. "Your brother just turned eighteen. He's being introduced to a world that will shake him to his very foundation. If you want to help him…you're going to have to open up. Now, tell me of the relationship between your father and brother."

Val shifted her eyes toward the ceiling. She took a deep breath before she addressed his question. "Larry is a good kid. So much was put on him at an early age.

You see, I was twelve and Larry was nine when my older siblings left the house. They couldn't take my daddy anymo'…his drinkin' started destroyin' the family. My mother always had an excuse for his violent behavior. She'd always say that he started drinkin' because of the pressure he was under tryin' to find out what happened to Terrell and Pooky."

"Who are Terrell and Pooky, and what happened to them?" the journalist asked.

Summer OF 1950

It took Margaret all of five minutes to drive over to Val's place.

"The last time any of us saw Pooky alive was the night we were rehearsing for a gospel fest." The distraught mother took a deep breath and she exhaled loudly.

Jonathan sipped his coffee. "Your daughter told me that he was hung. Was anyone ever charged with his murder?"

"In this place? In 1950? You're bein' a little naïve, Jonathan," Margaret ventured.

Val made herself comfortable next to her mother. "How is knowin' about Mr. Jackson gonna help you find the evidence that could free my brother?"

"I'm not sure but I'm the kind of person that covers all the bases."

Margaret stared at the journalist for several seconds before she would suggest, "Well, you should make yourself comfortable…it's a long story."

The newspaperman placed his cup on the cocktail table and then sat back before crossing his legs.

Margaret's daughter hated hearing the story surrounding James "Pooky" Jackson's final hours. She knew that her mother was still battling with the agony of losing someone that she felt so close to, even though thirty years had passed. Although Val had only heard the story twice—it seemed like her mother had told that story a million times. Each time Margaret revisited that painful night, the sorrowful look in her eyes and the pain in her voice were always the same.

Pooky Jackson was a close and very dear friend who was murdered on the same night Margaret revealed that she was about to bring a life into the world.

Pastor Walter Edwards, Jr. had presided over the church for nearly six years. In that time he played witness to Greater Faith Baptist being shot full of holes, derogatory and hateful graffiti being painted all over it, crosses burnt on the front lawn, and finally, being fire bombed.

Throughout all of the evil that was aimed toward Greater Faith, the pastor never once lost his vision, his faith, nor his resolve. On each occasion, when faced with the daunting task of refurbishing the house of worship, the young pastor always found a way to do so.

The church served as a sanctuary in a community besieged with violence that was initiated by the white men who assembled with the intent of intimidating or mangling the residents of the Bottoms.

There were many times when Perry's best friend

Pooky could be seen painting, patching and trying to restore the church himself. Funny thing about seeing him working so hard to get the church back to service-able condition was that Pooky wasn't a parishioner. Hell, he didn't even believe in God—he and his family were atheists. When asked why he took the time to do repairs, he simply stated, "Have you ever heard my best friend's girl sing?"

In the summer of 1950, a group of young wannabe White Knights threw several Molotov cocktails through the windows of the church. The damage was not exten-sive because several people in the neighborhood rushed from their homes and over to the church in time to contain the fire, but there was some smoke damage.

The pastor felt that until the damages were addressed, and as long as the weather held up, erecting a tent in back of the church and holding Sunday service outdoors until the repairs were made would be a nice change of pace.

The spiritual leader wanted to find a way to raise the money for repairs without making the congregation feel obligated to donate their hard-earned pennies. So, the very first Sunday that services were held outdoors, Pastor Edwards suggested that the church orchestrate a gospel fest and cookout to raise the money so that repairs to the ten-year-old structure could be made. Everyone in the community, regardless of his or her affiliation, wanted to help in the revitalization process, including a large contingent of choirs around the county, who had pledged their support and promised to take part.

The fest was scheduled to take place two weeks following the attack.

Some of the members of Greater Faith's choir gathered at the pulpit; they needed a break from the torturous rehearsal. Choir director Ms. Hattie Mae Scott felt that the strenuous preparation was necessary if Greater Faith were to represent. There were some very strong choirs in Morris County, and she didn't want hers to be embarrassed.

Gloria was Margaret's best friend in the whole world. They both were high school seniors.

The night of the first rehearsal, Margaret wasn't her usual jovial self, and Gloria knew something was wrong. She followed Margaret to the back of the church because she was determined to find out what was bothering her. They made themselves comfortable on the back pew before Gloria confronted her. She said that she could tell that Margaret had something heavy on her mind.

The most popular girl in Webber High School told Gloria that she was simply worried about whether Perry's parents liked her or not. Margaret knew that her boyfriend's mother and father didn't really think that Perry should be so serious about any girl—they felt that he was too young to rush into a committed relationship.

Perry's folks had never attended Greater Faith—they

were God-fearing people; just not churchgoing people. But after hearing Pooky rave over Margaret's ability to touch people through her voice, Perry's parents promised that they would attend the fest. Pooky hoped that once Perry's parents heard Margaret sing, they would see that their son and his girlfriend were perfect for each other.

Perry's folks really liked and respected Pooky because they knew that he loved their son like a brother. Everyone liked Pooky. He was a young man who always went out of his way to help others.

Gloria wasn't going to buy Margaret's excuse—she saw something in her friend's eyes, something that told her that whatever it was that was bothering Margaret went far deeper than her concerns about Perry's parents.

She was right.

Gloria harassed her best friend for several minutes before she finally opened up and told her that she was pregnant.

Margaret's girlfriend since grade school screamed—it was more of a squeal than anything, but it drew the attention of everyone in attendance. After realizing that she was a bit loud, she used her hands to cover her shocked expression. But it was too late. Ms. Scott asked the girls, in her usual rude manner, to share their conversation with the rest of the choir.

Now, there was no way that either girl was going to share anything with anyone in that church; especially Ms. Scott. That woman would have told everyone in the county that Margaret was expecting and she was not ready for anyone else to know. The only other person who knew was Pooky.

Pooky knew Perry better than anybody, so Margaret had to tell him. She needed to get his opinion on how to break the news to her boyfriend. Their plan was to have Pooky bring Perry to the rehearsal under the pretense of picking the girls up. Pooky, a dark-complexioned, stocky, high school football offensive guard had no problem with the plan because he would get a chance to run into Gloria. Pooky had an unbelievable crush on Margaret's best friend.

"If you're pregnant...are you gonna keep it?" Gloria asked in a whisper.

Margaret's eyes began to water. "Perry's gonna wanna marry me, if I am. I don't want him to marry me because I'm pregnant. He has dreams...I can't be the one responsible for him not goin' after them. Plus, his parents wouldn't let him marry me anyway. This could cause big problems with him and his mother for sure."

"He'd marry you in a heartbeat; regardless of what his mother might say. Perry loves you. Everyone knows that." Gloria's giddiness was evident. She moved closer to Margaret.

The two girls held hands before Gloria continued, "Girl, you're so lucky that he's the father. He's so sweet. Every girl in school, at one time or another, tried throwing themselves at him...but he's stuck on you."

The fifty-eight-year-old music teacher clapped her hands several times. "Okay, everyone, let's try this again…"

The choir began to gather, but Margaret and Gloria ignored Ms. Scott.

Hattie Mae was not one to be ignored; the two hundred and twenty-nine pounds on her five foot six frame was intimidating to most. Therefore, when the two girls in the back pew didn't respond—the choir director's nerve-wracking glare was aimed at them.

"Would you two fast-tail girls like to join us? We're gonna rehearse these songs of worship and praise until we get them right. We're not going to be humiliated at our own fest. I'll see to that; even if we have to do this all night." Her harsh commanding voice echoed throughout the church.

Embarrassed, the girls stood before Gloria asked Margaret, "When are you gonna tell him?"

"I gonna tell him after rehearsal. He and Pooky are gonna be waitin' for us outside," Margaret whispered.

Perry stood alongside his best friend on the steps of Greater Faith in awe of Margaret's solo a cappella version of "Amazing Grace," which resonated through the church's broken windows.

Pooky nudged Perry with his elbow, then said, "Man, I got goosebumps on my arms. Your girl can sing."

Perry didn't react—he was amazed that Margaret's angelic voice seemed to brighten every star that filled the night sky. His girlfriend had sung to him on many occasions—each time he was reminded how much he loved her. This time was no different.

He stood with his eyes locked on the church's entrance; his mouth suspended open—his heart flurried, he felt totally inspirited—as if his spiritual fuel tank was being filled.

Pooky instantly realized that his friend's mind had taken him on some sort of love struck journey; he shook his head in disbelief before saying, "Man…you need to go on and marry her."

He wasn't able to break the hypnotic hold that Margaret's voice had on his friend, so Pooky turned his attention to the beautiful night sky. For several seconds, he ingested the fresh air produced by a glorious evening. He glared intently toward a sky that was completely void of a single cloud; the Milky Way seemed within arm's reach.

Pooky would have gotten lost in the stars if he hadn't noticed, out of the corner of his eye, a blue 1950 Chevy parked a block from the church under a dimly lit streetlight. He was certain that that same car had followed him and Perry for much of that evening. He wasn't sure what was going on, but seeing that vehicle again made him feel a little uncomfortable.

Maybe it was the rednecks from town that we had a confrontation with earlier, he thought.

Pooky attempted to interrupt Perry's dreamy solitude;

he nudged him with his elbow once again, then mumbled without ever taking his eyes off of the vehicle. "P...hey, Perry, man...that car, it's down the block."

The singing, which echoed so radiantly from the church, stopped.

Aggravated after being nudged several times, Perry finally responded, "What...?"

"It's that car again." Pooky pointed. "It followed us from town."

Perry's eyes followed the path of his best friend's finger. "Who is that?"

"I don't know."

Pooky and Perry immediately locked eyes on the entrance as the doors to the church suddenly swung open. Several members of the choir rushed out; they gathered on the walkway and conversed under the moonlight.

Margaret and Gloria were amongst the last to step from the sacred gathering spot.

"Hey, Margaret...there's your man." Gloria playfully pointed toward Perry—he and Pooky stood on the steps, dividing their attention between the car and the girls.

Perry continued to split his attention as he headed up the steps. He greeted Margaret with an embrace. "Hey, baby girl."

"What's goin' on, Gloria?" Pooky asked before turning his attention toward his best friend's girl. "...Margaret... How you two doing tonight?"

"I'm okay, Pooky...how 'bout you," Gloria replied, her wide grin directed toward Perry.

They moved from the steps to the lawn in front of the house of worship.

Ms. Scott ordered, as she strolled past them, "You girls make sure you get yo' rest. We're gonna do this again tomorrow night. So take yo' behinds home."

"Okay, Ms. Scott." Gloria giggled.

"Take care of yourself, Ms. Scott!" the boys politely uttered to the nosy high school music teacher.

Margaret's girlfriend continued to direct her goofy grin toward Perry. When he turned his attention from Ms. Scott and noticed Gloria's cheesy smile, he asked, "Why are you smilin' at me like that?"

Gloria ignored the question. "Margaret...I gotta get home...I'll see you tomorrow," she said as she kissed Perry on the cheek. "Perry...you take care of her... okay, sweetie."

Pooky attempted to follow Gloria.

"Pooky...take your butt home," Gloria playfully said, as she began to walk away.

"Wait..." Pooky ordered.

Margaret's attractive, petite girlfriend stopped and placed her hands on her hips before directing her attention toward Perry's best friend. "What's yo' problem, boy?"

Pooky attempted to split his attention between the sassy, attractive young lady for whom he had a crush and Perry. "We can't let her walk by herself...that car; we don't know who's been followin' us." He pointed toward the vehicle. "That car has been followin' me and Perry all night."

"Baby...what's goin' on?" Margaret gazed at the Chevy for several seconds.

Perry didn't immediately respond to the question—his eyes were locked on the vehicle. He mumbled as he made his way toward the street. "We'll all walk together. Hold on for a second."

Margaret's handsome suitor stopped in the middle of the road and he glared in an attempt to bring the occupants into focus. He could see Ms. Scott out of the corner of his eye, as she headed down the sidewalk across from the illegally parked vehicle.

Unable to clearly make out who was behind the three shadowy silhouettes that occupied the car, Perry felt that he had to get closer in order to make an identification. He was determined to observe the inhabitants of the mysterious vehicle, so he slowly made his way toward it.

"Perry! Don't go over there. Let's get outta here," Pooky insisted.

Suddenly, the Chevy's engine roared to life. Perry froze in his tracks for several seconds. He was hesitant, but decided to continue to make his way toward the vehicle.

The occupants of the Chevy revved the engine. They hoped that the sound would be intimidating enough to dissuade him from continuing his approach.

When Perry increased his once nonchalant pace, the Chevy was quickly shifted into reverse. Its screeching tires frightened the twelve people that were still in front of the church. They all pleaded for him to give up his quest. "Come on, Perry...let's go!"

Undaunted, Perry began to chase the car, as it moved swiftly in reverse.

Ms. Scott stopped and observed the Chevy, as it backed past her at an alarming speed. She immediately turned her attention toward Perry, and wondered why he was in the middle of the street chasing after the car.

"Perry Henderson...what in God's name is goin' on?" she asked.

The music teacher stepped from the curb; she attempted to split her attention between the car and Perry as she headed toward him.

Suddenly, the car came to an abrupt halt, and so did Perry.

Ms. Scott continued toward the young man. "Perry... what in blue blazes is goin' on?"

The Chevy's tires began to spin rapidly. The car was shifted into drive. Ms. Scott stood paralyzed with fear. The vehicle was headed toward her at an alarming speed.

Perry ran toward the choir director, and pushed her out of harm's way. He and Ms. Scott lay dormant on the ground. They watched as the Chevy disappeared into the night like it was a participant in a drag race.

"Pooky walked Gloria home that night. They must've gotten him when he was on his way to his house," Margaret whispered. "Pooky was found lynched. We all believe that the people in that car were responsible for killin' him."

Jonathan asked, "Did you guys ever find out who was in that car?"

For months Detective Jake Aaron and his partner attempted to shed some light on the deaths of several individuals presumed to have been involved with the murder of Terrell Johnson, in the fall of 1967. Graphic crime scene photographs of those unsolved mysterious deaths, and their associated coroner's reports, covered the conference room table.

The investigation into three of the homicides went cold nearly fifteen years prior; yet, Jake was sure, that the recent murders of seven other men were connected. The public didn't exactly exude confidence in the police department's ability into solving either, because the families of the three that were killed in 1967 still didn't have closure.

"The connections are…Johnson…retribution-type slayings…and the Knights," Jake said as he and his part-ner meticulously searched through the materials before them.

Harris could tell that frustration had consumed his partner when Jake threw the report he was viewing to the table, and got to his feet.

"Four of these bodies were discovered in the Bottoms... Jasper Collins was the first...and he was the only one of the group to frequent that area. He did so because he ran a business down there for over twenty years. The coroner's report indicated that Jasper's body was viciously ripped apart after he was already dead."

Jake picked up a photograph of Jasper's mutilated body before he continued, "The report goes on to describe the deep gashes that covered the corpse as bein' inflicted by canines..."

The detective stared intently at the autopsy photograph. "His body was discovered in his store, but there was no indication that that's where the murder took place. So, his body was obviously placed there."

Jake tossed the photograph back to the table before he began to pace.

"Then there's Billy Forrester. He was nearly beaten to death with a blunt object...possibly a bat...then drowned. His body was found floatin' in Morris Creek."

His partner interjected, "Al Blaine was also pulled from the creek."

Harris began to search for Blaine's photographs and autopsy report. The fourteen-year veteran grabbed, and then opened, the file. He stood before continuing.

"According to this...the coroner believed that Blaine had a chain tied to his ankles. The evidence supports that the chain was attached to a vehicle of some sort. Blaine's body was then dragged by that vehicle at what the coroner described as a moderate speed over rough terrain."

Jake countered, "That one is puzzlin'. The coroner said that he was hung after he was dragged. That was the only victim tortured in that manner." Jake continued to pace. "We've had two that were hung, two that appeared to have been forcibly drowned." He wondered aloud, "There's somethin' really strange goin' on."

Jake's investigative intuition told him that Terrell Johnson's case was the key to solving all the unsolved homicides before him. He grabbed the Johnson file and peered through it. "Someone is tryin' to send some sort of message."

The Daily News video research room was empty when Jonathan entered. He immediately began going through microfiche in search of articles written on the murder of Terrell Johnson, and or James "Pooky" Jackson.

Article after article flashed on the microfiche screen.

The reporter's eyes began to water and tire. Jonathan rubbed them several times as he continued his search through the mound of fiche.

"I can't believe that no one thought this story was worth covering...even back then." He leaned back and stretched his arms to the heavens; his long, drawn-out body extension was accompanied by an exhausted yawn.

After relieving himself of the body knots created by sitting for a long period of time, the reporter sat forward once again. He then replaced the microfiche that was in the machine with another before he resumed his search.

Twenty minutes, and a half-dozen microfiche later, Jonathan finally came across an article written about Terrell Johnson:

On Thursday morning the body of a nineteen-year-old Negro was pulled from Morris Creek. A coroner's report suggests that the death of Terrell Johnson, a freshman at LeHigh Community College, was a direct result of an apparent suicide. The coroner believes that there were no signs that Johnson had been lynched, as was previously speculated. Accusations swirled around for days that Johnson's death was at the hand of the White Knights, and that he was in fact lynched. It was believed that after the lynching the boy's corpse was stuffed into a potato sack and dumped into Morris Creek.

Jonathan was shocked at what he had read. He was even more surprised at who had actually written the article. The reporter quickly printed the commentary, and then began to sift through more microfiche.

It was obvious to the investigative reporter that a cover-up of some sort had taken place. There was no doubt that the Klan murdered Terrell. Everything that Jonathan had heard about Terrell Johnson's death pointed to the hate mongers, and not a suicide. The powers that be had covered up the truth, and continued to do so.

While Jonathan was from the Midwest, he was well

aware that law enforcement in the South during the sixties wasn't at all concerned with justice for Blacks. So the Klan would not have been investigated. He understood that the individuals that were hired to uphold law and order south of the Mason-Dixon Line were the very ones committing the lamentable crimes against people of color. Jonathan also realized that crimes committed against people of color would not receive the coverage, or the sense of urgency, from newspapers or television.

Eric Maxwell was seated at his desk going over an article when Jonathan walked in with a piece of paper in hand.

"Eric...the Terrell Johnson case...you wrote the only article that covered his murder...why was it written up like a suicide?" the veteran reporter asked. He placed a copy of the story on his boss's desk before he continued, "I can't believe that you would have been so irresponsible?"

The editor picked up the printout that his reporter placed before him. He leaned back in his chair—his green eyes locked on the article. Eric's mind drifted into the past. For years, Terrell Johnson's murder had haunted him. Johnson's death was his first real opportunity at covering a story, his very first cutting-edge assignment after receiving his degree in Journalism from the University of Alabama.

"This story was my first. I still haven't been able to put this to rest in my mind. I was told that I could write a small piece...I think that they put me on the story because I wasn't a threat, being just out of school and all. They figured that I wouldn't raise a stink. I wrote a story based on the information that I uncovered. I wanted to impress, so I dug deep.

"This was not what I had written—it was changed during editorial. I pitched a fit. My photographs and my original piece were destroyed. The photos alone could have proven that that boy didn't take his own life. It was definitely murder... The *powers that be* didn't want me pushing the story any further." The tall, slender, dark-haired editor got to his feet and began to pace his office.

Eric mumbled, "The only investigation into Johnson's death besides mine was done by a second year police officer."

Jonathan's response was knowing. "Perry Henderson..."

"Yes, he told me that Terrell was his nephew and that he wasn't gonna stop lookin' into his murder until he uncovered the truth." Eric retook his seat, then said, "Terrell Johnson's death was meaningless."

"Tell me more?" Jonathan asked. He sat down on the couch and waited patiently for his boss to explain.

1967

Perry followed a man dressed in overalls.

The white male tried desperately to hide his identity by keeping his worn baseball cap snug to his head as they maneuvered through thick brush toward a swampy area near Morris Creek.

Jasper looked up from under the bill of his cap. It was obvious that he was concerned—and extremely nervous. The redneck periodically peered over his shoulder in an effort to ensure that no one had followed them.

"It's okay…nobody followed me…" Perry insisted.

"They gon' kill me if they find out I brough'cha here…" the anxious redneck mumbled.

Two squirrels playing several yards away distracted Jasper. He stopped and scanned his surroundings. Terrified, Jasper whispered, "What was that?"

"Nobody's followin' us…don't worry," Perry insisted.

The panic-stricken informant pointed. "What I want you to see…it's right over there."

The two men made their way over to an old Ford pickup truck, which was completely burned out. Its crushed front end was barely submerged in the swampy waters.

Perry began to examine the wreckage; he stepped into the marshy lagoon, and slowly circled the vehicle, before saying, "Whose truck is this…?"

Jasper continued to fearfully scan the area. "Doesn't matter…all you gotta know is that this is the truck he tried to get away in."

Perry Henderson knelt by the driver's side door and used his fingers to examine the bullet holes.

"I thought you said he didn't get shot…? How could he not have been?"

PRESENT

Eric picked up the copy of his sabotaged first article. He gazed at the column for several seconds before making eye contact with his best reporter. The chief editor could see that the journalist was expecting more details.

"Jasper Collins told Henderson everything…with the exception of the people involved. They dragged the creek and found Terrell Johnson's body…a couple hours after pulling that kid from the creek, Perry discovered Jasper's mutilated corpse."

"Where was Collins' body found?" Jonathan asked.

Eric once again got to his feet before he answered, "For years, Collins ran a grocery store in the Bottoms. Henderson found Collins' body in that store. Why so much interest in the Johnson case?"

"Because I feel that Terrell Johnson's case is somehow connected to Miran Thompson's. I have one other question. Do you know anything about a high school friend of Henderson's? He was lynched in 1950. His name was James *Pooky* Jackson."

Eric made himself comfortable on the edge of his desk. "Can't say that I do."

Perry Henderson had held his position as the director of public affairs for a little over a year. His new title came with a promotion to the grade of lieutenant, and of course, a lot more responsibilities. The rapid increase in black-on-black crime, which was no longer exclusive to the Bottoms, was the department's main reason for Officer Henderson's appointment.

Since people of color were allowed to migrate from the Bottoms and into the heart of Jacob, the mayor and the chief of police believed that the man who'd endured and overcome the racial discord and hostility that at one time embodied their municipality was the logical choice to play liaison between the department and the community.

Perry's office was white-glove neat. He could walk into his workspace blindfolded and would be able to locate anything he needed.

The door to his office was closed, the blinds drawn.

Perry, still covered with soot, a sign of his early morning heroics, sat at his desk with a phone to his ear. "I know that…"

He opened the bottom drawer of his desk and pulled from it a fifth of Ole Grand Dad and a shot glass. The distressed officer poured himself a shot. "I understand… but…"

Perry downed his drink as he listened to the person on the other end of his conversation. The nervous officer quickly put his bottle and glass back into its place after a sudden tap at his door startled him. He closed his desk drawer, and then quickly covered the mouthpiece of the phone. "Come in."

Jonathan Edwards entered. Perry gestured for him to wait before he continued with his phone conversation.

"Look...I understand that he has to wait for two weeks before he can have visitors. And, I understand that you won't make any exceptions...I also understand that you won't allow him to come to the phone. All I'm askin' is that the warden makes special provision for him. He's still a child."

Perry's frustration was very evident to the news reporter as Jonathan viewed the officer slam the phone to its cradle.

"Damn it..." Perry yelled as he quickly directed his attention toward his guest. "Who are you...and what can I do for you?"

The reporter stood before the officer and extended his hand, "I'm Jonathan Edwards from the *Daily News*."

"How are you, Mr. Edwards?" Perry stood. He then shook the reporter's hand. "What can I do for you?" the officer asked again.

Jonathan smiled. "First, you can begin by calling me Jonathan."

"Have a seat, Jonathan."

The reporter made himself comfortable in a chair that was positioned at the side of Perry's desk.

Perry retook his seat before saying, "What's on your mind?"

"Looks like you had a rough day."

The officer turned his attention to the soot that covered his uniform. "Yeah, I guess you could say that." He immediately redirected his attention toward the journalist. "You coverin' that fire?"

"No, I'm covering your son's story. When I first walked in, you were on the phone. Was that the prison?"

Perry gazed reluctantly at the reporter.

After several seconds of silence, he replied, "Look, I don't like talkin' to reporters. The last time I attempted to trust one of you, I was disappointed. Back in '67 I felt that my only way of gettin' to the truth was to inform the papers. That turned out to be a mistake. You guys hung me out to dry. One damn article and that one suggested that my nephew's death was a suicide; after I was promised that he would do everythin' he could to help me reveal the truth. He only wrote one damn article and it was filled with lies. I don't trust none of you and I'm not about to entrust any of you with my son's life."

Are They Comin'
FOR ME?

Every barracks on the grounds was required to pass Sergeant Morris' white-glove inspections. Andre "Mop" Turner was the person responsible for ensuring that Camp 29 lived up to the CO's high standards.

The buffed aisle that separated twenty-two bunk beds, eleven to a side (duel wall locker sat next to each bunk) got maximum marks during the day's inspection. Everything was in tiptop order, except the shower/latrine area and Sergeant Morris expressed his disappointment to the six-foot-five, two hundred and eighty-pound barracks leader.

"YOU'RE THE ONE RESPONSIBLE FOR THIS MESS..." Morris yelled as he pointed his gloved right index finger into Mop's face. "Look at this grimy shit... Camp 29 used to be considered topnotch. You been slippin'...asshole!"

The irate guard resumed his inspection. His next stop was the shower area. Without hesitation, he made his way toward the toilets; Mop followed.

The other inmates stood at parade rest next to their

bunks; three CO's paced the aisle to ensure that the prisoners remained in the military position while Morris conducted his inspection.

Every occupant of Camp 29 understood that when Morris wasn't happy, Mop certainly wasn't going to be; so, it was a given that everyone would definitely pay for his displeasure. They all cringed when they heard the CO yell.

"DAMN IT, MOP...WHO THE HELL YOU THINK SMALL IS GONNA CHEW OUT WHEN HE SEE THIS?"

He stuck the index finger of his left gloved hand into the mammoth inmate's face.

"IS THIS PISS? PISS... MOP...IF YOU CAN'T GET THESE SORRY SON-OF-A BITCHES TO CLEAN THIS SHIT...THEN MAYBE YOU SHOULD..."

Larry was assigned the bottom bed of the bunk closet to the shower/latrine area, which gave a clear view to the restroom.

Even though the inmate was ordered to keep his eyes straight ahead during inspections, the baby faced prisoner disobeyed the command and shifted his eyes to his left. Upon doing so, he was able to see Morris' rage.

He played witness to Morris and Mop standing toe-to-toe. Larry watched as saliva spewed from the angry sergeant's mouth and into the face of the barrack's leader.

Morris screamed, "I'M GIVEN YO' ASS UNTIL

THE DAY BEFORE SMALL'S INSPECTION TO GET THIS SHIT RIGHT…! YOU HAVE TWO DAMN DAYS…IF I SEE THIS TYPE OF SHIT AGAIN…YO' ASS IS OUT…I'M GONNA TURN OVER THE RESPONSIBILITY OF THIS BARRACKS TO SOMEONE THAT I CAN TRUST WILL DO A BETTER JOB!"

The CO's rage was unmistakable. He stormed out of the latrine before throwing his white inspection gloves at an inmate. Morris motioned for his subordinates to follow; they then exited the barracks.

The barracks supervisor waited several seconds after the corrections officers departed Camp 29 before he entered the common area. He stood at the entrance of the latrine with his hand on his hips; anger depicted on his face. The inmates stood frozen; everyone braced themselves in anticipation of Mop's retribution.

He was restless and unable to sleep because he feared the unknown. The new inmate tossed and turned for what seemed like an eternity; Mop's fury echoed about in Larry's head. The barracks supervisor had gone ballistic after being scolded by Morris and, for some strange reason, Larry felt that Mop's scolding wasn't over. He felt something in the air—something bad was about to happen.

To Larry's right was darkness; an obscurity that imparted pending doom. When he turned his head to the left, his eyes were introduced to a glow, generated from the firelight mounted on the latrine wall. It wasn't bright, but it was light just the same. Like a frightened child afraid of the dark, in an effort to chase his fears, Larry stared at what was to be his nightlight.

Just when he felt that he had conquered the hours of darkness, the squeaking of beds, a sure sign that two or three in-mates had gotten out of their bunks, brought back his fearful reality.

Larry nervously turned his head; he could see three huge shadows huddled together in the middle of the aisle.

Are they coming for me—hell...what should I do? he thought as his body began to tense. The youngest inmate in the entire facility felt an anxiety attack coming on. His stomach was in knots—he began to perspire profusely.

The three shadows broke their huddle and began to head in his direction.

Everyone else was sound asleep, but Larry desperately wanted to wake each from their slumber because he wanted everyone to play witness to what was about to happen to him.

The frightened prisoner closed his eyes; he then balled his fists. Larry tried to picture what he needed to do in order to fend off his anticipated aggressors. The young inmate had watched a lot of Bruce Lee movies as a kid; now was his chance to use the knowledge he had

obtained from *Enter The Dragon*, or even *The Green Hornet*…he would play Kato.

I don't wanna hurt them…but I will…Master Lee…I can do it… I know I can. His tremble intensified. *Damn…who am I kiddin'…they gon' kill me*…he thought to himself.

Larry could feel someone standing over him. He tightened his fists harder and began nibbling on his bottom lip. The person whose presence loomed as a shadowy figure in Larry's mind whispered. His communication directed toward the guy in the bed above.

"Stinky…you know the three I want…send 'em into my office…one at a time…in five-minute intervals."

The scared young inmate opened his eyes before turning his head in time to see the three shadowy figures disappear into the restroom. Seconds later, the inmate assigned to the bed above Larry's (Ronald Cells, aka Stinky) hopped down off of his bunk.

Stinky's hair was braided in cornrows, his was complexion dark; the inmate was dressed in boxers and a T-shirt. Larry watched curiously as the short, very thin, convicted criminal made his way over to a bunk across the aisle.

Stinky shook a sleeping inmate, whispering to him, "Hey, Terrence…wake up."

The woozy prisoner peeked up at the man that had awakened him. "What up, Stinky…" His voice was groggy.

"Get up…Mop wants to see you in his office…bring your toothbrush."

"What?" Terrence questioned.

"Bring your damn toothbrush."

Terrence immediately got out of his bed, opened a locker that was positioned next to his bed, and removed a toothbrush before following the messenger toward the restroom.

Stinky stood guard outside as Terrence entered.

Larry, without hesitation, sat up in his bed when he heard the grunts of a man that was obviously being beaten. Fear engulfed his very being; he wondered if he could be next. Once Mop and his goons finished with Terrence, would they turn their rage toward him?

Larry's bunkmate didn't seem at all fazed by the moans of anguish; it was clear to him that the pint-sized con was used to what was taking place in the lavatory.

While listening to the commotion in the restroom, Stinky caught a glimpse of a terrified Larry as he peered through the darkness. He tipped over to his bunk and whispered to the new inmate, "Go to sleep, *FISH*…you don't want no parts of this… If they see you up…you'll be next."

In a half-hour span, Larry saw a total of six people entered the latrine. However, only three exited. The three inmates that Mop blamed for the scolding he received from Morris had paid the price. The young convict heard each being beaten, and he feared that they lay dead on the floor of the shower. He spent the next three hours with his eyes locked on the entrance, hoping that they would stagger out.

He found it impossible to sleep so Larry decided to try and beat the morning rush. He was a little nervous about going into the shower before everyone else got up. He didn't want to be the one that discovered the three dead inmates, but he also didn't want to spend his first shower with the thought that everyone would be watching him, and waiting for their chance to take his manhood. Larry got out of his bed, grabbed his towel, toothbrush and paste, and headed for the latrine. Upon entering, he was relieved to see the inmates that had been summoned by the barracks leader. Although they had been severely beaten, they were alive. The three were forced to stay up the entire night cleaning the latrine area with their toothbrushes.

"Hey, man...should we tell that fish that he shouldn't be in here before Mop?" one inmate whispered to the others. Terrence insisted that Larry needed to learn "on-the-job-training" like the rest of them. The three inmates watched as Larry got into the shower before they continued cleaning.

Larry felt the eyes of everyone in Camp 29 locked on him as he dressed.

Why weren't they trying to take a shower? He heard the water running but only one person was in there. It seemed like a waste. After all, ten people could shower at the same time. He wondered why everyone seemed to be patiently waiting, and why they were standing around gawking at him. He felt that he was the topic of their conversations.

Suddenly, he heard a monstrous roar echoing from the latrine; it was a menacing scream that instantly stripped the attention away from him.

"WHAT THE HELL!!! THIS SHIT IS COLD!!! WHO WAS THE LAST SON-OF-BITCH TO COME OUTTA HERE?"

Paralyzed with a nervous energy, Larry finally realized why everyone else was gawking at him. Mop came storming out of the shower with a towel wrapped around his waist. The angry barracks leader immediately began his search for the New Fish.

Larry couldn't understand how the water got cold so quickly, he'd only spent about four minutes in the shower. From the devilish statements of the faces of the three individuals who were forced to spend several hours cleaning the latrine, Larry knew that they were the men responsible for setting him up. He figured that the battered convicts more than likely ran the hot water long enough to cause it to go cold in the middle of Mop's morning ritual.

"Yo!! Young blood…did you use up all the hot water?" he asked while approaching Larry with lethal intent.

"Huh!!" The young inmate's eyes widened.

"Don't 'huh' me…muthafucka!!! You used up all the damn hot water! Look here, BITCH! Don't nobody take a fuckin' shower until I have! I'm gonna have to teach yo' ass a lesson…" the angry behemoth snarled.

Larry was completely unaware of the barracks leader's

position as it related to him being the first to shower in the morning, but he was about to get a firsthand lesson. Without warning, Mop hit Larry so hard that the young inmate fell flat on his ass.

Larry immediately got to his feet. With his hand firmly pressed against his jaw, he said, "Man... What the hell!!!"

Without hesitation, Mop hit Larry for a second time.

Blood spewed from his mouth as he stumbled back several steps before he once again collapsed to the floor. The teen's eyes rolled up in his head. Larry's vision was distorted. Unable to fully zero in on his adversary, the dazed inmate spat out more of the crimson fluid. He blinked several times before he was finally able to bring Mop into focus.

Larry's gaze at the barracks supervisor was trance-like; his mind superimposed Mop's face with that of his father. He watched Mop move toward him, readying to kick. Camp 29's leader was in full-fledged attack mode.

To the dazed youngster, everything appeared to be moving in slow motion.

Larry quickly got to his feet and rushed his attacker. He rammed his shoulder into Mop's sternum, and then wrapped his arms around the waist of his aggressor, attempting to make a tackle. Nevertheless, the one hundred and sixty-pound boy was no match for the hardened criminal. It was like a fly attempting to topple an elephant.

Every resident of Camp 29 gathered around. They screamed and yelled. They outright instigated.

"COME ON, LITTLE MAN...COME ON! YOU CAN TAKE HIM..." they screamed. Everyone realized that Larry didn't stand a chance against Mop; their encouragement was meant to incite rage in their leader.

"I know yo' little ass don't think you can take me..." Mop said as he punched Larry with blow after blow. Several of his shots lifted the youngster completely off his feet, but the new convict held on. Larry refused to let go.

An uppercut was the key that unlocked Larry's grip; he fell to the floor. His eyes were swollen; blood flowed freely from his nostrils.

"I know you don't want no mo... Yo' little ass better get in line. I'ma let yo' ass go this time...but you won't be so lucky if that shit happens again," Mop said as he stood over Larry adjusting his towel.

"Make sure yo' ass don't get into the shower until I'm out!!!" the intimidating figure said as he turned and headed toward the latrine.

Larry struggled to his feet; he staggered toward Mop. The other inmates clapped and screamed their approval. "COME ON, LITTLE MAN... HE'S GONNA GET YO' ASS... MOP!!!

The barracks leader redirected his attention just in time to see the gutsy young convict stumble toward him with his arms extended. Larry's inability to maintain his balance prompted the corners of Mop's mouth to turn up; he was amused. The half-naked monster stepped to the side as Larry lunged toward him. Larry grabbed nothing but air as he fell helplessly to the floor yet again.

"Stay yo' little ass down, young blood!!!" Mop insisted.

Larry managed to struggle to his feet once again. He staggered in Mop's direction—the punch-drunk inmate still envisioned his opponent as his father.

Mop hit him with a devastating right hand to the jaw—the other inmates viewed Larry's face as it shook from side to side as if he'd been electrocuted. Blood and saliva sprayed from his mouth. Badly wounded, Larry once again collapsed helplessly to the floor.

The jeers and cheers of the inmates ceased to echo about the wooden structure. The only sound was the grunts of the embattled New Fish, who once again attempted to get to his feet.

The other inmates were shocked to see the bloody Fish attempt to recover. He had a difficult time catching his breath but he grabbed his stomach as he got to his feet.

"Stay down, young blood...stay down!!!" the inmates shouted.

Mop gazed at the young criminal before he advised, "Listen to them, young blood...stay down before I drop yo' ass again!!!"

"You gonna have to keep on droppin' me...'cause I'm gonna keep gettin' back up..." After four very painful steps, Larry dropped to a knee, but he kept his eyes locked on Mop.

The barrack's leader shook his head in disbelief. He

couldn't believe Larry's heart. Mop instructed Stinky to help the bloody kid to his feet and over to his bunk.

Everyone continued to gawk, which pissed off the short, self-conscious inmate.

Stinky yelled, "Mind yo' damn business."

Mop turned to the others. "Get ya'll asses ready."

Ronald Cells helped Larry to his feet.

Larry wobbled. He nearly collapsed but Stinky was able to steady him. They both watched as Mop returned to the latrine. Once he disappeared, the two made their way toward the bunk. Larry was exhausted and in pain. He dropped to a knee before they could make it to his bunk.

Another inmate ran over to help him. He helped Stinky lift Larry to his feet and over to his bunk.

"Stinky…what's that name all about?" The youngster's question was barely audible. He promptly coughed up blood. Ronald Cells wasn't at all interested in answering. The two inmates eased the battered youngster to his bed.

"Come on, man…you gotta let me know what that name is about," Larry insisted. He protectively clutched his arms close to his ribs. The grimace on his swollen face was heart-wrenching, even for the hardest criminal.

Stinky grabbed Larry's towel and disappeared into the latrine. He rushed back out with the damp material. Ronald "Stinky" Cells began to wipe away some of the blood that covered the young boy's face.

"So...why do they call you Stinky?"

"Because...when I first got here...those son-of-a-bitches tried to rape me...but I was ready for their asses..."

Larry moaned in pain while he clutched at his stomach.

"When they tried to take this ass...they had a surprise waitin' on 'em..."

Larry grimaced. "What?"

"When they pulled my drawers down...they found out what it's like when a nigga don't wipe his ass for weeks... You should have seen them muthas take off when they smelled that shit...and I do mean shit..."

Larry's laughter brought about more pain. "Ouch! You lyin'!!! Ouch!!! This shit hurts..." The young inmate held his jaw before he continued, "Shit..." His laughter continued. "Did they ever try it again?"

Stinky announced with a smile. "Would you?"

Jake
AND THE DA

District Attorney Louis Calvert escorted Detective Jake Aaron into his office. The probing law enforcement officer was determined to get the prosecutor's take on Larry Henderson's allocution. Jake wanted to hear why the DA's office moved so quickly. He wanted to know what made them believe a child who was obviously frightened. The detective wanted to know if the DA realized that there wasn't any evidence that pointed to Larry's guilt. Moreover, Jake couldn't understand why the kid confessed. Perry's explanation simply didn't make sense.

The DA made his way over to his desk. Jake made himself comfortable in one of two chairs positioned in front of the legal representative for Morris County, which included the fifty thousand or so residents of Jacob.

"You know that that boy didn't kill Miran Thompson," Jake stated.

The DA was confused.

Louis leaned back in his seat. "He confessed. Plus, his own father thinks he did it."

"What do you mean, that his father thinks he did it?"

The headman in the prosecutor's office couldn't understand why Jake, of all people, would want to make waves. Everyone knew that he didn't like Perry, and that Miran was his best friend. Louis thought that the detective would be ecstatic to have the Black officer by the proverbial nuts. The district attorney was also under the impression that Perry had discussed his son's case with the rest of the department.

"You mean to tell me that Henderson didn't tell you guys that he felt his own son was guilty?" Louis asked. "He spent thirty minutes trying to convince me of his son's guilt."

Why didn't the lieutenant tell me what he had told the District Attorney's Office? Perry gave me some sorry excuse about death row. He told me that he knew his son was innocent, the detective thought to himself. With his mouth suspended open, Jake stared intently into the eyes of the DA.

"You're kiddin'…Henderson actually told you that his son was guilty?"

The buzzer to Louis' intercom rang out, but before he would respond, the DA excused himself, "Give me a second, please."

Louis pushed the bottom to his voice box. "Yes…!"

"He's here, sir," a voice echoed.

"Send him in." Louis made eye contact with his guest before saying, "I called myself giving the lieutenant a break. I felt bad for him; that's why I didn't have a problem makin' the deal. You're not the only one that feels that the kid was innocent. But, he confessed. Then there's Lieutenant Henderson's insistence that his son was guilty. What would you have suggested I do?"

The prosecutor got to his feet as the door opened.

Jake peered over his shoulder and watched as Jonathan Edwards entered. The journalist headed straight for Louis with his hand extended. "I really appreciate you taking the time to see me, Mr. Calvert."

The two shook hands.

"It's quite alright...I love your work. If you're lookin' into this, then you must feel that somethin' has been overlooked."

Louis pointed to Jake. "Mr. Edwards...this is Detective Jake Aaron...lead investigator of Jacob's police department. Jake, this is Jonathan Edwards, reporter from the *Daily News*."

Jake got to his feet and extended his hand to the reporter. "Nice to see you again, Jonathan."

The two exchanged a friendly handshake.

"I see that you two are acquainted," whispered the DA.

"For some time now," said the detective.

The prosecutor retook his seat, after which, he emphasized, "I asked that you both come here because of your shared interest in the Henderson case. While I think that you might have valid reasons for concerns, the mayor's wish is that this case be put to sleep."

"Why?" Jake blurted.

DA Louis glared at the detective. "He thinks that your time can best be served looking into the recent unsolved homicides and not involving yourselves in a case in which the taxpayers were lucky enough to save a lot of money. You see that boy's confession, and our subsequent agreement, prevented a lengthy trial that would have eventually resulted in the death penalty. It would have also drawn unwanted attention toward the police department because of who the perpetrator was. The son of a police lieutenant and I don't mean just any police officer. It's a known fact that Henderson and Miran Thompson had a history."

Jonathan intervened, "Who's puttin' pressure on the mayor and why?"

"What makes you think anybody is puttin' pressure on him?" Louis' gentlemanly Southern drawl was razor-sharp.

"This stinks of a political cover-up. Why would the mayor be concerned about this case?" Jonathan questioned.

Jake directed his response toward the inquiring journalist. "Because Miran Thompson was special assistant to Senator Gavin Willington."

"You're kidding…" It was a revelation to the reporter to hear Miran's connection with Senator Willington. Jonathan slowly bobbed his head up and then down several times, like a light bulb had gone off. "Willington had a known racist as his special assistant." He immediately realized why the mayor wanted to put the case to rest. "...So that means that the mayor is trying to help the senator keep that piece of news quiet because of his reelection bid."

Louis stood abruptly. The District Attorney was not at all comfortable with the direction that the conversation was headed. "I've heard that you're a good journalist... I've heard you never print information based on speculation. What you are suggesting is not based on fact. Miran Thompson had nothing to do with Willington. The senator did not employ Thompson in any capacity."

The prosecutor directed his next statement toward the detective. "Jake, I don't know where you got your information but I'm certain that the senator wouldn't appreciate you giving anyone the impression that your accusations are founded."

Senator Gavin Willington was seated in the back of a limousine.

His chauffeur had his attention locked on the road as he weaved in and out of traffic en route to Willington's campaign headquarters. Seated across from the elected official were two members of the Secret Service, along with the senator's campaign advisor.

His dedicated consultant frantically fumbled through paperwork, while the Senator carefully reviewed projected returns. The senator sighed as he continued to flip through

the reports. "The race is close. I wasn't expecting this...
I'm projected to lose a lot of my constituency."

His advisor countered, "Sir...it's like we discussed. As
long as you're not associated with the Knights...accord-
ing to this report...you'll pick up a lot of the Negro vote."

The campaign advisor passed several pieces of paper
to the senator. "This shows that, with that demographic,
you'll win in a landslide."

"Well, we have to ensure that those unfounded accusations die down as quickly as they've surfaced. I think
that you should contact LT. Tell him we have three
issues that I wanna address. Then contact Detective
Jack Aaron and that journalist from the *Daily News*...
Jonathan Edwards. Tell both of them that I wanna see
them as soon as possible. We need to put an end to this
as quickly as possible. Those two are the keys to doing
just that." He looked up from his paperwork. "Remove
any possible obstacles."

The chauffeur eased the car to a stop directly in front
of Willington's campaign headquarters. From the crowd
of people that lined the streets holding signs and cheering, it was obvious that the senator had an awful lot of
supporters.

Photographers positioned themselves to take pictures,
while reporters attempted to maneuver through the
crowd for a chance at a possible interview.

The chauffeur opened the door and the senator's security force exited the black limousine—the suited Secret

Service contingent attempted to hold off the crowd in anticipation of the senator stepping from the vehicle.

As Willington exited his car to the cheers of hundreds, he waved, and mouthed the words "thank you" before heading up the walkway.

Senator Gavin Willington was once again throwing his hat into the ring to represent his state in the senate. Born and raised in Jacob, the senator was a third-generation member of the governing body. Like his father and grandfather before him, Gavin spent the majority of his adult life serving the state in one capacity or another. Having served two terms as governor, the youngest son of the most prominent family in the country was bidding for his third opportunity to represent Jacob in the senate.

The senator's grandfatherly appearance, strong chin, brownish-graying hair, blue eyes and soft-spoken demeanor were a campaign manager's dream. It didn't hurt at all that the sixty-two-year-old pedant had the political pedigree.

The likable politician wasn't at all happy that his opponent had apparently leaked information that connected Gavin with having affiliation with a supremacist group known as the White Knights.

The ex-governor was prepared. He understood that as soon as he stepped from the car that he was going to be bombarded with questions about his relationship with the group of violent individuals that had wreaked havoc around Morris County for decades.

As he headed up the walkway shaking hands, and waving to his supporters, he noticed several reporters attempting to fight past one another in an effort to question him.

"Senator…how do you like your chances?" one reporter yelled.

Another screamed, "Senator…according to the projections…you might lose this election…I'd like to know your thoughts on that."

"Senator…senator…what's your connection to the White Knights?" another shouted.

The beautiful antique oak desk that Gavin sat behind was third generation—he could remember playing in his grandfather's study and hiding under the desk just as JFK, Jr. did in the White House. His guest was seated in a butter-soft, fine-looking leather chair, which was positioned in front of the elected official.

"Your brother was handlin' things for me…I'm turnin' that job over to you because you earned it. I need you to be as inconspicuous as your brother was. No one can know that you're doin' work for me…I mean no one!" The senator opened his desk drawer and began rummaging through it before he continued, "There are three important things that you're gonna have to be aware of."

His intercom beeped and interrupted his thoughts. Gavin excused himself with a hand gesture before answering, "What is it, Cynthia?"

His secretary's voice resonated over the intercom. "Senator, Detective Jake Aaron is here."

"Give me thirty seconds before you send him in. I have to conclude a call," the senator said calmly. After disconnecting his secretary, he redirected his attention back to his guest before he closed his desk drawer.

His visitor seemed confused—almost in a state of panic.

"It's okay…I asked him to come…I wanna hear from him…" Gavin pointed to a chair in the far corner of his office, out of the view of anyone that would enter. "Take a seat over there."

Jake Aaron entered the office several seconds later. The detective walked up to Gavin and, of course, extended his hand. The senator politely stood and greeted the law enforcement officer.

"I'd like to congratulate you, senator…I really believe that you're gonna be reelected," Jake said as the two men shook hands.

"I've really appreciated your support over the years. When I was governor, you were right there for me. Please have a seat, Jake."

As Jake readied himself to sit, he happened to catch a glimpse of someone out of the corner of his eye. He made himself comfortable in the beautiful leather chair in front of Gavin's desk before turning his attention to the senator's visitor. The police officer politely acknowledged the man who was sitting in the corner. "Lee…"

Jake immediately turned his shocked expression toward

the senator. "What's goin' on, Gavin...what's he doin' here?"

Lee got to his feet and spoke as he headed toward the police officer. "Jake...what's this I hear you tryin' to prove that that porch monkey didn't kill my brother? I'm here because I would like the senator to look in to you. I don't appreciate what you're tryin' to do."

"Don't act like you cared about Miran." Jake turned his back to the infuriated redneck. Lee immediately made himself comfortable in the chair next to the detective.

"Senator...I don't believe that we have the right guy," said Jake.

Lee quickly got to his feet; he was outraged. "What!"

The senator used a calming hand gesture toward Lee. "Take it easy, Lee...sit back down, please." He pointed to the chair in the corner, suggesting that Lee return to the seat that he had vacated. Lee hesitated, but promptly reconsidered after he recognized a look in the eyes of the politician that he was all too familiar with.

Gavin Willington waited for Lee to return to the far corner of his office before he redirected his attention toward Jake.

"I hear that you're tryin' to connect Miran's case to some of the previous and recent unsolved homicides. What's the status of those cases?" the senator asked.

"It's reached seven now and I do believe that the three unsolved cases in '67 are connected to these seven. I also believe that Miran's death was not the result of an attempted robbery, and in fact, it ties in with the others. I do believe that someone wants me to think Miran's death was not related. Thus, the framing of Henderson's kid."

The senator quickly countered, "If you can't immediately tie those other cases to this one, stop your investigation. Leave that boy in prison for Miran's murder."

"Why?" Jake questioned.

"I don't want the papers gettin' any ideas. I don't want them feelin' that there's a story where none exists. You guys got that Henderson kid to confess that he killed Miran, so he should pay."

Jake sat forward in his chair. "But...what if he didn't kill Miran?" He looked over his shoulder; the detective made eye contact with Lee before he continued, "...don't you want the person responsible for killin' your brother to pay for it?"

"The person that killed him is payin'...don't mess it up," Lee insisted. He got to his feet and once again walked up to the senator's desk. "Senator Willington... please don't let 'em dishonor my brother. Miran would turn over in his grave if that nigga got away with killin' him..."

Jonathan Edwards made his way through McCarran International Airport; the gateway to Sin City. He carried an overnight bag over his right shoulder, while attempting to maneuver through the crowded hub. The journalist nearly got rear-ended by a courtesy cart; the customer services agent honked his horn but the investigative reporter didn't move out of the way as fast as the man driving the motorized cart would have liked. As the agent zoomed by, he gave an apologetic hand gesture.

Jonathan returned the contrite gesture with one of his very own; he realized that the near collision was his fault because he was deep in thought. The journalist had two people that he wanted to speak with, both of whom would not only shed light on Larry's character, but also on his whereabouts the night that Miran was gunned down. It wouldn't be enough evidence to free him. However, it would most definitely satisfy any doubt that the newspaperman may have had about Larry's guilt, or innocence.

A stifling dry heat, akin to the desert, hit Jonathan full-face when the automatic double doors whooshed open. As he stepped into the midday one hundred and three-degree searing high temperature, Jonathan was sure that the exhaust generated by the traffic jam at the airport arrival section had pushed the heat index up several more degrees.

The reporter quickly realized that he wasn't going to be able to immediately escape the dry, suffocating heat by taking refuge in an air-conditioned cab. There was a line awaiting transportation and the boiling high temperatures had seemingly taken their toll on everyone. The irritable commuters pushed and shoved for positioning.

After fifteen minutes of water dripping off of him like a thawing turkey, it was finally his turn to flee what felt like the devil's living room. Jonathan's taxi pulled to the curb. The reporter opened the door, and then tossed his bag into the backseat; he slid in next to his luggage. The journalist felt instant relief as he closed the door, trapping the cool air.

"Where to, mister?" the cabby asked.

The journalist used the sleeve of his shirt to wipe his brow. "Take me to the Vegas Hilton."

When the driver pulled off, he immediately found himself in a battle with traffic. The congestion was bumper to bumper. Jonathan's chauffeur honked his horn in an effort to motivate the motorists ahead of him to move.

"Is traffic always like this?" the reporter asked.

The cabby replied, "Twenty-four seven."

Jonathan glared at his driver, who seemed to suddenly be hit with the spirit of a New York cabby. He honked his horn, hit the gas, turned his wheel sharply to the left, and then to the right, as he maneuvered past several vehicles.

He stopped suddenly as he closed in on a car's bumper; his braking without warning caused the reporter's body to jerk. The driver hit the gas again; his passenger's head jerked back. The chauffeur rolled down and then yelled out his open window just as he passed the car that he had nearly collided with.

"Where the hell did ya'll get ya'll license?" he screamed out the window.

Jonathan insisted, "Look here...I'm in no hurry."

The yellow cab headed northwest up Route 515. The hot desert sun created a mirage that made the asphalt appear to be blanketed with water. Jonathan's body was drained of moisture, and looking at the hallucination played with his mind. He was growing thirstier by the second.

Twenty-five minutes into the ride, the cab pulled in front of the Vegas Hilton. The newsman gave the cab-driver a twenty.

"Keep the change," he said, as he grabbed his bag and got out of the car.

Later THAT EVENING

Jonathan followed closely behind as the chef made his rounds through the chaotic kitchen. The high-energy activities made it very difficult for the reporter to get the supervising cook's attention long enough for him to answer questions.

The kitchen supervisor stepped to one of his line chefs, who was busy prepping his station, and said to his underling, "What are you trying to do? This is not right...the Pesce Spada...swordfish for you idiots that don't know what Pesce Spada is…you have to roll it in breadcrumbs, herbs, salmoriglio and caponata… Do you even know the name of the dish?"

"Yes, chef…Involtini di Pesce Spada!" the nervous line chef responded.

Several waiters nearly knocked Jonathan off of his feet as they pushed by him in their attempt to get the prepared dishes.

"Excuse me, sir…" Jonathan said in an effort to vie for the chef's attention. "I'm Jonathan Edwards…and I'm a reporter." He extended his hand, but the chef ignored him. "I'm doing a story about a young man that worked for you for about three weeks."

"I'm very busy now…this is really not a good time," the chef insisted.

The chef's disappointment in his staff's efforts was evident when he screamed, "GET IT RIGHT, PEOPLE! …MY REPUTATION IS AT STAKE…!"

Jonathan tapped the fuming cuisine specialist on his shoulder. "I only have a few questions… Do you remember Larry Henderson?"

The chef stopped suddenly and quickly directed his full attention toward the reporter. "Yes…I heard that he was having problems… Is he okay?"

"No…he's in prison."

The chef was stunned. "What…?"

"He's serving twenty-five years for murder."

The food professional moved closer to Jonathan.

"You've gotta be kiddin' me…that kid…I don't believe that. How can I help?"

"You can answer my questions. First, did he come to work every day?"

The chef quickly replied, "Early, usually one and a half…to two hours. Apart from two days a week. On those two days, he was taking classes to get his GED. Even on those days, I could count on him to be here at least an hour early. He said that he and his father were having problems…so his mother sent him here to live with his aunt. He had to quit school, but he promised his mother that he would continue his education. That kid had a lot of heart. He would help out around here without being asked. I wish that I had more like him."

"So…he never missed a day, and he was never late?"

The chef was adamant with his reply, "Never!"

"Did he ever leave work early?"

"I had a hard time getting him to go home after his shift. No, he never left early."

"Do you guys keep time cards?" Jonathan asked.

"Sure…follow me…" the chef said as he led Jonathan to his office.

The journalist stood at the side of the file cabinet as the supervising cook searched for the information that the reporter requested. He stopped suddenly, "They're not here." He began his search again. "…I usually keep them for a year…I can't seem to find his…they're gone."

The PROFESSOR

Several very heavily barred picture windows allowed the natural sunlight to fill the area. The cafeteria was huge; thirty-four long steel gray tables were neatly aligned. There were twelve seats surrounding each table, which put the capacity at four hundred and eight convicts in the dining facility at one given time. The schedule was set so that the cafeteria would practically be at capacity most of the time.

Larry was a bit antsy as he stood in line waiting to be served; it didn't help that his altercation with Mop had Larry's mind on edge. The noise generated by the cons that were moving about was intimidating to the young inmate. But the pushing and shoving that took place in line unnerved him more. Young Larry became even more ill at ease after the slop was dumped on his tray and it was time for him to find someplace to sit. Seeing the high-energy activity taking place around him, as his eyes roamed the hundreds of individuals, made him feel like he would get into a dispute; no matter where he attempted to sit. He had eaten his meals in the administration building upon his arrival; which was a more controlled environment. But now mayhem was everywhere he looked.

Larry noticed two inmates leaving a table in the far corner of the mess hall, so he headed in that direction. He was a bit surprised that no one harassed him as he made himself comfortable.

The young inmate was a physical mess. His eyes were swollen; his face was black and blue. He was still in excruciating pain after his morning encounter with his barracks leader. The broken youngster played at his food with a fork that he held in his left hand. He had his right arm protectively pressed against his rib cage.

He casually looked up, at which time he noticed Stinky, who was making his way through the crowded mess hall over to Larry.

Ronald Cells was a highly intelligent individual who had learned quickly how to survive in prison. His height alone put him at a severe disadvantage in an environment where stature and muscle would at least give the appearance that one was capable of protecting themselves. But the puny ones; they had to use their brains in order for them to live to tell the tale. Such was the four-year struggle of Stinky Cells.

As a sixteen-year-old, Ronald possessed remarkable skills; he had been a star point guard for his high school. He played the game of basketball much taller than his five-foot-six frame. Ronald was so skilled that several top-ranked major universities were scouting him. They were all aware that he would more than likely not grow much taller, but they felt that his abilities were something that they couldn't pass on.

After his arrest and subsequent incarceration, Ronald would use his basketball talents to gain favor with prison officials and his fellow inmates.

Stinky placed his tray on the table before making himself comfortable next to his bunkmate.

Three guards patrolled the jam-packed prison cafeteria. One of the corrections officers felt that the inmates were making a little too much noise as they prepared to eat. He yelled, "THOSE THAT DON'T SHUT UP... YOU GON' HAVE TO GET OUT OF HERE... NOW SHUT UP...AND EAT."

Stinky whispered to Larry, "Man...you gon' have to be low-key... Stay away from Mop..." He checked to ensure that the guard wasn't looking before he continued, "Look...I'ma give you the scoop on this place..." Stinky stuffed a piece of bread into his mouth. "First, you already met Mop. He's the worst of the worst in this joint... He ain't even suppose'ta be in the barracks...he should be at the big house. This area is suppose'ta be for dudes like us. But that murderin' son-of-a-bitch got big connections...he runs this shit."

"That's obvious," Larry said.

"Mop ain't never let nobody off like he let you off... That man don't take no shorts... He usually finishes off what he starts." Stinky stuffed more bread into his mouth.

He spewed breadcrumbs as he continued, "Most inmates who've run across his path, they usually end up dead."

Larry replied, "Well... If it makes you feel any better, I feel like I'm dying." He grunted; then continued to play at his food.

Larry's bunkmate was worried that the youngster might need medical attention. For several minutes, he watched Larry continually clutch at his ribs; grimacing in pain.

With concern, he asked, "You gonna be alright?"

Larry slowly moved his head up, then down.

"What'cha in for...?" Stinky asked.

Larry reluctantly replied, "Murder..."

"What...how'd you end up in this area...?" Stinky babbled, "I guess...'cause of yo' age. Anyway...that's gonna get you some points..." He drank some of his milk.

"What'cha mean?" Larry managed.

Stinky again peered around before whispering, "Little *niggas* like us need something that'll keep these stupid fucks off of our ass...mine is basketball. You...bein' in lockdown for murder, that automatically puts you on a different level..."

"On a different level...?" Curiosity made up Larry's statement.

"Yeah...your rep has been established...these fools know that you ain't afraid to take a life."

"Man, I don't wanna kill nobody...I didn't kill the guy that I was accused of."

Stinky immediately placed his finger to his lips. "Shss…" He looked around slyly. Larry's new friend wanted to ensure that no one heard what was being said.

When he was convinced that no one was paying any attention to their conversation, he said forcefully, "Shss!!! Don't ever…and I mean ever, tell these guys that you didn't do it. You see…with the ass kickin' you took from Mop…" Stinky's eyes veered once again. "…and…the fact that you in here for murder…it'll make it a little easier for you if they think that you killed that man. It'll help for a while…at least until someone new comes in lookin' to make a rep for themselves. Or until one of these fools gets a stick up their ass and simply wants to fuck with you. Either way, you gon' have to find some other way to hold them at bay."

"How did you hold them off?" Larry asked.

Stinky made eye contact with his bunkmate. "B ball, my friend?"

Larry's hunched shoulders prompted Stinky to continue. "I got skills on the court…certain people appreciate my game so they won't let nobody fuck with me. A little nigga like me… well, I wouldn't have a chance in hell if I couldn't dribble a basketball."

"What'cha in for?" Larry asked.

Stinky wasn't ready to discuss that; he stuffed food in his mouth and chewed slowly. Larry got the hint and attempted to eat a little himself.

Several minutes into their meal, both of the inmates noticed Mop heading their way. Larry dropped his eyes; his hope was that the man that had beaten the shit out of him would ignore the fact that he was in the cafeteria. But Mop, with tray in hand, spotted Larry and Stinky. He walked over to the two inmates with several of his boys following.

The bald, muscle-bound tyrant tapped Larry on the shoulder. "Hey, young blood!!! You got heart…but don't get it twisted, if there is a next time…yo' ass is mine…" Mop nodded, gave a half-grin, and then made his way over to his table.

Margaret had revealed to Jonathan that her son attended classes two nights a week and that, according to his schedule, he should've been in school the night of Miran's murder.

The chef at the Vegas Hilton confirmed that Larry was in class preparing for general educational development testing the night that Miran Thompson was gunned down. He insisted that there was absolutely no way that Larry could have made the journey back to his hometown, committed the murder, and made it back in time to attend class—let alone be at work almost two hours early; unless he was Superman and could fly.

Did he ever talk about his teacher…do you have a name…

where did he attend class? The questions that Jonathan posed to the chef invaded his thoughts as he maneuvered his way through a crowded university hallway.

He stopped several students and asked for directions to the administration office.

The investigative journalist was in search of a particular professor from the university, one that volunteered his time teaching high school dropouts at Farnsworth High School located on the lower east side of Vegas. The chef didn't know the professor by name. He was only aware, through previous conversations with Larry, that his teacher was a professor at the university.

Jonathan couldn't obtain the name of the professor from Farnsworth because it was closed for the summer. The reporter was unaware that the high schools in Vegas closed for vacation a month earlier than those in Jacob— thus he needed to go straight to the source. He had to figure out a clever way of gathering the information from the administrators at the institution of higher education.

A student pointed. "Keep straight down this hallway. You'll see a sign that says Buckley Hall. The admin office is in Buckley."

"Mister, like I said before…I really can't help you. I'm not allowed to give out any information about our staff," the secretary insisted as she continued stapling papers and answering the phones behind a fiberglass counter that separated her from visitors entering the office. Jonathan rested his arms on top of the neatly kept display case. "Ms., I've traveled a great distance. Is there anyone that I can speak with?"

Before the secretary could respond, a white-haired woman dressed in gray business attire stepped from her office.

The office assistant pointed to Jonathan. "Ms. Shaw, could you help this gentleman?" she asked before she turned her attention toward two students that entered the office.

Ilene Shaw approached the journalist. "What can I do for you, Sir?"

"My name is Jonathan Edwards." He extended his hand toward Ms. Shaw before he continued, "I'm a freelance reporter doing a human interest piece. I'm gathering information from all across the country. My story brings to light the many educational professionals who are willing to volunteer their time to help educated high school dropouts."

The two shook hands before Jonathan went on to say, "I'm told that you have a professor on staff that volunteers his time at Farnsworth High School."

"Yes...Gerald Careri has been teaching night classes for over three years at that high school. He's a professor of art history here at the university."

"Is he here today?"

Ms. Shaw glared at the handsome journalist before she responded, "He's giving a lecture."

The lights in the classroom were dimmed. The light from the hallway drew everyone's attention when Jonathan Edwards eased opened the door and entered. He stood at the top of the lecture hall steps and allowed his eyes to adjust to his surroundings. It took several seconds before he could clearly see that Professor Careri's lecture was at full capacity, standing room only. Jonathan immediately leaned his back against the wall and locked his eyes on a brilliant piece of art.

The art history professor stood at the podium with a pointer in hand. Behind him was a painting of Native American art being projected on a screen by an overhead projector.

"Christopher Rowland was born on the Northern Cheyenne Reservation. He used painting as an escape from the tough life associated with his surroundings. This young man is destined to be one of the more prolific oil painters of our times. He has sold several of his works to some of the more prominent collectors around the country."

The professor used his pointer to direct everyone's attention toward another painting. "This particular eighteen-by-twenty-four oil painting was sold for one hundred dollars…it's worth ten, maybe twenty times more than he sold it for. In four or five years, it'll be worth much more than that. Ironically, his art teacher told him that his paintings would never sell…he insisted that the young artist wasn't any good. As you can see by the rest of these oils, Mr. Rowland possesses everything that defines a great artist." Professor Careri changed to the next slide.

Visiting
DAY

L arry had found himself in a battle with several convicted criminals during his two weeks of incarceration. If it hadn't been for Stinky, he would have found himself in more altercations. Some of his assailants weren't at all concerned with the fact that they themselves had children older than the youngster. Their only objective was intimidation, but Larry wasn't going to be demoralized. His determination, along with his refusal to be bullied, magnified his reputation as a scrapper. He'd already received a nickname. *Bring Yo' Lunch* was his moniker. He was given that name because in his two short weeks behind bars, he had proven that if anyone confronted him, it wasn't going to be easy. Although they might beat him like he stole something, Larry would never give up.

Larry was escorted into the visiting room on a day that was designated for New Fish. Upon entering, he immediately spotted Leroy Burns and Wesley Hobbs. The two sat at a table with the same female visitor. Both winked and blew a cynical kiss in the direction of the young inmate as he passed.

Burns mouthed, "I'ma still show you how much of a freak I am."

Bring Yo Lunch was so caught up in the macabre duo that he hadn't noticed his own visitors. He knew that it was only a matter of time before the two would find their way over to Camp 29, or corner him in the yard.

Larry's mother and sibling got to their feet. They shielded their poignant reaction with their hands upon seeing the bruises that covered Larry's face. The two family members also noticed the concern manifesting from his weary eyes as he stared down a couple of gruesome looking convicts. Margaret began to cry as she hugged her battle-tested son. "Baby, I'm so sorry…I love you so much." She placed both hands to his face and stared intently into his eyes for several seconds. "What have they done to my baby?"

The angry mother locked eyes on Burns and Hobbs. "Did them boys sittin' in that corner do this to you?" she asked with a vengeful fervor.

"I'm okay, Momma," Larry whispered.

She wanted to protect her son but, once again, blamed herself because she was unable to do so. Margaret softly kissed him around his bruises, and then pulled him back into a protective embrace.

Valeria wrapped her arms around both of them, and whispered, "It wasn't our fault, Larry. Daddy didn't tell us what was goin' on…they said that you had to be in here fo' two weeks before they would let us see you."

Margaret continued to cry. She took her son by the hands and stared at him once again. "Baby…you okay… who did this to you?"

When he took his seat, Larry's eyes were locked directly on the white man who was seated at his table. However, his conversation was directed toward his family. "I been fightin' ever since I got here. Two guys jumped me yesterday. But I'm okay…I need to get out of here. What are you guys doin' to get me out? Ya'll know I didn't kill nobody…did Daddy check with my job?" His babbling was calm; not one word was laced with fear.

Margaret wasn't at all happy. She could see the change. In two short weeks, her son was not the same. He was hard, yet troubled. Her son was distant and he seemed heartless.

"We gotta do what we can…we can't depend on yo' father," said Margaret. Larry's mother pointed to her guest before she continued, "This gentleman is gonna try to help us. Baby, this is Mr. Jonathan Edwards…he's a reporter from the *Daily News*." She took Jonathan by the hand. "Mr. Edwards, this is my baby."

Larry looked confused. "What the hell is a reporter gonna do? I need a lawyer!"

"I'm going to find the evidence. I've heard a great deal of wonderful things about you. I truly believe that you are an innocent man, and I'm gonna do whatever it takes to prove it." Jonathan extended his hand toward Larry.

Larry was reluctant; he didn't trust anyone. He couldn't even trust his own family, so he wasn't about to take a stranger's word. Jonathan Edwards was going to have to show him something.

The newspaperman understood why Larry was reluctant to shake his hand, but Margaret didn't. "Baby, don't be so rude… he's here to help. You can shake his hand."

Larry ignored his mother. "Well, you can start with my job."

Jonathan lowered his hand, saying, "I've already spoken to your boss, and to Professor Careri. They both think very highly of you. I tried to get your timecards, but they seemed to have been misplaced. They're willing to testify but our problem is that you've already confessed." Jonathan whispered, "Larry, I'm not gonna kid you. This is not going to be easy." The reporter crossed his legs. "Tell me something, why did you confess?"

Larry leaned forward. "My father told me that my alibi wouldn't hold up. He told me that in order to avoid the death penalty, I had to confess."

"Your mother and sister told me why you were sent to live with your aunt…I want you to tell me your version."

Larry was confused; he didn't understand the relevance. Jonathan immediately noticed the teen's bewildered expression. The award-winning journalist's appeal was calm. "Larry, I realize that this doesn't seem important to you. However, to me, it may be the difference in my understanding of the entire picture. Just trust me; tell me why your mother felt it was best for you to live with your aunt?"

"Me and my father began to have problems when I turned thirteen. I got tired of him hittin' on my mother… but I think he really had it out for me when I caught him with my teacher." Larry leaned closer to the reporter; he didn't want anyone to hear his story. "My father had purchased a gas station several years back. It was his way of setting up his retirement plan. Anyway, the day before I went to Vegas, he told me he was gonna go fishin'…so I was left in charge. I was kinda mad because my friends and I wanted to ride our bikes from the Bottoms to Jacob. We liked doing that because it was a pretty good journey, and we had fun every single time we did it. When my friends found out that I had to work, they came by the station. I was surprised because they never came by before; they didn't wanna run into my dad."

Days before MOVING TO VEGAS

The main artery into what was known as Chocolate City intersected with a dirt thoroughfare. The two infrastructures interconnected at Route 39 and the bridge that extended over Morris Creek, which led into Junction Three. At the fork in the road, one could see red paint on an isolated old brick structure, situated off the unpaved road. It was a prime location.

A couple of gas pumps were positioned twenty-five yards from the building. An old sedan sat in front of one of the pumps. The sign on the worn structure read, *HENDERSONS.*

Several vehicles, in need of repair, were in an open garage attached to the brick building. A police cruiser was parked to the side of the gas station's garage.

Larry wiped his hands with a rag as he watched the sedan he had just serviced speed off down the unpaved road. The road was the rear entrance to the Bottoms.

He stuffed the rag into the back pocket of his overalls before he headed for the station's entrance.

Lieutenant Henderson, dressed in shorts and a T-shirt, carried a fishing rod and tackle box as he made his way from the back office. "Hey, boy!!! I'm gonna go catch a couple fish. You close up the shop for me. Mr. Thomas' wagon is ready to go. If he calls, tell him that he can come get it."

Larry smiled. "Okay... Can I pull it out of the garage?"

"You know that you ain't suppose'ta be drivin'...you ain't got no license," Perry said with a smile as he walked out of the station. His son followed.

As a teen, the proud father was taught how to repair engines by his own father. He walked to the side of the garage and over to his patrol car, then opened the door placing his rod and tackle in. Perry's eyes veered over to his son, standing between the pumps.

"Just out of the garage, no further...as a matter of fact, put it here, in my spot. Make sure you wash it before you move it," he said. Larry's father slid into the car next to his fishing gear.

"Okay," Larry eagerly replied. The thought of getting behind the wheel had him energized. "What time do you want me to lock up?"

Perry closed his door before he answered, "After Mr. Thomas picks up his car." He started the engine. "If you want, you can come to the creek and do some fishin' with me after you close."

Perry was sure that his son would refuse his offer. He knew that Larry didn't enjoy hanging around him anymore. He wasn't at all surprised when he heard his son's reply.

"I'm gonna go bike ridin' with John, Alex and Rico after I leave here."

Perry pulled his car up to the pumps; he then leaned his head out of the window, before saying, "I don't like you hangin' 'round them...those boys ain't nothin' but trouble."

"They're cool...they ain't as bad as you try to make 'em out to be..."

"You stay out of trouble...you hear!" the father ordered before he pulled off.

It took Larry forty-five minutes to wash the station wagon.

While marveling at his labor, he whispered to himself, "Not bad..." He wiped at a minuscule piece of lint, left behind from his towel.

Larry shook the towel as he continued to circle the

vehicle. He tossed the cloth atop the hood, and walked to the driver's side door. Before he could get into the vehicle, he noticed his friends riding up on their bikes.

When Rico, John, and Alex saw their friend get into the car and start the engine, their faces lit up with enthusiasm. The trio literally jumped off their bicycles while in motion. They all ran toward the garage. Rico, being the fastest, jumped into the front seat. There was no way that either John or Alex had a chance to outrun their slender friend. Rico was one of the fastest kids in high school.

Alex was out of breath by the time he made it to the car. He rarely attempted to exert that much energy; especially with the running thing. His pudgy body wasn't up to the strain. The slightly overweight youth puffed several times before he opened the door and got in. Pimply-faced John had already made himself comfortable in the back seat.

"What the hell are you chumps doin'?" Larry questioned with a smile.

John replied quickly, "Goin' with you."

"I'm gonna pull the car out and park it next to the garage," Larry said as he put the car in gear.

Alex was still puffing. In between gasps, he managed to say, "Oh! Okay, go ahead…drive."

Larry eased off the brake, and the car slowly moved forward.

"Ya'll some real brave muthas today. How'd you know my old man wasn't here?"

John quickly blasted, "'Cause we saw yo' playboy pops with Ms. Jackson a little while ago."

Larry wasn't really fazed by anything that came out of John's mouth. The boy was considered the jokester of the group. At any given time, the kid, who was described as being the most handsome of the group, could blurt out anything. He was definitely the class clown.

"Are you talkin' about Ms. Jackson…Ms. Jackson?" Larry asked with a smile.

John responded quickly, "Yeah…fine-ass Ms. Jackson!"

"You lyin'…my pops went fishin'!"

He continued to back the car up in an attempt to park it according to his father's instructions.

"He's fishin' all right…but not the kind of fishin' you talkin' 'bout." John joked.

Larry was annoyed. "You don't know what you talkin' 'bout!!!"

"It's true, Larry…we saw ya pops slobbin' Ms. Jackson… they were down by the creek…they looked like they were 'bout ready to do the dirty nasty…" Alex whispered.

Larry stopped the car. He stared at Alex and John through the rearview mirror. The two boys nodded slowly in agreement. Young Henderson then directed his attention toward his front passenger. Rico's nod acknowledged that they in fact had witnessed Larry's father engaged in some sort of sexual encounter with their teacher.

Rico broke the awkward silence when he said, "Drive by the creek…you'll see…"

Larry got out of the car. He locked up the gas station, and then jumped back into the vehicle and peeled off.

Ten minutes later, they pulled over into a wooded area. They were some thirty yards off the dirt back road. The four boys got out of the vehicle and began to make their way down to a path that would lead them toward Morris Creek.

Larry peeked from around a big oak tree. His father was lying on a blanket with a very attractive female. He immediately recognized the woman as his history teacher, Ms. Silva Jackson. The two lay on a blanket entangled in each other's arms, their lips locked.

Larry's mind went blank.

He didn't know what to think about his father. Although this wasn't the first time that he had caught his dad cheating on his mother, the boy was still taken aback. Larry had played witness to his father's adulterous behavior on several occasions. He'd even seen his father with his teacher before, but Perry had convinced his son that he and Ms. Jackson were only friends, and that Silva Jackson was the sister of his high school best friend. Larry really wanted to believe his father's lies. He wanted to believe that his father would not stoop so low as to have an affair with a woman that his mother looked at as being a friend.

Both Ms. Jackson and Perry had their tops off as they passionately rolled around on the blanket. An intense anger engulfed Larry as he continued to stare.

When John saw a single tear make its way down his friend's cheek, he attempted to persuade him to leave.

"Come on, man, haven't you seen enough?" John whispered. He turned his attention toward the two others and said, "I knew we shouldnt've told him. Look at him, ya'll."

Alex grabbed Larry by the arm as he stood zombie-like. He whispered, "Come on, man."

Larry didn't budge. He continued to stare intently. Alex tugged harder at his friend's arm. "Come on, Larry, fo' real… let's get out of here," he insisted.

They began to lead a disinclined Larry toward the car.

Perry and his female companion stopped and tried to identify unusual noises that they heard coming from the woods.

Silva sat up and quickly used her arms to cover her exposed breasts. "Did you hear that?"

While both were curiously scanning their surroundings, Silva saw her chubby student as he clumsily trudged through the thick brush. She pointed, "There…over there." The embarrassed history teacher immediately put on her T-shirt and got to her feet.

Larry and friends sped down the back road in Mr. Thomas' station wagon. The faster Larry accelerated the more his mind was cluttered. He wanted to kill his father—he wanted to ensure that that man didn't harm his mother again.

PRESENT

Larry turned his attention toward his mother. "That was the day when I crashed Mr. Thomas' car… remember…ya'll thought that Daddy was mad at me for wreckin' it." Larry turned his attention toward the reporter. "My father went into our backyard…he cut a fan belt from a perfectly good car…he then used it to beat the shit out of me. I'm sure that he was mad at me for taking the car…but his real anger came from the fact that I saw him gettin' ready to fuck my teacher in the woods!"

"Larry…baby, your mouth…you sound like you were raised in a sewer," Margaret said with disappointment.

Larry ignored his mother.

"He knew that I would tell my mother. Beating me with a fan belt was his way of sendin' me a message. That's why my mother put me on that bus to Vegas. My momma knew that if I stayed…something was gonna give. It was either gonna be him…or me."

Leroy Burns and Wesley Hobbs winked at Larry as they were being escorted from the visiting room. The two inmates' attempt at intimidation was overshadowed by the anger Larry felt toward his father. The *new fish* completely dismissed the convicts' gestures. He directed his attention toward Jonathan just in time to see his new ally push a newspaper in front of him. The journalist pointed toward an article. Larry picked up the paper and began reading:

It was a chilly evening when Miran Thompson entered Harry's Liquor Store. He was apparently preparing for a party since he bought several cases of beer and over two hundred dollars' worth of liquor. His purchase was to be delivered to his Samona Hills home. When Miran exited the store located on Chamber Drive—he had no idea that it would be his last visit to the store.

As tragic as the death of Miran Thompson was to some people within the community, the real catastrophe came with the arrest of the seventeen-year-old who was accused of his murder.

Larry Henderson, the son of Jacob Police Lieutenant Perry Henderson, was arrested and subsequently confessed to robbing and murdering someone who was on record as being his father's mortal enemy. Despite his confession, there are a number of reasons that make this reporter feel that the youngster's declaration of guilt may have been coerced, so I am dedicated to uncovering the truth, which I am sure will lead to his exoneration.

Larry looked up from the article and delivered a half-smile of appreciation toward the journalist before he continued to read.

The sun shined brightly on a crowded Lorene Park. Several park-goers lounged on the grass, soaking up the rays. Others played with dogs, and children played on swings and in sandboxes. The elderly sat on benches reading papers, magazines, and books.

Perry and Silva strolled through the park, both licking on ice cream cones as they watched others enjoy the beautiful day. Several screaming children playing tag attempted to use the schoolteacher and police officer as shields in an effort to separate themselves. The two adults allowed themselves to be exploited by the giggling children, who circled them while screaming, "You didn't get me!"

"Yes, I did…you're it!"

Silva ignored the stampede of little people; she licked the chocolate cream atop her cone before saying, "I had to leave… I packed my things and left right after Pooky's memorial service."

Perry smiled at the sight of ice cream on the teacher's lips. He used his finger to whip the chocolate away. "When he died the only thing that I wanted was to kill Miran's ass."

"You still believe that Miran and Jake killed my brother?"

The two stopped; they turned their attention to a group of children playing on a set of swings. "They were the ones that tried to jump us in town that night. I think they followed us and waited for Pooky and me to split up. Then they snatched him. Both of them wanted to be in the Klan. I think that Pooky was their initiation." The two went silent for several seconds before

Perry said, "I didn't see your brother again until I went out lookin' for him. I followed his shortcut from church to your house. He always used to cut through the woods. That's when I found him hangin' from that tree."

She really wanted to change the subject, so Silva quickly interrupted. "How's your son? Did he really kill Miran?"

"I can't prove it right now…but, no." He licked at the vanilla cream that slowly made its way down the side of his cone.

Silva peered into her escort's eyes. "Perry, I was told that you were the one that pointed the finger at your son. Did you do it because he told your wife about us?"

The two made themselves comfortable on a park bench before she continued, "Perry, you hit her in front of me. I've been scared of you ever since. Then I hear that you threatened to get Larry. I'm not sure who you are anymore. At one time, you would have given your life for your children."

Jonathan and Margaret watched as Val traveled up the walkway that led to her trailer. The reporter waited for Margaret's daughter to enter her residence before he pulled off.

"You told me that Terrell was thought to have been involved with Senator Willington's daughter."

"That was the rumor, Jonathan. I wanted to wait until

my daughter left before I told you this," Margaret whispered.

The reporter turned his attention toward his passenger. "Tell me what?"

Margaret directed her attention toward Jonathan. "My husband…" She quickly dropped eye contact.

"What's going on, Margaret?" He could tell that she was embarrassed about something because she wouldn't look at him. "What's the problem?"

When she did look up, her eyes were watery. "You can't let anyone know what I'm going to tell you!"

"What?"

"You asked me if I thought that my husband was capable of framing his son. You also wanted to know if he still felt that Miran was behind murdering Terrell. Well, I can tell you this… although Perry and Larry had their problems, my husband loves our son. As far as Miran is concerned…I know of several occasions were Perry stalked Miran. He did it for months after my nephew was murdered. Jonathan, I really believe that Perry, if given the opportunity, would have put a bullet in Miran's head. But I don't think that he would have done so and then blamed it on our child. I can't believe that he would do anything like that."

The prison yard was overrun with cons. Like any penitentiary, the enclosure was divided into cliques. When

Larry entered the grounds for his yard time, the bruised teen laid eyes on over a hundred inmates. Some played basketball, and others shot craps. There was a dice game that was causing a ruckus; several that participated began pushing and shoving.

Larry walked past a few cons that were exercising, lifting weights, doing pushups, or hitting a heavy bag. He happened to overhear a group of inmates that belonged to a prison gang jawning at one another. As he continued his stroll, he became privy to four prisoners discussing the transportation of drugs.

One of the gang members spotted the teenaged inmate. He pointed toward Larry and said, "Hey, ya'll, ain't that the kid that they said fought with Mop…?" The inquiring gang member placed a cigarette behind his ear as he continued to stare at the young con.

"I'ma get that boy for our set…I hear he got heart…" The inmate began to make his way over to him. "Hey, PIMPIN…!" he shouted.

Another inmate interceded before the con could get within earshot of Larry, "Hey, Jas…you hollerin' at *Bring Yo Lunch?*"

Jas turned his attention toward the inmate that approached him. "That's the dude?"

"Yeah…that cat got heart…so if you 'bout ready to step to him…"

Jas interrupted, "Nah…nothin' like that. We heard he got down with Mop… You tellin' me that he was the same dude that took on those two cats yesterday?"

"Yeah...that's him. He got the shit beat outta him... but he kept on pluggin' away."

Jas nodded his approval. "We wanna put him down with our set." The dark, well-built lifer continued his approached toward Larry. The con used a hand gesture when he got within shouting distance. "HEY, YOU!!!"

Larry ignored the thug's approach, he made his way over to a set of bleachers positioned at the side on the basketball court.

"You tryin' to ignore me?" Jas asked.

Larry made himself comfortable on the top of the bleachers. Jas followed.

"Hey, man...I ain't tryin' to give you no beef," the lifer said. "Look here, my peoples...they like yo' heart. If you wanna stop some of the shit you been goin' through, you need to be down with my set," Jas said. He turned his attention away from Larry and toward the activity that was going on around them.

Larry slowly shook his head from side to side.

He wasn't looking for gang affiliation. He didn't want the stress of having to deal with another boss. He already had to abide by the rules set forth under the penal colony's mandate. He also had to take orders from his barracks leader. Larry was not about to take instructions from a gang leader. He'd rather take his chances staying on neutral ground.

He understood that being associated with a gang could alleviate some of the pressure of having to fight every single day. However, he was also aware that the other gangs would make his life just as miserable.

Larry ducked his head and stared at his shoelaces. "I'd rather not...I just wanna do my time. I don't wanna get on nobody's bad side."

"Young blood...if you down wit' us...you be on easy street." Jas pointed toward each group. "Each one of them out there...they gonna want somethin' from yo' ass at one time or another. If you ain't got nobody behind you, yo' ass is gon be the one that's gon' have to *Bring Yo Lunch*. You gon' have to watch yo' back fo' the rest of the time you behind these bars. Wit' us, you'll have an entire crew watchin' out for you."

A Secret
REVEALED

C andles that were strategically placed around the living room generated the only light and clearly created the desired ambience. The fragrance of expensive cologne filtered through, its aromatic mist was slightly stronger than that of the scented candles. A bottle of Cabernet Sauvignon and two wine glasses sat atop the cocktail table.

Romance was certainly in the air in the Henderson household.

Perry entered the room dressed in a blue, full-length silk robe. He gazed at the décor. It suddenly dawned on him that the atmosphere was missing one very important ingredient. The dead silence wasn't exactly a mood setter, so Perry walked over to and then began to search through a stack of albums that sat next to a phonograph. The husband and father, whom everyone believed had lost his way, removed an album from the pile. He stared at it for several seconds. The romantic police officer sang softly as he removed the record from its jacket. *"I hear the bells...oh...oh...ringin'...in my ears..."*

The frivolous Billy Dee wannabe placed the phonograph's needle to the album, which was produced by Motown and performed by The Originals.

"Yeah…that's it…" He snapped his fingers in beat with the harmony.

The bluish-yellow illumination, which flickered off the tip of the candles, seemed to sputter in rhythm to the smooth tenor voice of Freddy Gorman.

Margaret was unaware of her husband's plans for romance until she sashayed into the living room to the beat of the music. Her head swayed from side to side. Dressed in a white, full-length terrycloth robe, she seemed absolutely stunned at her husband's efforts.

Margaret's heart fluttered.

What was before her was something that she was accustomed to; one of the things that drew her to him was his romanticism. The man she loved always had a very passionate side to him.

Perry immediately grabbed his wife and spun her around several times before he pulled her closer to him. They began to dance cheek to cheek.

Margaret went red in the face. "What's gotten into you? I'm not sayin' that I don't like it…but I certainly wasn't expectin' it…"

"I just feel good. I'm happy because they let you visit with Larry today. Plus, I followed up on some leads earlier; they look pretty good. I don't wanna say anything about them, until I make verification. But I know for sure that somebody got into the house and got my backup weapon. Whoever did it…I think was tryin' to set me up for Miran's murder. Why else would they bring it back?" He smiled, then spun his wife once again before he pulled her back into his embrace.

The blushing bride locked eyes with her husband. "But…they said that someone described Larry."

"I think that they were tryin' to describe me," he said nonchalantly. Perry held his wife tight in his arms.

Margaret placed the palm of her hands to Perry's chest; she pushed him forcibly away from her. "So you had Larry confess to save yourself?"

Perry attempted to explain. "If I had gotten locked up, who would find the evidence needed to get me out? Look, I need to find out who's tryin' to frame me."

Margaret blasted, "I can't believe that you used your own son!" She hit him in the chest several times. "You good for nothin' bastard."

Perry stood frozen. "Marg!" Before her husband of twenty-nine years could completely call out her name, she stormed from the room.

Perry stood with his mouth suspended open for several seconds. He dejectedly flung his arms in the air. "Damn!"

The frustrated husband quickly turned and walked over to, then grabbed a bottle of his favorite liquor, Ole Grand Dad, from his miniature bar. He quickly made his way over to the sofa and lifelessly deposited his body onto the soft cushions. Perry opened the bottle and placed it to his lips. The depressed husband guzzled a third of its content.

With his bottle firmly gripped in hand, Perry leaned back and stared at the ceiling, allowing his mind to drift.

Summer of '67

Lloyd Steward had held his position as the chief of police for over twenty years. He was a down-home boy who outwardly objected to the city council and the mayor's insistence that Perry Henderson be allowed to join the force.

Perry began his quest to protect and serve at the age of twenty; except, he wasn't given an opportunity until he reached the tender age of thirty-two.

For twelve years, the arrogant bigot who headed the police department intentionally misplaced, and or made changes to Perry's official application to join the force; thus, impeding the process. If it were left up to Steward, Perry would still be trying.

Once the known racist accepted that he couldn't prevent Perry's instatement, he turned his attention into making the Negro's life as a police officer as miserable as he possibly could. Perry's first patrol was in an area overrun with an insurgent of rednecks; a place Steward felt would eat away at the Black officer's resolve. If that wasn't bad enough, the police chief ordered the racist citizens of that area to harass Perry every chance they got.

Perry headed up the walkway of a tenement for which he responded to a domestic violence call. Before he could make it to the porch, several rednecks rushed from the house armed with baseball bats. This wasn't the first time that he had been ambushed—he knew that as long as Steward headed the department it wasn't going to be his last.

"What's this all about, fellas…?" the stunned officer asked. He put his hand on his gun and slowly backed away.

The men surrounded him. "What'cha think, Nigga…!"

"I don't want no problems with ya'll…I came here to do my job…" Perry stopped after he realized several others had approached from the rear. In an attempt to identify as many as he could, he turned slowly in an effort to lock every face into his memory. "Look…you don't wanna do this. I'll have the entire force come down on you…you know you won't get away with this…" the officer said as several more racists gathered around him. They didn't seem intimidated by his threats at all.

Perry pulled his gun; without hesitation he pointed and fired. His victim was half-bald, short and chubby. His panic-stricken green eyes widened as he hit the ground after being struck in the shoulder.

"Ahh! He shot me…the nigga shot me…!" the bigot screamed as he squirmed.

The others were sickened as blood flowed freely. Upon seeing that the band of extremists had lost their nerve, one of the men anxiously shouted, "He can't get all of us…"

Perry immediately turned his gun on him and fired a round into his leg.

"Ahh…shit…!" the man anguished.

"Nobody said that that nigga was crazy," one of the men shouted, as he dropped his bat and ran.

All of the other men followed; they hightailed into the night and out of sight.

The chief of police was not too pleased to have federal investigators digging into the precarious way in which he upheld law and order. Steward's anger was directed at one of his very own employees. The down-home country redneck had issues with his patrolman for teaming up with outsiders and attempting to shine the light on his lack of concern toward the Negro citizens of Jacob.

The desk sergeant led two FBI agents into the chief's office. "Chief, those two Feds is back. They asked to see you again," said the desk sergeant as he stepped aside and allowed the agents to enter.

"Well…well…well…come in, gentlemen." His Southern drawl was as thick as the manure he was prepared to shovel. "I still think ya'll wasted yo' time comin' to these parts…" The chief stood and extended his hand. "But I'll be mo' than happy to help you folk any way I can."

The lead agent extended his hand to the chief of police. "It's not a waste of time; it's our job."

"Well…what can I do for you gentlemen of the federal gov'ment…?"

The gentlemen took a seat. The desk sergeant leaned against the door.

"Billy…close the door on yo' way out…" the chief insisted before he made himself comfortable.

The burly desk sergeant stared into the eyes of his boss. Steward's bloodshot baby blues seemed to scream at the sloppy officer that stood at the entrance to his office. The overweight policeman got the hint; he reluctantly closed the door as he left.

"You know why we're here…and I told you that we're not leaving until we find out why you refused to look into the death of Perry Henderson's nephew," the agent stated.

The chief filled his oral cavity with chew before he mouthed, "We don't have the time or the personnel to search fo' every nigga that come up missin'… The son-of-a-bitch is mo' than likely hidin' out in the Bottoms… He the type of boy that like puttin' his hands on white women… The boys in these parts don't tolerate that sorta thang. Looky here, boys, we don't have no indication that that boy was murdered."

"Has anybody seen or heard from him?" the agent asked.

The chief spat some of his grimy chew into an oilcan before he responded, "Na…just how would you expect I would know that…" He spat again.

"If you did yo' damn, job you would probably have an idea," the agent mocked.

The chief stared at the federal employee. "You tryin'a be funny, boy?"

"We were told that you were asked to authorize the department to drag Morris Creek in search of Terrell Johnson's body. Your officer said that he had gotten a tip that the teen's mutilated corpse was dumped in the waterway after he was murdered."

Once again, the burly chief spat a stream of slimy tobacco into his filthy oilcan. "I didn't authorize that cause that arrogant Nigga that works for me wouldn't tell me who his source was. How would I know if it was a 'credible tip?"

"Let me tell you something…you racist fuck…I've ordered that the state police drag that river." The agent's anger was evident as he got to his feet. He placed both hands on the chief's desk, then leaned forward and said with conviction, "If that boy's body is found…I'm personally comin' after yo' ass…"

Steward spat again. This time, the black saliva missed his oilcan and splattered on his desk, inches away from the agent's hand. He looked up at the agent, his response unflappable. "Is that a threat, boy…?"

The perturbed agent turned—he gave a hand gesture to his partner at which time both men exited Steward's office. As they made their way down the narrow hall leading from the chief's office and into the squad room, they immediately noticed Officer Henderson enter the station with two white men; they were cuffed to one another—one bled from the shoulder, and the other from the leg.

The man with the injured leg begged as he limped. "Somebody help us…this nigga won't take us to the hospital…he shot us fo' no damn reason."

Several individuals seated in chairs aligning the wall in front of the large L-shaped wooden counter were horrified at the sight of Perry's bloody suspects.

Cuffed to one of the chairs was a middle-aged Black man dressed in worn overalls. The nappy-headed detainee giggled after playing witness to the redneck's misery. His outward display of satisfaction drew the attention of the group that was seated next to him.

"You see somthin' funny, boy!" an elderly white man asked as he stepped in front of the dark-skinned individual who was being detained on a drunk and disorderly charge.

Having yet to fully recover from his alcohol-induced belligerence, the Black man's slurred speech was directed to the racist standing before him. "You might wanna get yo' fat ass out of my face."

Without warning, the angry grandfather struck his drunken foe in the face with an open hand. "Don't no nigga talk to me like that!"

The desk sergeant immediately made his way from behind the wooden counter—but couldn't decide whether to attend to the ruckus taking place between the drunk and the racist, or checking out the severity of the injuries to the men that Perry Henderson had escorted into the building. He froze in his tracks for several seconds.

When he heard someone yell, "What the *hell* have you done, Henderson...?" his mind was made up for him. The sergeant motioned for another officer to break up the altercation that was getting a little out of hand, while he made his way over to Henderson.

"They're not hurt bad...those are flesh wounds..." Perry uttered. The Black officer immediately went into his explanation. "I got a call to respond to a domestic violence complaint. When I got there...these clowns and a few of their friends were waitin' to ambush me."

When Perry looked up, he noticed two men dressed in dark suits. The men were definitely out of place; the cop immediately pegged them as federal agents. Out of curiosity, he left his prisoners, leaving the desk sergeant and several other officers to attend to them as he approached the government employees.

"You two from the FBI?" Perry questioned.

Both agents nodded, affirming that they in fact represented the Federal Bureau of Investigation. The lead officer stepped forward with his hand extended. "I'm Agent Jarrod...and this is my partner, Agent Scott."

The men exchanged handshakes.

The desk sergeant, while attending to Perry's suspects, split his attention between the two wounded men before him, the officer who stepped between the ruckus created by the drunken Black man, the Black officer, and his federal visitors. He watched as Officer Henderson motioned for, and then led the agents out the door into a beautiful, star-filled evening.

The nosy sergeant slyly slid away from the crowd that had congregated around Perry's two suspects and over to the door. He peered through the window. The two streetlights in front of headquarters provided him ample lighting to see the three men as they stood on the steps leading to the building. Unable to hear, the nerdy, half-bald police officer eased the door open in hopes that he would be privy to their conversation.

"That chief of yours is a piece of work... We profiled him as a racist when we first met with him this afternoon. I think there's a strong possibility that he might be involved," Jarrod said as he leaned against the railing. "Anyway...we're having the creek dragged at dawn. Now...about your informant; we need to speak to this Jasper Collins..." Agent Jarrod was totally unaware that Perry was in a trance of some sort. At least not until his eyes veered in the direction of the officer.

The government official said, "Officer Henderson..." Still unable to get the officer's attention, the agent dialed his tone up an octave higher. "Henderson!"

Perry continued to stare at the bright stars that filled the night sky. To the FBI agents, Perry seemed lost in the clearly defined constellation.

It wasn't until the two men nudged the dazed public servant that they were finally able to break his concentration. The patrol officer's thoughts were on his inability to protect his own family, and friends. Perry never could shake the feeling he had after finding his best friend's body dangling from a tree. Even though it had been seventeen years, it was like yesterday to Perry. It was a little too surreal that two of the people in his life, for which a special bond was created, died an unthinkable death.

He wouldn't let that happen again. He wouldn't let anyone get that close to him. For their own sake, he had to find a way to detach himself from all that he loved. As ludicrous as it sounded to him, Perry felt that he was cursed.

"Officer Henderson...did you hear what I said?" the lead agent asked for the third time.

The chilly lingering dampness was a direct result of hurricane-type winds and rain that hit the city of Jacob a few days prior. Although the sun began to peek over the horizon, it did nothing to curtail the early morning breeze that washed over the waterway. The steady gust kept the temperature well below what would normally be expected for that time of year.

A dozen or so state employees (bold yellow lettering

him, the officer who stepped between the ruckus created by the drunken Black man, the Black officer, and his federal visitors. He watched as Officer Henderson motioned for, and then led the agents out the door into a beautiful, star-filled evening.

The nosy sergeant slyly slid away from the crowd that had congregated around Perry's two suspects and over to the door. He peered through the window. The two streetlights in front of headquarters provided him ample lighting to see the three men as they stood on the steps leading to the building. Unable to hear, the nerdy, half-bald police officer eased the door open in hopes that he would be privy to their conversation.

"That chief of yours is a piece of work… We profiled him as a racist when we first met with him this afternoon. I think there's a strong possibility that he might be involved," Jarrod said as he leaned against the railing. "Anyway…we're having the creek dragged at dawn. Now…about your informant; we need to speak to this Jasper Collins…" Agent Jarrod was totally unaware that Perry was in a trance of some sort. At least not until his eyes veered in the direction of the officer.

The government official said, "Officer Henderson…" Still unable to get the officer's attention, the agent dialed his tone up an octave higher. "Henderson!"

Perry continued to stare at the bright stars that filled the night sky. To the FBI agents, Perry seemed lost in the clearly defined constellation.

It wasn't until the two men nudged the dazed public servant that they were finally able to break his concentration. The patrol officer's thoughts were on his inability to protect his own family, and friends. Perry never could shake the feeling he had after finding his best friend's body dangling from a tree. Even though it had been seventeen years, it was like yesterday to Perry. It was a little too surreal that two of the people in his life, for which a special bond was created, died an unthinkable death.

He wouldn't let that happen again. He wouldn't let anyone get that close to him. For their own sake, he had to find a way to detach himself from all that he loved. As ludicrous as it sounded to him, Perry felt that he was cursed.

"Officer Henderson…did you hear what I said?" the lead agent asked for the third time.

The chilly lingering dampness was a direct result of hurricane-type winds and rain that hit the city of Jacob a few days prior. Although the sun began to peek over the horizon, it did nothing to curtail the early morning breeze that washed over the waterway. The steady gust kept the temperature well below what would normally be expected for that time of year.

A dozen or so state employees (bold yellow lettering

the active crime scene. Pulling his vehicle off on the side of the dirt road, Perry was taken aback when he noticed dozens of reporters behind crime scene tape being kept at bay by Jacob police.

No one noticed him heading through the wooded area and toward the crowd, gathered at the clearing. As Perry got closer, he could hear the journalists attempting to pose questions to the sheriff and state law enforcement officials that roamed the sixty or so yards of clearance that led to the edge of Morris Creek.

Several hours after their arrival, the men that stood on the bank of the creek, watched as the four officers assigned to the small boats snagged their dragging poles onto something.

"We got something!" one of the policemen yelled. He and his partner stood as they tugged and yanked on their poles. Their boat rocked from side to side. Whatever they had caught on the end of their hooks was not budging.

The second group of officers maneuvered their boat over to help out.

They stood, causing their boat to teeter. The slightly rocking vessel didn't sway them; the two officers placed their poles into the water in an effort to assist their co-workers.

They immediately hooked onto something.

Finally able to dislodge the heavy object from the bottom of the creek, the men slowly pulled what looked to be a potato sack to the surface.

Two uniformed state troopers removed their shoes and then rolled up their pants legs before they stepped into the stream and waited for the four troopers to bring the waterlogged, weighted sack close enough to allow them to render assistance in dragging it ashore.

Perry reluctantly approached the creek; the two federal agents followed. All three watched intently as the state troopers pulled the huge, algae covered sack up the bank and onto dry ground. Everyone that was involved with the search began to gather around in anticipation of the revealing of the bag's contents, but the state troopers patiently waited for the approaching agents and their escort.

As Perry, Agent Jarrod and his partner, Federal Agent Scott, assembled, one of the troopers removed a pocket-knife from his trousers. He then cut the rope that bound the sack. The officers slowly opened the dripping, muddy, extremely heavy bag. Upon doing so, the stench was overwhelming. Both officers quickly turned their heads away from the waterlogged corpse.

Perry took two steps toward the bag and apprehensively peered in.

A single tear escaped the officer's emotion-filled eyes. His sister's son, a boy that he'd loved as his own—a young man with so much hope and promise had had his life senselessly cut short. Terrell Johnson's mutilated frame was too much for the loving uncle to bear. He turned away and, with little hesitation, the grief-stricken officer regurgitated.

Agent Jarrod patted the slumped over, extremely disoriented officer on his back. "Henderson, you okay?"

Bent at the waist with his hands on his knees, the officer managed to speak in between his moments of sickness. "Yeah," Perry spat.

The agent leaned over and whispered into Perry's ear. "We need to go see Jasper Collins."

Out of all the stores that aligned the two blocks that made up the business district in the Bottoms, Jasper was the only one expected to have already started his day. It was still early, yet it was an hour past the storeowner's usual time. Perry was concerned. He couldn't remember the last time that Jasper's doors weren't open at sunrise.

The police officer of two years tapped on the screen.

Agents Scott and Jarrod attempted to shield their eyes from the early morning orange-yellow rays as they peered through the wide windows, which overlooked the street and several trees of motionless green. The sunlight lit up the thirty-eight-hundred-square-foot store, and brilliantly reflected off of the seven rolls of well-stocked shelves that were in the center of JC's grocery store.

"He should've been open an hour ago," Perry said as he opened the screen door and tried the knob. The tinkling chimes that hung over the door were meant to alert the proprietor that someone had entered, but no one responded.

All three stood at the entrance for several seconds before Perry used hand gestures to tell the agents where to go. Each pulled their weapons and slowly separated. They moved with military precision, allowing their pistols to lead the way as they surveyed the mom-and-pop supermarket.

There were two fully stocked meat coolers, separated by a door. Each was thirteen feet long and stretched the length of the back wall. When Perry and the federal agents met up in front of the porterhouse steaks, Perry pointed to the door. The men locked their weapons on the entrance to the storeroom.

"Jasper…you in there…JASPER!" Perry barked as he slowly headed toward the storage room. With weapons drawn, the two agents followed.

Perry opened the door. Upon peering in, he eased his weapon into his holster and dropped his head.

"What is it?" Jarrod asked. The two agents curiously eased toward Henderson with their weapons still locked on the door. Both Jarrod and his partner peeked into the storage room. All they could do was shake their heads at the sight. The FBI agents holstered their pistols. Scott swiftly walked across the storage room floor and over to the far corner. He knelt beside a mutilated body, which lay lifeless next to several cases of stacked sodas bottles. Scott put his index finger to the neck of the corpse in an effort to feel for a pulse.

❧

It had been a very long shift for Perry.

He had worked his regular twelve hours and several hours of overtime. He was tired, but afraid to sleep. Perry knew that his mind wouldn't allow him to rest. Terrell's blotted face, as well as Jasper's mutilated corpse, played in his head while he was up. He knew what would happen if he fell asleep.

The agents that sat in the car with him also suffered from anxiety caused by what they had witnessed upon their arrival in Jacob.

Silence filled Perry's patrol car.

He and the two federal agents headed toward Junction Three. They'd been in the Bottoms much of the day. After the horrific discovery of the two bodies, the federal employees were determined to confront Chief Steward.

Before leaving the Bottoms, Agent Jarrod made it a point to request that more agents be dispersed to the Southern town so that a complete and thorough investigation could be conducted. He also reached out to the state's attorney general and informed him of the situation. The agent's hypostasis intrigued the state's top legal representative who assured the government envoy that all the resources of his office were at the disposal of the Federal Bureau of Investigation.

Perry drove the back road out of the Bottoms. He passed several worn trailer homes on either side of the dirt road. The decaying dwellings stood for several years before eventually being abandoned and later engulfed by the greenery that surrounded them. For years they would resemble a row of tree houses.

Further up the dirt road, a few yards away from where it intersected with Route 39 that led to and from the heart of the Bottoms, and the bridge that expanded over Morris Creek into Junction Three, sat Collins' filling station, a property that the Black officer would purchase.

The patrol car sped over the bridge and onto the gravel-laden, two-lane vein. The road, which gave access to the nine-mile stretch of farmland and two miles of neglected trailers scattered along the Junction, was purposely left unpaved. The city council thought it would be a waste of taxpayers' money to have to continually pave a road that would only need it done over and over due to the farm equipment that was forced to travel it.

"How long will it take us to get to the station?" Jarrod asked as he glared at the various farm animals left to graze in the open fields on either side of the road.

"About twenty minutes...I could probably do it in less," Perry said, pressing aggressively on the gas.

Four oaks and a three-foot-high hedge grew along the edges of the sidewalk-less road in front of the trailer where Miran and Lee Thompson were raised. A '59

Ford pickup, a 1960, '62 and '64 Dodge, all with various mechanical issues, were surrounded by mufflers, engine parts, tires and other rusted out pieces of the vehicles. Two hound dogs were tied to a pole from which a Confederate flag flew. Leaning on the vehicle and or playing with the dogs were several members of the radical group, headed by Miran Thompson.

The men had assembled to discuss Jasper Collins' unexpected death; although it hadn't been reported yet. Only law enforcement were privy to his demise.

Several of the rednecks openly drank beer and had been doing so for hours, although it was barely noon.

"I can't believe that somebody murdered Jasper..." Lee stated to the group of men that surrounded him.

Miran quickly chimed in. "I don't know if it was true or not...but I was told that Jasper was talkin' to the law... If he was...we don't know how much he revealed. So we're gonna have to assume that them gov'ment people know who we are."

Billy, the desk sergeant from police headquarters who still in his uniform, noticed Perry's cruiser as it tore up Junction Three past the Thompson property. He pointed. "Hey fellas...there they go."

All the men turned their attention toward the road, but the car had already sped by. Before the men could pick up their discussion, they heard the sound of tires digging into gravel; a sure sign that a vehicle had stopped abruptly on the road.

Perry shifted his car into reverse. "I saw them racist bastards; they're probably celebratin'...those are the degenerates you need to question."

The patrol officer pressed on the gas; the car sped in reverse. Perry cut his wheel and his cruiser barreled backward onto the Thompson property, its rear end barely missing one of the oaks.

Those that had assembled on the Thompson property watched as the patrol car came to a sudden stop. Before the dust could settle, Billy ducked his head and rushed into Lee's rundown trailer. The desk sergeant couldn't afford to be seen with the racists.

The dogs became rowdy, barking aggressively as they tried desperately to free themselves from the ropes that bound them to the flagpole.

Perry Henderson heatedly exited his vehicle; the two federal agents hot on his heels. Like the Three Musketeers, the public servants hastily approached the stunned gathering. Miran quickly maneuvered through his group and headed toward Perry and the two members of the FBI.

The two men closest to the dogs knelt beside them with beer cans in hand. They used their free hands to stroke the dogs. The men waited, hoping that Miran would order them to release the trained hunters.

"What the hell are you doin' on my brother's property? Ya'll ain't got no cause to be here..." Miran said.

"Miran, these gentlemen have some questions for you and them fools that follow you," Perry interjected.

The elder Thompson brother turned his attention toward his friends—he quickly shifted his focus to his uninvited guests before saying, "Them boys can have all the questions they wanna...I ain't got no answers for 'em..."

"I'll get each and every one of you for what you did to my nephew!" He pointed toward the two men that were playing with the barking dogs. "Oscar! You know I'ma get yo' ass!" Perry insisted.

Al Blaine donned worn overalls and a baseball cap. He held a beer in his hand as he leaned against the broken-down '62 Dodge. Perry aimed his rage toward the short, dumpy coward. "Al...you gutless bastard! You can believe that I won't rest until I bury yo' ass."

The dorky, overweight drunk ignored the officer. He walked over to the out-of-control dogs and knelt, then began using his free hand to stroke the animals.

"I mean it...each and every one of you will pay!" Perry pointed to the shadow he noticed peeking from the window of the house. "That includes you, too, Billy..."

PRESENT

Thump, thump, thump; every second the annoying sound echoed about the entire house. It was a sound that the children were afraid to interrupt for fear of having to deal with their father.

The wicks on the candles, which once burnt bright in the living room, had lost some of their intensity. They had been burning for much of the night. For hours, Perry lay unconscious. His romantic evening, which he had meticulously planned, was a complete disaster. His wife was none too pleased when she discovered that the father of her children had neglected his responsibilities. Margaret felt that her husband's first duty as a father was to protect their children at any cost. To her children's detriment, Perry was miserable at his job as a parent. Margaret was unaware that Perry purposely made it a point to distance himself from all whom he loved.

Perry's head hung over the arm of the sofa; drool slowly made its way out of the corner of his mouth. He barely held onto the bottle of Ole Grand Dad; liquor slowly dripped to the wooden floor. The drunken cop spent much of the night in an alcoholic stupor; his mind reminiscing about a day that he would never forget.

Margaret was up by 4:30 a.m.

She had to prepare for a trip; it would be her second journey in as many days. The outing would require her to be on the road for several hours. Thanks to Jonathan, this was to be another opportunity to visit with her baby. The journalist had called in some favors and was granted an unscheduled visit with her child, so he invited her to tag along.

When the anxious mother walked into the living room, her attention was immediately directed toward the phonograph as it made an annoying thumping sound; an indication that the needle was stuck in the same spot as the record continued its revolutions.

Margaret gazed at her slumbering husband. He was passed out on the sofa; his liquor bottle had obviously slipped from his hand and shattered on the floor beneath him. Margaret shook her head in antipathy. Disgusted at the sight of her husband, she simply turned and left the room.

I Found
PLASTIC

The red and blue flashes of light that flickered in the sky originated from the half-dozen vehicles that idled in front of a neatly kept bungalow. The house was erected in the center of the middle-income street. The somewhat picturesque residential neighborhood wasn't without flaws. Two of the homes were neglected, creating a conflict between neighbors concerned about property value. Gray paint peeled from one; the other had been primed several years prior but was never painted. The two homes were without grass, and the fencing that surrounded the dwellings backyards was in desperate need of repair. The carports also needed upkeep, as did the front screen door of both habitations.

The two unkempt parcels of land were on either side of the well-maintained yellow, white-trimmed home where the police had congregated.

Several residents of the neighborhood curiously gathered together; some in robes, while others had nothing to protect them from the balmy night air as they stood under the streetlights opposite the commotion. None were surprised to see that police had been summoned;

they were shocked that so many vehicles responded. Everyone was under the impression that the Hatfield McCoy-type feud that had been going on between the families occupying the three homes was in need of lawful intervention.

An elderly white woman peeked from her window and saw dozens of her neighbors standing on the side-walk in front of her home. She had become accustomed to seeing one or two patrol cars at the residence across from hers because of the fighting, but unmarked vehicles, and a coroner's truck were something new. The woman wanted to know what was going on.

A nervous anxiety could be felt as those who were watching attempted to get as close as they could. Law enforcement continually forced them back to the side-walk.

The neighbors of 1456 Hudson Street were not only curious; a few were frightened to death after being told of the situation. They were sure that what had occurred was not the result of neighborhood feuding. Men were dying; white men, racist white men—and those affiliated with them were afraid that they could be next.

The community, as a whole, began to feel that the deaths were the work of, as they put it, an angry Negro. But who could be clever enough to commit the acts without leaving any evidence?

The elderly woman exited her home from the side door. With her blue cotton robe pulled snug to her body, she headed down her driveway; the flip-flop of her house shoes against the concrete alerted those standing in front of her home that she was approaching.

"What in the world is goin' on out here?" she questioned.

Her thirty-seven-year-old next-door neighbor was the first to reply. "Someone shot OB..." said the mother of two.

"Was it those fools...?" The old lady's eyes veered toward both of the neglected homes on either side of the crime scene.

"No...everyone believes that some crazy nigga is on the loose," the mother responded.

The police were dumbfounded to learn that no one in the neighborhood seemed to have heard the fatal gunshot. The homes on Hudson Street sat so close together— separated by only the three-by-three-foot fencing that connected to the carports in each driveway. Law enforcement was amazed that no one heard anything.

Neither Jake nor his partner could immediately see the body as they stood in the middle of street.

"What's goin' on here, Ehrman...?" Detective Jake Aaron asked the officer responsible for securing the crime scene.

Officer Ehrman filled the detectives in on the victim's history. The officer could tell that Aaron immediately recognized the victim, based on the information provided, so the uniformed officer went on to say, "Oscar Bowman's body was found over there." The policeman pointed toward an oil-stained driveway. "He didn't get along with his neighbors on either side of him."

Jake replied, "Do you think that there was enough hostility to cause either party to result to physical violence?"

"In my opinion...no way! They argued all the time... a patrol car was here every weekend. But they never came close to killing one another. It was just words. Plus, all of these people are the type to handle their disputes face to face. What I'm saying is, the entire neighborhood would have played witness to the killing, if any of those individuals were involved."

The men directed their attention toward the carport.

An old gray Pontiac Bonneville was pulled into the shelter. The sedan blocked everyone's view of the body that lay on the ground at the hood of the vehicle.

"They verbally fought over property issues...you know, beautification type stuff..." Officer Ehrman said, "Follow me!" as he led the way.

When the detectives entered the carport, they noticed a puddle of blood surrounding the passenger side tire. The weary law enforcement officials had a hard time dealing with the fact that they had no suspects for any of the previous homicides. Now, they had another to deal with. The county prosecutor had already threatened them. Louis Calvert told the detectives that he would assemble a special investigative team from the sheriff's department to take over the investigation if Jake and his people didn't make progress quickly. On top of that, they were starting to feel pressure from the media, Senator Willington and the mayor, as well as the citizens of Jacob.

"Someone give me a flashlight," Jake requested. There wasn't enough visibility—the car blocked the streetlight and created an elongated shadow around the body.

A uniformed officer immediately handed the detective a police-issued heavy duty light. With the flashlight in hand, Jake knelt beside the bloody corpse; the body was faced down. The detective carefully examined the entry and exit wounds in the victim's skull. Still kneeling, he allowed his eyes to soak up every detail—from the blood splatter on the windshield to the position of the body in relationship to the bloodstained bumper.

Detective Aaron hypothesized that the victim exited his vehicle and walked toward the front of the car. Then, as he made his way between the front end and the back of the carport, he was probably gunned down.

The veteran cop peered up and noticed that the back of the wooden carport had a gaping hole. The window was missing that should have been there to further protect the vehicle from the rain.

Jake got to his feet, carefully stepped over the body, and then began examining the gap. The officer didn't have the slightest idea what he expected to find as he meticulously covered every inch of the opening. It wasn't until he walked out of the port, hopped the fence into the backyard, and examined the shelter from the rear that he realized his diligence had paid off. Jake discovered minuscule pieces of plastic lodged in the wooden structure. Upon closer examination, he realized that the tips of the fragments seemed to be burnt. The detective knelt and began examining the grass around the carport.

Jonathan Edwards got out of his car and approached Jake Aaron's crime scene. The reporter walked up to the first citizen he saw. "Who was murdered?"

"Oscar...someone shot him in the head," the jittery, elderly female mouthed, never once looking his way.

Jake hopped back over the fence and made his way inside. He and his partner once again knelt beside the body and he shined his light on the victim's head.

Harris used the tip of his pencil as a pointer. "What is that in the wound? It looks like..."

"Plastic!" Jake interrupted.

Harris turned his curious expression toward his partner. "What!"

"I found plastic imbedded in the window sill." He pointed to the window. "I also found bits of it on the ground in the backyard. The shooter was in the yard. It looks like he might have used a plastic bottle as a silencer...could be why no one heard a gunshot."

"So...the killer was extremely careful about not being spotted. I questioned a few of the residents...no one seemed to have noticed anything out of the ordinary. I still think that someone saw something but just don't realize that they did," Harris said.

"You could be right...we're gonna have to question

them again," Jake said as he continued to maneuver his flashlight around the body.

One of the more outspoken neighborhood residents could suddenly be heard shouting, "THEM NIGGAS DONE GONE CRAZY…!" He turned to the others and attempted to incite a riot. "We gon' have to kill 'em all before them son-of-a-bitches get us…"

The people gathered began to stir. "If the police can't do nothin' 'bout what's goin' on…then we will. Everybody! Go get yo' guns…let's get 'em."

Jake erected himself and slowly made his way from the crime scene over to the rowdy crowd. The cop was aggravated already and wasn't in the mood to hear the frustration of a group of people looking for an excuse to take matters in their own hands. "Ya'll better calm ya'll asses down. The first one of ya'll to step out of line… I'ma personally put a bullet in you…and you know that I will…nah…get the hell out of here."

No one budged.

The detective screamed, "GET AWAY FROM HERE…NOW!"

The angry mob slowly and reluctantly began to disperse; one of them yelled as he headed away, "THIS AIN'T OVER!"

"It better be!" Jake ordered before he redirected his attention back to the activity around the body."

Jonathan shouted to Jake, "Aaron…!"

The detective glanced over his shoulder and saw Jonathan in the clutches of a uniformed officer attempting to prevent the reporter from entering the perimeter. Jake gave the newsman a hand gesture before saying, "Give me a second!"

Harris approached his partner, then pointed toward the dispersing angry mob. "Jake...they gonna do somethin' stupid."

"I realize that...that's why we're gonna have to solve this quickly. If we don't...we could have a race war on our hands."

Harris put his hand on Jake's back and led his partner toward the carport. "So, you wanna keep this investigation focused on the possibility that the murders are a part of some kind of vendetta?"

"We can't overlook that. If we use that theory then we have to go back to what happened in '67," said Jake.

"What do you suggest?"

Jake looked over to his partner. "Find who's behind these murders."

Harris couldn't help but notice Jake's skeptical expression. He quickly spoke, "I realize that Henderson is a far-fetched theory...but what else do we have?"

Jake began to pace.

He glanced over at the body, then toward his partner. The lead detective stopped and, for several seconds, directed his attention back to the activity around the corpse. Harris could tell that his partner was deep in thought; he realized that Jake was seriously pondering his assumption. At that moment, Jake walked up to his partner and whispered in his ear.

"Henderson…he would know how not to leave evidence…and he allowed his son to confess to Miran's murder although he knew that it was impossible for his son to have been involved. I really do think that we should turn our investigation toward him." He didn't know what to think about Perry's possible involvement. But the detective knew that he couldn't conduct a serious investigation without at least considering the possibility that the Black officer may have been complicit. "Listen, keep this between us. Don't tell anyone what we're doing."

"Thing is…could Henderson have come into this neighborhood without being spotted? I don't know, Jake. How could Henderson have known that OB would be coming home at that particular time? There's absolutely no way that he could lay in wait for so long…in this neighborhood. These people hate Blacks…if they saw a Black man in this neighborhood we would have known. Nah…as much as I would like to think so…he's not the person we're lookin' for."

"Jake Aaron…!" Jonathan called out, motioning for the detective to approach.

The detective tapped his partner on the shoulder, a gesture meant to excuse himself, then headed toward the perimeter's edge. "What's goin' on, Edwards?"

"You tell me…was this guy one of the people involved in the lynching of Terrell Johnson?" Jonathan asked. He backed away from the officer responsible for holding him at bay to allow the detective enough room to duck under the yellow crime scene tape.

Jake Aaron put his hand on Jonathan's shoulder and slowly led him down the street. "And if he were involved in the Johnson case?"

The reporter quickly responded, "Then I would say that there were only three more to go…"

The detective stopped and stared intently into the eyes of one of the best investigative reporters in the business. There were several seconds of silence before he spoke. "What the hell are you saying?"

"I think that all of these homicides…and the three that occurred in '67 are all tied to the death of Terrell Johnson. If that's the case…then there are three more thought to have had something to do with Johnson's death. I also believe that you need to turn your investigation internal."

Jake had come to respect Jonathan's investigative ingenuity. He placed his hands on his hips, before allowing his eyes to veer toward the crime scene and his partner, who was instructing an officer to back the Bonneville out of the carport.

Without breaking his gaze , he whispered, "Who do you suggest that our investigation should focus on?"

Digging DEEP

I t was once an old courthouse but anyone walking up the twelve concrete steps still got the feeling that lady justice was waiting to greet them at the front door. The building on the corner of Ellis Street had been converted into a sanctuary where the struggles of a people were housed. Although the building wasn't in stellar condition, no one cared. The relics that were on display within the one hundred-eight-year-old structure would take its visitors on an historical journey from slavery toward equality. The Black leaders of the surrounding communities had fought for years to have a place where their children could learn of the struggles of their ancestors.

Jonathan made his way up the steps of the only African American Historical Museum within a hundred-mile radius. He had to dodge several busloads of children as they ran from the vehicles. The excited youth, who were on a class field trip, blocked access while they eagerly awaited entrance to the converted museum. Jonathan had to carefully maneuver around the ten- to twelve-year-olds in order to get in.

Upon entering the once hallowed halls of justice, the journalist made his way toward the procurement office at the far end of the building. In doing so, he was captivated by a display of the Reverend Martin Luther King, Jr. and the Civil Rights Movement. He stopped and peered at an exhibit depicting frightened Black citizens being hosed and attacked by dogs. The sight of the mistreatment caused the reporter to move on, shaking his head in disgust. It wasn't until he passed photographs of shackled slaves being forced off of ships that he decided to get on with the task at hand.

After arriving to the office, he tapped on the door.

"Come in…" a female voice responded.

Upon entering, Jonathan's eyes were immediately locked on a brunette. She wore a form-fitting red dress with a smartly cut white polyester jacket. The woman was stuffing paperwork into a file cabinet. When she directed her attention toward the reporter, he immediately noticed her green eyes and the ruby red lipstick that accentuated her beauty.

Her sweet Southern drawl was intoxicating. "Can I help you?"

"I'm looking for Sara Willington," Jonathan said as he stood at the door.

Sara took a seat behind her desk. "You've found her."

The reporter made his way over to the woman. He extended his hand and spoke softly. "I'm Jonathan Edwards…I'm a reporter from the *Daily News*."

Sara stood and quickly placed her soft, delicate, well-manicured hand into his. "What can I do for you?"

"I have a few questions about your relationship with a young Black boy named Terrell Johnson."

Sara retook her seat. She gestured for her guest to make himself relaxed. "Please…make yourself comfortable."

The reporter sat in the black leather chair in front of Sara's desk.

"I've heard that, before his death, you and Terrell were extremely close."

Sara was puzzled—it had been a very long time since Terrell's name had been mentioned in her presence. She always thought about him but never felt that she could open up to anyone. She wondered why her past seemed to walk into the door alongside of the journalist. The daughter of Senator Gavin Willington fell deep in thought.

Summer of '67

All she could do was pray. The heat had intensified and any hope of survival seemed unlikely. The high temperatures and thick black smoke generated by the blaze stripped her of oxygen. The heat scorched her throat. Her cough was hard and frequent.

"Our Father who…" The prayer seemed to calm her, but her cough interrupted her overture to God once again. Her eyes rolled up in the back of her head.

The blue Trans Am rested on its roof, the front end tilted toward the ground. A Ford pickup that was obviously involved in the Trans Am's situation had veered head-on into a telephone pole. The lines rested across the hood. The driver of that vehicle was thrown through the windshield. He lay sprawled out on the hood with pieces of glass imbedded all over his body. Blood flowed freely from his young, battered, pale white face.

Sparks from the hot electrical lines had ignited a trail of gasoline that flowed from the ruptured gas tank of the Trans Am. The flames immediately set both vehicles ablaze.

Sara Willington was dazed and scared. She made one last attempt to escape the wreckage but found that she couldn't move her legs. The roof was crushed on both the driver and passenger sides. Even if she could free herself, she saw no way of escape. She couldn't squeeze through either window and there was absolutely no way for her to get through the windshield.

Because of the harsh smoke, Sara's screams had turned into panic-filled whispering pleas. "Help me... Please, someone...!"

Barely clinging to life, Sara was ready to give up on her fight for survival. She felt as if she were walking down a tunnel. In the far distance, she saw people heading toward a light.

As she stared intently toward that same light, Sara saw a stunning woman in a beautiful, free-flowing silky white gown walking away from the light as others walked into it. The woman seemed to float with every stride as she headed toward Sara. Although the woman in the gown didn't seem to be getting any closer to Sara, the girl found it a bit strange that she was able to make out her face; it was her mother.

Sara saw her mother frantically waving; insisting that she go back. Her mother was telling her that it wasn't her time. But with every step toward her mother, Sara felt an unbelievable peace.

Ignoring her mother's gesture, Sara eagerly continued to move toward the light.

She wanted her mother; she wanted to feel the warm, comforting embrace of the woman that had given birth to her. Sara couldn't understand why her mother didn't want her; why she began to move in the opposite direction. Why, without warning, her mother suddenly vanished. Once again, Cynthia Willington's little girl was immediately hit with a feeling of abandonment upon watching her mother disappear. For the second time in her life, her mother had left her without so much as a good-bye.

"DON'T GO NEAR THAT CAR, BOY! ...GET BACK!" Someone yelled, "BOTH OF THEM ARE GONNA BLOW...! GET AWAY, BOY...SHE'S DEAD ALREADY!" She couldn't believe that everyone thought that she was dead.

Sara summoned enough strength to struggle in an

attempt to free herself. All the while, she wondered why her life would end with her being burned alive. She needed to understand why God would allow her to suffer a gruesome ending.

Sara's entire life flashed before her.

She could remember that at the age of three, her parents had taken her to the woods in the middle of the night. On that evening, Sara remembered being completely surrounded by flames, and what she thought to be ghosts. She could remember seeing dozens upon dozens of spirits standing around burning scarecrows. She would later come to know that she, in fact, was paying witness to a Klan gathering, her first of many to follow. What she saw as burning scarecrows were actually crosses that had been set ablaze.

Her parents were so proud when it came time to dress her up in the white ceremonial cloak. She had wrestled with what had taken place on that particular night for much of her life. That horrific evening continued to haunt her dreams.

For years, she wondered how two people, that showed her undying love and affection and taught her of God's unconditional love, could in one breath teach her to do the right thing, and in the next, expose her to something so inhumane. How could they expose their baby girl to such evil?

Like so many other children that she had grown up with, Sara Willington was taught to hate all that was different from her. She never really understood why, but the love she had for her parents made her need for understanding irrelevant. She was taught as a child that fire symbolized cleansing: that whenever it burned high, she should always be reminded that their mission was the elimination of an inferior race.

The sound of glass shattering put a stop to the memories from her childhood.

She struggled slightly in a last desperate attempt to free herself. Unable to do so, without demur she closed her eyes for what she felt would be the last time.

"Lady...can you move at all?"

Sara thought that she was dreaming. When she opened her eyes, she couldn't see anyone, but someone was there. She knew that she had heard someone. It wasn't until he appeared from the thick smoke that she realized it wasn't a dream. There he was—a Negro. In her eyes, he had the most beautiful reassuring smile on his dark face. She had been taught that this man—the wonderful Black man who was risking his life for hers, was a selfish, uncaring man; one that couldn't be trusted.

Her would-be hero was crawling through the intense blaze through her back window. Why? Why would someone like him risk his life to save hers? She was raised to despise his race; and yet, one was willing to do what her own wouldn't.

The Negro struggled to push the seat off the trapped woman. She could clearly hear people shouting in the background. "THAT NIGGA'S CRAZY! ...AIN'T NO WAY IN THE WORLD HE GON' GET HER OUT...SHE ALREADY DEAD!"

PRESENT

Jonathan whispered again, "Ms. Willington, are you okay?"

Sara snapped out of her trance. "What's this all about?" the procurement officer asked.

Jonathan could see that Sara was anguished, so he got straight to the point. "I'm working on a story about the recent homicides in Jacob. I really think that they might all be linked to what happened to Terrell Johnson. I heard that you two went to LeHigh Community College together. I was wondering, with your family's wealth, why you didn't attend a major university?"

"I told my father that I didn't wanna go to the university because I wanted to be with him after my mother's death. But that wasn't the truth." She gazed at the man seated across from her. Sara's thoughts were on why she should open up to a stranger. He hadn't given her any reason to. After all, she could not care less that a bunch of rednecks were being murdered. In fact, she was happy that the men responsible for Terrell's death were being punished. She leaned back in her chair before saying, "Why should I talk to you? I don't care about those men."

"Tell me something…were you and Terrell Johnson close?"

"Yes, I really loved him. But our relationship wasn't like it was being portrayed back then. It wasn't that I didn't want it to be more but Terrell only wanted us to be friends. He was scared of getting too close. One thing is true; I was in love with him." She gazed curiously at her guest. "What do my feelings toward Terrell have to do with your story?"

"I really do understand that you want the people who murdered him to pay. And apparently they are paying for their sins. My concern is Terrell's cousin. He was sent to prison for murdering Miran Thompson."

"I read about that."

"So, would you be willing to help me…help him?"

"How could I possibly be of help?"

"First, let's start with background information. How did you and Terrell meet?"

"Terrell had just completed his registration at LeHigh. He was on his way home when he saw me trapped in my car. It had burst into flames. Terrell risked his life saving mine. After that our friendship grew. I later convinced my father that I didn't want to go to a university. My father wasn't happy about me turning down a chance to go, but he was happy that I would be close to him, so he agreed. If my father had found out that I really wanted to go to LeHigh because I wanted to be close to Terrell, he would have lost his mind.

"Anyway, Terrell Johnson was a beautiful, caring individual. He was the only person that ever tried to understand me. He loved his family; especially his uncle and little cousin. All he talked about was how proud he was of his uncle for making the force…and how smart his little cousin was."

"Do you think that Miran Thompson had anything to do with Terrell's disappearance?" Jonathan asked.

"My father was running for governor back then. Miran Thompson was working on my father's campaign. Miran's son, Donald, also attended LeHigh. Donald convinced his father that Terrell and I were more than friends. Miran believed that our relationship would hurt my father's chances at winning the election. He warned me to stay clear of Terrell. The last time I saw Terrell Johnson was after classes the day he came up missing. I overheard Donald telling a friend of his what had happened the day that Terrell was snatched."

Sara WILLINGTON

Terrell and I had been the subject of ridicule and harassment throughout the campus for several weeks. Folk in the school put out the rumor that Terrell and I were dating. Of course, when my father heard the rumor, it caused him "embarrassment"—as he put it— the Willington name was being ruined by my actions.

You see, I was raised to hate Blacks.

Back then, the prejudice that surrounded our community was well documented. Although Blacks were given more rights under the constitution, Morris County had a bad habit of ignoring those Constitutional privileges.

The movement for equality became my focus after Terrell pulled me from that burning car. I vowed that I would no longer live life with hatred in my heart, despite being surrounded by the narrow-mindedness of my father, and the majority of the community; including most of the staff and students at LeHigh.

I loved and respected my father dearly, but I wasn't going to stop being Terrell's friend, despite my daddy's continuous objections.

Terrell was warned several times to stay away from me.

Donald Thompson figured that Terrell wasn't worried about being threatened, so Miran's ignorant son turned his threats toward me. He told Terrell that he and his friends would hurt me if his black ass didn't keep away.

Although I was always petite, Terrell used to say I was a firecracker.

I wasn't worried about Donald's fat butt, nor was I in the least bit concerned about his dumb ass friends. I was more concerned with Terrell. He wasn't a big guy, being five-feet-eleven and somewhere around one hundred and sixty pounds. I was more afraid that Donald and his friends would do something to him. I really believed that Donald aimed his threats toward me as a diversion. They always intended on going after Terrell.

I know that my father wouldn't have allowed those

guys to bother me, but he certainly didn't do anything to curtail their threats.

People didn't understand how special Terrell was to me. It wasn't because he saved my life. It's true that I probably wouldn't have given him the time of day before he pulled me from that car, but once I got to know him, I realized that I was limiting myself by hating a group of people that I knew absolutely nothing about.

My handsome, quiet, unassuming classmate had more manners and integrity than anyone that I had ever encountered. Terrell was a very respectful young man with a wonderful heart.

If my father had only taken the time to get to know him, I'm sure that he would have been able to see him for the exceptional individual he was.

Terrell teased me for being a debutante. He was so easy to talk to, and he always seemed to be able to get me to think, which caused me to come up with the solutions to my own problems. Terrell was good at that; he was always willing to listen.

Anyway, evening classes at LeHigh Community College had just concluded.

Several male Caucasian students were gathered on the steps of the predominately white institution as it emptied. It was 8:30 p.m. and the sun was setting, but the humidity was still high. Although a hurricane was predicted, it was so hot that Donald and his two friends began removing their shirts as they leaned against the railing in front of the school.

Terrell Johnson was one of a handful of Black students attending the college. He and I exited with books in hand. We were laughing and joking—talking about a test that we had to prepare for. I wanted to set up a study date, so we made a date to return to the campus library. The stares, the jokes and taunting geared toward Black students in LeHigh's library were just as bad as in Jacob's public library.

As we descended the concrete stairs, leading from Holland House, the building adjacent to the administration building, Donald and his two shirtless friends began their usual asinine taunting.

"Hey, Sara...you doin' that coon?" Donald Thompson blurted to the delight of his cronies.

I answered, "I'd rather do him than interfere with what you and yo momma have goin' on...!"

The others that stood around began to laugh at the look on Donald's face.

"Look here, you *NIGGA LOVER*..."

"No...you look here...take your ignorance someplace else..." I said forcefully.

Terrell grabbed me by the arm with his left hand, which caused me to drop one of my books.

As Terrell picked up the book, he said, "Come on, Sara...let's get out of here."

Donald quickly replied, "Yeah, Sara...you better listen to yo *HOUSE NIGGA!*"

Of course, I quickly countered. "Donald, I hear that congratulations are in order...you're about to be a father…I hear that yo' momma's pregnant again, huh…?"

Terrell pulled me off the steps and away from the ensuing verbal battle. He laughed as we began to walk toward the bus stop. "Girl…you're crazy," he said, handing me the history book that I had dropped.

"He gets on my nerves. He's mad because I won't date his stupid ass. I can't bring myself to go out with him. He's been going to LeHigh since I was twelve," I said with a giggle.

Terrell looked at me like a heroine. He was my hero. Anyway, he said, "Sara, you can't keep jumpin' down people's throats about me."

"Nobody has the right to treat you with disrespect."

Terrell stated, "I'm used to it, you can't keep gettin' involved." He continued as we walked casually, "Your father is gonna really get mad at you, if he hears about you takin' up for me…ain't no tellin' what he'll do to you." He was very concerned. "I knew Donald was gonna say somethin' to you after we left the building. They were botherin' me all day. When you came into the hallway and heard them…everyone knew that you were gonna say somethin'. That's why they were waitin' on us when we left the building."

Donald and his friend made him nervous, but he was much more afraid of my father. "Don't worry about my father and me. You're the best friend I've ever had. And, I'm not about to lose your friendship due to someone else's ignorance."

Terrell looked over his shoulder and saw Donald and his friends standing on the sidewalk, staring at us. He was more fearful of what they could do to me than him. What a sweetheart he was, always thinking that he had to protect me.

"You're gonna have to be careful, girl. I'm gonna walk you home," he insisted.

"No…that's okay…I'll be fine. I only live two blocks from the bus stop. Plus, those clowns know who my father is. They won't dare try anything with me."

As we stood in front of the cross-town bus stop, I motioned for Terrell to come closer; like I wanted to whisper something in his ear. When he did, I caught him off guard. I kissed him on the cheek.

I had never done that before. Stunned, he placed his hand to his cheek and stared at me for several seconds. I think that we both were trying to figure out if we should unleash our passion. I had strong feelings for him, and I felt that he had feelings for me also.

Before we finally made up our minds, the cross-town bus turned the corner. We quickly backed off. When Terrell got on the bus, we waved bye to one another.

No one in his family thought that it was safe for him to attend LeHigh; especially at night, because of the racial tension. However, Terrell felt that he had no choice. He wanted to go to Michigan State University. He could have gone on a track scholarship but his mother had fallen ill. Terrell wasn't about to leave town with her being sick. He told me that he had spoken with officials at MSU, and they both agreed that he would attend the university the following year.

Neither Terrell nor I had noticed that someone was sitting in a pickup truck parked one block from the bus stop. Its occupants were watching our every move. As the bus pulled off, the mysterious black truck's headlights came on. I remember seeing the truck, but I didn't put two and two together until I overheard Donald.

From this point, I'll be telling the story as I heard it from Donald.

The truck pulled off. It passed right by me as I headed home. I turned just in time to see the truck pull up to the curb and watch Donald jump in.

According to Donald, there wasn't much traffic traveling the road on that evening. Although it was hot, a hurricane was predicted. People were trying to prepare, so the streets were relatively clear.

The bus made several stops before it finally reached Terrell's first stop where he needed to transfer.

I overheard Donald say that they watched Terrell get off the bus and cross the street. Miran's son said Terrell sped up after noticing that their truck was following him. They approached him with their headlights out.

Terrell stepped to the curb in front of his second bus stop.

Donald went on to say that they could tell that Terrell became nervous as he looked around and didn't see many people.

The vehicle's pace allowed Terrell to see the occupants of the black pickup: Lee Thompson, Donald, and Jasper, who attempted to hide himself behind a worn baseball cap.

As the truck passed, Lee tauntingly pointed to the confederate flag in the back window of the vehicle. It was an intimidation move—meant to keep Terrell on edge. Donald said that they kept their eyes on my friend as they turned the corner to ensure that he didn't look like he was going to leave.

He said that they waited for two minutes, then they parked around the corner, put on ski masks and snuck up on Terrell and surrounded him.

His books fell from his hands as he attempted to use his arms to protect himself from being bashed in the face by several baseball bats. As he fell to the ground, the savage, brutal attack continued. They kicked, stomped and repeatedly struck him. Donald laughed when he described the blood splattering as they beat Terrell with their Louisville Sluggers.

"I play those events in my head every single night. Terrell was special to me. The way in which he died will haunt me for the rest of my life." Sara began to cry.

Jonathan gave Sara his handkerchief. She dabbed the cloth at her eyes before she continued, "When he got on that bus…that was the last time I saw him."

The reporter countered, "Did you ever confront Donald?"

"There was no need; he would have simply denied ever being involved."

"What about your father? Do you think that he was involved?"

"I know he was. I talked to my father about it after Terrell's body was discovered."

"Off the record, would you tell me what you talked to your father about?"

"I told him that I saw Lee Thompson pull up behind the bus in a black pickup. I told him that Lee picked up Donald and they followed that bus. After I heard that Terrell had been lynched, I immediately knew who was responsible. I confronted my father later that night. Of course, he denied being involved. Miran came over to the house that night. I overheard him tell my father that he had taken care of the problem." She sniffled.

"Did he say what problem? He could have been talking about anything?"

Her response was filled with confidence. "He was talking about Terrell...I know he was."

"So, you truly believe that your father was involved?"

She dabbed the handkerchief to her eyes once again. "At the time, I didn't want to believe he would be. I was hoping that my father would have never taken the life of the person responsible for saving mine. Several things made me believe that he was involved so I began to distance myself from him. I haven't really spoken with him in years."

"Look…I need you to do me a favor. I realize that you and your father don't speak but can you call him?"

Sara stared at her guest. "For what?"

"This is what I want you to do."

Missed OPPORTUNITIES

Larry was responsible for keeping the latrine spotless. He understood the consequences of leaving any hint of filth and was very meticulous in his cleaning. For two weeks he scrubbed and polished. He mopped and sanitized every nook and cranny of the restroom.

The Friday morning of his second week was when his primary assignment was finally handed down. Larry was on his knees cleaning around a toilet when Lieutenant Frank Small entered. The man who, for the most part, ran the entire facility, stood behind Larry unnoticed. The CO listened to him as he hummed while he worked. Small couldn't quite figure out the musical murmur that the inmate was humming.

Lieutenant Small barked, "Inmate!"

Startled, Larry immediately dropped the rag that he was using and hopped to attention. "Yes sir, boss!"

"You been doin' a good job in here," Small said. He slowly made his way around the spotless lavatory. "I hope that you'll be able to do as good of a job workin' on the grounds as you been doin' in here. I want you to report to Elden Howard. You have been assigned to work on the grounds crew."

Larry was ecstatic. He was relieved that he would be working outdoors and no longer had to deal with the smell of ammonia and or any of the other cleaning solvents that tortured his nostrils every morning for his first fourteen days of latrine duty.

Being involved with landscaping was his opportunity to take in the morning air. Breathing in the sunrise would remind him of the good times he had fishing during the early morning hours at the banks of Morris Creek.

Larry and five others were responsible for the four hundred square yards that surrounded the administration building. The six cons were to ensure that the grass that bordered the building stayed green, watered, cut and edged; and that the shrubbery was neatly manicured.

The prisoners that were already assigned to the landscaping group knew the importance of their job. They all were very much aware that the only person that Frank Small had to report to operated out of that building.

If the warden rained down on Big Frank, then the man that actually ran the prison would lay hand on each and every one of the prisoners responsible for bringing heat on the hard-core prison official. Small ran the prison like a military boot camp. After all, the training that the ex-Marine received was a part of his persona, engraved in him for the rest of his life.

Larry snapped out of his daydream, after accidentally

running over a rock with the push mower. The blades made a loud grinding sound as it came into contact with the solid object. The landscaping supervisor, who was on a knee digging in preparation of planting lilies, turned his attention toward the newest member of his grounds crew.

"Young blood…you need to watch what you're doin'. We have to keep the equipment that's assigned to us in top shape," he said calmly.

The elderly, gray-headed Black man with the worn tired face got to his feet. He wiped his hands on his pants legs before dragging his sleeve across his dark chocolate face. He then made his way over to his underling.

"Look here, son, if we damage this equipment to the point where I can't personally repair it, then I have to go to the man and try and persuade him that we need new equipment. I really don't want to deal with the hassle of doin' that." He motioned for Larry to follow him.

Elden Pappi Howard had been doing the same job for twenty-eight years and he never had to make a request to replace broken equipment. Prison officials replaced most of the tools necessary for upkeep every ten years or so. In between that time, Pappi fixed what he could, or simply made do.

"Come over here and let me show you what else you're gonna have to learn."

The old con was a fixture in the prison—forty-eight years, six months, twenty-two days and fourteen hours:

but who was counting; he was never getting out. To Pappi, the only thing he had to look forward to were his mornings—where he could fill his lungs with fresh air, work on the grounds, and receive his usual array of compliments for a job well done. The warden and Corrections Officer Small always made it a point to acknowledge the lifer's efforts.

Larry followed the old-timer over to an area where dirt had been turned in preparation for planting a new bed of flowers. They both knelt down.

"I know you were told that my name is Elden but nobody calls me that. Folk 'round here call me Pappi." He began to move dirt around with his hand. "I hear they don' tagged you '*Bring Yo Lunch.*' I also hear that you like to fight."

"I don't like fightin'. Actually I hate it. But I ain't gon' let nobody whip on me," Larry said.

Pappi laughed.

He looked at Larry's bruised face as he continued to use his hands to move the dirt. "Looks to me like you been whipped on a little bit already." The sixty-eight-year-old inmate pointed toward a crate filled with an assortment of flowers waiting to be planted. "Pick up one of those potted plants, then remove the plant from the pot and hand it to me."

As Larry complied, he noticed Lieutenant Frank Small exit the four-story, tan-brick admin building. Larry, the two inmates that were assigned to trim the grass, and the two that were responsible for trimming the bushes, immediately snapped to attention.

Pappi continued to work.

This was the first time since Larry had been incarcerated that he had witnessed anyone, including guards, not stand at attention in the presence of Lieutenant Small.

Small descended the six steps and made his way over to where Pappi worked. Small signaled for the others to resume their chores as he passed.

Larry knelt back down next to his supervisor as Small approached. The young inmate whispered, "Pappi…here he comes."

"I know, young blood…he always stops by and speaks to me," the elderly man replied softly as he placed the lilies into the hole that he had dug.

Frank's massive body seemed to eclipse the rising sun as he stood before Larry and Pappi. "Good mornin', Ole Timer."

"How goes it, boss?" Pappi replied as he patted dirt around the lilies that he'd planted.

Small scanned the landscaping. "You have this place lookin' like the Botanical Gardens. Pappi…I've always been impressed wit yo' work…"

"Why, thank you, boss." The inmate never took his eyes off his project.

The CO didn't say another word—he continued scanning the grounds as he casually walked away.

After turning his attention from Small, who was headed

toward the entrance of the electrified fencing, Larry shifted his concentration in the direction of the elderly gardener. "How is it that they don't make you stand at attention when he's around?"

"I'm too old for that nonsense…I been in this joint too damn long for anybody not to show me respect."

Larry gazed at Pappi. "How long have you been in here?"

"I been in here fo 'bout forty-eight…forty-nine years…" Pappi said as he gestured for Larry to give him more flowers. Larry removed another set of lilies from the crate that sat in the wheelbarrow and then gently pulled them from the pot before he handed them to the master gardener.

"Pappi…you killed somebody?" he questioned.

With his focus directed toward his task, the elderly inmate once again wiped at his brow with his shirt sleeve. Pappi then whispered, "I don't like talkin' 'bout why I'm here. You shouldn't either. That makes you question if you could have done anythin' differently. Leave it alone. It's easier to deal with."

Larry could tell that the older gentleman wasn't about to open up to him so he turned his attention to the task at hand. The two continued to work in silence.

A few hours had passed and it was time for the gardeners to prepare for lunch. Larry carried two rakes and Pappi pushed a wheelbarrow filled with garden tools toward a shed positioned forty yards to the left of the administration building. Larry could see the four other members of Pappi's team sitting in front of the shed. They were patiently waiting on their supervisor.

"Pappi, I hope I didn't offend you when I was askin' questions 'bout how you ended up here. It was just conversation. You see…I feel lost. I was hopin' that you might be able to help me find my way around," Larry mumbled shyly.

Pappi looked toward Larry as he pushed. "*Lunchman*," he said with a grin. His halfhearted attempt at humor was in reference to Larry's moniker of *Bring Yo' Lunch*. "Just kiddin'. Look, son, I don't know why ya here, and I don't wanna know. You need'ta keep that to yo' self."

"I was accused of killin' a white man. He was a racist who headed a group of Klansmen. He murdered my cousin. I just needed to tell you."

"Let me guess. You didn't kill 'em?" Pappi asked sarcastically.

Larry insisted, "Nah…I didn't."

Larry allowed his eyes to soak up the rich greenery that surrounded him. He then turned and peered to his right. The double electrified fencing that enclosed the massive red structure and the dozen or so barracks that were situated some four hundred yards behind the enormous prison, came to view. Larry still found it hard to believe that he was on the wrong side of the barbed wire.

He shook his head in bewilderment.

As his eyes darted around, his thoughts shifted to the

thousands of inmates that were housed in the facility.

Pappi noticed the naïve expression on Larry's face. He knew that his new worker was lost. After all, Larry had been thrown into a cage with some of the more hardened criminal elements this side of the Mason-Dixon Line.

The battered teen was obviously scared. Plus, it didn't take long before he was acclimated to the harsh reality of life behind bars. Pappi felt for the boy, so, for the first time since he had been locked up, the old man had thoughts of taking someone under his wing.

Whether he committed the crime that resulted in his incarceration or not, Larry was there and he had a lot to learn in order to survive.

"Looky here, boy, everybody in this place, with the exception of me, is innocent. I killed the bastard that murdered my wife and son. I didn't try to hide it and I would do it again. I murdered a white man who broke into my house and raped my wife while I was workin' in his field tryin' to earn enough money to feed my family. The only reason that I didn't get the death penalty was 'cause he did the same thang to a white woman."

He picked up the wheelbarrow and they resumed their journey toward the shed. "All I'm tryin' to tell you is to deal with the hand that you've been dealt."

"Yo' situation is totally different from mine. My father convinced me to confess. I think that he killed that man. He told me that I was gonna get the death penalty if I didn't confess."

"So you believe that yo' daddy would wrong you?" Pappi questioned.

Larry stared straight ahead. "I use'ta lay in wait on him. I wanted to kill him 'cause he kept puttin' his hands on my momma. He knew that I wanted to kill him so yeah, he would wrong me…"

Larry HENDERSON

I was fifteen when I really got fed up and was readying myself to take him out. On this particular day, I had come home early from school and discovered that my mother had been subjected to another brutal beating from my father. I was determined to confront the abusive alcoholic yet again; I wanted to put a stop to his tirades.

I was at the end of my rope, so that night I had fallen asleep on the couch with a butcher's knife under my pillow.

It was really late when he came in; everyone in the house was sleeping.

I sat straight up when I heard the front door open. My father was drunk as hell, which wasn't a surprise. You would think that a cop would be respectful of his uniform, but my father didn't care. It was embarrassing to know that he walked around drunk in his uniform.

He was still in his gray and blues when he tripped and fell while staggering into the living room.

Once I got to my feet and grabbed my weapon, I quickly made my way over to a dark corner of the living room and attempted to prepare myself. With the butcher's knife firmly gripped in my right hand, I took a deep breath and slowly exhaled.

Anytime that my father would come home late from a night of drinking, he'd always crash out on the sofa, so I leaned my back against the wall and patiently waited for him to enter.

The drunk fought to get to his feet. I was engaged, filled with nervous energy as I peered through the darkness and into the foyer. I couldn't believe that I was actually readying myself to put an end to my father's reign of terror.

I was so caught up in the moment that I wasn't aware that my mother had made her way into the darkened living room. As I raised the knife in anticipation of my father stumbling in, I felt someone's hand firmly grip mine.

My mother whispered into my ear, "Give me the knife, baby...give me the knife...and go to bed."

I reluctantly released the weapon to my mother; she hugged me just as my father stumbled into the living room. That bastard didn't even notice me or my mother standing in the corner; just allowed his body to fall lifelessly to the couch.

For several seconds, while we hugged, my mother and I stared through the darkness at that mumbling, slobbering, good for nothing asshole. He was seconds away from passing out.

After a restless night, unable to sleep, and very much distressed because I was unable to bury the anger and frustration that triggered my murderous rage, I spent all night planning my next attempt on my father's life. I knew that the only way that I would be able to successfully rid my family of my father's madness was to plan to do it where my mother wouldn't be able to stop me.

At one time, I wanted so badly to understand why my father felt a need to beat on my mother—why he was filled with so much anger. But, I was tired. I was no longer interested in why he did the things he did. I was fed up with my mother's uneasiness and her change of demeanor at seven o'clock each evening.

My mother was always extremely nervous when it was time for her husband to come home from work because she didn't know what his mood would be. And I felt that that was not the way for anyone to live; especially my mother.

When I entered our family gas station the following morning, I had every intention of carrying out what I was unable to do the previous evening. I really didn't have a plan when I noticed my father under a car that had been jacked up. The country music was playing loudly, so my father didn't realized that I had entered. In my mind, the perfect opportunity had presented itself. Killing my father and making it look like a robbery crossed my mind.

I stood frozen and glared at my father's feet dangling

from under the vehicle. My thoughts were on kicking the jack that supported the car. I pictured the car falling on top of my old man. I imagined no one being able to hear his screams because the Everly Brothers would drown them out.

My thoughts were so caught up in takin' that son-of-a-bitch out, that I hadn't realized that my sister had entered the garage.

Val told me later that she had immediately noticed the crazed look in my eyes. She said that she knew what I was thinkin', so she slowly approached me and whispered into my ear, "Hey, Larry…how ya doin', baby boy?"

I didn't acknowledge her; I continued to stare at the car jack. Val hugged me, and then whispered again, "Let's go home…"

PRESENT

Larry's eyes darted around the packed, high-energy cafeteria as he stood in the chow line behind Pappi and the other members of his gardening team. They all waited patiently for the slop of the day to be dumped onto their trays.

"On several occasions I had made up my mind that I was gonna get my father, but something always happened to stop me," Larry whispered.

Pappi was stunned that Larry had planned to end his father's life but he understood why Larry felt the need to do whatever it took to defend his mother. The old man was developing an admiration for the young kid.

It was Pappi's turn to be served. As he held his tray toward the inmate responsible for dishing out his portion, he never took his eyes off of Larry.

Seeing Larry stand with his mouth suspended open brought about a sense of déjà vu for Pappi.

Almost a half-century prior, the elder statesman of the prison had the same bewildered expression while watching the cons around him. Everywhere Larry turned he saw the bigger, stronger inmates intimidating their smaller counterparts. He had watched with interest as the weaker cons appeased the bullies by giving up portions of their lunch.

The old man and Larry headed down the aisle. As they made their way toward a table at the far end of the cafeteria, a muscular, heavily tattooed Caucasian inmate (with empty tray in hand) intentionally bumped Larry, nearly causing him to drop his tray.

While Pappi's monotone was respectful, the mild-mannered lifer's bloodshot dark brown eyes were stern. "Bruno…!" It didn't matter if the prisoner was Black, White or Chicano, even the guards knew that giving the old man a hard time could result in them feeling the wrath of not just Small, but the Warden as well.

The bald, scandalous perpetrator of crime responded with a very respectful head gesture toward both Larry and the prison's most revered resident. "Sorry, ole-timer…didn't know he was wit' you."

Pappi returned the con's head gesture with one of his

own. Then he and Larry continued down the active aisle. Ten prisoners occupied the table, leaving two seats available at the long gray picnic bench.

Pappi could tell that Larry's mind was still on the inmate that had bumped him. He whispered to him as they sat, "Let it go...deal with the now...be quick to let go of the past."

Larry didn't hear Pappi—he was caught up in what had just taken place. The white guy that attempted to intimidate him with the known jailhouse method of establishing dominance had quickly backed off because of a gaze from an old man.

Larry had questions, but wasn't going to ask any because he didn't want to upset the man that sat next to him.

The young con played at his food with his fork; a habit that he'd developed as a child. As a kid, he never felt that he could relax while eating because his father was so unpredictable. Perry would, on occasions, come in drunk and ruin everyone's meal.

When his father was home in time to sit with the family, Larry still found himself playing at his food; he would lock his eyes on his father, expecting him to go into a rage at any second. Often, he was unable to eat until he was convinced his father was not looking for a fight.

Larry redirected his attention toward a man that he hoped would be his mentor. "Pappi...what barracks are you in?"

"I'm in Camp 12…if you keep out of trouble…you can be there," the elderly gentleman responded as he began to stuff bread into his mouth.

"Is Camp 12 special or somethin'?"

Before Pappi could answer, Stinky walked over to the table with tray in hand. He immediately made himself comfortable next to the young inmate as the person previously seated next to Larry had left.

Stinky greeted Larry. "What up, baby boy?" Then he directed his attention toward the senior convict. "How you doin', Pappi?"

The elderly con responded without ever making eye contact. "Ronald…how ya' been?"

"Very good…Pappi." Stinky stuffed bread into his mouth. "Hey, Fish…you play ball?"

"Yeah…" Larry replied before he scooped up a fork filled with macaroni.

Ronald CELLS

The state championship was on the line—there were fourteen seconds left in the game. We had the ball. Henry Ford High was up by two. Coach Fillmore drew up a play that would put the ball in my hands.

While we were in a timeout, most of the team wasn't even paying attention to what the coach was saying. For one, they knew the play was coming to me and, two, they had their eyes elsewhere.

Blue and white were the colors they wore; same as the team they represented. The skimpily clad cheerleaders that represented Henry Ford High had once again snatched my teammates' attention. The perfectly built girls stood at center court of our gymnasium and entertained the capacity crowd with their sexiest routine.

Most of the visitors that sat in our stands had heard about me, but had never seen me play. I was sixteen years old, and, as a sophomore, I started at point guard for my team. There was talk going around that I was the best high school athlete in the nation; I tried not to let that kind of talk go to my head.

When I looked up into the stands, my eyes were greeted by a cheering, tension-filled crowd. Thing was, my mom was always a part of the contingent, but for some reason, the person that ensured that I stayed grounded wasn't in her usual seat on this day. I was really worried because she had never missed a game. Something drastic would have had to occur for Elaine Cells to miss a game; especially this one.

My coach was told at the beginning of the fourth quarter why my mother wasn't at the game, but he felt that it was best that he didn't tell me until the game was over.

The horn blew and the referees motioned for the players to take the court. The ball was given to the small forward for my team.

I broke free—the ball was passed in to me.

I stood at the top of the key (the back of the free throw line) and gazed at the clock. I let four seconds run off before I made my move. Being the shortest guy on the court made it easy for me to split two defenders as I headed for the basket. I elevated and put the ball up. Just as I did, I was fouled. The ball seemed to roll around the rim forever before it fell through. That basket tied the game. I went to the line and made the foul shot.

We won the game.

In the midst of our celebration, coach pulled me to the side and told me that my mother had suffered a stroke. The very moment that he told me, I hated him and I hated basketball. I felt that he should have told me the instant that he was informed. In my eyes, basketball had come between my mother and me. I should have been at my mother's side instead of scoring twenty-one points in the fourth quarter.

My mother was paralyzed on the right side of her body. She couldn't talk either. The state was trying to split us up. They wanted to put my two sisters and me in foster care; they said that my mother couldn't care for us.

I wasn't going to let that happen.

Anyway, I dropped out of school to help out around the house. I had to get a job. My coach wanted to help us so that I could stay in school. But, I looked at him, and basketball, as the reason that I wasn't with my mother when she suffered her stroke. I felt that if I was there, then maybe, I might have been able to do something. It took me a long time to realize that there was nothing that I could have done. Meanwhile, I had taken a side job—running drugs. It was the quickest way for me to bring money into the house. I had worked two jobs prior to that. One at a grocery store, and another where I was sweeping the floor of a barbershop. I wasn't making enough money to get my mother's medicine and take care of the girls. I saw peddling drugs as my only option.

To make a long story short—the next year my mother passed away. The state split my sisters and me up, but I hit the streets heavy. They couldn't find me to put me in foster care. Hell, I was seventeen and I could take care of myself.

For years, I survived by running drugs. But that's not what I wanted to do with my life, so I enrolled in a GED program. You see, I wanted my sisters, and the only way that I was going to be able to get them was to reshape who I had become.

After four years of living my life dealing drugs, I quit because I had saved enough money. My plan was to enroll in a community college, get back into basketball, and get my family under the same roof.

Everything was going as planned; I was in school preparing for the season when the guy that had gotten me started in the drug game stepped to me and told me that he needed me to do him a favor. I was really reluctant, but he told me that he knew where my sisters were. He told me that if I ran a shipment to New York for him, that he would give me all the information that he had on my family.

Call it naïve, but I believed him.

I left his house in a car that he had rented but before

I could get a mile away, I was busted. I been in this place ever since.

Stinky's explanation touched Larry. While they continued dribbling around the court, Larry explained in detail how he ended up behind bars. He and his miniature-sized bunkmate would go on to develop a special kinship and become each other's strongest ally.

It didn't take either of them long before they both felt comfortable enough to talk about anything. They opened every door of their families' closets. Every morning, waiting their opportunity to take a shower, the two would sit on Larry's bunk and talk. It was as if they were long lost relatives trying to catch up on missed years.

There was no doubt in Larry's mind that Ronald missed his sisters dearly. He could tell that his bunkmate blamed himself for the girls being put into foster care. Ronald made it clear that his biggest mistake came when he didn't refuse to make that last dope run.

Larry convinced Stinky that he was just doing what he thought was best for his sisters—and that he shouldn't blame himself.

Stinky was so grateful at Larry's attempts to ease his personal torment that he vowed to do what he could to put a end to the harassment Larry had had to endure since arriving.

"I'm gonna help you as much as I can. First, you need

to join the Military Academy that Small set up. One thing though, it kinda helps…and hurts, at the same time."

"What do you mean?" Larry asked.

"Joining the Academy means that Small will look at you differently…he'll have your back. But, the cons will resent you…they'll come at you every chance they get. You already have something working in your favor."

"What's that?" asked Larry.

"Pappi!"

"Pappi?" Larry questioned.

The End
OF A LEGACY

Jonathan had obviously pushed a button. He could clearly see that the elected official was in an agitated state. He also noticed that the senator was trying his best to maintain some semblance of self-control while glancing over documents that would impact him in a negative way.

Several seconds into his read, the senator angrily tossed the papers to his desk. Total frustration was depicted in his demeanor. Gavin took a deep breath, shook his head slowly in disgust, and then directed his question toward the investigative reporter, "How in the hell did you come to this conclusion?"

"I followed the trails," Jonathan countered. He then gestured toward the pile of paperwork that sat before the senator. "That stuff that I gave you outlines the individuals that I believe were involved. Everything that I have come across points to you being the person who ordered Terrell's murder."

Senator Willington curled his bottom lip. "Your accusations are incomprehensible!" He squinted his eyes; an obvious sign that anger was building. "Sara is behind this."

"No, I'm behind this. Your daughter has nothing to do with my findings."

"Then why are you digging up the past?"

"Because, at the time of his death, no one seemed at all interested in uncovering the truth. Tell me, Senator. Were you in any way involved in the death of Terrell Johnson?"

He could no longer contain his displeasure.

"How dare you!" Gavin stood; he emphatically placed the palms of his hands to the surface of his desk, then leaned forward before saying with malice, "If you continue with these outrageous and unfounded accusations, I'll be forced to come at you with everything I have. It is not in your best interest to print these lies. If you do, I'll make damn sure that your life won't be worth living."

"So, you're threatening me?"

It suddenly dawned on Gavin that issuing threats to someone like Jonathan Edwards was useless. The patriarch of the Willington fortune was mindful that when it came to getting a story, Jonathan would literally rather walk through a brick wall than back down; no matter what the threat to his personal safety. It was known that the journalist had very tough skin, so the senator had to figure out a better way of handling the newspaperman.

First of all, he needed to know how many people Jonathan had shared his findings with, so he asked, "Who have you made privy to this outlandish hogwash?"

"That's not important. What is important is that you

are able to convince me that you had nothing to do with what happened to Terrell Johnson."

The senator's response was reactionary as he blurted, "Who the hell do you think you're talking to, boy! I don't have to prove myself to you." In an effort to get his thoughts under control, Gavin casually began to pace his office.

"Well, good luck explaining yourself to your constituents. Believe me, they'll be the least of your worries."

"So you're telling me..." He walked over to his desk and picked up the documents. "...that you're gonna print these lies?"

"What I'm telling you, senator...is that I am going to expose those responsible for killing a young kid. If you weren't involved...then you have nothing to worry about."

"Your insinuations are enough to bring my administration into question," he insisted.

The senator was shaken; his world was closing in on him. It was painfully clear to him that with Jake and Jonathan both digging into his past, skeletons would be uncovered. This was about more than how the people whom elected him into office would perceive him; this was about the possible collapse of the Willington legacy.

"This is your chance to speak on or off the record. If you don't have anything to say, then I'll go with what I've uncovered thus far."

"I've already spoken with the police about this, so I don't have a problem speaking with you."

The journalist was taken aback. "You spoke with the police concerning Terrell Johnson?" he questioned.

"I spoke with detectives yesterday."

Jonathan couldn't believe what he was hearing. The police gave no indication that a case, which had been closed for over a decade, was of interest to them. In fact, Aaron had shrugged off any such suggestions.

"You mean to tell me that the police have been investigating this case? Who's leading the investigation?"

"Jake Aaron," the senator offered before he stopped pacing and directed his attention toward the newspaperman. "He thinks that that boy's death has something to do with the recent murders in Jacob."

Twenty minutes with Senator Gavin Willington did nothing to sway the journalist's opinion. In fact, Jonathan was certain that the information he had already uncovered was solid; he didn't need the senator to refute or confirm what his findings already conveyed. The reporter was about to blow the lid on a decade long mystery.

But, before he would reveal his information to the public, Jonathan felt that he should seek out and talk with the detective who was spearheading a murder investigation that was most likely connected.

Jonathan's eyes darted around the jam-packed police station as soon as he stepped through the doors that led into headquarters. While making his way through the squad room, the journalist spotted Perry Henderson. Perry held a cup of coffee in his hand as he stood at the desk of a uniformed officer. Jonathan watched as Perry's colleague handed him several manila folders.

Upon seeing the newspaperman making his way through the station, Perry hurriedly scurried into his office and closed the door before drawing his blinds. He was in no mood to speak with the press. Especially Jonathan; he was a little too pushy for Perry's taste. Jonathan had gotten his teeth into a story, and Perry knew that the journalist wasn't about to let it go. Perry felt that Jonathan's efforts would cause more problems than he and his family were prepared to deal with.

Jonathan could not care less that Perry had hightailed it out of sight. He had no interest in speaking with the fleeing officer. He needed Jake, so he briskly walked past Perry's office and headed for the far end of the squad room, where Jake's workspace was located.

For eight straight days, there was a suffocating heat that hung over the prison. The sweltering warmth produced by the sun seemed to tug at the air, literally stripping oxygen from the many shirtless inmates that roamed the yard. The sweaty cons didn't see staying in the barracks as being a way to combat the record-breaking temperatures because the three fans that were allocated to the wooden quarters didn't do anything but move the hot air around.

Most people wore cutoff blue jeans and sleeveless T-shirts. Stinky dribbled a basketball as he and Larry headed toward the court.

There was a group of cons at one end of the asphalt covered basketball court; the inmates were participating in a fierce game of three on three, so Larry and his friend headed toward the opposite end.

"Have you spoken with Pappi yet?" Stinky asked, then fired a shot fifteen feet away from the basket.

"Yeah! I did," replied Larry. He grabbed the ball as it fell from the netting, then immediately fired the sphere back to his partner.

The short con was surprised. "You did!" He shot the ball from the same spot, with the same results. "I thought you didn't want no part of those cadets."

"I don't…but I gotta do what I gotta do," Larry responded as he laid the ball off of the backboard; he then patiently waited for it to free itself from the netting.

Stinky jogged toward Larry. "Have you finally come to grips with the fact that you ain't gettin' out of here until you serve yo' time?" he asked, pushing Larry away from the bouncing ball.

Larry's once upbeat disposition turned to depression.

The young inmate whispered solemnly, "Yeah…I realize that I'm not goin' anywhere. Not since they died.

All of my hopes were tied up in that journalist, and that police detective. They were the only ones fightin' to clear me. Now I have no one. I don't even have my family. Hell, my mother and sister haven't even visited me. It's been months since I heard from them."

Stinky could clearly see that the conversation was altering his friend's attitude. He casually dribbled the ball in front of Larry, who stood under the basket. his mind was clearly not on basketball.

"Hey, man, you gon' be okay?" Ronald *"Stinky"* Cells was concerned.

Larry didn't respond—he was lost in his dilemma.

His bunkmate tapped him on the shoulder. "I know how you feel. I think you oughta talk about it." He began to ramble. "For a long time, all I could think about was doin' good by my sisters…that's what I'm gonna do when I finally get out, do right by them. You should think about what you gon' do when you get out, not about how much time you got."

From behind his bewildered expression, Larry managed to ask, "What is there to talk about?"

"You need to talk about what happened with that journalist, and the detective. What their deaths mean?" Stinky stopped dribbling and stood directly in front of Larry. With all sincerity, he uttered, "They were tryin' to help you when they were killed. You can't keep blamin' yourself? You not gon' be able to deal with that guilt, tryin' to survive in here."

Larry needed to learn how to cope.

Larry snatched the ball from Stinky before asking, "How do you deal? We've talked about a lot of things, but you have a tendency to avoid that particular question by putting it on you playin' basketball for the prison."

"To be perfectly honest, I write," said Stinky. He snatched the ball back from his young friend before throwing it up toward the backboard.

Of all the conversations and secrets they had shared, Ronald never mentioned anything about writing. "You what?" Larry asked with a smirk.

It wasn't that he didn't believe that his friend could write—it was more about Stinky's patience. Larry understood that writing took discipline, and his bunk-mate seemed to only possess that particular trait when it came to basketball.

"I write…I've written a bunch of short stories 'bout my life, 'bout my sisters; and 'bout how I'm gonna make things right for them when I get out of here. I have a little money put away, it's enough for me to self-publish some of my stuff."

"You serious, ain't you?"

"Damn right," Stinky insisted. He picked up the loose ball before turning his undivided attention toward Larry. "I've been writin' for a long time."

"I'd like to read some of your work."

"I've never let anybody read my stuff."

"Why not?"

"I don't know…I guess I didn't want anyone to think

that they knew me." Before he could go into more of an explanation, he noticed that the game on the other end of the court had concluded. Stinky motioned for Larry to follow him.

The two joined several other inmates who were waiting to start a new game. Stinky approached the shirtless con that was trying to select the right combination of talent to take on the winning team.

"Hey, Bubba!" Stinky shouted. He snatched the ball from the six foot seven inch convicted car thief before continuing, "Me and my man here wanna run."

Bubba directed his question toward Larry. "So...what you got, young blood...you got any skills?"

Larry nodded in response to the lanky inmate's query.

Stinky ignored both of them; he shot the ball from twenty-three feet away from the basket. It went through the hoop and barely touched the bottom of the worn nylon. Larry was totally impressed with his friend's skills. He thought to himself that his bunkmate was really good—basketball was definitely his forte.

The tall, gangling inmate in the cutoff slacks tapped Larry on the shoulder in an effort to regain his attention. "You play well?"

"I'm okay. I can hold my own," Larry insisted.

Bubba shouted to Stinky, "Come on, Ron...you and the *Lunch Man* can run with me."

Stinky dribbled the ball over to Larry and Bubba. "We gon' run against those clowns that just won?"

"Yeah," Bubba replied.

Larry was taken by surprise when he turned and saw Wesley Hobbs and Leroy Burns approaching from the rear. Three other cons accompanied the men that threatened to make Larry's life behind bars as miserable as they could. He clearly remembered what he had said about Burns' freakiest behavior upon their arrival several months before.

"What's wrong with you?" Stinky asked.

Larry managed to mumble, "Two of those guys." He gave a head gesture in the direction of Hobbs and Burns, before continuing, "They got it in for me."

"Which two?" Stinky peered in the direction of the five men.

"The two without shirts."

"You talkin' 'bout Hobbs and Burns?"

"Yeah...you know them?"

"At one time both worked for Mop dealing drugs inside the big house."

Larry's next statement was laced with a nervous energy. "I thought that the inmates assigned to the big house weren't allowed to come over here."

Stinky placed a calming hand on his partner's shoulder, before saying,

"They've been reassigned to our barracks. Don't worry; I'll keep them away from you."

"How do you think that you're gonna be able to manage that?"

Larry was aware that Ronald Cells had clout. His value

to the prison basketball team afforded him certain privileges. But Larry wasn't sure how that would benefit him.

An argument erupted between Bubba and another inmate, the dispute was over who really had the next game. While they exchanged verbal insults, Larry and Stinky seemed to be the only cons that noticed Hobbs and Burns heading toward them, three others inmates accompanied the pair.

Hobbs intentionally walked as close to Larry as he could and elbowed him as he passed.

"What yo' bitch ass doin' on the asphalt?" Hobbs growled as he threw an elbow to Larry's neck.

"Fuck!" Larry screamed. He grabbed at the spot where he was struck. It hurt like hell. Stinky, without thinking, threw and walloped Hobbs in the head with the ball.

Infused with anger, Hobbs and his boys simultaneously directed their attention toward the pint-sized inmate who had taken it upon himself to stand up for young Larry Henderson.

Stinky instantly realized that he was headed for a beat-down. Instead of waiting for the fight to come to him, he ducked his head and ran toward Hobbs readying to make a tackle.

The brutish criminal pounded on Larry's bunkmate with a destructive forearm to the back of his head; instantly knocking Stinky face down to the ground.

Larry immediately ran over to assist Stinky. He knelt beside his wounded friend. "Are you okay?" he asked.

Stinky moaned, before he managed to whisper, "Yeah…"

Larry stood; he then aimed his rage toward Hobbs. "That's where you made yo' mistake! I'm gon' beat the shit out of you!"

Hobbs laughed, and then barked, "You comin' at me, fool?" He headed toward Larry; his approach menacing. But, before he could say or do anything, he heard the voice of authority.

"Step yo' asses off!"

Everyone on the court froze. All eyes turned in the direction of the raspy order. The power and strength behind the command meant one thing; Mop was coming. The most feared prisoner at the facility led twelve of the roughest individuals known to walk the grounds toward the pending altercation.

Larry and Stinky's tormentor attempted to ignore the big *Dawgs* approach—they turned their attention to Bubba.

"Me and my crew wanna run…anybody that wanna run a game for cash, step yo' ass right up and let's do this!" Hobbs yelled.

Upon hearing the challenge, the inmate that was arguing with Bubba immediately reneged; he wanted no part of any game that included the inmates standing at center court.

Hobbs walked up to the bald, dark-skinned inmate and said, "Bubba…you gon' run against me and my boys?"

While Larry helped Stinky to his feet, Burns and Hobbs stood in the middle of the court and watched as Mop led his entourage to the bleachers.

Bubba walked over to Larry. "Fish…can you really play?" he asked.

"Yeah…but I ain't got no money."

"Don't worry 'bout it…I'll cover that." He looked over to Stinky and asked, "You still wanna run?

"Hell yeah!" was the injured con's reply. Stinky moved his head from side to side in an effort to loosen the stiffness that Hobbs' blow had caused. "Let's do this," he said with excitement.

Larry was extremely concerned about playing a game against Hobbs' group. They were much bigger and stronger than he and Stinky. Plus, they would be playing with a grudge. The new inmate glanced at his bunkmate. Ron didn't seem at all concerned about the overall size difference.

Bubba picked up two other cons who appeared to be skilled and they both stood about six-feet, five inches.

Stinky could see the concern in Larry's eyes. "Listen, Fish…the fastest way to gain respect from these clowns is to *whup* their asses on the asphalt."

Larry could hear what his friend was saying, but his thoughts were on why it seemed like everyone had dropped what they were doing. He made a very slow turn, witnessing a mass of humanity moving with a sense of urgency. Inmates had begun to gather around the court.

It was if they were filing into Madison Square Garden to watch a matinee game featuring the New York Knicks and the Los Angeles Lakers.

The young inmate's eyes finally locked in on Pappi; he watched as the old con strolled over to the bleachers. A horde of inmates followed the senior statesman.

Some of those that had assembled were preparing to place bets. A few walked the baseline while waiting to see Stinky take on yet another challenge.

Bubba, in an effort to regain Larry's attention, said, "I want you to guard that guy…" He pointed to a con that stood several inches taller than Larry's five-foot-ten frame. The inmate was at least sixty-eight pounds heavier than Larry's one hundred and sixty-five pounds.

"You sure?" Larry questioned, a bit intimidated.

"Believe me, you're faster. We'll play a lot of help defense."

When Larry saw Pappi smile at him from the top seat in the bleachers, he was a bit motivated. He and his supervisor had developed a great relationship, and the young convicted criminal was always looking for a way to impress the old con. His once nonchalant demeanor was uplifted when he realized that Pappi would be watching.

Larry was astute enough to realize that psychologically his desires to impress Pappi stemmed from his inability to develop a decent relationship with his own father. Nevertheless, the man that had taken him under his wing was the closest thing that he had to a father figure.

Bubba reminded Larry what to look out for when playing against Hobbs and his crew. "They're good at controlling the boards and dunking. The only one that can shoot from anywhere outside of five feet is the guy you're going to be guarding. You down?"

"I guess…"

"I'ma tell you somethin'."

"What?"

"They gon' knock you on yo' ass…especially if you got game."

He struggled to lift his eyelids; his vision was blurred.

The lighting above was plentiful but did absolutely nothing to help his focus. He had no clue where he was. Hell, at that time, he hadn't the foggiest idea who he was.

Although he was dazed and confused, he did recognize that someone was touching his face. Whoever it was, was trying to assist him in keeping his right eye open. Without warning, a sharp beam of light, which was aimed directly at his eyeball, annoyed him. His first reaction was to turn his face away because the concentrated beam ignited a throbbing pain in his head.

"Take it easy…I have to check," a voice whispered.

He fought to focus, but was unable to do so.

A hand was placed on his chin, his head was pulled back, and once again his eyelid was forced open. The sharp light was aimed at his right eyeball for several seconds before being directed toward his left.

"How are you feeling?" he was asked.

He moaned before saying, "My head hurts really bad." He moaned a second time, and then asked, "What happened?"

"I think you suffered a concussion," the person standing over him said as he continued to use the light in an effort to verify his diagnosis.

"Do you know where you are?"

He blinked several times and his focus was slowly returning as his eyes darted around. Based on the eggshell white walls, the silver pushcarts, the twelve beds (three occupied), and the intravenous drip that led to his arm, he took a stab at his location.

"I guess I'm in the infirmary..." he hesitated, and then continued as if he weren't sure, "I think."

"What's your name?" Doctor Freeman asked, flicking the light at his patient's eyes.

"Larry...Larry Henderson."

"Do you remember what happened?"

"No..."

The doctor that had examined him upon his arrival at the prison put his ear tips in their proper place, then placed the cold stethoscope to Larry's chest. "You feel pain anywhere else?" he asked, checking Larry's heart rate.

Still a bit confused, Larry barely managed, "No...not really."

"That's good. By the way, you have two people waiting to see you." Freeman completed his examination. He signaled to a nurse, who was heading out the door. "Nancy, please show the gentlemen in."

Larry closed his eyes. He was determined to search through the cobwebs and fog of his mind in an attempt to remember what had led to his being in the infirmary.

"Hey, man, how you feelin'?"

Larry was barely able to open his eyes, but he recognized the voice. Stinky eased down on the bed next to him. When Larry attempted to scoot over to give his friend more room, a pain shot through his head with the intensity of two freight trains colliding.

His head hurt so bad that he hadn't noticed Pappi was also at his bedside.

Stinky examined the nasty welt under Larry's right eye. "Man, this was my fault," he said with sincerity. "I'm sorry."

"What are you talkin' 'bout...how was this yo' fault?" Larry managed.

"You don't remember?"

While holding his head and with his eyes closed, Larry said, "The last thing I remember was that we were one point away from winning. I had takin' the ball out. I threw it in to you, and you drove the lane."

Stinky filled in the blanks. "Hobbs elbowed me in the stomach as I elevated for my shot...he hit me so hard that I flipped over and landed on my back. I thought I had cracked my spine. Anyway, when you saw what happened, you rushed Hobbs. I gotta say, you spaced out, you was callin' him Daddy. You got in a couple shots, but his boys *whooped* yo' ass. The bruise under yo' eye, that came from Hobbs kneein' you." He touched Larry's face before saying, "That's what knocked you out."

"Did we win?" Larry questioned.

With pride, Stinky responded, "Hell yeah!"

"Bring Yo' Lunch! I'm havin' you transferred over to Camp 12," Pappi said.

Larry whispered in astonishment, "Pappi...I didn't even know you was here." He turned his head in the direction of his supervisor's voice, then tried to open his eyes, but immediately gave up on the idea when he was once again hit with a tremendous pain. In between moans of agony, he said, "You can have me transferred?"

"Of course..."

"What about Ron?"

Stinky chimed in, "I'm not interested in transferring..."

"Why?" Larry asked.

"Because he has a warped sense of loyalty to Mop," Pappi went on to say, "Ron could have transferred a long time ago."

The BODY

She was worn out upon entering the house.

As if all desire to live had been drained from her body, Margaret nonchalantly dropped her car keys on the coffee table before she half-heartedly strolled through the living room and toward her picture window. The weary mother folded her arms and, with a sigh, peered out into her front yard.

For a brief second she was enthralled with two squirrels as they tangled and taunted each other. She watched the two carefree furry creatures as intently as she would have her own children when they chased one another across her well-kept lawn. The thought of seeing Larry running after Valeria caused the corners of her mouth to turn up; her mind wandered.

She needed help; Larry's mother had nowhere else to turn since the deaths of her two strongest allies. No one was even willing to consider the possibility that her son had the slightest chance of being exonerated. Her last shred of optimism was laid to rest with Harlan's negative response after she pleaded for his help.

Margaret's thoughts drifted to Harlan Coyle's green, sympathetic eyes.

Harlan was very familiar with Larry Henderson's plight; he'd been following his situation from day one. His interest stemmed from his seventeen-year-old son's relationship with Margaret's youngest boy; the two were high school classmates.

The managing partner of Coyle, Fitzgerald, and Bernstein was no stranger to the chaos created by the man whom Larry was accused of murdering. Harlan grew up with Miran and was very much aware of the rumors that circulated about the racist's involvement in several unsolved lynchings.

Although she could feel his compassion, it hurt her to hear him say, "As much as I would like to help you, there's nothing I can do. Your son confessed. He agreed to a plea, and he had his father present when that plea was accepted."

"But, he was tricked into signing the agreement," she remembered saying. "My husband didn't have my son's best interest in mind when that agreement was made."

"What do you mean?" the attorney asked.

Margaret recalled Harlan sitting at his desk while he attentively listened to her reveal her husband's unhealthy hatred toward their son. She went on to tell him the reason she felt that Perry set her child up for Miran's murder.

She thought about how embarrassed she was after she

said, "The only reason he hates that boy so much is because Larry is the only person in the entire county that wouldn't back down from him. You see, my husband beats me…and my son lived much of his young life trying to run interference. I'm supposed to protect him, but he was always trying to protect me. No one else ever attempted to stop my husband, because everyone knows how vindictive he is."

The forty-seven-year-old attorney felt for Margaret, he really did, but the truth was, nothing that she shared with him could help her son out of his predicament. As much as Harlan sympathized with her, he found her story to be a little farfetched. If he were to present her accusations to any judge, he would be laughed out of court.

After being in his office for more than an hour trying to convince him that her son would never take a life, and that her husband was behind everything surrounding Larry's incarceration, she finally got the hint. She didn't have enough to pursue any legal actions. Perry had once again gotten what he wanted.

She pictured the well-dressed attorney extending a hand to her while saying, "I am truly sorry, ma'am…but we don't have enough to work with."

Her last words to Harlan were of a desperate nature. "What am I gonna do?"

Much of her day was spent searching for someone that could help. Unfortunately, her mission turned out to be futile. She was unable to find anyone that was the least bit interested in getting involved. Like Harlan, the other legal minds that she had visited saw Larry's state of affairs as being next to impossible to rectify.

Margaret's eyes veered to her right; she watched as the two squirrels scurried up the old giant oak that took root in her yard. Out of the corner of her eye, she saw something that caught her attention. Her eyes swayed from the playful rodents and toward the three-foot-high hedges that separated her lawn from the sidewalk. Margaret watched as her husband's squad car pulled to the curb and stopped. She hadn't left enough room in the driveway for him to pull in because she wasn't expecting him to be home before she had a chance to pick up the kids from school.

It was time for her to change into her crossing guard uniform, so she headed up the stairs before her husband could step from his vehicle.

Perry didn't put his hat on until he stood in the street. As he closed his door, he acknowledged his elderly next-door neighbor and her girlfriend as the two headed up the sidewalk.

"Hello, Ms. Wilcox," he said. He touched his right index finger to the bill of his hat, while acknowledging his neighbor's friend, "Ma'am…"

"How you doin', Perry?" Ms. Wilcox replied.

"That's one sharp lookin' man," whispered Ethel Wilcox's sixty-nine-year-old friend. Perry's blue and gray uniform fit him like that of a military guard positioned in front of the White House. She slyly smiled, then waved at Perry like she was flirting.

"You young ladies enjoy this beautiful day," Perry said as he made his way toward his front door.

"Where are you?" he yelled upon entering the house.

Her voice echoed through the hall and down the stairs. "I'm upstairs!"

Margaret had already removed her blue jeans and pink silk blouse, so she was in her bra and panties readying to slip into her crossing guard uniform (which lay neatly across her bed), when her husband walked into the bedroom.

Their queen-sized bed separated the two.

"What you been doin' all day? I tried callin' you earlier."

"I had a little runnin' 'round to do," she replied, walking over to her dresser. She removed a black slip from her top drawer. "Take your hat off in the house; you know that's bad luck." She mumbled under her breath, "Lord knows we can use all the luck we can get."

Perry took off his hat, tossed it on the bed, and then walked over and positioned himself in front of his wife. "Have you been tryin' to help Larry?"

With slip in hand, she attempted to pass him, but he refused to move out of her way. "Answer my question, woman!" The tone of his voice made her nervous but she was determined to stand strong. She wasn't going to let him intimidate her.

"Yes," she said. Margaret gave up trying to move past him; she put on her slip from where she stood.

He spoke to her like one of his children. "I told you to leave it alone!"

"I'm not about to leave it alone...that's my son."

He grabbed her firmly by her arms. "I told yo' ass... everybody that has tried to get involved with this has been hurt. We got other children to think about," Perry barked with all seriousness.

"Get your hands off of me!" she shouted, snatching from his grip.

Out of the blue, he slapped her across her face with an open hand. The force of his blow caused her to stagger. She screamed in agony as she stumbled backward; the dressers prevented her from falling to the floor. Margaret used her hands to cover her throbbing face.

Perry's stunned wife dropped her hands to her side as her husband moved toward her like a prizefighter determined to end the fight with a knockout.

Something about her made him stop in his tracks. He stood frozen for several seconds; he couldn't quite put his finger on it. It wasn't until he saw her ball her fist that he realized the fear was missing. Margaret's eyes were not weighed down with trepidation. He could see, at that moment, his wife was ready to go toe-to-toe with him.

The physically and mentally abused woman was fed up. Margaret had undoubtedly reached her boiling point. She took a deep breath. With power behind her quiver,

she insisted, "If you ever put your hands on me again…
expect not to wake up the next morning."

When Detective Simon Harris' car pulled off Junction
Three and onto Lee Thompson's property, he immediately noticed, directly in front of him, three uniformed
officers standing between two patrol cars.

Scattered about the one and a half acres of neglected
property were junk heaps that the man had never bothered to repair or move. With the patches of weeds and
grass that surrounded the scrap metal, it was obvious
that the wrecks had been sitting in front of the trailer
for years.

Simon Harris pulled behind one of the marked vehicles
and cut his engine.

Three hounds drew the detective's attention as he
stepped from his vehicle. The dogs were chained to a tree
some forty yards to the left of the trailer. He watched as
they barked and jumped wildly.

The officers that were on site had reported to dispatch
that there was no need for an investigation, so they were
a bit surprised that the veteran cop bothered to make
the drive from town.

Officer Nolan was the first to speak to the approaching, no-nonsense lawman. He shrugged his shoulders in
dejection, "Detective, sorry about your partner."

"I appreciate that…" His reply was heartfelt. "What's goin' on here?"

Nolan offered, "It's not a homicide; it's suicide. We're just waiting on the coroner."

Harris stepped in front of the young officer. "I was unaware that you had been promoted to detective," he said sarcastically. As he headed toward the trailer, the cynical prick blurted over the out of control dogs, "I hope no one touched that body!"

Another officer said, "Those dogs looks like they're fixin' to rip Harris a new asshole."

"I wish they would; I can't stand his ass."

A small porthole-type window over the cluttered kitchen sink allowed a ray of sunlight to ease into an otherwise dark trailer house. The other windows around the 1962 Royal Mansion Spartan trailer were covered with black paint. Lee covered his other windows as a way of blocking out direct sunlight. He felt that men with curtains were feminine.

Simon stood at the front door and allowed his eyes to adjust.

The inside of the trailer was littered with filth; to the immediate right of the detective was a pile of dirty clothes. To his left, garbage, beer cans, and an assortment of other trash.

The stench of urine, animal feces, rodents and stale funk was over shadowed by a rank, abrasive, and much more unpleasant smell—that of death.

Simon once again glared to his right, at which time he saw a rat rummaging through trash down the musty hallway.

A uniformed officer exiting a room with a handkerchief to his face (an obvious attempt to shield his nose from the aroma) drew Simon's attention away from the feasting rodent.

The detective had to step over several hefty bags that were filled with pizza boxes, whiskey bottles and old newspapers in order to make it to the room the officer had just left.

As Simon stood at the entrance of yet another debris filled room, he allowed his eyes to soak up everything.

The smell was getting to him, so he reached into the inside pocket of his blazer and removed a handkerchief. He immediately placed the cloth to his face. The cranky law enforcement professional shook his head in disbelief. It was a gruesome sight. No matter how evil he was known to be, Lee's lifeless, decomposing body dangling from a support beam in his bedroom was not a welcome site.

Lee's room looked tossed purposely; the contents of his dresser drawers had been dumped, everything in his closet was scattered about. His mattress had been flipped over.

Underneath Lee's dangling body laid a wooden chair; it appeared that the victim had used it to assist him in hanging himself. Harris examined the chair's position in relationship to that of the body.

Before he began to scrutinize the corpse, Harris noticed the other officers (all holding handkerchiefs to their noses) stood at the entrance watching his every move.

Five Years
LATER

Two five-year-old girls chased one another around the fifteen stations that made up the visiting area. They wove around, and then crawled under, the fifteen silver, four-legged round aluminum tables that were scattered about.

The children playfully twisted and squirmed their way between the legs of those that were seated.

The tykes' giggles were infectious.

Most of the individuals in the visiting room were tickled by the activity of the children that played around them. Several of the adults couldn't seem to take their eyes off of the kids, so they split their attention between the cute pigtailed girls and the person seated before them.

Some of the inmates allowed their minds to mentally transport them back to their childhood; allowing periodic cerebral voyages was the only way that they could escape their mundane existence.

The two Black children, on their knees, swiftly crawled from under one table and over to where Larry and his mother sat. Both stopped and peered up like two puppies attempting to get permission to continue their adventure.

Larry's smile was the children's green light—they made their way under his table.

"How are you holdin' up?" Margaret's question drew Larry's attention away from the kids.

"Mom, you haven't bothered to visit me in five years and now you're interested in how I'm doin'?" There was disdain in his tone. "That's a joke!"

Margaret expected her son to be contemptuous, but she had hoped that he would understand why she had stayed away.

"Baby, everyone that tried to help me help you has died. After that reporter and Jake Aaron were killed, your father made me realize that we have other children to think about. I wanted to visit you, but I couldn't take that chance." She pleaded with her eyes before saying, "Baby, I know that I had stopped writing at one time, but I had to wait until things died down. Do you think that you'll ever be able to forgive me?"

Larry buried his face in his hands. He wanted so badly to be mad at his mother. He felt that there was no excuse for her not keeping track of him.

How dare she not go out of her way to see about me? After all, I stepped up for her every time she needed me, he thought to himself.

Margaret could feel her son's disappointment. She knew that she had let her little boy down. Thing was, he wasn't so little anymore. Larry had put on a few pounds over the five years that he had been incarcerated. Her boy had grown up. When she looked at him, she saw her husband. Larry was the spitting image of his father at age twenty-three.

"Baby, keep your faith in God. He'll see you through."

"I don't wanna hear nothin' about yo' God," he said in anger.

Margaret was shocked by her son's blasphemy. "What's gotten into you? You've never spoken like that. You've never spoken against God."

"What the hell has God done for me? If there was a God, as much as you praised Him, then why did He let you get yo' ass beat all the time?"

Margaret couldn't hide her disappointment in her son. "Don't you dare blame God for what happened to me, or for your situation. If He hasn't seen fit to get you out of here, then He must have His reasons."

"Momma, you can take that shit somewhere else. I don't wanna hear nothin' about God, Jesus, or no damn body else that has anything to do with faith. You see, I ain't got no damn faith in nothin'. I ain't got no faith in you, or in God. If you plan on comin' here tryin' to convince me of your beliefs, then you might as well not come."

Margaret placed both of her hands to her mouth. She was emotionally traumatized. Her son was very bitter and, as much as she understood why he had such acrimony, she wouldn't condone his attitude.

"I understand how you must feel, but to dismiss your

faith, to dismiss the way in which you were raised, you can't let the devil trick you, baby." Her muffled whispers resonated from behind her cuffed hands.

"Fuck that; you have no idea what I've gone through. And, you can't make me believe that, if there were a God…that He would allow me to be locked up for the better part of my life for somethin' that I didn't do."

Larry's mother abruptly got to her feet. "Boy, I don't care what you've gone through since you've been here; no child of mind will speak that way."

"Momma, in case you haven't noticed, I ain't no child no mo'. I ain't been no child for a long time. You allowed your husband to take that away from me the first time you didn't stand up for yourself."

Before the two could continue with their conversation, a female guard walked over to their table. She directed her question to Margaret, "Excuse me, ma'am…are you okay?"

"Yeah…she fine," Larry interrupted. "I'm ready to go."

At that moment, Margaret knew that it would be a long time before she saw her son again. Larry was different. His spirit had been beaten down. With that, he obviously had lost all respect for her, and he no longer had belief in God.

Margaret was treading in new territory. Of all her children, she never thought that she would lose her baby boy. As she watched him being escorted from the visiting room, a tear eased from her weary eyes.

❦

She stood five foot six inches, her butterscotch complexion was flawless, and her medium-size Afro, neat—every curve on her firm body was accentuated by the tailored, state issued uniform she wore. She physically worked out; there was no doubt about it.

As she escorted Larry down the hall that led toward the door to the yard, she could see the young con trying to catch a glimpse of her every chance he got.

Just before she was readying herself to open the door, Larry began making small talk. "I've never seen you before." He peeked at her nametag. "What's your first name, CO Taylor?"

"Inmate, you've been here long enough to know that you don't speak to me unless I speak to you." She pushed the door open. The afternoon sunlight overwhelmed the doorway. Before Larry could head out into the mid-summer afternoon, the guard reached into her shirt pocket and pulled from it an envelope. "This is for you." She handed it to the disgruntled convict.

"What's this?" he asked, closely examining the un-sealed envelope.

Of all of my children, I envisioned you as being the most successful. My foresight wasn't because you were smart, or because you were brave—it was because of your heart. You have always had a heart of gold. Ever since you were old enough to understand what kindness was, you have exemplified benevolence.

My dear son, I owe you and your siblings an apology. I realize that I didn't handle my duties as a mother the right way when it came to my willingness to sacrifice myself for my children. In other words, there was absolutely no way in the world that I should have subjected my children to the abuse and ridicule that was your father. For years, I made excuses on why it was important that I did nothing to upset a man who had issues that he himself needed to work through. Your father was once the best person that I had ever met—his willingness to extend himself for any and everyone, in their time of need, is why I fell in love with him.

At one time, your father was the bravest man in all of Morris County. What he did by joining the force in the midst of the bigotry and hatred that surrounded our community was an act of courage that no one in the county will ever forget. Larry, that's the man that I want you to remember, to be proud of.

I'm not writing this letter to you to ask for forgiveness for me. I'm asking you to search in your heart for a way to find forgiveness for your father. I wanted you to know that, for the last few years, he hasn't lifted a finger in anger toward me.

I want you to know that ever since Jonathan and Jake Aaron passed away, your father has been trying, as quietly as possible, to search for the evidence necessary to prove your innocence. Everyone in church refers to your situation as "Caged Innocence," and believe you me, they are all looking to support you any way they can.

Larry wasn't at all impressed with the letter that his mother had left with the new guard. As he sat on his bed reading, he felt nothing but anger. The letter went on to give details of the family and the births of his new nieces and nephews. Hearing about the new generation was the best part of the letter. He could care less about his father being promoted to captain, or his mother taking over as choir director for her church. The two people whose job it was to protect him didn't live up to their duties as parents, so he had no interest in their lives.

Larry folded up the letter, stuck it back into its envelope, and then lay on his bed. He stared at the bottom of the top bunk for several seconds before closing his eyes. His mind was cluttered. For five years his family had acted as if he were dead to them. Now, based on the letter that he had lying next to him, they all claimed that he was missed.

For five years he fought to keep his spirit, he fought to understand God's reason for putting him in a situation where he had to fight for his right to a peaceful existence. Nothing made sense to him, so he gave up that fight and turned his attention to survival. Larry was determined to do whatever it took to stay alive.

"Hey, Lunch Man," a tired, grieving voice whispered. "What's this I hear 'bout you stormin' out of the visitin' room? You been waitin' for that visit for years."

Larry could feel his bed move; an indication that his old friend had sat next to him.

"I don't wanna talk about it…" was Larry's annoyed reply.

"Listen, boy, I've gone out of my way to help you… but it's time that you start helping yourself. I tried my best to put you in the greatest possible position to do yo' time. I did for you what I had never done for anyone." He glanced at Larry before saying, "Open yo' damn eyes and look at me when I'm talkin' to you."

When he caught the look in Pappi's eyes, Larry immediately sat up, and then asked, "How did you hear about my visit? I ain't too long ago left the visitin' room…"

"You been here long enough to know that I got eyes everywhere." Pappi quickly got back to his point. "Looky here, young blood…you gotta stop feelin' sorry for yourself. People have made the ultimate sacrifice for you. Not many folk can say that someone died tryin' to help them. Okay, things didn't work out…but don't you, for one second, believe that you're the only innocent con behind these bars." He lowered his voice when he asked, "Is it true that you told the woman that gave birth to you that you didn't have faith in her, or in her faith?"

"Pappi, what has God ever done for folk like you and me?"

"Don't you ever include me in your blasphemy. God has always been good to me. My Lord didn't make me murder that man."

"But, He didn't protect your family."

"That was my job. I knew that workin' for the red-neck that murdered my family was not a good decision when I took the job. I had heard 'bout the things he did to others that went to work for him. It was my greed that made me take that job. He offered three times what everyone else was payin' for the same work. He couldn't get folks to work for him because they all knew that he was a sick bastard. So, you see, I put my family in that position."

"But what did I do? I didn't do nothin'!"

"Boy, it ain't 'bout what you did; it's' bout what you gon' do."

Larry was confused. "What?"

"Look here, son, sometimes people ask *'why them?'*. They look at a situation the wrong way, then blame God for puttin' them in that situation. When all along it was them that put themselves there, like me. Then there's people like you. You not supposed'ta think 'bout bein' wronged; you supposed to prepare yo' self for why you was wronged. God figured that no one else on this planet would be able to deal with yo' situation better than you. And He was right; He's always right. So when you get out, just do what He tells you."

"What is He gon' tell me?"

"Who knows? It's up to you to listen." Pappi got to his feet before he would continue, "First, I want you to take the cadets seriously…I don't know if I'm gonna be able to give Small any more excuses for you. You promised him that you would sign up to take your GED as a condition for you bein' in this barrack…you haven't done that. But first, you gon' have to find a way to get God back into yo' life. You a good kid, bad things have happened to you…don't live the rest of yo' life usin' those bad things as excuses. Society can lock you up, but, when you get yo' spirit back, don't you ever let them take it again. You got five years before you go up for parole. Havin' yo' education, the cadets…and any other thing that you can do to enhance your chance of gettin' out of here, is gonna be yo' number one priority from this point on," said the seventy-three-year-old lifer.

Larry listened, but he wasn't ready to hear what his mentor was saying. At that time, his anger defied words, no matter how profound. He knew what Pappi had said was true. He just didn't care.

He also realized that if it hadn't been for Pappi sticking up for him, he would have surely been kicked out of the cadets and transferred back to Camp 29.

Lord knows he didn't want to go back to Camp 29—Wesley Hobbs and Leroy Burns were waiting on him to screw up. After five years, those two still wanted to beat his ass, but as long as Larry was in the cadets, he was untouchable. But he couldn't get past the anger that he felt toward his family, and nothing that Pappi could say at that time was going to change that.

Margaret Henderson's baby boy watched as Pappi slowly walked the aisle leading toward the exit. The way the old man moved indicated that his arthritic knees were bothering him. Years of crawling around on his hands and knees had taken a toll on his entire body. Smoking three packs a day also contributed to his declining health.

Larry had no idea that when Pappi walked through the doors of Camp 12 that day, he would never see the old con again.

Elden *"Pappi"* Howard suffered a massive heart attack while heading toward the prison chapel. Larry was told that the old man's last words were, "I gotta put in a prayer for the *Lunch Man*. I gotta ask God to forgive him."

His inexpensive suit was blue, it didn't quite fit his thin frame, almost a size larger than he would have liked, but it did give him a confidence that normally eluded him. He appeared refined, his hair neatly trimmed. For the first time in years he didn't attempt to flip four or five strands of hair from the left side of his head in an effort to camouflage the bald spot atop his cranium.

In his normal attire, which consisted of blue jeans or corduroys, his bowlegs were pronounced. He was a cowboy through and through. But wearing a suit for the first time made him stand tall. He was proud. While he wasn't *GQ* magazine qualified, he could have made the cover of *Redneck Least Likely to Refine*, if for nothing else but the shock value, because he had never, ever, attempted to gussy up.

At that moment he understood why Miran was stuck

on himself. Why his brother's entire demeanor changed once he went to work for the senator some thirteen years prior. Wearing a suit altered his attitude, although his wasn't tailored like his brother's were.

Willington's maid escorted him across the marble floors of the palatial estate and toward the Senator's study. Lee had never stepped foot inside the mansion because the Willington estate was his brother's domain. Miran was the liaison between the White Knights and the government official, and he never allowed any of them access to Gavin.

"Make yourself comfortable, sir...the senator will be right with you."

Sir! No one had ever treated him with such respect. Gavin's maid stepped aside and allowed Lee Thompson access to the study. Miran's little brother couldn't seem to take his eyes off of the elderly woman as he passed her. She had made him feel like a member of the upper class.

Once the good ole boy entered the senator's sanctuary, the maid closed the double doors behind him. The red wood panels, bookshelves, antique furniture and the way that the sunlight eased in through the stained win-dowpanes made one feel as if they were walking into an old English library.

Lee was totally fascinated with how the wealthy lived—as his eyes soaked in the allure, his delight sud-denly turned to anger. He was upset that his brother didn't allow him to behold the splendor of good living.

Miran didn't think that he was smart enough to do anything; and Lee knew that his brother was embarrassed by him.

The fiery redneck was so engrossed with the antique trinkets that were scattered about that he didn't notice the door ease open. Gavin quietly made his way over to Lee. The senator's guest held a Maritime antique telescope, which bore an engraving that suggested the eyepiece was from the 1800's.

"That's been in the family for years…" Gavin's comment startled his guest.

Lee fumbled with the telescope. "Oh, I'm sorry…" he said, trying to put it in its proper place.

"That's okay," the senator countered. Gavin walked over to his desk and made himself comfortable.

"What's so important that you had to see me? Yo phone call sounded urgent?" Lee asked. The redneck made his way over to a black leather chair that was positioned in front of his boss.

"We need to talk about the evidence that you have," said Gavin. "I need to know why you feel it necessary to have evidence that would implicate me. I told you that the job is yours. You get all the perks that your brother got."

"It ain't 'bout the perks…not even the job."

"Then what is it?"

"You done had everybody that was involved in that Johnson boy's lynchin' murdered to protect yo' family's name. Miran told me that you was gon' make sho' that nothin' would point back to you. Nah, I know that all ya'll think that I'm stupid, but I ain't. I wanna make sho' you don't have somebody come after me."

"Nobody thinks you're stupid, least of all me. That's why I gave you your brother's job. I always admired the way you handle yourself. I had you get rid of your brother because he was a liability, like the rest of those weak son-of-a-bitches. But you and me, we on the same page."

"I didn't want you to think that you was gon' be able to get rid of me. I got me some, what they call, insurance. And I don't care how many private investigators or detectives that you have, ain't nobody gon find it unless somethin' happens to me."

"Lee, I don't want what you have to fall into the wrong hands."

"As long as nothin' don't happen to me, it won't. Nah, if I happen to get struck by lightnin', or hit by a car, then you got worries."

"So I guess that I had better make sure you live the life of luxury, huh?"

"You got that right."

"I'm very impressed with your work, Lee. The way you rigged that reporter's car to blow…and then making sure that Jake Aaron was with him…you got two birds with one stone."

"I had help with that one, and we didn't make no

mistakes, not like when I tried to frame Henderson for killin' my stepbrother."

"Tell me...how did you do that again?" The senator attempted to sound interested.

Lee THOMPSON

I went to that nigga's house that Sunday mornin'. I knew that they went to church early, and stayed most of the day; sometimes into the night. I'd been keepin' an eye on Henderson for a quite a spell. I hate that son-of-a-bitch! Anyways, I breaks into the house through the back do'. I was gon' search for somethin', anythin' that would let me know how much he knew.

That wife of his sho' kept that house neat.

I walked through the kitchen and made my way down the hall. Just outside the kitchen, to the right, was a door that led to a bedroom. I looked in. It was a lot of sewin' stuff on the bed. There was a sewin' machine set up in the middle of the floor. I figured that there was nothin' in there that would tell me what Henderson was up to, so I continued down the hall and toward the living room. I figured that if I was gonna find anythin', I would have to go to his bedroom.

Once I made it to the staircase I knew I had to be careful. The curtains to the livin' room window was left open. I could see people movin' around out front. The hedges in front of the house was only 'bout three feet high. Seeing people made me realize that if I could see them, then if they looked in, they would be able to see me headin' up the stairs.

I had to wait in the hall for a couple minutes because two old women was standin' on the sidewalk in front of their house—they was jawin' for a long time. I decided that as soon as they turned their attention toward the street, I would run up the stairs.

I damn near broke my neck tryin' to dart up them there steps.

All the doors was closed. I stopped in the hallway tryin' to figure out what door led to his room. I wasted several seconds before decidin' to open the first door on my right...it was a bathroom.

I ended up opening three doors before I discovered his room.

If I .didn't know better I would've thought that Henderson was soft. That room looked so girly. Seemed like a hundred pillows was on the bed; perfume bottles all over the dresser. I didn't see nothin' that looked like a man slept in that room. If I hadn't seen one of the shirts to his uniform draped over the vanity chair, I would have mistaken that room for his daughter's.

Anyways, I searched under the bed, under the mattress, and in the dresser drawers, and I didn't find nothin'. That's when I went into the closet.

When I looked up, I saw a shoebox. I pulled it off the shelf; then opened it. In the box I found several folded pieces of paper, and a handgun. I walked over to his bed and set the box on it. Then I pulled out the papers and began to read what turned out to be comments.

His notes indicated that he felt he was gettin' closer to provin' Miran murdered his nephew, on yo' orders, and that Aaron and Miran lynched that Jackson boy when we was in high school. His notes said that Miran was weakening under his pressure; that Miran was drinkin' a lot, and runnin' his mouth to people.

That's when I got the idea that I would take Henderson's gun and put a bullet in Miran's good for nothin' head. I don't know what happened to that boy. From the day that we formulated our plan to tie up loose ends, he'd been actin' funny. He didn't wanna kill the boys that were involved in lynchin' Henderson's nephew. He told me that that would be a mistake. That you were wrong for even askin' us to do it. Miran said that if we killed them boys, it wouldn't be long before you got rid of us. My brother insisted that yo' plan to frame Henderson for murderin' White Knights in retaliation for what happened to his nephew wasn't gonna work.

Miran had gotten soft. He had to go.

When my brother left yo' place, he headed to Harry's Liquor Sto'. I watched him as he pulled into the parkin' lot. He usually parked in front of the entrance, but there were already four or five cars pulled in front, so he pulled to the side and parked.

I watched as he stepped from his car. He left the car door open, removed his black tie, and tossed it into his front seat before closin' it. I remember thinkin' that I was gon' make sho' that he would never be able to belittle me again.

I waited until the three customers that were ahead of Miran exited. Then I pulled my truck around the block, put my ski mask in the pocket of my black hooded sweater, and then ran back to the sto'. I hid behind a tree that was about ten yards from Miran's car.

Several seconds later, my brother came out of the sto' with a paper bag in hand. He stood in front and looked around. It was dark, very little lighting around the sto'. Wit' the ski mask and hood on, I walked up from behind him as he went toward his car. I stuck Henderson's gun to Miran's back. I had always wanted to hit him. I saw that as the perfect time. Without sayin' a word, I hit him as hard as I could with the butt of the gun.

Miran screamed in pain, his knees buckled but he managed to maintain his balance while grabbin' at his head with his free hand.

I played it calm. I might've been a little too calm. Miran seemed to recognize me; even though I had on a ski mask and a hooded sweater.

"Lee…boy, is that you?" he asked, holding his hand to his head.

The pain that he was experiencin' was overshadowed by his anger toward me. When his jaws tightened, and his bottom lip curled, that's when I realized that he knew it was me.

At that moment, without hesitation, I placed the gun to his head, and fired.

When you kill somebody like that, everythin' seems to happen in slow motion. I watched as the paper bag he was carryin' flew through the air. It was like it took forever for that bottle and his body to hit the ground. Funny thin 'bout seein' Miran layin' on the ground, bleedin' 'bout the head; I didn't feel nothin'.

After I shot 'em, I went through his wallet and made it look like a robbery gon' bad. I figured that the police would look at it as bein' staged, and blame Henderson's black ass.

Who would've thought that he was cold enough to blame his son?

When I snuck the gun back into his house, I almost got caught. His wife and they pickaninnys didn't get home 'til I was puttin' the gun back into the shoebox. I had to climb out a second floor bedroom window and dart through the back yard. Them damn chickens made so much noise that I thought I was gon' be seen.

You ordered Miran to take out Jasper and the other two because they was readyin' themselves to talk wit them gov'ment boys back in '67. Miran didn't mind killin' them boys. As a matter of fact, he enjoyed doin' some of the things we did to those boys.

But my stepbrother was mad as hell when you told him to get rid of OB. That's when he really felt that we would be next; he was sho' you would have to get rid of us. He wasn't gonna do Oscar. In fact, he told Oscar that you would be comin' after him.

It wasn't difficult at all for the senator to remember

every detail of his last encounter with Lee Thompson.
His recollection of that last meeting several years prior
was something that he had never forgotten. Lee let him
know that he was in a position to destroy everything
that the Willington name was built on.

"So, Lee told you that he had something on you, but
he wouldn't tell you what?" asked Gavin Willington's
specially invited guest.

The senator leaned back in his seat. "That's right."

"Senator, it's been five years…nothing has come up…
why are you still concerned?"

"Because, if it does come up, my family will be
ruined."

"Well, before I ended his life, I tortured him. He was
a tough cookie…that guy wasn't gonna tell me nothing
about what he had. All he would say is that his information would sink my ship as well. He said that when the
time was right, everyone would know what we did. He
said that he laid it out from 1950. Lee wasn't with us
when we snatched that Jackson boy. We followed him
and Henderson to that church after they got smart with
us in town. We were really mad at them niggas, thinking
that they could talk to us any kind of way. Lee didn't
show up until that nigga was hangin' from the tree."

The Senator insisted, "You have just as much to be
concerned with as I do…so find the shit that Lee had!"

I Need
YOUR HELP

It was cloudy, overcast, and outright dreary. Periodic bursts of heavy rainfall added to the inmates' misery. The weather matched the mood of most—everyone in the entire prison felt a bit melancholy. Thoughts of their own mortality toyed with some, while others were forced to deal with the fact that they would never live another day outside the prison.

He had no relatives; there was no one to claim his body. Those around him were his family. Inmates, no matter what color, respected him, and he, them.

There weren't very many that didn't seek his advice at one time or another. Pappi was the bridge between the races, the mediator in regard to disputes.

Throughout his time behind bars, Pappi had made it a point not to share his personal dilemma with anyone. For reasons that Larry would later discover, the old inmate was driven to open up to him.

Pappi felt that it was his calling to nurture and protect Larry; in that, he needed to prepare the youngster for the tyranny that made up prison life. After spending more than fifty years behind bars, the old con wanted to ensure that Larry didn't fall prey to his surroundings, that he didn't allow his situation to define the rest of his life.

At times, he found that he had to be hard on the young prisoner, yet he was able to do so without toying with Larry's psyche. He allowed his protégé enough rope to recognize his own mistakes, while reminding the youngster that there were really only two choices that he could make in life—the right one, or the wrong one. He explained to Larry that if he were to look at life with that in mind, things would become a lot easier.

Pappi once told Larry that it was common to go through states of depression; he said that it was human nature, especially when one has been wronged.

The wise old man explained that there is a big difference in being successful in life, and having success in living life. He assured Larry that the latter was much more enriching.

Larry was allowed to be on burial detail. As Larry stood alone at the gravesite of his mentor, the last thing on his mind was the slight drizzle. His thoughts were on the many conversations that he and the old con had as they perspired while doing their jobs under the hot sun.

He could clearly hear Pappi say, 'I don't expect that you'll understand what it is I've been tryin' to put into that cinder block head of yours, until it's time. When it's time, you'll say…I got it.'

No one on the compound was surprised that Pappi left all of his personal possessions to the Lunch Man.

Larry, dressed in a sleeveless T-shirt and blue jeans, was waterlogged. The box that he was carrying was covered with his shirt, his way of protecting the contents from the elements. The distressed mourner entered the empty barracks and headed down the buffed aisle, and over to his bunk.

He sat the box atop his bed, and then removed his shirt before hanging it on the door of his locker, which was erected next to his bunk. He then made himself comfortable beside the box. As he stared at the contents, he reminisced about what the warden had said to him while handing him the cardboard container.

"Listen, son, Pappi thought a lot about you. He told me that you wanted to get a business degree. I'll tell you what…if you show me what you showed Pappi, I'll keep my word to him by giving you a job in the canteen. As you know, that's one of the best jobs on the compound. Plus, I'll speak up for you when it comes time for you to go up for parole."

After several seconds of contemplation, Larry began rummaging through what amounted to be Elden "Pappi" Howard's life. He found letters addressed to his wife and child. Larry found that to be strange; seeing how their murders were why he was in prison in the first place. Pappi had apparently been writing to his wife and son for over fifty years.

Larry pulled out several books, all spiritually based. The one that caught his attention was the first works of

Maya Angelou—*I Know Why The Caged Bird Sings*. The title alone fit his predicament. He opened, and then began glancing over the philosophical works of an author he would come to cherish.

Subsequent to his realizing that he had more of Pappi's things to go through before the others were released from their work assignments, he placed the book on his bed before he reached into, and then pulled from the box, a photo album.

Larry braced his back to the wall and began flipping through the pictures. He thought about his childhood when he saw a photograph that depicted Pappi holding his two-year-old son. Upon seeing a snapshot of Pappi, his wife and child, it was hard for Larry to understand why the old man wasn't bitter.

After spending five minutes viewing Elden Howard's memories, Larry began to sort through the letters that lay atop his bunk. One envelope caught his attention.

It read: *To Larry (My son)*

He opened the envelope and pulled out the letter. Larry unfolded the correspondence and began to read.

Dear Lunch Man,

It was written that you be here, it was your life's destiny. You were meant to be in this cage, there was nothing that you were going to be able to do to alter that.

Larry, I've studied religious doctrine—I've written articles on spirituality. None were ever published, not because they weren't any good, but because the editors at the magazines that I submitted my work to found out that they were written by a con. Not just any con, one who was serving a life's sentence for the ultimate crime, the taking of a life.

I tell you this because I wanted you to know where my strength came from. It's very true that through good works comes peace.

Anyway, our two paths were meant to cross. It was the key to me being able to see my Ethel again. You see, without you coming into my life, I don't believe that my Ethel would have come to visit with me; it was because of you that she appeared.

Ethel was my dear wife.

She was a woman of few words, but boy, when she spoke— you had better be listening. Nevertheless, she came to me the day before I met you. She told me that a child would be coming into my life, one who possessed the same quality spirit as our son, Calvin.

Lunch Man, my wife told me that I would know him when I saw him. Now, at the time, none of that made any sense to me. I was going to meet a child, hell; I'm in prison for the rest of my life.

I thought to myself, how in the world was I gonna meet a child. Then suddenly, I meet this little eighteen-year-old kid.

If you're reading this letter, either you were released, or I'm with my wife and son. Either way, I want you to know that I hadn't met anyone as bright, and as thoughtful as yourself since my Ethel. It took me a while to understand why she appeared on your behalf.

It was my place to take you into my heart, to share with you my life's journey. To teach you what it really means to be a man, not just any man—but a man of God. I wasn't trying to force feed you religion; my job was to teach you how to stay in tune with your spirit.

Larry, learn who you are, seek out and become one with your inner self, because you have a good heart. Feed your mind, heart and spirits with all that is necessary for you to be the best that you can possibly be.

If I have passed on, I want you to know that Ethel, Calvin and I will be looking down on you. Remember, although they could lock you up, they don't have the authority to imprison your mind. Be Good! Be Blessed!

Larry refolded the letter and placed it back into the envelope before directing his attention back to the box. He pulled from the box one of several scrolls of paper. Larry was completely surprised when he unrolled it.

"A bachelor's degree in theology," he said to himself. Larry placed the certificate on his bed and immediately pulled from the box another scroll. He opened it and saw that Pappi had also obtained his master's in theology.

The contents of the box also included several very inspiriting articles that Pappi had written, the rejection letters from the magazines that he had submitted to, the bibles of various religions, and research information on Buddhism, Hinduism, Christianity, and the Muslim faith.

For years he studied extremely hard.

Before prison, Larry was a really good student—but with the time to concentrate, and the motivation to land a job that only few even had a shot at, he pursued his educational endeavors with the vigor of a scholar.

If he felt himself losing interest, he'd pull from his shirt pocket a letter that he would carry for the rest of his life. It was a letter that inspirited him to the highest degree; he would read Pappi's letter, then neatly fold it and place it back into its rightful place, next to his heart.

For a little over three years he pursued a bachelor's degree in Business. Larry attributed his success in obtaining his degree to the fact that he was as determined as ever to make someone who believed in him proud.

No one in his family had any idea what Larry had accomplished; they were unaware that the prison Military Academy had promoted him to the rank of colonel and that the warden was posturing him for parole. They had no idea that he was in the upper echelon, as a matter of fact, first academically in the college program that led to his degree.

None of his family was aware of his successes because they hadn't tried to contact him in over eight years.

As promised by the warden, Larry was put in charge of a canteen; and in a short period of time he was able to impress the prison's governing body of one. The young con was able to keep operating expenses down, yet sales were up.

With everything that Larry had managed to accomplish, the warden declared him rehabilitated.

Summer of 1989

Mop sat on his bed going over his day's take.

Wesley Hobbs and Leroy Burns, along with his two most reliable henchmen, were the only ones allowed in the barracks while the prison's most manipulative and intimidating inmate went over his receipts.

Mop quickly discovered that someone hadn't reported in, so the imposing con ordered one of his flunkies to bring Larry's best friend back from the basketball court.

Stinky hadn't turned in his day's receipts and Mop was beginning to feel that his best hustler was slacking because he was scheduled to be paroled in less than two weeks.

Upon Ronald Cells taking on the title of ex-con, he was expected to be answerable for the couriers that smuggled drugs into the prison. The soon-to-be released inmate wasn't thrilled about his forthcoming assignment. To tell the truth, he had no intention of living up to his promise—but he certainly wasn't going to refuse Mop's orders before he got out.

Stinky didn't realize that his boss of nine years had a feeling that he wasn't going to live up to his word. Because of Mop's intuition, he had a surprise in store for Ronald Cells.

With a towel draped around his neck, the sweaty inmate entered the barracks. When his eyes locked in on Mop, Stinky immediately knew why he had been summoned.

"What up, boss?" he said before making his way over toward Mop's bed.

His barracks leader didn't bother looking up when he said, "You and me...we need to talk." Without taking his eyes off of his task, he calmly issued an order to those around him. "Ya'll break...I need to talk to my boy."

Mop's staff made their way out of the barracks—at which time, Stinky sat on the bunk across from the gang's accountant-slash-boss.

"I haven't forgotten...it's just that I haven't completed my runs. I wanted to give you all the money at one time."

The diligent accountant never looked up. "I'm not really concerned about that. If I were, I would have called you on all the money you been skimming off the top."

Stinky's face was drenched with bewilderment. He wondered how it was possible that Mop knew of his deception. He felt that he was extremely careful with the way in which he operated his scheme to financially prepare for his release from prison.

"Boss..."

Mop quickly interrupted, "Look...don't play with my intelligence, son," he said with a taste of arrogance. Fully locked in on what he was doing, he insisted, "You gon' have to make up for your indiscretions."

"What do you mean?" Stinky was curious, but at the same time he wasn't about to confess to Mop's accusations.

❧

The eight shelves were four feet high, they stretched twelve feet in length, and all were well-stocked. The display racks were evenly spaced in the middle of the canteen floor. Everything that a prisoner could want and more was available at the right price.

Underwear, socks, snacks and an assortment of blue jeans were located on the shelves furthest from the entrance. If a customer were to walk that aisle they would also locate pencils, paper and binders.

Against the wall behind the clothing aisle was a cooler that was stocked with pints of ice cream and Popsicles. Larry sold everything that he was allowed to stock in the canteen. Orange juice, sodas and milk, candy, cookies, potato chips, canned goods, lunchmeat, peanut butter, jelly, and bread were also available. He also had plastic spoons, paper plates and cups, newspapers, books and magazines.

To the immediate right upon entering was an L-shaped glass encased checkout counter; behind Larry's workstation was a door that led to his living quarters. Inmates that were responsible for running a canteen were actually allowed to sleep in the store, which was a major perk for that position.

Stinky was carrying a large box when he entered the canteen. He immediately headed over to Larry, who was standing behind the counter.

Larry's confidante seemed very agitated; his monotone was without its usual pep. "Hey, my man, what's goin' on?" said the soon-to-be released inmate as he rested his cardboard container on top of Larry's candy display case.

The canteen manager smiled at his friend. "What's wrong?"

"I need for you to keep this for me. Hold on to it until I'm ready to get out of here."

"What is it?"

"The things that I cherish most."

"What's really goin' on, Ron?"

Has Anyone
SEEN RON?

The jingle jangle produced by the bell that Larry hung at the door was rigged to alert him of a customer's arrival. The store manager got the idea to use the country store technique from the quaint little mom and pop stores that he frequented as a child.

With clipboard in hand, Larry's head was stuck in the ice cream cooler when his primitive alarm sounded. Correction Officer Stacy Taylor had entered the canteen. She immediately spotted the inmate working; it was quite apparent to her that he was doing inventory.

Larry's cocoa complexion, thin mustache and neatly trimmed Afro caught her attention the very first time she saw him. And, she was truly impressed with his exemplary record, and educational achievements. Stacy had heard about his situation and believed that she had come across the very first convict who was truly innocent.

"Be right with you!" he said without ever taking his head out of the cooler.

"Take your time, inmate!"

It was intense. His heart raced like a car piston. Hearing her voice caused his body to react in a way that would be expected from a young man who had never experienced the pleasure of female company.

He nearly put a hole in his head as it struck the sliding door of the cooler when he attempted to snatch it from the icebox—her presence truly startled him.

Larry was embarrassed. He wasn't sure if she had caught his clumsy reaction.

When he was finally able to gather himself, he pulled his aching head from the cooler before peering over his right shoulder. "How's it going, Officer Taylor?" His question was filled with a combination of humiliation and giddiness.

She smiled at him.

He wanted to rub the spot on his head where the sharp pain originated, but to do so would merely draw attention to what he had done.

"I told you that my name is Stacy…"

He responded with a nod.

"How are you doing today, inmate Henderson?" asked the corrections officer as she approached.

"I insist that you call me Larry," he replied, prior to closing the cooler. Like a schoolboy being called to the chalkboard in the middle of an erotic daydream, Larry shyly used his clipboard to camouflage the bulge in his pant.

"So, how are you doing, Larry?"

"I'm doin' okay…" was his response from behind a flirtatious smile.

"I think you're doing an outstanding job running this place."

"Well, I can't take the credit. It's the business courses that I took."

"That's another thing. You're certainly trying to do something with your time. The fact that you're keepin' out of trouble and pursuing an education will work in your favor when you go up for parole. Keep up the good work…"

Larry kept his response appreciatively simple. "Thanks."

"Remember, if you ever need to talk, I'm here for you."

"I appreciate that. By the way, thanks so much for the bible you left on my bed yesterday."

"You're quite welcome. The last time we spoke, you said that you were ready to educate your spirit…that's admirable."

"When I was telling you that, it wasn't a hint for a bible. I have several from different faiths. I never got into reading any of them because, for a long time, I was angry with God. But over the years, something that I was once told by an old wise man got me to thinking. So now, I'm prepared to edify myself spiritually." Larry followed the corrections officer toward the counter. "Tell me something, Stacy."

"What's that?"

"Could you ever be interested in someone like me?" She made her way behind the counter.

"I gotta inspect your room," Stacy said, reaching for the doorknob that led to his living area. As she disappeared behind the door, he heard her say, "I'm very interested in you!"

The infatuated inmate couldn't seem to remove the smirk; the blushing felt permanent. Larry rested the clipboard on the counter as he tried to catch a glimpse of the woman who had made his life bearable.

For several seconds, Stacy stood next to his locker and allowed her eyes to ingest his space. Stacy noticed an *Ebony* magazine lying atop Larry's neatly made bunk. She hadn't seen the new issue, so she walked over to his bed, picked it up, and began flipping through the pages.

After browsing the popular publication, she placed the magazine back on the bunk. Stacy then casually resumed her visual examination of the room, contemplating where to begin her inspection.

The CO walked over to the inmate's desk. She noticed a handwritten letter lying next to the bible she had given him.

Stacy picked up the handwritten communication and began to read:

Val...I haven't heard from you in years. I received your last letter three years ago. What happened to you trying to get me help? Why didn't you do what you told me you would do? You said that you would get me a lawyer. None of you have tried to help me prove my innocence.

Mamma hasn't bothered to write or visit me. I guess she's still mad at the way I acted the last time she came to see me. I feel that she should have gotten over that by now. After all, it's been years.

I had every right to react the way I did. Tell me something, why is it that no one seems to understand that my reaction was predicated by my situation? First of all, I was young; and second, I was—and still am, innocent.

I lost all hope when I heard that Jonathan and Jake had been killed. Jake Aaron had visited me several times before he died—he said that he was going to prove that I didn't kill Miran Thompson.

You know; although it was reported that Jonathan's car malfunctioned and blew up because of a gas leakage while he and Jake were together, I still believe that they were murdered. They were onto something…they were both sure that they would be able to help me get out of here.

But their deaths have nothing to do with my displeasure with you guys.

I've written hundreds of letters and no one has taken the time to write me back, no birthday cards, Christmas cards, or anything.

Anyway, I'm working hard trying to make myself eligible for parole. My hearing is coming up. The warden is very impressed with my efforts to educate myself, both academically and spiritually. Yeah, you read what I said correctly. I'm into the bible again. I hadn't picked up one since we were kids.

As far as schooling, I'm already putting my education to

work for me. I've been put in charge of a canteen, that's a store on prison grounds.

Yeah, we have stores.

The warden told me that if I keep going in the direction I'm headed, I'm gonna probably get paroled on good behavior. He says that I have a real good chance.

Parole is my only hope of getting out of here.

By the way, I met this female guard. She's really nice to me. I sorta developed a crush on her. I wish that I could get the guts to tell her how I feel. But she probably doesn't notice me like that. If I weren't in here, she would be someone that I would try to get close to.

Look, I'm still not sure why no one in the family has tried to reach out to me. It's not like I'm hard to find.

By the way, I hate your father for making me waste away in this prison. I'm trying my best not to hold so much hatred, but it's hard. It's gonna take time before I'm able to get past this hate I feel. Reading the bible helps a little.

I know it's because of him that you and the rest of the family are acting like I'm dead. But that's okay because I'm real confident that I will be home in time for Christmas.

Life has been hell, but I'm surviving.

I love you so much, Val. I miss you a lot.

I've cried many nights, trying to understand how I ended up in here. It all comes back down to your father. That man hated me from the time I was born.

Val, I'm really disappointed in you. Of everyone in the family, I never thought that you would desert me. As mad as

I am with you, I can't help but to forgive you. I can forgive
everyone except your father. I HATE HIM with a passion.
The hatred I feel toward him cannot be put into words.

Hey, enough of that. How many nieces and nephews do I
have now?

The letter touched Stacy. She had already formed an
opinion on Larry's character before reading the correspondence that was addressed to his sister.

The single mother of one truly believed that the man
standing on the opposite side of the door had been ter-
ribly wronged. As much as she wanted to help him,
there was nothing that she could do aside from praying
that he have success at securing parole.

After placing the letter back in its proper place, Stacy
continued with her inspection. She searched under the
bed, under his mattress, and then went through his
locker. Stacy pulled books from two shelves that were
mounted on his wall. She inspected between the pages
of novels, trade books, and the Bibles that were left to
Larry by Elden "Pappi" Howard.

There were two boxes (covered with sheets), which
sat at either side of his bed—like nightstands. They were
the last items remaining in her inspection.

As she removed the sheet from the box on the left
side, she heard voices echoing from the storefront.

"You gon' be treated like every other mutha fucka
that runs these shit stores…"

Stacy was unable to identify the voice behind the threatening tone, so she moved closer to the door in an effort to distinguish who was attempting to intimidate the store's proprietor.

"Look...I can't give you money that don't belong to me..." Stacy heard Larry say.

"You ain't got no choice...you either come across with the money...or...I'll lay yo' ass out..."

Larry's response was totally off the subject. "What happened to Ronald?" the store manager asked with concern.

"Don't fuckin' worry 'bout Stinky's ass...you worry 'bout gettin' me that cash...or it's yo' ass..."

Stacy managed to catch a glimpse of Mop, Wesley Hobbs and Leroy Burns as she peeked from Larry's living space and into the storefront.

Wesley and Leroy were in the back of the store digging through the potato chips bin. She could tell by their mannerisms that the two cons had no intention of paying for what they had taken.

Both inmates opened their bags of barbecue Frito Lays, guarding the entrance. Hobbs and Burns began eating the chips while they waited for their boss to conclude his business.

"Mop, you don't scare me one damn bit! I may not be able to whip yo' ass but I ain't goin' down like no punk!"

"You willin' to die for this? This ain't even yo' shit!"

"I don't know if I'm ready to die, all I know is that I ain't givin' up somethin' that don't belong to me. Look, man, I go up for parole in a few months. I don't wanna screw that up. Why don't you give me a break?"

He raised his voice. His tone was menacing. "I don't give fuckin' breaks! If you don't get on the same page with everybody else, then I'm gonna have to make sure that you don't be around for that parole that yo' ass is hopin' for," Mop said in anger.

The prison's biggest thug was annoyed. He turned and headed for the door. His two potato chip eating cronies followed their boss out of the store.

Shock was engraved on her face when she exited Larry's room. "What the hell was that all about?" Stacy asked.

"That guy is crazy. He's extorting money from everybody. He's backed a friend of mine in a corner and he's putting serious pressure on him." Frustrated, Larry rested his crossed arms atop the counter and buried his face between them.

Before she could show support, someone's voice followed the static coming from her shoulder-harnessed walkie-talkie.

"Taylor...this is Command...do you read me? Over!!!"

Stacy spoke into the mouthpiece, "This is Taylor... go ahead!!!"

"Taylor...we need you back at Command...over!!!"

"Ten-four...I'm on my way...I'll be there in five minutes...OUT!!!"

After concluding her communications, Stacy directed her attention toward Larry.

"Mr. Henderson, I'm working a double tonight, so if

you leave the door open…I'll come and tuck you in," she said from behind a seductive smile.

For most of the day, and into the evening, he wondered if she were playing games with his head, if she had any intention of returning.

The clock mounted on the wall over the ice cream cooler wasn't moving fast enough for him. He stood behind the counter and literally counted every second.

At the end of the day, when it was time for him to close, he did so in record time. Closing usually took him nearly thirty minutes, but on this day, he only needed ten.

After counting the cash receipts and storing the money in the small safe provided by the prison, Larry locked the door. He then turned out all the lights in the storefront before heading to his room.

For years Larry had to listen to some of the cons talk about their conjugal visits. He was envious. Larry certainly wasn't about to tell the other inmates that he was a virgin. That was a part of his life that he didn't even share with Ronald.

Some of the inmates got married so they, too, could relieve themselves once a month.

Hearing the inmates share their conjugal exploits only served to inflame Larry's hatred toward his father. Here was yet another experience that his father's deception had cheated him out of. For a long time, Larry felt that he would never experience that kind of intimacy, being that he was scheduled to be in prison for the better part of his life.

Hell, to simply see a female naked would have been satisfying.

Larry had no idea if Stacy was going to show up. Just in case, he was determined to have everything right.

The horny inmate took some cologne and poured a little into the top of a shoe polish can; he lit it, and then began fanning the fragrance around the room with his hands.

Larry then sat nervously on his bed—he reached for, and began fiddling with the dial of his transistor radio, which sat atop his makeshift nightstand. His intent was to find a smooth-jazz radio station.

He had watched a lot of movies, and from that he learned that a romantic setting was always the key. If this was going to be his first sexual encounter, he wanted to make certain that he had the proper ambiance.

Hours went by.

Every now and then he found himself standing at the arch of his bedroom door, staring through the darkness of the store in anticipation.

When his mind wasn't on how he could go about ensuring that he didn't disappoint the woman whom he expected to liaise with, his thoughts were on his missing friend.

It had been two days since Stinky dropped off his personal treasures for Larry to safeguard. He hadn't seen his pint-sized friend after that.

Larry had questioned everyone in Camp 29. He had also spoken with Captain Small and several other guards. Everyone that he had confronted gave him the same answer. Larry was told that Ronald Cells had been released several days before he was scheduled. But Larry knew that his friend would never leave without saying goodbye.

His short stories, and game ball from his high school regional championship game (everyone on his team had signed it), photographs, letters that he had written to his sisters (never mailed them, because he didn't have their address) and an assortment of other personal items were in the box that Ronald left with Larry. He would never have left without it.

He couldn't understand why Small would not confide in him, why the supervising corrections officer didn't provide him with the truth. Everyone's insistence that Ronald was released early made absolutely no sense.

The transistor was holding up its end. The music certainly fit the situation. Larry had heard from the cons that Kenny G's music had a way of setting the mood. Boy, were they right.

In only his tighty whiteys, Larry had his guest braced

against the wall. They kissed passionately as he attempted to work Stacy out of her state-issued gear.

While wrapped in each other's embrace, the two continued their sultry lip lock. Neither had any interest in keeping their hands off of the other—they exchanged delicate caresses.

As if dancing an erotic mating ritual, they twirled and spun while making their way over to his bed. The two allowed their bodies to fall to his mattress.

He attempted to act seasoned but Stacy could tell that she was dealing with a virgin, or at least someone with limited experience. This stunning revelation turned her on even more.

She would not embarrass him. Instead she took his hands and placed them where they would be most effective. She seductively caressed the shaft of his manhood, hoping that he would use his hands just as gently on her. When he reacted as she felt he would, she knew that he was a quick study.

As anxious as Larry was to experience penetration, he was more interested in pleasing her. He took his time and allowed himself the opportunity to appreciate the sensations created by foreplay.

After an unbelievable exchange of passion, the two lay naked in bed. Both were readying to light a cigarette. Larry stared at Stacy. His gaze was that of a man who had just gotten his world completely rocked.

"Wow! That was incredible," he barely managed to say.

Stacy couldn't believe that someone with little to no

previous experience was able to set her off like Larry did.

Larry was completely caught by surprise when the woman who snuggled up to him, unexpectedly said, "I'm gonna get Mop for extortion."

"No, Stacy," Larry sat up before continuing, "leave him alone. That cat is dangerous. He wouldn't hesitate to kill you, if you got in his way."

"He's not that crazy," she quickly responded.

With concern, Larry countered, "You don't know him. He doesn't give a shit. I mean, he's already in here for life." Larry put his cigarette out, and then buried his face in his hands before saying, "This ain't gonna be good. I go up for parole soon and this man wants me to give that all up."

"I'll see what I can do to keep him off your back," she said before kissing him on his chest. She gently removed his hands from his face, and then tenderly kissed him on the cheek.

Larry stared into her eyes, and again, with concern, he mumbled, "Don't get involved. If you do, they're gonna think I told you."

She assured him, "I can do it without his knowledge..."

"How?"

"I got friends over in twenty-nine. I'll handle it. I'll take care of those clowns. I'll have Mr. Man assigned to the Big House," Stacy said as she caressed him seductively. "You keep doin' what you doin'. Keep making me feel like this." She again kissed him on his chest.

"It'll be my pleasure," Larry said. He locked his arms around her as the two resumed their lust-filled tryst.

The following day, Larry, clad in his cadet uniform (silver bird on his collar, indicating his rank of colonel) took his seat in his morning class. Before he got comfortable, Captain Small approached his desk.

"Cadet, I need to speak with you in the hallway," Small ordered before maneuvering his way past the other cadets who were making their way into the classroom.

When Larry entered the hallway, he and his commanding officer walked over to an isolated corner. Small was none too pleased with Larry's insistence that something had happened to Ronald Cells.

"I told you that he was released. I don't want you goin' around makin' it seem like some kind of conspiracy has taken place. You been doin' really good 'round here. Don't go wastin' yo' time, or jeopardize your parole with this nonsense."

Larry already believed that foul play was at the helm of his friend's disappearance. But witnessing his commander's attitude, and his suggestion that Larry's questioning people about Ronald's whereabouts could somehow influence his chances at parole, verified his feelings. Something was definitely wrong.

Larry never invaded his friend's privacy because Ron

had revealed to him what was in the box that was left in his care. But the more he thought about their last conversation, he wondered if his friend was trying to tell him something.

After his mandatory cadet's class on military strategies, Larry immediately headed back to the canteen. Apparently, his investigative intuition was hereditary. He felt that there might be something in his friend's possessions that could give him a clue into what was going on.

Upon his return to the canteen, Larry put the "Closed" sign in the window, locked the door, and then made his way to his quarters. To ensure that no one walking by would disturb him, he closed the door to his room.

The cadet tossed his hat on his bed. Without hesitation, he made his way over to the homemade nightstand. He removed his transistor radio and placed it to the floor. Larry removed the sheet, sat on the bed and then began rummaging through the box's contents.

As he removed the basketball, he thought to himself that it looked a little warped. After examining the signatures of Ronald's high school teammates, he tossed the ball to the bed and continued his search.

He didn't find anything that would give him insight, so he loosened his tie, braced his back against the wall, and started reading Ron's short stories.

Larry was very impressed with his friend's literary skills.

Ron wasn't a great speller, but he certainly could tell

a good story. One compelling narrative after another, each one made Larry more interested in the next. By the time he got to the fifth of twelve, he realized what was going on.

Ron was very clever. Within his stories he laid out a twisted web of deception. It was a story so bizarre that Larry literally hopped out of bed when he came across it.

The more he read, the more he hoped that creative license was in play. If not, his parole hearing couldn't come fast enough.

The Parole
BOARD

"Over the last few months I've ensured that all of your things were sent to your sister's house as you requested. I've even had a chance to speak with her several times," Stacy said as she straightened the tie to his uniform.

Larry smiled. "Thanks for everything."

Stacy could tell that he was a bit nervous. "Are you gonna be okay?"

"Yeah, but I'm a little edgy," said Larry. He took a deep breath before slowly exhaling.

"Don't worry; everything is gonna work out."

"I'm sure it will. It's just that I can't believe that this day is finally here. Everyone has put in a good word, but, for some reason…" He never finished his statement. Larry turned his attention to his belt; it didn't align with his zipper so he adjusted it. He gave Stacy a quick peck. "You've been so good for me. Once I get this parole I would like to pursue a lasting relationship with you," he said, heading to the door.

"Go get that parole, baby," Stacy eagerly said. Her encouraging words brought about a smile from the man that she hoped to have a future with. She followed Larry out of the canteen.

❦

The administration building was a sight for sore eyes. He'd dreamt of the day that he would be invited to stand before a group of individuals that would be willing to hear his side of the story, to hear about the circumstances that led to his being forced to live behind bars.

Larry wasn't about to let his opportunity go for not.

Perception was fifty percent of the battle, so he ensured that his hair was neatly trimmed. He had a spit shine on his shoes that would make any Marine proud. Dressed in his tapered cadet's uniform (Captain Small's suggestion) Larry appeared as if he were about to be promoted by the President himself.

The cadet sat in the well-buffed hallway of Section 3 Yellow, the area where parole hearings were held.

As could be expected, the anticipation of going before the members of the board made him feel a bit uneasy; but Larry felt that as long as he maintained military decorum, he would do fine. He felt that everything he had gone through—from cadet training, receiving his bachelor's, and being assigned to run a canteen—had prepared him for what he was about to experience. Those thoughts brought a sense of calm to his cluttered mind.

A guard stepped from room 333 and motioned for Larry to approach.

The three members of the Parole Board occupied the long, deeply varnished table that faced the entrance. The only other furniture in the room consisted of one folding chair, positioned directly in front of the panel.

The decision makers were going over and discussing the information provided to them concerning the next individual scheduled to stand before them.

The members simultaneously looked up from their conversation as Larry stepped through the door with his hat tucked under his armpit.

The cadet locked his arms to his side; he stood as stiff as a board, just as a top notch soldier would in the company of his superiors. Larry never made eye contact; he picked out a spot on the wall behind the panel and stared.

One of the individuals responsible for deciding his fate looked to be a compassionate person. Her white hair and studious features made Larry feel that she might be someone that he could count on when it came to deciding his fate. He was confident that the grandmotherly looking woman would feel compassion for him once she heard his story.

That meant one down and two to go.

Upon entering, he also noticed that the other two panel members were middle-aged Caucasian men. One had the look of a banker; the other appeared to be a stuffed shirt.

The one who appeared to be the head of a financial institution was the first to speak. "You can have a seat."

"Thank you, sir," Larry said as he made himself comfortable.

The man asked, "Are you Larry Henderson?"

"Yes, sir."

The stuffed shirt introduced himself as Louis Padell, chairman of the panel. He pointed to the right of him and introduced Julie Davis, and to his left, was Mark Sizemore. He went on to say, "The purpose of this hearing is to determine whether or not you should be considered for early release." He glared at Larry before continuing, "We're gonna ask you a few questions and we would like for you to answer honestly. My first question to you, Mr. Henderson, is do you think that you've paid for your crime?"

Larry assumed the posture of a confident man. He made eye contact with the man asking the question, and then replied, "Well, Sir, I'm really not sure how to answer that."

"What do you mean?" the chairman responded.

"I'm a victim. You see, sir, I didn't commit the crime."

The chairman quickly countered, "Did you, or didn't you agree to a plea?"

"Yes, sir, I did." Larry's raised eyebrows alerted the panel that he had more to say, so they listened. "At that particular time…I saw that I had no choice but to accept the plea."

Ms. Davis interjected, "Please elaborate."

Larry's eyes veered in the direction of the one person on the panel that his instincts led him to believe would be sympathetic. He locked in on her gray green eyes, "Well, ma'am, my father convinced me to accept the plea agreement; although he knew that I was innocent," he stated with conviction.

His statement baffled all in attendance. Sizemore ran his fingers through his brown hair before chiming in. "Why would your father allow you to do that?"

"I'm not sure, sir." Larry eyes shifted to the bewildered man.

"Your father is a police captain, isn't he?" Sizemore asked.

"Yes, that's what I hear."

Chairman Padell posed the next question. "So, let me get this straight. Your father had you plead guilty, knowing that you were innocent?"

"Yes."

The panel members whispered amongst one another for several seconds. After that the chairman pulled out an envelope from one of the files that sat before him. He held it up and said, "I would like for you to explain this letter that we received from one of your siblings. It asks us to please be careful in considering you for early release.

"According to this sibling, you are a threat to your father. This family member seems to think that you will harm your father, if you are freed. What are your thoughts on that?"

Larry was not only shocked, he was disappointed to know that someone else in his family would be working against him. "I guess you're not gonna tell me which one of my siblings feels that I'm a threat to my father, huh?" he asked begrudgingly.

"That's not important," Sizemore replied.

"Well, the only thing I have to say about that is I feel that my father sacrificed my life. I'm really not sure why."

Ms. Davis' face was filled with curiosity when she asked, "Do you really believe that?"

"Yes. My father convinced me that I didn't stand a chance going to trial for that crime. I was only a kid… he was supposed to protect me… I was real young…he worked on my mind… Do you know that my father didn't even let me get a lawyer? Isn't that wrong?"

The chairman was in attack mode. "So, you harbor resentment toward your father?"

"Naturally."

"Do you see yourself as being a threat to your father?" The chairman's question was a fair one, considering the information that had been provided.

"He's my father, sir. I don't see myself as being a threat to him, or anyone else for that matter."

The chairman went on to say, "According to your file, you have been a model prisoner. The warden entrusted you with seven hundred dollars and the keys to a canteen on the grounds in 1983. You've been running the store for a long time. That's impressive. We also see that you've taken advantage of the educational programs that the prison provides. Military Trained Cadet... holding the rank of Colonel. All impressive. But, I must say, Mr. Henderson, this letter that we received from one of your siblings has us concerned." He stared at Larry for a brief second, and then turned his attention to the panel.

The group whispered while going through his file. It took them all of thirty seconds before the chairman turned toward Larry and said, "Mr. Henderson, give us a few minutes so that we can discuss your situation. Would you please wait in the hall until we have had time to review your case?"

For more than ten minutes, Larry wondered which one of his siblings was out to ruin his chances of getting out of prison. As hard as he tried, he couldn't figure out why any one of them would be so spiteful. The more he thought about it, the more he was convinced that none of the Henderson children were behind that letter.

His eyes roamed the hallway.

Several other inmates were sitting on benches outside of their perspective hearing rooms. Some seemed confident, while others possessed the same bewildered expression that he did.

Based on his stellar record, Larry deserved to be released on good behavior. But, he wasn't very optimistic after seeing the faces of his panel as they discussed that letter. All three seemed conflicted. Larry knew that everything hinged on the weight placed on that letter.

His stomach tied up in knots when he saw the guard exit the hearing room and motion for him to return.

Larry was escorted back into the hearing room. When he reentered, none of the members acknowledged his presence.

The parole seeker was directed to his seat by the guard.

When the chairman finally made eye contact, chills went up Larry's spine. He knew that things weren't going in the direction that would be beneficial to him.

The chairman spoke, "Mr. Henderson, because of the nature of your original crime, and the fact that you don't seem to be able to come to grips with what you've been incarcerated for, it's hard to set you free. But looking at your record since you've been incarcerated, along with the many recommendations we received from the warden and some of the guards, I find it very hard to honestly say that you would be a threat to anyone. Nevertheless…" The man announcing Larry's fate held up the letter. "Based on this letter, your own family feels you're capable of committing a lamentable act against your own father." Mr. Padell put the letter down and continued while opening the file, "Mr. Henderson, please stand."

Larry snapped to attention, his hat under his armpit.

"Mr. Henderson, we find you to be a danger to your father, and order that your parole request be denied."

Larry was devastated but he wasn't going to allow the panel to see that he was distraught. He was a soldier and he would conduct himself as such.

"May I have permission to speak?"

Ms. Davis whispered, "Yes."

"I would like to thank the panel for allowing me a chance to make my case. I do believe that I should be given a chance to live a life that had previously been snatched away from me. If you expect me to have remorse, then I guess that I'll never be released. I didn't commit the crime and I'm never going to say that I did."

"Young man, it's not that we don't believe that you're not deserving of an opportunity to be set free, but we do believe that you pose a threat. You seem to be a very focused individual. So believe you me, making a decision on your life was the hardest thing that we as a panel have had to do," the chairman answered.

Larry was escorted to the administrative office after leaving his hearing. Paperwork had to be done. Of course, he was totally disappointed that he had been denied parole—the rejection meant that he would have to wait another five years before he could try again.

Moreover, he was aware that he was living on borrowed

time. Word was going around that Mop was out for revenge. Apparently, he had been made aware that Larry had something to do with him being transferred to the big house; and, the recently rejected inmate had absolutely no idea that the prison gang leader had finagled his way back to the barracks.

While Larry waited to complete the paperwork that he was required to fill out, he found himself thinking about Ron's disappearance. It was at that moment that he realized that his friend would have had to go through the very office that he found himself sitting in. Larry felt that he was being presented with the perfect opportunity to gather information on Ron.

Upon stepping from the administration building, he immediately used his right hand in an attempt to shield his eyes from the mid-afternoon sun. Two hours prior, the rising sun was an introduction to hope—but at that moment, it merely represented another meaningless day.

As he was being escorted toward the double electrified fencing, nothing seemed to register; at least, not until he glanced over his shoulder. Seeing the building reminded him that he had been hit with two devastating bombs.

Being rejected for parole was bad, but Ron's situation had hit him even harder. His friend's dilemma far exceeded that of his own.

Watching the heavily wired gates swing open sent a cold chill throughout his body. Entering the first checkpoint brought back the memory of his arrival. By the time he walked the twenty yards that it took to get to the second checkpoint, Larry was outright fearful for his life.

Stacy had been waiting with baited breath on his return. Her hope was that he had received his parole. If he were released, there was nothing under prison policy that would prevent her from continuing her relationship. But, if for some reason he had been denied, she would be taking a serious chance continuing a relationship with the inmate.

She tried her best to maintain discretion when Larry entered the yard. Stacy immediately made herself visible to him by barking out an order to two inmates as they were roughhousing several yards from her position.

His face showed no sign of the results. As hard as she tried, she couldn't determine whether his hearing had a positive outcome or not. As soon as the two locked eyes, Stacy gestured with her head for him to make his way toward the bleachers. Looking like a strapping soldier returning home after the war, he walked around the court so as not to disrupt a game that was taking place.

Larry made it to the bleachers before she could.

As the cadet was about to be seated (bottom row, first seat), he noticed Mop and his cronies heading toward him from the opposite side of the yard. With Stacy closing in from the left, and Mop pushing his way through the middle of a basketball game, Larry couldn't tell who would arrive first.

By the grace of God, Stacy stepped to the bleachers just as Mop did. The guard and gang leader made eye contact. The female guard gave him a no-nonsense stare. The muscular con aimed his finger at Larry like it was a gun, and then he slowly pulled the trigger.

Mop motioned for his entourage of six to follow him after Stacy pointed her finger at him.

As Larry and Stacy watched the hoods walk away, she said to Larry, "Did you get paroled?"

"No, I didn't. But I'll tell you about that later. Right now, I need your help. I know what happened to Ronald."

On THE RUN

The prison infirmary known as Long View had a distinct reputation; an urban legend-type aura hung over the facility like a dark cloud. It wasn't nicknamed Frankenstein's lair for nothing, some people described it as a way station for death. Eighty-seven percent of the inmates that entered were taken out in body bags.

With a limited amount of beds, only the most serious were admitted. This accounted for the startling death rate. The facility's reputation actually worked in the favor of those that were charged with running the infirmary. No one faked injury because they were too afraid that they themselves would be added to the body count.

Only twelve out of the twenty beds were occupied.

Two doctors, along with several nurses, made their way around the ward, each checking on the patients' monitors, and injecting morphine into IVs, fluffing pillows and establishing heart rates.

One particular patient's injuries were life-threatening. He was the most critically injured individual on the compound and not expected to pull through.

In a catatonic state, he rested in a bed that was located at the far corner of the ward. His bed and monitors weren't visible because of the curtain that surrounded them.

Stacy entered the main infirmary as inconspicuously as she could.

The guard allowed her eyes to scan the beds in an effort to identify one specific person. For a brief second, she felt misinformed. He wasn't there. The person that she was in search of was nowhere to be found.

It wasn't until she saw a nurse disappear behind the curtains at the far end of the infirmary that she realized she had missed a bed.

Stacy nonchalantly strolled toward the curtain.

She stood outside the drawn partition, trying to make up her mind whether she should enter. The nurse came out.

"Excuse me, may I help you?" the nurse asked.

The guard smiled. "Just checking in on the inmate. You don't mind, do you?"

"Not at all," said the nurse. She opened the curtain and allowed Stacy access.

He had an abnormal amount of monitors and tubes connected to his body. His face was totally unrecognizable, badly disfigured. There was a stitched wound on the base of his skull. Doctors were very concerned because he hadn't regained consciousness since he was admitted more than a week prior.

In Stacy's thirty-two years of life, she had never seen anybody beaten as badly as the inmate lying on the bed before her.

Several folding chairs had been placed in room 333 of the administration building. The room normally used for parole hearings was being used to conduct a meeting between Captain Small and several other corrections officers.

The supervisor sat on the end of a table designated for use by the parole panel. The seven guards that he needed to speak with sat before him.

"This situation is going to bring unwanted attention to our endeavors. Mistakes were made and now, we're gonna have to weather the storm. First, I want all of you to turn your attention to combating this problem; there will not be business as usual until this is cleared up. We're here to get our stories together."

One of the guards said, "They're putting pressure on us. I don't know how long I can hold up."

Two others quickly joined in.

They both talked about how they were taken into custody and interrogated for hours. It was obvious to Small that his men were scared. Each felt that it was only a matter of time before their secrets were revealed to law enforcement

Small's biggest concern was how his youngest officer would hold up. He was truly their weakest link, as far as the ex-Marine was concerned.

The supervisor turned his attention to his twenty-year-old guard. "Holly, how you holdin' up?"

"I can handle it, sir," he said with an arrogance that none of the others seemed to possess.

Doctor Freeman was going over the medical chart of a patient. He didn't notice Captain Small attempting to come in as he was readying to exit the infirmary. The door swung and nearly hit the supervising guard.

"Oh, excuse me, Captain," said the doctor.

"The door missed. I'm okay."

"What an unexpected surprise," Freeman said.

"I'm here to check on an inmate."

"Let me guess which one. His prognosis is not very good. He's still critical. There's been no change in the inmate's condition. I'm not sure if he'll regain consciousness," Freeman conveyed. "Have you been able to contact his family?"

"I'm not sure. I'm not the one handling that." Small changed the subject. "Would it be alright if I looked in on him?"

"Sure. You guards really like this guy, huh?"

"What'cha mean?"

"Taylor's visiting with him now."

"Oh yeah," he responded. The corrections officer quickly excused himself. "I'll speak to you later, doc." Small was very curious to know why one of his staff was visiting an inmate. He swiftly made his way down the aisle toward the last bed.

She'd been asking a lot of questions lately. At first, he really didn't think anything of it. But now he wanted answers. He wanted to know if she was working with law enforcement.

Small snatched the curtain back like a magician exposing his assistant and there she was, standing at the side of the injured inmate's bed. The compassion in her eyes concerned him. He couldn't have anyone working for him that felt empathy for an inmate, no matter the circumstances.

"What the hell are you doing here, Taylor?"

Stacy moved toward her boss. "Sir, why did you tell everyone that Ronald Cells was released early?"

"That's not your concern. I wanna know why you're here."

Before she could answer, she noticed two women standing at the curtain with shocked expressions. Tears instantly flowed from their eyes as they gazed in disbelief.

Stacy could see that the younger one was beginning to tremble, attempting to use her hand to mask her trauma.

The older woman managed to whisper in dismay, "Oh my God...who did this to him?"

Small didn't want any part of explaining the situation so he quickly excused himself. "Excuse me, I have to go. Taylor, you and I will speak later." He maneuvered past the women without acknowledging their presence.

The two women stepped inside the curtain before drawing them closed.

"Who did this to my brother?"

Stacy walked over to the woman that posed the question. "You must be Valeria." She extended her hand.

"Yes," said Val as she took Stacy's hand into hers. Having given birth to three children since last seeing her brother, Larry's sister carried her years well.

"I'm Margaret, his mother. You must be Stacy."

"Yes." She smiled before extending a hand to Larry's mother. "Mrs. Henderson, I'm so glad to meet you."

"My daughter has told me that you've been looking out for my baby," Margaret said from behind an appreciative smile.

Stacy whispered, "He's a really nice guy." The guard refocused on Val. "Yours was the only number I had. When I couldn't get you on the phone, I didn't know what else to do."

"I'm sorry, but my husband and I took the kids on vacation. I apologize that you were unable to reach me until yesterday." There was a quiver in her voice when she questioned, "What happened to Larry?"

"He tried to escape; this is the result of his capture."

"What!" both women blurted in unison.

"The day after he was denied parole, he escaped," Stacy whispered.

Summer of 1994

He was seventy-one years young.

Retired, but unwilling to spend the rest of his life fishing, Donald Harris was able to convince his son to employ him part-time. He would help his son write briefs, develop strategies for cases, and whatever else Don, Jr., asked of him.

Donald, Sr. knew that retirement wouldn't last. Hell, he had spent half of his life running one of the top law firms in the Midwest. Other than his children and grandchildren, law was the only other thing that had meaning to him. His wife had passed several years prior. If he couldn't work, he felt that he might as well be dead, too.

Heart problems led to his decision to leave the stresses created by criminal law. But Don felt that not having someone to fight for was much more stressful—so, he was determined to keep his mind sharp. When he wasn't working with his son, the slightly overweight, distinguished gentleman volunteered time to the ACLU.

When the phone call came in, Don was seated behind his son's desk going over briefs. The grandfather of seven removed his reading glasses and picked up his son's phone.

"Denise, my son hasn't come back, so whomever you have on the line, tell them to call back later."

His son's secretary immediately responded, "I'm sorry, Mr. Harris, but there's a Mr. Hector from the ACLU on the line. He wants to speak with you about the Henderson case. He says it's important."

"Put him through," Don insisted. With the receiver pressed to his ear, the retired attorney's wait wasn't long.

The individual on the other end of the phone said, "Don, this is Alphonso Hector."

"Mr. Hector, what can I do for you?"

"You've heard about the Henderson case, right?"

"Yes! It's a shame that the results of that trial went in favor of those out of control guards."

"Well, that's the reason that I'm calling you. Don, the ACLU has stepped in. We're looking at bringing those involved up on charges of violating Henderson's civil rights."

"That's great…something should be done. That was a clear cut case of civil rights being violated."

"Don, how would you like to chair this case?"

"Are you serious?" the retired attorney asked with excitement.

"Yes…I don't feel anyone else could bring the type of energy that this case requires."

"I'd like to meet with him first. Can you arrange a meeting?" Don asked.

"I've already made arrangements for you to see him. One thing, Don…"

"What's that?"

"I don't want you to be surprised to learn that he's been placed in solitary confinement. It's for his own safety."

They had no intention of leading Don into the room designated for his visit with his client without harassing him. The guards made it clear to the attorney that it would be in his best interest to forgo the Henderson case. They harassed and taunted the elderly attorney as he waited patiently for them to rummage through the contents of his briefcase. Suddenly, they rudely dumped his things atop the checkpoint table.

In an effort to continue with their harassment, they pushed the old man against a wall—then began to frisk him.

One guard's Southern enunciation was heavy. "I don't understand why you big city attorneys think that you can come down here and change things... You need to take yo' ass back to the city. This ain't yo' *damn* business!"

Intentionally mocking the guard's down home country boy accent, Don said, "You might as well get use'ta seein' me...'cause I ain't goin no where until I expose the boys behind the brutality that nearly killed my client."

Don's mocking touched a nerve. The guard that was patting him down used his forearm to pin the attorney against the wall, then said, "You think you funny, boy!"

"Take it easy." Don peered over his shoulder, made

eye contact with his tormentor, then said, "All you fellas have done is aggravated the hell out of me."

Don was released. The attorney immediately gathered his papers and began stuffing them back into his briefcase.

The guards continued to taunt him as they watched.

"Life in these parts can be brutal on old folk," one guard said in a threatening manner, leaning against the wall.

"You threatening me?" Don countered as he stuffed the last of his paperwork into his briefcase.

"Ain't nobody threatenin' nobody. Follow me?" another guard interceded. He then unlocked the steel door that gave access to the hallway.

The guard escorted Larry's attorney toward a specially designated room. The warden had assured Don that the area provided would be private.

Don walked over to the table, and rested his briefcase. He nonchalantly paced the room, inspecting for listening devices or cameras. After satisfying his paranoia, he sat at the table. With his back to the door, he removed a file from his briefcase. He wanted to go over a few things before Larry was escorted into the room.

Don still couldn't get over Larry's entire situation. How he ended up in prison in the first place was baffling to the attorney. Then there was the fact that he was turned down for parole based on a letter that Don believed was written by Larry's father.

The attorney's attention was suddenly drawn to his

rear when he heard the door being forced open. Looking over his shoulder, he watched as Larry was escorted into the room. The inmate was bound from his wrists to his ankles, and the shackles severely restricted his movements.

The once savagely beaten inmate had healed well.

Photographs taken of him after the attack depicted a man whose face was so severely swollen that every bone in it appeared to have had been broken. The compassionate attorney was happy to see that his client was without permanent disfigurement.

Don got to his feet, turned, and then extended a hand. The elderly lawyer felt a bit foolish after realizing that Larry was unable to shake his hand due to the his restricting leg irons.

The lawyer shifted his eyes toward the guard. "Could you remove his restraints, please?" Larry's new attorney asked.

The guard quickly refused, "I'm not supposed to."

"Then I need to speak with the warden because he neglected to tell me that my client would be forced to go through our meeting being uncomfortable."

Reluctantly, the arrogant guard removed the burdensome restraints.

After rubbing his wrists to get the blood flowing, Larry shook Don's hand. "I was told that you would be coming. Mr. Hector from the ACLU speaks very highly of you.

The two sat down before Larry continued, "I guess you heard that the first trial was a complete sham."

"Yeah, I pretty much knew that you weren't going to get justice in that trial."

"You followed it?"

"Yes. It's not every day that injustices like yours are brought to light. When they are, they're worth following. So I kept up with you, and your story."

"How does this civil rights violation thing work?"

"Since you didn't resist, they had no lawful reason to strike you. Everyone that was involved will be serving time for not taking you into custody without brutality." Don pulled several files from his briefcase. "First, you and I have to go over a few things. I need to know everything about your situation. Let's start with what led up to your escape attempt."

"What I tell you is under attorney client privilege, right?"

Don was a little bewildered, "Yeah...why?"

"Because someone helped me. Although she's no longer employed by the prison, I don't want her to be involved."

"Tell me what's going on."

"Well, it's like this." Larry leaned closer; he lowered his voice. "That night, it was raining real badly."

Larry **HENDERSON**

The day I was turned down for parole, the prison thug threatened my life.

On top of that, I had just found out that my best friend had supposedly committed suicide. The strange thing was, my friend was scheduled to be paroled less than a week before allegedly taking his own life.

I hadn't seen him in several days, so I made a few inquiries. When I started asking questions about Ron, I was told that he had been released earlier than scheduled; they didn't say anything about him killing himself. Of course, I thought him being released early was a bit strange because he had given me his personal possessions for safekeeping. He never came by to pick them up, or to say bye. So, of course, I wasn't buying the guards' story of him being released.

With all that was going on that day, it got to be a bit much; I couldn't take it. I wasn't about to let Mop get his hands on me; and I didn't know whether or not the guards felt that Ron had told me what he knew about them. Simply put, I felt that my life was in danger.

When I was transferred over to Camp 12, I met and befriended a guard. Stacy was really nice to me. She believed that I was innocent. Anyway, after my parole hearing I met up with her in the yard. That's when she saw Mop threaten my life. After that warning, I filled her in on what happened to Ron. She was convinced, as I was—that my life was in jeopardy.

She and I devised a plan for me to escape the following day.

The night of the escape, she came to the canteen carrying a gym bag.

There was a torrential rainstorm; she was soaked when she entered the store—dripped water all over my buffed floor. I remember joking with her.

"Girl, I hope you brought your mop," I said. It was an effort to disguise my anxiety. I couldn't believe that I was really going to go through with it. I was going to take the biggest chance of my life, but I had no choice.

She placed the bag on the counter and then said, "Everything that you'll need is in this bag."

After Donald Harris Sr. completed his one-on-one with his new client, he tracked down and then paid a visit to Stacy Taylor. He also contacted the guard that was standing at the gate on the rainy night of Larry's escape. Don had one other person that he wanted to see; Larry felt that his attorney might be able to flip a guard by the name of Eric Holly. The inmate told Don that that particular guard was young. Larry claimed that Holly didn't seem to have any interest in participating in the attack on him.

The watering hole was high energy—patrons shoved one another in an effort to better position themselves as they fought to order drinks. A confederate flag covered the wall behind the enclosed bar. In the corner of the establishment several drunken correction officers begin to mix it up.

Don Harris entered the pub. He stood at the entrance and allowed his eyes to adjust to the dim lighting. Upon identifying the subject of his interest, with all the grace of television's Matlock, he maneuvered through the sea of bodies and over to the bar, where Officer Holly stood. The young CO was attempting to slip away from the ferocious crew. With beer in hand, he noticed an empty stool at the far end of the bar, so that's where he was headed. Don walked up to the guard just as Holly sat.

Larry's attorney leaned against the bar next to Holly. The guard attempted to ignore the elderly gentleman standing next to him.

It took the attorney several seconds before he was finally able to get the bartender's attention.

"What'cha drinkin?" the bartender asked.

"Scotch on the rocks, please…" he said in response to the barkeep. After placing his order, the attorney turned his attention toward the patron seated next to him.

"Your buddies seem to be having a disagreement." There was a ruckus taking place between two of the other defendants who were mixing it up by the juke-box.

"What are you doing here? I can't talk to you…" Holly said slyly, sipping on his drink.

The bartender handed Don his Scotch.

The attorney stared at his drink—he attempted to speak to Holly discreetly. "Look…I can tell that this whole thing is eating at you. It's obvious that you have integrity. Your parents told me that you don't drink but yet here you are."

"You spoke to my parents!" Holly was not at all pleased with Don's intrusiveness. "You had no right to do that." Never taking his eyes off of his drink, he questioned, "What do you want from me?"

"I have some people that I want you to talk to."

"I have to live and work here. You wanna get me killed?"

"I want you to do what's right. You guys nearly killed that man, and for what? He didn't try to resist. Is it about him being Black? Is that what you're about?" He placed a business card on the bar. "Talk to this guy?"

The other guards finally noticed the old attorney standing next to Holly; they made their way over toward them. "WHAT THE HELL ARE YOU DOIN' IN HERE...YOU NIGGA LOVER?" one yelled over the country music.

At that moment, Don felt that he finally pieced together his accounts of the night that Larry executed his daring escape from one of the largest penal facilities in the South.

Night OF ESCAPE

A driving rain ravaged the compound.

Idling at the gate was a 1978 gray Delta 88 Oldsmobile.

Its trunk was up. A guard, wearing state-issued rain gear was going through the trunk's contents. The female corrections officer responsible for conducting the search closed the trunk and quickly scurried toward the driver's side window; she wanted to get out of the rain as fast as possible.

The Black woman behind the wheel had long, flowing hair, a mocha complexion, and a mole under her bottom lip. She waited patiently for the guard to give her permission to drive off of prison grounds.

Twenty minutes after the car was allowed to leave, one of the prison's staff was escorting a group of cons through the downpour, from the Spiritual Life Center, when he noticed that Stacy's car was not in the employee parking lot.

Corrections Officer Stacy Taylor was informed that her vehicle was missing; she had no choice but to report it. She walked over to a phone that was mounted on the wall of Camp 12's guardhouse.

"This is Officer Taylor over here at Camp 12. Mr. Stanley just escorted several inmates back from the Spiritual Life Center... He informed me that my car is missing..."

The guard was asked to describe her vehicle; at which time she said, "It's a 1978 gray Delta 88...license plate number is 1 BRT 125..." She was then asked if she could account for the prisoners assigned to Camp 12. "My original count is good..." was her response.

After gathering the information on the missing vehicle, the command center guard called the employee gate and asked if the guards on duty noticed the car in question. The rain was coming down so hard that the command center CO making the query could hear it pound against the booth as he waited for the duty guard to respond.

"Sir, I did see that car...it approached the gate at approximately 8:52. At which time I inspected it and found it to be clean," the duty guard stated.

"Can you describe the individual driving?"

"Female, Black... kinda homely... Long-black hair... a mole on her face..."

Twenty-nine minutes after the car first being reported missing, the guards within the command center were frantically going over all the scenarios that could have resulted in the car being taken off of the compound.

Lieutenant Morris wanted all camps to report to him with an accurate account of the inmates assigned.

"Camp 10...this is the Command Center...can you verify your count once again...this count should include everyone..." His request meant that they were to check inmates assigned to sleeping in areas other than the barracks.

While Morris waited for a response, Stacy entered the center and approached her immediate supervisor. She tapped him on the shoulder; he turned and gestured for her to wait until he concluded his call. Several seconds later, he placed the receiver on its cradle. Morris then turned his undivided attention to the female guard.

Stacy was reluctant, but she knew that she had to speak up. "Lieutenant, I can't account for one inmate."

"Which one?"

"Inmate Henderson, Larry, #353891," she said.

It took the Lieutenant all of seven minutes to assemble his crash team.

The nine fully armed individuals were dressed in their riot gear as they prepared a full assault of the canteen for which inmate #353891 was given responsibility.

As they stood outside the canteen battling the elements, Lieutenant Morris fiddled with a set of keys in an effort to find the one that would fit the keyhole.

There was very little lighting on the two-lane, newly paved, ten-mile stretch of road that led to and from the prison. With the rain disrupting what little visibility there was, driving, especially at a high rate of speed, was difficult.

Larry, dressed as a woman, found himself rocking back and forth, full of nervous energy as he tried to find his way down the dark road and through the hurricane-like rainstorm. The escaped prisoner's mind was on Stacy risking her own freedom to help him gain his. He remembered her telling him where to stash the car, and that a second vehicle would be waiting for him in the parking lot of a motel some ten miles from the prison.

Seeing her come into the store dripping wet, carrying

a gym bag, made him a bit reluctant about going through with their plan. If it didn't work, she would end up in the very situation that he was in; incarcerated. When Stacy opened her bag and revealed the clothing that Larry would use to disguise himself, he became even jitterier.

Stacy followed Larry into his room—the two were readying to transform him into the woman that he had to become in order for the first part of their elaborate plan to be realized.

Larry explained to Don Harris that his visibility was extremely poor, that if he were standing in the rain, he wouldn't have been able to see his hand in front of his face. But regardless of the poor visibility, he continued to press aggressively on the gas. His nerves were on edge, he wanted to get away as fast as he could, but in order to do that he had to be able to see. Larry searched the floorboard with his foot in an effort to find the high beam button.

The high heels that he was wearing were really tight, cutting off his circulation, and making it next to impossible for him to feel, let alone manipulate the headlights.

Larry had been locked up for so long that he was completely unaware of the modifications that had taken place within the auto industry. Little things like the high beam control being moved from the floorboard to the steering column. So, as he used his hand to search the floor for the button that he could not seem to find with his foot, he lost control of the car.

The automobile flipped several times, causing glass to shatter. Tiny pieces of the windshield embedded itself in his face. Larry had violently struck his head on various parts of the interior before the vehicle came to a disastrous halt on its roof.

Although the caved-in roof nearly trapped the escapee, Larry managed to crawl out of the wreckage. He stood in the middle of the open field, dazed and confused. The heavy rains pounding on his face seemed to help him regain his composure. He suddenly remembered that he was in the middle of an escape attempt; so he quickly reached back into the vehicle and pulled from it, his purse. Within the purse was seven hundred dollars, money he needed to secure his safe passage to Detroit, Michigan—where he and Stacy planned to rendezvous several days after the escape.

Larry straightened his wig, pushed up on his makeshift breasts, and peered around through the heavy rain. That's when he noticed a dense wooded area some two hundred yards from where he stood. The desperate escapee draped the purse on his arm and began to run in the direction of the woods.

The soggy ground began to slowly attempt to devour the heels of his pumps. As he unknowingly ran, desperate for freedom, it wasn't long before the mud sucked his shoes right off of his feet.

The TRIAL

Judge Edwin Childress was readying to preside over a trial that would decide whether several guards, who assisted in Larry's capture, would be held criminally accountable for violating his civil rights.

The Honorable Judge Childress was a twelve-year veteran of the court. He was known to be a no-nonsense individual who despised racism. His Honor was a frail, Barney Fife looking man in stature, but a very strong man when it came to moral standing.

It took a year before the case reached Judge Childress' docket, adequate time for Don Harris to put together the elements he needed. Don felt that he was as prepared as he could be.

The guards charged didn't want to sever. They asked that all three defense attorneys work as one in an effort to present their cases.

Then there was the jury—the seven men and five women seemed very interested in getting to the truth, but some appeared to know from the start that they were going to have a hard time keeping track of testimony. Thus, a question had been posed to the judge in regard to taking notes.

"You are permitted to take notes regarding the evidence presented to you in court. However, you must not allow your note taking to distract you from the ongoing proceedings... You are instructed that your notes, if you decide to take them, are only aides to your memory, and are not conclusive. They should not be given precedence over your independent recollection of the facts. A juror who does not take notes should rely on his or her independent recollection of the evidence, and not be influenced by another juror's notes. The contents of your notes must not be disclosed; except to your fellow jurors... I hope that clears up the questions of note-taking..."

Judge Edwin Childress continued as he directed his attention toward the plaintiff.

"Now, back to what I was saying before the question was raised. Larry Henderson also claims that the acts of the defendants were done willfully, intentionally, and with callus and reckless disregard, or deliberate indifference to plaintiff's constitutional rights, so as to entitle him to an award of punitive damages against each of the defendants..." The judge shifted his attention toward the five defendants before saying, "...in addition to compensatory, and/or nominal damages, you should take into consideration the character and degree of the wrong, as shown by the evidence, and the necessity of preventing similar wrong... Punitive damages are not compulsory, but should only be imposed if, in your discretion, you consider the facts, and circumstances to warrant punitive damages against a specific defendant... If, in your discretion, you determine to impose punitive damages upon a defendant, your award should reflect the following factors: 1. The harm likely to result from the defendant's conduct—as well as the harm that actually has occurred... 2. The degree of reprehensive ability of the defendant's conduct... 3. The duration of that conduct, the defendant's awareness, any concealment, and the existence and frequency of similar past conduct..." The judge directed his attention to a bailiff, who was standing at the entrance to his courtroom.

"Any further questions before I allow my bailiff to open the courtroom?"

Judge Childress was well aware of the global interest that had been stirred up by Alphonso Hector of the ACLU. The man chosen to preside over a case that was receiving national attention wanted nothing more than to maintain control of the proceedings. Larry's situation had sparked the indignation of a nation.

After forfeiting his initial trial, thirty-two-year-old Larry Henderson was seeking justice—something that had eluded him for over fourteen years.

On the witness stand sat Tony Scale, an inmate Dog Boy from Camp 18—the canine unit. Larry's seventy-two-year-old attorney questioned him. "Mr. Scale, how many inmates reside in Camp Eighteen?"

"About twenty-five..." the inmate replied.

"Would you tell the court in your own words what

transpired the evening of September 18, 1991?" Don asked as he moved to the side of the witness chair to give the jury a perfect view of Tony's face.

"Huh...well, I was one of six canine trackers called... Two others from my unit were with me, Brown and Simmons. Huh... What happened was, we received a call from the State Police while we were already out searching... They radioed that they had found the car reported stolen from the prison grounds. Once we got to the scene...we began searching around the wreck. We split up, looking for foot trails... At that time, I watched as CO Small inspected the wrecked stolen car. I could hear him say that there was blood in the car..."

Don made his way over to the plaintiff's table and retrieved some photographs before asking, "Did you ever look in that car yourself?"

Curious to where his line of questioning was headed, Tony replied, "Yes!"

Holding up photographs of injuries Larry sustained on the day of his capture, Don asked, "In your opinion, was there enough blood in that car to lead you to believe that the injuries depicted in these photographs— marked as exhibit 146C—were caused by my client wrecking that car?"

One of the defendant's representatives quickly stood. "Objection... Your Honor, this witness is not—"

"Withdrawn!!" Don interrupted. "Mr. Scales, would you please continue..." the attorney insisted as he placed the photograph back on the table before he approached the witness.

Dog Boy continued, "CO Small then ordered me to get a dog from the canine vehicle, I did... Upon doing so—Small, CO Greene, and myself, started toward the woods... We searched throughout the night..."

"When did you learn that Mr. Henderson had been captured?"

"I first learned that Henderson had been located sitting in my assigned truck, with inmate Hank Dixon—at that location..." Tony Scales replied.

As Don made his way back over to his table, he asked, "How many others were on the scene when you arrived?"

"At the time that I arrived at the abandoned house, there were several other trucks there, but I can't remember who, or how many."

"What happened next?" the attorney asked as he took a seat.

"We saw Officer Raymond pushing what looked to be a woman out of the house; he aimed his weapon in the air and fired to signal that Henderson had been captured... I then pulled down by the house and parked the truck approximately fifty yards away."

Dog Boy could feel the corrections officers' eyes locked on him. So he locked eyes with one of the jurors before he continued, "Officer Raymond pushed Henderson with the butt of his rifle, forcing him from the porch... then CO Crockett met Raymond and Henderson outside…Raymond put Henderson on the ground face down… At that time, I saw Holly, who was standing next to the porch… I think he may even have been in the house at one time…he walked up to Henderson. I observed Officer Holly put his foot on the back of Henderson's head… pinning him to the ground. At that time, I saw Raymond push Holly's foot away. He was on Henderson's left side, and CO Johns was on his right side. They were preparing to lift him up…" The witness paused, as if he were prepared to continue with his testimony.

Don said. "Go ahead, and remember…you're under oath."

"Suddenly, CO Small ran up to Henderson and kicked him in the side of the face three to four times…"

"Objection!" screamed one of the attorneys for the defense.

"Overruled," said the judge.

Don redirected his focus to the witness stand. "Are you sure you saw Small kick my client?"

"It was definitely CO Small… I'll never forget…you see, as hard as he kicked him, Henderson never cried out. My boy Slim, Otis Boyd…was standing next to me; when he saw Small kicking Henderson, he started yelling, 'That's enough, that's enough…' But Officer Holly told him to keep quiet or the rest of us would get beaten too… After he said that—they began to beat the shit out of Henderson…"

Everyone in the gallery began to mumble—causing

Judge Childress to strike his gavel several times, his command radiated power. "Order...I want order in my courtroom."

The judge directed his attention toward Don Harris. "Please continue your questioning of the witness, counselor."

"Thank you, your Honor." Don redirected his attention from the judge and back to the man on the witness stand. "Now, Mr. Scales...you testified in the first trial, did you not?"

The inmate could see the defendants whispering amongst each other out of the corner of his eye. "Yes, I did."

"Was your testimony the same as it is today?"

"No..." the inmate mumbled.

"Why?"

"Man... I have five years left before I'm released. I have to live there," Scales nervously stated.

"Were you threatened at anytime during the first trial...?"

Scales turned his attention toward the defendants before answering, "Indirectly..."

"Elaborate for us, please..."

"They have their ways of getting their point across... can I leave it at that?"

"What made you tell the truth now?"

A defense attorney quickly stood. "Objection..."

"I'll rephrase... Mr. Scales...why did you change your testimony?"

"Because it wasn't right...what they did to Henderson

wasn't right. Sure, Larry Henderson had escaped from the institution, but that didn't give them the right to beat him...he wasn't resisting—he was scared," Scales said with conviction.

Larry's attorney sat down. "No further questions," Don said as he began shuffling through paperwork.

Attorney Daniel Livingston insisted as he stood. "Mr. Scales, isn't it true that your testimony today is the result of a deal that you made with the government? Isn't it true that you changed your testimony because you had time taken off your original sentence...and that you've been promised a transfer to a different facility?"

"I've been a trustee four of the six years I've been incarcerated... I've been nothing but a model prisoner. Sure, I didn't tell the truth during the first trial—but they would have ruined my chances for parole. I wasn't gonna say nothin' because I didn't wanna stay in that hole longer than I had to. Even today...I wasn't gonna tell the truth because I didn't believe that they were gonna protect me. But when I took the stand and you tried to make it look like Mr. Henderson was a threat to all them CO's...I had to tell the truth," Scales rambled.

The heavy rains had made their job more difficult. The individual responsible for locating and securing the escapee had trudged through mud and fought with the elements for half the night.

When they came upon the abandoned house, which sat in the middle of roughly three thousand square feet of prime acreage, daylight was approaching. The sun, which barely peeked over the horizon, exposed that the rain clouds responsible for wreaking havoc on their recovery efforts were swiftly moving west.

Several pickup trucks, which had assembled at the isolated area, were splattered with mud, and the tires of those vehicles had sunk into the earth, a pure indication of how heavy the rains were.

A dozen or so individuals hopped out of, and off, the back of their assigned vehicles.

While most were discussing the areas to be searched, Corrections Officer Raymond, with shotgun in hand, slipped away. He headed toward the tenement, some twenty-five yards to his immediate left.

Tony Scales (Dog Boy) was the first to see Raymond exit the tenement with what appeared to be a raggedy, barefoot, defeated looking woman. Raymond apparently didn't give the woman a chance to straighten the wig atop her head. He continually forced her to move by pushing the butt of his rifle to her back.

To ensure that everyone was aware that he had secured the escapee, the CO aimed his rifle toward the sky, and fired. That was the procedure for all captures. The gun-fire instantly drew the attention of everyone present. Upon realizing that the escapee was in custody, the men responsible for the search rushed toward the tenement, and immediately wrestled the inmate to the ground.

With photographs before him, Don sat at the table in his hotel room filtering through the images of Larry's capture. When he allowed his imagination to explore the beating, when he pictured the guards using the butts of their guns, state issued flashlights and or batons to strike Larry repeatedly about the head, when he imagined the force that it took to open up a wound in his client's skull that would require over seventy stitches to close, all he could do was cringe.

If not for the ringing of his phone, Don could have easily gotten lost within his horrific thoughts. The elderly attorney shook his head, wiped at his watering eyes, got to his feet, and then walked over to his bed. He made himself comfortable before reaching for the receiver.

"Hello!" He was a bit choked up, so he cleared his throat before repeating,

"Hello!"

The voice on the other end was all too familiar. "Don, are you okay?" Denise asked.

"Yes…a little tired is all. How's my son doing?"

"He's fine, sir… Don, I called because I have what you asked me for."

"Thank you…fax it to 555-0134, you know the area code."

Before Don could finish his thoughts, without warning, his hotel room window shattered—the suddenness of the unprovoked attack startled the hell out of the lawyer. The phone flew from his hand as he dropped to the floor and covered his head with his hands.

Denise heard the explosion. Don could hear her frantically screaming into the receiver, "DON! DON... WHAT HAPPENED, DON? ARE YOU OKAY?"

After several seconds of listening to his son's assistant screaming through the receiver, Don looked up. He allowed his eyes to scan the room. It didn't take him long to spot the red brick that rested under the table. He had been sitting at that table for half the night. From where the brick ended up, Don was sure that if not for that phone call, he would have been hit with that brick.

After getting to his feet, he didn't bother about picking up the phone. The nervous old man walked over to the table and retrieved the brick. Written on the concrete material, in black magic marker was, '*Nigga Lover*'.

Don would lay his message on the table after realizing that his son was on the line screaming to no end. "DAD! WHAT THE HELL IS GOING ON!"

"Hello, son," he said into the receiver.

Donald, Jr. was frantic, "Dad...what happened?"

"I guess some folks around here don't realize that we're living in the 1990's. I'm okay."

"I want you to drop that case. Come home, Dad. You're too old to be going through this."

"Son, I'm not walking away from this."

AUGUST 23, 1995

Court was about to reconvene for the eighth day of testimony.

Judge Edwin Childress entered the courtroom as everyone stood. He picked up his gavel and struck it before saying, "Order..."

Everyone took a seat.

The judge directed his question toward Don. "Do you have anymore witnesses?"

For good measure, he decided to put Holly on the stand. The defense team felt that it would work to their benefit simply because Holly was the youngest, most inexperienced officer on site the night of Larry's capture.

Don began playing on the jury's sympathy by struggling to get out of his seat.

He wanted the jury to be convinced that if an elderly attorney, someone who was willing to fight through obvious physical pain, was determined to be the voice for Larry Henderson, then he must see something in the inmate's allegations.

Don used the railing around the witness box to steady himself. "When your catfish business went under...what did you do about finding work?"

"I put in an application at the State Department of Corrections," Holly replied.

"Did your family want you to work there?"

"No, sir...not really..."

The judge asked, "Counsel, what relevance does this

have? Can we get on to something pertinent to this case?"

"Your Honor, I'll show relevance, if you would give me a little rope."

"Go ahead."

"Thank you." He turned back to the witness. "Officer Holly, why didn't your parents think that working for the state in the capacity of a prison guard was such a good idea?"

"They felt that the people in prison still posed a danger. They didn't want me in that environment because they felt that the inmates could decide to stage a revolt at any time."

"Did your parents ever show any concern for the guards themselves?"

Holly allowed his eyes to scan the packed courtroom before he would answer. "Well, my father was a guard at one time. He quit when he discovered that a few of his coworkers were sneaking drugs into the facility. My dad didn't want any part of what was going on so he didn't want me working in that type of environment."

"When did you go to work for the prison system?"

"In 1991."

"When this incident happened on September 18th, 1991, about how many months had you been working at the prison?"

"Two, I think."

"Where were you when you got the word that there had been an escape?"

Holly went on to explain that he was at his parents' eating dinner when he got a call informing him that it was mandatory that all guards report back to the prison. Holly said that he felt great when Captain Small requested that he be a part of the search team. The young guard also stated that he became the designated tracker because he was very familiar with the area where the search was being conducted.

"All right... In spending the night tracking the inmate, can you tell about how many miles he went on foot before he got back to that tenant house?" Don asked.

"It was several miles...five or six, in a circle..."

"Where was the inmate when you first saw him?"

"Lying on the ground."

"Were there any people around him?"

"Yes, sir..."

"What were the people doing?"

Holly didn't want to answer that question. He looked at the defense table, then the judge, before finally getting back to Don.

"Officer Holly, what were they doing when you arrived?"

"Standing next to Henderson. They had him on the ground."

"Who struck Henderson first?"

Livingston stood. "Objection!"

"I'll rephrase: 'Did you see anyone strike my client?'"

Again, the young guard was reluctant. He gazed at the jury, and then redirected his attention back to Don.

It was like someone had used Krazy Glue to seal his lips completely shut. He wouldn't say a word.

The judge said, "Son, answer the question."

"Your Honor, do I have to?"

"I'm afraid so," the judge answered.

Holly's head slowly turned away from the judge and back to the man standing before him. "The first person to strike the inmate was Captain Small." Once again, the gallery began to moan. The judge got everyone's attention when he pounded his gavel.

"There will be order in this courtroom! Please don't make me say that again!"

Holly looked confused, and quickly said, "But you have to understand that the captain was very upset that Henderson had betrayed his trust. The captain had gone out of his way to set Henderson up in the canteen. He gave the inmate a shot at being a cadet. He helped Henderson more than any other con in the facility."

"How would you know that? You'd only been at the facility for two months prior to Henderson's escape attempt?"

"Well, that's what I had heard."

"When?"

Holly was confused. "When what?"

"When had you heard that Henderson was Captain Small's pet project?"

"At a meeting that the guards had while Henderson was hospitalized."

After several minutes of questioning, Holly finally

revealed that he played witness to the brutality that led to Larry's injuries.

❧

The next morning Don sat in the visiting room waiting for his client. He had purchased Larry a brand-new suit, which was draped over the table before him.

The attorney was very satisfied in how things had worked out in court the previous day. Don could tell that the jurors were becoming more and more sympathetic toward his client. After all, when the defense presented its case, they weren't prepared to hear the Dog Boy change his testimony; everyone was totally blown away when his testimony went in favor of the plaintiff. But it was Holly that really turned the tables. Being a guard, his testimony had credibility.

Don kept his eyes locked on his client as he was being escorted into the visiting room. Time hadn't changed anything; the inmate was still bound as if he were Dr. Hannibal Lecter, preparing to have a one-on-one with FBI Agent Clarice Starling.

"Hello, how you doin' today, Mr. Harris?" Larry asked with delight. He himself felt that Don had done great thus far. His attorney was truly a godsend. He felt that his dear departed friend, Elden "Pappi" Howard, had a hand in sending the gentle old man to his rescue.

Don got to his feet and patiently waited for Larry's shackles to be removed. "I told you to call me Don."

The attorney cleared his throat. "I'm putting you on the stand after Dr. North."

When the last of his restraints were removed, Larry extended a hand to his attorney. The two shook before taking a seat. They both waited for the guards to leave before continuing with their conversation.

"I bought you a new suit for today," Don said as he pushed the suit in Larry's direction. The attorney then hung his head solemnly.

Larry immediately felt the misery that had suddenly engulfed his attorney's demeanor. "What's goin on, Don?"

They made eye contact before Don said, "Larry, your father is ill…"

Doctor
NORTH

"Today's proceedings will consist of the plaintiff presenting his case. Mr. Harris, you may call your first witness."

Don stood, before saying, "Thank you, Your Honor, we would like to call Dr. Maurice North."

Medical expert Dr. Maurice North took the stand. He was a very studious-looking gentleman, with salt and pepper hair and bifocals. As he approached the bench, it was obvious that he was a bit arthritic; he walked with a slight hunch.

Before the courtroom were pictures taken of various injuries that were inflicted the day of Larry's capture.

Don approached the witness with pad in hand. "Dr. North…when and why were you introduced to my client?"

The scholarly man turned his attention toward a notepad that he removed from the inside pocket of his brown blazer, before saying, "At approximately eleven a.m. on the 27th of September 1991, I was introduced to Mr. Henderson—at which time I was given two weapons to compare to the wound patterns found on

Mr. Henderson... A Smith and Wesson Model 66-2 and a Beretta 92-F...also six pairs of boots and shoes were brought for comparison. I was told to look for wounds that could have occurred on, or around, the 18th of September. Mr. Henderson told me that the pistols had struck him several times. Once on the left lateral aspect of the head...once to the right face, and at least once across the left clavicle. He also stated that he had been kicked several times, all over his body. Henderson also stated that there were burns on his back and buttocks, which were caused by cigarettes." Don asked, "What were your findings?"

The doctor flipped a couple of pages. "An area of laceration was noted on the left lateral aspect of his head. An abrasion pattern was noted above his left clavicle. Another abrasion pattern was noted around his right eye. Twelve areas of abrasion were noted on his back, neck and the backs of both arms..."

"In your opinion, were these injuries consistent with my client's claim of physical abuse by the defendants?"

"Blows from a Smith and Wesson model 66-2 made the wound patterns found on the left aspect of his head and left clavicle. The blow, which made the pattern noted around the right eye, was from a Beretta model 92-F. The abrasions found on his back were consistent with being kicked and not an MVA—Motor Vehicle Accident. But, no comparison to the shoes could be made. He had cigarette burns on his rectum and on the back of his right hand. The cigarette burns on the back of his hand were not inflicted on the eighteenth. The age of these wounds are at least two-and-a-half weeks old, minimum. To answer your question, yes…"

While the proceedings were taking place before him, Larry Henderson's mind had slipped into his past. He began to think about every aspect of his life; everything that led to his trial, his incarceration, and what he perceived as a lack of concern from his family.

Alcohol had consumed Perry, turning him into an evil, vindictive, self-centered human. But Larry was used to hearing excuses being made for a man he once pegged as his hero. Why stop now?

Larry's thoughts swayed to what he considered to be the epicenter of his father's change—in his mind, it all came down to Terrell's murder.

Everyone's eyes were locked on the witness stand as Larry gave his account of the morning that he was brutally assaulted.

Don stood to the side of the witness stand to give the jury the perfect view of his client. Larry gazed at the jury while he told his story. Pictures of the abandoned tenement in which Larry was found were on display for the jury.

"On the morning of my capture, I was found lying in the fetal position on the floor of that house that you're looking at. I was lying under a wooden door when Lt. Raymond found me. Lt. Raymond pulled the door off me…and told me to roll over. He frisked me, after which, he told me to get to my feet. I was about to do what he told me to do, but Raymond helped me up before I could get completely up on my own. He then forced me outside; he kept pushing me with the butt of his rifle. When I got outside and stepped from the decaying wooden porch, several CO's wrestled me to the ground. I looked up just in time to see Officer Parker approaching. Parker walked over to me and asked me where the money was."

"Money!" Don asked. "What money?"

"I ran the canteen closest to Camp 12. I took the money from the canteen to assist me in my escape…"

"Continue…" the attorney insisted.

"I told Parker that the money was in the house, right where I was lying. As soon as I said where the money was, they all began kicking me. I was kicked in the face, my ribs, and my back, approximately fifteen to twenty times. I must've blanked out, 'cause I don't remember the guns and walkie-talkies being used at that time. But, if I had to, I would estimate that I was on the ground eight to nine minutes. It was really weird."

Although Don knew exactly what Larry was about to say, he acted like they had never gone over his testimony. "What was really weird?" the clever attorney asked.

"I felt like my spirit left my body. I couldn't feel anything. I kept hearing, you are the redeemed, forgive them." He placed an index finger to his temple before saying, "in my head. You are the redeemed...if you forgive...is what I kept hearing." Larry directed his next statement to the jury. "It was really strange, the more they beat me, the less I felt..." The sadness in his eyes touched a twenty-six-year-old Caucasian juror—she didn't bother to wipe the tear that escaped her weary eyes.

Larry watched as she slowly shook her head, as if to say, 'It's a shame the way they treated you.'

"I came to as they were about to toss me in the back of a truck... I don't know whose truck it was. Anyway, four or five of them got into the back of the truck with me. I heard someone ask a guy by the name of Terrance a question. I remember this guy Terrance saying that... once I got to thirty-two, that his boys would finish the job on me..."

Don asked, "Do you know who Terrance is?"

"Based on the conversation I was hearing...I was under the impression that Terrance was the administrator...or something at Unit 32C."

Two of the defense attorneys stood simultaneously and screamed, "Objection!"

"Sustained," the judge countered.

Don went on to ask, "What else do you remember?"

"When they had me in that truck...that's when they cuffed me. One of them put a cigarette out on my butt... I clearly remember the heat from the cigarette."

"Can you describe the officer that put the cigarette out on you...?" was Don's next question.

"A white male, short...stocky, about 210 pounds, brownish hair and a mustache...he was wearing a camouflage jacket and hat."

"Do you see him in court today?"

Everyone followed Larry's finger as he pointed to one of the defendants. "It was him!"

"Let the record show that Orin Carter has been positively identified as the individual responsible for the cigarette burns." He pointed to the easels the photographs of the cigarette torture rested on.

The judge's response was, "So noted!"

Don stepped back to the witness stand. "What happened next?"

"After they beat me again...they put me in a sleeping bag and tossed me off the truck..."

Terrified at the brutality described, moans of anguish echoed from the gallery.

The judge struck his gavel several times. "There will be order in my courtroom."

"At that time...thoughts of stories told to me about my cousin Terrell came rushing to my head. You see... the Klan murdered Terrell when I was a kid...they put his body in a potato sack and threw him into Morris Creek. I must have been knocked out when I hit the ground...because I don't remember anything else until I woke up and saw this old farmer looking at me..."

Don turned to the defense, then the elderly attorney whispered, "Your witness!"

The three legal minds seated at the defense table seemed confused, like they couldn't decide who would be conducting the cross-examination.

It took the judge to speed up their decision process. "Gentlemen, we're approaching the end of the day. Do you plan on starting cross?

He seemed very cocky; he stood a little over six feet. His expensive suit led Don to believe that his rates were fare more than the defendants could afford. James O'Connor got to his feet; briefly split his attention between Larry and the jury before stepping toward the jurors.

With his eyes locked on the twelve men and women, he said, "Isn't it true, Mr. Henderson…that your injuries were in fact caused by your accident?"

O'Connor went at Larry's character, he attacked him by calling him a convicted murderer. He posed questions that forced Larry to admit that he wanted to kill his father. Any time Larry attempted to elaborate, the defense attorney cut him off.

The judge cut off the aggression of the defense attorney when he said, "Because of the hour…we'll resume with these proceedings on Monday morning…" He struck his gavel while announcing, "We're adjourned until Monday at nine a.m… Have a nice weekend, everyone."

The Long
JOURNEY HOME

Several Days Later

Margaret and Valeria wanted so much to believe that Larry would finally have something work in his favor. They both realized that whatever decision was agreed on by the jury, Larry would still have to serve out the rest of his time. They also realized that he would most likely have more time added to his sentence for his escape attempt, but—they would deal with that when they had to.

All eyes veered toward Larry. He was being escorted into the courtroom by two bailiffs. He winked at his mother and sister while taking a seat at the table directly in front of them.

While he was shaking the hand of his attorney, Val reached over and tapped her brother on the shoulder. When Larry directed his attention toward his sister, she handed him two old notebooks, then blew him a kiss.

Larry immediately handed the books to his attorney before whispering, "Don, this is the information that I was telling you about. This is from my friend, Ronald Cells. It outlines the guards' participation in drugs and extortion. He also hints that several deaths within the prison were, in fact, at the hands of the guards. I know that it's not evidence but do you think that it's enough for you to get the state to look into it?"

Don leaned closer to his client. "I'll do what I can."

Suddenly, a bailiff could be heard saying, "All rise!"

Everyone got to their feet and stared in the direction of the judge as he made his way to the bench.

Most everyone was ecstatic when it was announced that the defendants were found guilty of violating the civil rights of Larry Henderson. The compensation awarded was substantial— but no one expected that he would ever see a penny.

Over the next two years, Don Harris worked hand in hand with the ACLU and Federal Bureau of Investigation. They discovered that several deaths, including that of Ronald Cells, were the result of murder. One by one, Small and six other guards were arrested and convicted on murder, conspiracy, and a whole slew of other charges.

Unfortunately, Donald Harris, Sr. didn't get a chance to see the guards pay. He passed away from a massive heart attack during their trials.

Summer of 2001

He had a touch of gray on both of his temples, and on his mustache. He was no longer the little eighteen-year-old naïve kid that entered the prison. Larry had spent the better part of his life behind bars. It was hard for him to believe that he was in his forties.

He lay across his bed writing a letter. It would be his last as a ward of the state.

I've been in solitary confinement for ten years now. Twenty-three hours a day locked in this hole. My life has come full circle. Because of the time I've had to read God's word, I think I have a better understanding of why and how I ended up in this situation. We're all here to train for battle. A war is taking place each time one of God's children opens his or her eyes.

Our job is to learn what weapons we have at our disposal in order to fight this war.

I harbor no resentment.

This entire ordeal has made me a much better man. I have come to understand the spirit of God...along with my own spirit, which is of Him. Forgiveness has overtaken my life... God is giving me another chance to prove that I have grown, and that I understand my mission. I am the REDEEMED.

To my family, all I have to say is that I love each and every one of you. For, I am the REDEEMED. To my father, I forgive you. Because without that in my heart, I can't claim to be the REDEEMED...

I think I understand why you allowed me to accept blame for something you know I didn't do. I think that on the day that you saw Terrell's body in that potato sack—I truly believe that that was the beginning of your change.

I had a long time to sit back and think.

When you discovered that Sara Willington's father was behind Terrell's death—you were told by the powers that be that you were putting your family's lives in danger if you were to present that evidence. Well, that put you over the edge. I realize that combined with all the things you had to deal with being the only Black face wearing a uniform got to be too much for you. I didn't help matters either, me wanting to kill you every chance I got.

I know that you knew that I was laying in wait on many occasions.

But, I hated you for putting your hands on my mother. If I hadn't come here, you would have died. I'm glad that I didn't get that chance. You see, God leads my path now. I realize that over the past 21 years, when I felt so alone—I was really never alone, or abandoned, like I thought. He was with me at every turn. Every night, when I closed my eyes, He watched over me—He protected me.

A tear made its way down Larry's matured face.

LORD GOD ALMIGHTY, I thank you for this BLESSED day. I don't know what to expect when I walk out of these gates, but whatever awaits me I know that I don't have to deal with it alone. It's true what is said about Your guidance. I can do anything as long as I do it with You. THROUGH YOU, I have regained my SPIRIT—my reason for life. For that, I thank you for the BLESSINGS!

As he closed out his letter, a guard opened his cell and said, "Henderson, it's time for you to go, my friend."

He didn't tell anyone in his family that he was coming home.

Because of Val's letters, Larry was very much aware that his father had been diagnosed with alcoholic cirrhosis. Perry's liver tissues were completely scarred. He was bedridden and had been hospitalized for several weeks.

The first place that the ex-con headed was to Christ Hospital.

With his personal possessions packed away in the box he carried, Larry maneuvered around several people as he headed for the elevator.

Having only been out of prison for two hours, after having spent more than twenty years behind bars—he was headed to the last place on earth that anyone would expect he would be.

As Larry slowly walked the hall in search of room 428B, he fought against the negative thoughts that invaded his mind. Every step that brought him closer to his destination was marred with images of his past. Images of his father's abuse toward his mother, of him being chased from the house by his drunken father, armed with his fully loaded service revolver.

Larry's mind was playing tricks on him. He could have sworn he saw Elden "Pappi" Howard in one hospital room, and Ronald "Stinky" Cells in another, as he headed for a reunion with his father. Both of his friends seemed to be encouraging him to continue on his path of healing.

When Larry entered his father's room, he immediately noticed that there was no one by his side. The tubes and monitors leading to and from his body looked extremely restrictive.

Fighting through his mixed feelings, the ex-con stood at the door and simply stared at a man he once thought to be invincible. Perry seemed to be sleeping comfortably. Larry couldn't quite make up his mind whether he should wake him, or let him sleep and return later—or pull up a chair.

He decided on the latter.

Larry placed his box in the corner of the room before pulling a chair next to the bed.

He made himself comfortable.

Larry glared at his father. There he was, after so many years—the very man that had turned his back on his own son. The convicted murderer fought with his anger; he fought against his feelings of hate.

While he struggled with his own internal demons, he didn't notice a well-dressed man standing at the entrance to his father's room.

The man cleared his throat, an obvious attempt to get Larry's attention.

He looked official, but his gray hair and strong features reminded Larry of someone. The elderly gentleman casually strolled over to Larry with his hand extended. "Hello, Larry."

The confused, recently released prisoner got to his feet. He took the stranger's hand into his. "You look familiar…but I'm sorry, I don't quite remember."

"My father told me a lot about you. I'm Donald Harris, Jr."

"Wow! Nice to meet you…but, what are you doing here?"

"I came to see you."

"How did you know that I would be here?"

"My father told me the kind of person you were. Dad bet that the first place you would go upon your release would be to see your father. He didn't think that you would be going to see him out of revenge, but that you would want to forgive him in person," Don, Jr. said. He reached into the inside pocket of his blazer and removed from it an envelope. "This is for you."

"What is it?"

"The last thing that my father was working on before he passed. Open it!"

Larry opened and then pulled a piece of paper from the envelope—he was stunned when he unfolded the paper. Larry whispered while he read, "Thank you! Thank you so much."

"You're welcome. Dad said that it would mean a lot to you."

"It does…it really does."

❦

Perry wasn't sure who had taken up residence in the chair next to his bed. Whoever it was looked to be resting comfortably. He stared at the individual as he lay motionless.

Although in a weakened state, the old pioneer realized that it was his youngest son sleeping next to him.

For ten minutes Perry watched as his son slept.

The retired police captain realized by holding back the time cards that he had taken from the Vegas Hilton, he had essentially taken his son's freedom. Perry had no excuse for what he had done to his son.

The more Perry reflected on his transgressions, the more his eyes welled up with tears. He remembered Larry's birth and the first tear escaped. Another eased down his cheek when he pictured the look on his son's face the day that he was convinced to plead guilty to a crime that would send him away for the better part of his life.

What could he say to that boy? There was nothing that he could say that would begin to erase what he had done.

Perry fought so hard to stay alive; his intent was to live long enough to tell his son that he was sorry. He realized that his apology wouldn't be enough—it wouldn't restore his son's lost years.

He shifted his eyes toward the heavens, and then mouthed, "I love that boy." His watery eyes veered back to his sleeping son. He held that gaze for several seconds, and then slowly, he closed his eyelids for the last time.

The sound of flat lining monitors alerted nurses and doctors.

Larry was pulled from his slumber upon hearing the chaos taking place around his father's bed. He abruptly sat up—unable to clearly comprehend what was taking place around him. He stood. "What's going on?"

A nurse physically forced him away from this father's bed. "He's gone!" she said as she held him off.

"What!" he replied in shock, although he knew exactly what was being conveyed. Larry was not ready to accept the nurse's words as fact. "He can't be…there's no way that he would take this away from me." Larry attempted to get past the nurse.

He was filled with a nervous energy—he hadn't had a chance to tell his father that he had forgiven him. He needed to get to his dad's bed.

Larry was angry and sad at the same time; he fought to hold back the tears.

For years he wanted to kill that old bastard. All the hate that he worked through—this was to be the day that he shared what he had learned from God's word.

This was to be the day that he looked his father in the eyes long enough to say, "I forgive you…from the bottom of my heart…I really do forgive you."

"I'm sorry…but he's gone!" the nurse repeated.

❧

The morning before his father's funeral, Larry was sitting at his mother's kitchen table reading the newspaper when the doorbell rang. He was the only one in the house so he laid the paper on the table and made his way to the front door.

"Just a second!" he shouted before turning the knob.

She had milk chocolate skin; full lips and neatly styled hair added to her attraction. She was petite, about five-two and simply gorgeous.

"May I help you?"

Her sweet voice fit her package. "Yes, I'm looking for Larry Henderson."

"I'm Larry."

"I hear you've been looking for me."

He looked confused.

"Ronald Cells was my brother."

"Oh…Wow! Please come in."

For hours they talked about Ronald and what he meant to them. Ronald's sister explained that she hadn't seen her sister for years, and that she was attempting to find out where she was.

"I've already met your sister," Larry said from behind a caring grin.

His visitor sat up in her chair; she was all ears. "What! Are you kidding me?"

"Not at all. An attorney friend of mind found the both of you for me before he passed away. When I got out, his son passed that information on to me. I was able to get your sister through the information that he provided but your information turned out to be old. Your brother left a few things with me while we were in prison. I gave them to her."

It was as if all the spiritual forces had aligned. As Larry was readying to call Ron's other sister, the phone rang.

"Hello!" he said into the receiver.

"Larry…how are you? This is Ron's sister."

"I can't believe this!" he said, while smiling at his guest.

Larry wasn't able to get a word in edgewise. "Larry… you're not going to believe this. You know Ron's basketball, the one you gave me…I had given it to my son…" she continued to babble with excitement. "Well, out of the clear blue sky, it popped open. Larry, that ball was filled with money. Do you know were Ronny got so much money?"

Larry didn't even bother about explaining how Ron was taking money off the top of Mop's little enterprise. He simply said, "I have someone who wants to speak to you." He handed the phone to his guest.

As he was readying to recite a poem that meant so much to him, Larry looked out onto the assemblage of well-wishers who had taken the time to show support as he and his family mourned the passing of his father.

Larry was caught completely off guard when he noticed his old friend. Stacy Taylor appeared to be doing quite well for herself. The guard who helped him in his escape attempt stood next to Don Harris, Jr.

Out of respect to Larry, Ron's two sisters made it a point to have their reunion at the funeral.

Perry was really respected—officers from all around the county stood at attention; they looked real sharp in their dress blues. Everyone standing graveside waited patiently for Larry to recite Dr. Maya Angelou's "Still I Rise."

By the time that he had concluded his eulogy, there was not a dry eye at the gravesite.

After the twenty-one-gun salute, an officer played Taps on his trumpet while the casket was being lowered into the ground.

At the conclusion of the ceremony everyone, with the exception of Larry, made their way to their cars. Perry's youngest son stood alone by the grave of his father as he said his last goodbyes. He stared at the casket for a few minutes, and then gazed up to the heavens before whispering, "Ron, Pappi…watch out for him."

Suddenly, Larry was hit with a very strange feeling. For years he hadn't been touched with the thought of his cousin Terrell…but at that moment, it was like Terrell was calling him.

Larry could see that most of the people who attended the services were already pulling off—no doubt, headed to his mother's house to eat and share stories about his father. But he couldn't seem to head for the car that would take him.

The mystified ex-con scanned the gravesite in an effort to remember where his cousin was buried. It didn't take long before he was able to locate Terrell's headstone.

Larry knelt beside the grave of his cousin and stared.

He saw that the burial plot hadn't been kept—weeds were growing around it. He began pulling at the weeds, snatching them from the ground. Upon further examination, Larry saw that a decent sized vase had been turned over. He reached for it, and then turned the vase to an upright position. Upon doing so, something caught his eye.

Larry stuck his hand into the vase, and then removed a package that was inside a very large Ziploc bag. The curious mourner pulled the contents from the perfectly sealed bag.

Terrell's cousin was stunned at what he read.

The contents outlined every single murder thought to be connected to that of Terrell. Lee Thompson had apparently stashed it in a place that none of his co-conspirators would think to look. The information outlined the entire conspiracy.

It was true that Gavin Willington was at one time the leader of the Klan, like his father and grandfather before him. It was written that Gavin didn't like the fact that his daughter had a schoolgirl crush on the young Black teen who risked his life to save hers. So he ordered Terrell's murder.

As Gavin's aspirations for public office were realized, he believed that in order to protect himself, he would have to tie up loose ends, so he ordered the murders of everyone involved in Terrell's death. All of the information was a shock, but to Larry, the real shock came when he read that it wasn't Jake Aaron behind the death of Perry's best friend, James "Pooky" Jackson. In fact it was his partner, Simon Harris.

He had a lot of information to absorb. What would he do with it? Everyone involved was dead.

Then he realized that the information would prove that he didn't murder Miran. That when it came to him the system had truly, CAGED INNOCENCE.

THE END

About THE AUTHOR

A. P. Ri'Chard is a successful author and entrepreneur who writes for television and the silver screen, along with several literary projects in the works. The pilot for his made-for-television drama *The Market Place* is in development, and famed producer Fred Caruso has signed on to help with scripts. A. P. Ri'Chard lives in New Jersey. You may email the author at heartlike mind@aol.com or visit www.unitedspiritsllc.com